THE EL MURID WARS HAD BEGUN

North of Feagenbruch they came across the burned wagons of the Sparen carnival. Sparen himself was among the dead.

Mocker studied Sparen for a long time. "Was paranoid fool, sometimes, maybeso, this man. But was friend. In some way, even, was like father. There is blood now, Haroun bin Yousif. Same must be cleansed in blood."

The more Haroun observed his companion, the more he became sure Mocker would make a dangerous enemy. The fat and incurable optimism hid a lean, conscienceless killer. Haroun whispered, "They slew both my fathers."

It would be a long time before Mocker understood that remark.

WITH MERCY TOWARD NONE

GLEN COOK

A BAEN BOOK

WITH MERCY TOWARD NONE

A Baen Book

Baen Enterprises
8-10 W. 36th Street
New York, N.Y. 10018

First printing, February 1985

ISBN: 0-671-55925-7

Cover art by Dawn Wilson
Map by Glen Cook

Printed in the United States of America

Distributed by
SIMON & SCHUSTER
MASS MERCHANDISE SALES COMPANY
1230 Avenue of the Americas
New York, N.Y. 10020

DEDICATION

For Christian, Michael and their Mommy.

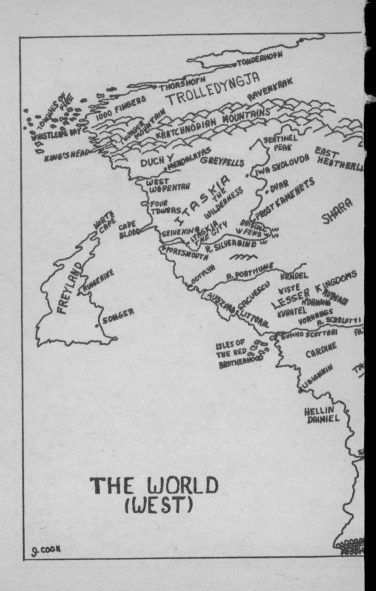

THE WORLD
(WEST)

J. COOK

WITH MERCY TOWARD NONE

What has gone before . . .

He came out of the smelted wastes, impossibly long after his family had been massacred by bandits. His name was Micah al Rhami, but now he called himself El Murid, the Disciple, and he was aflame with a holy vision. He came in a time of want, a time of troubles, a time of despair; and though he was but a boy his message fired half a kingdom.

He gathered the dreamers, the desperate, the dispossessed—and the opportunists. And declared relentless war upon the darkness. At his right hand rode Nassef, the Scourge of God, who became his brother-in-law, and whom he never dared entirely trust.

Those El Murid viewed as agents of darkness viewed *him* with great horror. They fought back. There was a boy, Haroun son of Yousif, youngest child of the prince in whose domains El Murid established himself. His fate became enmeshed with that of the Disciple. They met when Haroun was but a child, when Haroun caused El Murid's horse to throw him and permanently injure his leg.

There were battles and years, some lost, some won, but the power of the Disciple ever grew, till in his pride he ordered Nassef to mount an expedition against Al

1

Rhemish, the capital of his enemies, the unbelievers, the Royalists.

The Royalists met him at Wadi el Kuf, in the heart of the great erg, Hammad al Nakir (which means the Desert of Death, or Desolation of Abomination), and his insurgents were overwhelmed, shattered, obliterated, by the disciplined western mercenaries of Sir Tury Hawkwind. Wounded, he and Nassef survived only by hiding in a cave with the dead, drinking their own urine, till the enemy gave up and went away.

But survive they did, to rally the faithful again.

There was a third boy, Bragi Ragnarson, from the farthest north, a fugitive whose flight brought him and his brother south to enlist with the mercenaries. His company took service with Haroun's father. And so his life became mixed with that of Haroun, whom he rescued from death several times.

El Murid learned many lessons from the disaster at Wadi el Kuf, the greatest of which was to leave generaling to generals. In their hands his movement grew ever stronger, despite the ingenuity of Haroun's father and his captains. Haroun's family and followers were forced to abandon their province for Al Rhemish.

In time, El Murid moved against King and capital again, this time in small parties, following little-known trails. He attacked immediately, at night, and though outnumbered, panicked Al Rhemish's defenders.

Bragi, Haroun, and a handful of others attempted to break out of the killing trap—only to collide head-on with the Disciple and his household.

In the struggle that ensued El Murid's wife was slain, Haroun met the Disciple's daughter Yasmid momentarily, and the Royalists broke free. And Haroun knew that he was the last surviving member of the family with a blood claim upon the throne of Hammad al Nakir. He had become the man forever after known as The King Without A Throne.

He and Bragi, an army of two, fled into the desert

with the Scourge of God at their heels, seeking vengeance for the death of his sister.

El Murid had brought his faith to a desert empire. But the struggle was not done.

All this was told in *The Fire in His Hands*. Now begins *With Mercy Toward None*.

Chapter One: *THE DISCIPLE*

The moon splashed silver on the waste. The scrubby desert bushes looked like djinn squatting motionless, casting long shadows. There was no breeze. The scents of animals and men long unwashed hung heavy on the air. Though the raiders were still, waiting, their breathing and fidgeting drowned the scattered sounds of the night.

Micah al Rhami, called El Murid, the Disciple, concluded his prayer and dismissed his captains. His brother-in-law, Nassef, whom he had given the title Scourge of God, rode to the ridgeline a quarter mile away. Beyond lay Al Rhemish, capital of the desert kingdom Hammad al Nakir, site of the Most Holy Mrazkim Shrines, the center of the desert religion.

Micah eased his mount nearer that of his wife Meryem. "The moment is at hand. After so long. I can't believe it."

For twelve years he had battled the minions of the Evil One. For twelve years he had struggled to reshape and rekindle the faith of the people of Hammad al Nakir. Time and again the shadow had forestalled foundation of his Kingdom of Peace. Yet he had persevered in his

5

God-given mission. And here he was, on the brink of triumph.

Meryem squeezed his hand. "Don't be afraid. The Lord is with us."

He lied, "I'm not afraid." In truth, he was terrified. Four years earlier, at Wadi el Kuf, the Royalists had slain two-thirds of his followers. He and Nassef had survived only by cowering in a fox den for days, poisoning themselves with their own urine to stave off thirst, while he battled the agony of a broken arm. The pain and terror and exhaustion had branded themselves on his soul. He still sweated cold when he recalled Wadi el Kuf.

"The Lord is with us," Meryem said again. "I saw his angel."

"You did?" He was startled. No one else ever saw the angel who had chosen him Instrument of the Lord in this struggle for Truth.

"Crossing the moon a few minutes ago, riding a winged horse, just the way you described him."

"The Lord was with us at el Aswad," he said, fighting bitterness. Just months earlier, while besieging the fortress of his most savage enemy, Yousif, the Wahlig of el Aswad, he had fallen victim to a shaghûn's curse. The Wahlig's own son, Haroun, had cast a spell of pain. He could not shake it because a prime tenet of his Movement was total abjuration of sorcery.

"The children saw him too, Micah."

The Disciple glanced at his offspring. His son Sidi nodded, as always determinedly unimpressed. But his daughter, who yet bore no name, still had awe sparkling in her eyes. "He's up there, Father. We can't fail."

El Murid's nerves settled some. The angel had promised to help, but he had doubted. . . . He doubted. The very Champion of the Lord, and he doubted. The shadow kept insinuating itself into his heart. "Just a few days, little one, and you'll have your name."

The Disciple had come to Al Rhemish once before,

long ago, when the girl was but an infant. He had meant to proclaim the Lord's Word during the High Holy Days of Disharhun, and to christen his daughter on Massad, the most important Holy Day. The minions of the Dark One, the Royalists who ruled Hammad al Nakir, had accused him falsely of assaulting Yousif's son, Haroun. He had been condemned to exile. Meryem had sworn that her daughter would bear no name till it could be given on another Massad, in Most Holy Mrazkim Shrines liberated from the heretic.

Disharhun was but days away.

"Thank you, Papa. I think Uncle Nassef is coming."

"So he is."

Nassef swung in beside El Murid, thigh to thigh. Thus it had been from the beginning. Meryem and Nassef had been his first converts—though Nassef seemed more ambitious than dedicated to a dream.

"Lot of them down there," Nassef said.

"We expected that. Disharhun is close. You heard from your agents?" Nassef deserved his title. His tactics were innovative, his fighting savage, and his espionage activities cunning. He had agents in the Royal Tent itself.

"Uhm." Nassef spread a rolled parchment map. "We're here, on the eastern rim." The capital lay at the center of a large bowllike valley. "King Aboud's people are camped in no special order. They aren't suspicious. All the nobility have gathered at the King's quarters tonight. Our agents will attack when we do. The serpent should lose its head in the first breath of battle."

The Disciple squinted in the moonlight. "These things you have marked? What are they?"

"That's Hawkwind's camp on the far side." The Disciple shuddered. The mercenary Hawkwind had commanded enemy forces at Wadi el Kuf. His name stirred an almost pathological fear. "This by the Royal Compound is Yousif's camp. I thought both deserved special attention."

7

"Indeed. Catch me that brat of Yousif's. I want him to take his curse off me."

"Without fail, Lord. I'm assigning an entire company to the Wahlig's camp. None will escape."

"Meryem says she saw my angel. The children did too. He is with us tonight, Nassef."

The Scourge of God eyed him uncertainly. His faith, the Disciple suspected, was entirely of the lip. "Then we can't fail, can we?" Nassef gripped his shoulder momentarily. "Soon, Micah. Soon."

"Go, then. Begin."

"I'll send a messenger when we take the Shrines."

The sounds of battle reflected off the walls of the valley. They could not be heard outside. The voices of nightbirds were louder. One had to go to the rim to hear fighting. El Murid stood there staring at the soft glow of the amulet he wore on his left wrist. His angel had given it to him long ago. With it he could call down lightning from a cloudless sky. He was wondering if he would have to aid Nassef with its power.

Little was visible from his vantage. Only a few fires speckled the soupy darkness below. "How do you think it's going?" he asked Meryem. "I wish Nassef would send a messenger." He was frightened. This was a long chance taken on one pass of the dice. The enemy was vastly more powerful. "Maybe I should go down."

"Nassef is too busy to waste men reassuring us." Meryem watched the sky. War she had seen before, often. Her husband's angel, never. Till tonight she'd never entirely believed.

The Disciple grew increasingly uneasy, becoming convinced the battle was going badly. Each time he rode with his warriors something went wrong. . . . Well, not every time. Way back, when his daughter was an infant, he and Nassef had overrun Sebil el Selib in a night attack not unlike this. Sebil el Selib boasted the most important religious center outside Al Rhemish. From that victory all else had grown.

"Come relax," Meryem said. "You can't do anything here but upset yourself." She led him back through his white-robed Invincible bodyguards, to a mass of boulders where his household waited. Some were sleeping.

How could they? They might have to run at any moment.... He snorted. They slept now because they knew they would be in flight a long time if the battle went badly.

He, Meryem, and Sidi dismounted. His daughter rode off to inspect the pickets. "She's got the el Habib blood," he told Meryem. "Only twelve and already she's a little Nassef."

Meryem settled on a pallet provided by a servant. "Sit with me. Rest. Sidi, be a dear and see if Althafa made that lemon water." Meryem snuggled against her husband. "Chilly tonight."

His nerves had steadied. He smiled. "What would I do without you? Look. The bowl is starting to glow." He tried to rise. Meryem pulled him down.

"Relax. You hovering won't speed things. How do you feel?"

"Feel?"

"Any pain?"

"Not much. A few aches."

"Good. I don't like Esmat drugging you."

If there was anything he disliked about Meryem, it was her nagging about his physician. This time he ignored her. "Give me a kiss."

"Here? People will see."

"I'm the Disciple. I can do what I want." He snickered.

"Beast." She kissed him, sneezed. "Your beard. I wonder what's keeping Sidi?"

"Probably waiting for the lemon water to be made."

"Althafa is a lazy slut. I'll go see."

El Murid leaned back. "Don't dawdle." He closed his eyes and, to his surprise, felt sleep stealing up.

Screams startled him awake. Where? ... How long had he dozed? A strong glow from the valley now.... Shouts. Cries of fear. Charging horsemen limned against the glow, like demons storming from the fires of Hell, swords slashing....

He staggered to his feet, sleep-fuddled, trying to recall where he had left his sword. "Meryem! Sidi! Where are you?"

Must be fifty of the enemy. Coming straight at him. The Invincibles were too scattered to stop them. Already they were slaughtering his household.

The old terror seized him. He could think of nothing but flight. But there was no flying, as there had been none after Wadi el Kuf. He could not outrun a horseman. He had to hide....

A child ran toward him, crying. "Sidi!" he bellowed, fear forgotten.

A horseman swerved toward the boy. Another horse flashed in from the side. "Girl! You fool," El Murid breathed as his daughter blocked the enemy rider. She paused an instant, face to face, while Sidi raced for the rocks.

"Meryem!" His wife was running through the thick of it, chasing Sidi. The rider slid past the girl, slashed. Meryem cried out, stumbled, fell, began dragging herself toward the rocks.

"No!" With no better weapon at hand, El Murid hurled a stone. It missed. But for an instant Meryem's attacker looked his way.

"Haroun bin Yousif!" He swore. Then, "But who else?" His old enemies were always close. Yousif's family were the Evil One's leading champions. This youth had begun doing him evil at age six, when he had caused a horse to throw him. He had broken an ankle in the fall. It pained him still.

His amulet flared, bidding him call down the lightning and end this persistent plague.

The Invincibles beset Haroun and his henchmen. El

10

Murid lost track of the action. It drifted away as the Invincibles regained their composure. They outnumbered the attackers considerably. A half dozen remained around the Disciple and his wife.

He clutched Meryem to him, ignoring the blood wetting his clothing. He thought her gone till she squeaked, "I did it this time, didn't I?"

Startled, he laughed through his tears. "Yes. You did. Esmat! Where are you, Esmat?" He grabbed an Invincible. "Get the physician. Now!"

They found Esmat cowering in the shadow of an overhang, behind a pile of baggage, and dragged him forth. They were not gentle. They flung him down at the Disciple's feet.

"Esmat, Meryem is hurt. One of those hellspawn. . . . Fix her up, Esmat."

"Lord, I. . . ."

"Esmat, be still. Do what you're told." El Murid's voice was hard and cold. The physician got hold of himself, turned to Meryem. He was closer to his master than any man but the Scourge of God. Closer, in many ways. His master might collapse if he lost his wife. El Murid's faith, huge as it was, was not sufficient to keep him going.

Nassef rode up to where his brother-in-law paced. "We've won, Lord!" he enthused. "We've taken Al Rhemish. We've occupied the Mrazkim Shrines. They outnumbered us ten to one, but panic hit them like a plague. Even the mercenaries ran." Nassef glanced at the moon as though wondering if some high night rider hadn't stirred the panic on behalf of his chosen instrument. He shivered. He abhorred the supernatural. "Micah, will you stand still?"

"Huh?" The Disciple noticed Nassef for the first time. "What's that?"

The Scourge of God dismounted. He was a lean, hard, darkly handsome man of thirty who bore the scars of many battles. He was a general who rode at the head of a charge. "What's the matter, Micah? Damnit, stand still and talk to me."

"They attacked us."

"Here?"

"The Wahlig's brat. Haroun. And the foreigner, Megelin Radetic. They knew exactly where to come." El Murid gestured, indicating the casualties. "Sixty-two dead, Nassef. Good people. Some were with us from the beginning."

"Fortune is a fickle bitch, Micah. They fled, and by chance stumbled onto you. Unpleasant, but these accidents happen in war."

"There are no accidents, Nassef. The Lord and the shadow contend, and we move at their behest. They tried to kill Sidi. Meryem. . . ." He broke into tears. "What will I do without her, Nassef? She is my strength. My rock. Why does the Lord demand such sacrifices?"

Nassef wasn't listening. He was gone, seeking his sister. His stride was strong and his voice angry. The Disciple stumbled after him.

Meryem was conscious. She smiled weakly, but did not say anything. The physician shook while Nassef questioned him. The Scourge of God had a quick temper and grim reputation. El Murid knelt, took his wife's hand. Tears filled his eyes.

"Not so bad," Nassef said. "I've seen many a man survive worse." He patted his sister's shoulder. She flinched. She had refused Esmat's painkillers. "You'll be up for the girl's naming, little sister." His hand settled on the Disciple's shoulder, gripping so tightly El Murid almost cried out. "They will pay for this, brother. I promise." He beckoned an Invincible. "Find Hadj." Hadj was El Murid's chief bodyguard. "I'll give him a chance to rectify his lapse."

The Invincible gaped.

"Now, man." Nassef's voice was low, but so hard the warrior ran. Nassef said, "We lost a lot of men. Won't be able to follow through. Wish I could go after the mercenaries. Micah, go ahead into the city. The Shrines and Royal Compound should be cleaned by the time you get there."

"What're you going to do?"

"Go after Haroun and Megelin Radetic. They're all that's left of the Wahlig's family."

"King Aboud and Prince Ahmed?"

"Ahmed killed Aboud." Nassef chuckled. "He was my creature. Was he ever upset when I wouldn't let him become king."

The Disciple smelled the ambition hidden behind Nassef's gloating. Nassef wasn't a true believer. He served Nassef alone. He was dangerous—and indispensible. He had no peer on the battlefield, save perhaps Sir Tury Hawkwind. And that mercenary captain no longer had an employer.

"Must you go?"

"I want to do this myself." Again the wicked chuckle.

El Murid tried to argue. He did not want to be alone. If Meryem died. . . .

His son and daughter arrived during the exchange. Sidi looked bored. The girl was angry and hard. She was so like her uncle, yet had something more, an empathy absent in Nassef. Nassef recognized no limitations or feelings he did not experience himself. She held her father's hand, saying nothing. In moments he felt better, almost as if Esmat had given him a potion.

He realized that he hadn't needed Esmat's painkillers tonight. Stress usually aggravated his old injuries and the curse of that beast Haroun.

The Wahlig wasn't satisfied keeping the Movement bottled up in Sebil el Selib for a decade, he had to train his whelps in sorcery as well. The kingdom would be freed of that heresy! Soon, for tonight the Kingdom of Peace had undergone its final birth agonies.

He looked at Meryem, bravely trying to bear up, and

wondered if the price of heaven were not too steep. "Nassef?"

But Nassef was gone already, leading most of the bodyguard out after the Wahlig's brat. Tonight the boy had become the last Quesani pretender to Hammad al Nakir's Peacock Throne. Without him the Evil One's Royalist lackeys would be left without a rallying point.

A dark, angry, vengeful sore festered in the Disciple's heart, though love and forgiveness were the soul of his message to the Chosen. The riders clattered and rattled and creaked into the night. "Good luck," El Murid breathed, though he suspected that Nassef was not motivated by revenge alone.

His daughter squeezed his hand, rested her forehead against his chest. "Mother will be all right, won't she?"

"Of course she will. Of course." He sped a silent prayer up into the night.

Chapter Two: *THE FUGITIVES*

The desert smouldered like the forges of Hell, the sun hammering the waste with sledges of heat. The barrens flung the heat back in fiery defiance, shimmered with phantoms of old oceans. Charcoal-indigo islands reared in the north, the Kapenrung Mountains standing tall, forming reality's distant shoreline. Mirages and ifrit wind-devils pranced the intervening miles. There was little breeze, and no sound save that made by the animals and five youths stumbling toward the high country. There were no odors save their own. Heat and the dull ache of exhaustion were the only sensations they knew.

Haroun spotted a pool of shade in the solar lee of a sedimentary upthrust protruding from a slope of bare ochre earth and loose flat stones like the stern of some giant vessel sliding slowly into a devouring wave. A dry watercourse snaked around its foot. In the distance, four spires of orange-red rock stood like the chimneys of a burned and plundered city. Their skirts wore dots of sagey green, suggesting the occasional kiss of rain.

"We'll rest there." Haroun indicated the shadow. His companions did not lift their eyes.

They went on, tiny figures against the immensity of the waste, Haroun leading, three boys straggling in his footsteps, a mercenary named Bragi Ragnarson in the rear, struggling continuously with animals who wanted to lie down and die.

Behind somewhere, stuck to their trail like a beast of nightmare, came the Scourge of God.

They stumbled into the shadow, onto ground as yet unscorched by the wrath of the sun, and collapsed, oblivious of their beds of edged and pointed stones. After half an hour, during which his mind meandered in and out of sleep, flitting through a hundred unrelated images, Haroun levered himself up. "Might be water under that sand down there."

Ragnarson grunted. Their companions—the oldest was twelve—did not bestir themselves.

"How much water left?"

"Maybe two quarts. Not enough."

"We'll get to the mountains tomorrow. Be plenty of water there."

"You said that yesterday. And the day before. Maybe you're going around in circles."

Haroun was desert-born. He could navigate a straight course. Yet he was afraid Bragi was right. The mountains seemed no closer than yesterday. It was a strange land, this northern corner of the desert. It was as barren as teeth in an old skull, and haunted by shadows and memories of darker days. There might be things, dark forces, leading them astray. This strip, under the eyes of the Kapenrungs, was shunned by the most daring northern tribes.

"That tower where we ran into the old wizard. . . ."

"Where *you* ran into a wizard," Ragnarson corrected. "I never saw anything except maybe a ghost." The young mercenary seemed more vacant, more distant than their straits would command.

"What's the matter?" Haroun asked.

"Worried about my brother."

Haroun chuckled, a pale, tentative, strained excuse

16

for laughter. "He's better off than we are. Hawkwind is on a known road. And nobody will try to stop him."

"Be nice to know if Haaken is all right, though. Be nice if he knew I was all right." The attack on Al Rhemish had caught Bragi away from his camp, forcing him to throw in his lot with Haroun.

"How old are you?" Haroun had known the mercenary several months, but could not recall. A lot of small memories had vanished during their flight. His mind retained only the tools of survival. Maybe details would surface once he reached sanctuary.

"Seventeen. About a month older than Haaken. He's not really my brother. My father found him where somebody left him in the forest." Ragnarson rambled on, trying to articulate his longing for his distant northern homeland. Haroun, who had known nothing but the wastes of Hammad al Nakir, and had not seen vegetation more magnificent than the scrub brush on the western flanks of Jebal al Alf Dhulquarneni, could not picture the Trolledyngjan grandeur Bragi wanted to convey.

"So why did you leave?"

"Same reason as you. My dad wasn't no duke, but he picked the wrong side when the old king croaked and they fought it out for the crown. Everybody died but me and Haaken. We came south and signed on with the Mercenary's Guild. And look what that got us."

Haroun could not help smiling. "Yeah."

"How about you?"

"What?"

"How old?"

"Eighteen."

"The old guy that died. Megelin Radetic. He was special?"

Haroun winced. A week had not deadened the pain. "My teacher. Since I was four. He was more a father to me than my father was."

"Sorry."

17

"He couldn't have survived this even if he hadn't been hurt."

"What's it like, being a king?"

"Like a sour practical joke. The fates are splitting their sides. King of the biggest country in this end of the world, and I can't even control what I see. All I can do is run."

"Well, your majesty, what say let's see if there's water down there." Bragi levered himself up, collected a short, broad knife from the gear packed on one of the camels. The camels were bearing up still. Haroun drew his belt knife. They went down to the thread of sand. "I hope you know what you're looking for," Bragi said. "All I know is secondhand from your warriors back at el Aswad."

"I'll find water if it's there." While Megelin Radetic had been teaching him geometry, astronomy, botany, and languages, darker pedants out of the Jebal had instructed him in the skills of a shaghûn, a soldier-wizard. "Be quiet."

Haroun covered his eyes to negate the glare off the desert, let the weak form of the trance take him. He sent his shaghûn's senses roving. Down the bed of sand, down, bone-dry. Up, up, ten yards, fifty. . . . There! Under that pocket of shadow seldom dispersed by the sun, where the watercourse looped under the overhang. . . . Moisture.

Haroun shuddered, momentarily chilled. "Come on."

Ragnarson looked at him oddly but said nothing. He had seen Haroun do stranger things.

They loosened the sand with their knives, scooped it with their hands, and, lo! two feet down they found moisture. They scooped another foot of wet sand before encountering rock, then sat back, watched a pool form. Haroun dipped a finger, tasted. Bragi followed suit. "Pretty thick."

Haroun nodded. "Don't drink much. Let the horses have it. Bring them down one at a time."

It was slow business. They did not mind. It was an

excuse to stay in one place, in shade, instead of enduring the blazing lens of the sun.

Horses watered, Bragi brought the camels. He said, "Those kids aren't bouncing back. They're burned out."

"Yeah. If we can get them to the mountains. . . ."

"Who are they?"

Haroun shrugged. "Their fathers were in Aboud's court."

"Ain't that a bite? Busting our butts to save people we don't even know who they are."

"Part of being human, Megelin would have said."

A cry came from the clustered youngsters. The oldest waved, pointed. Far away, a streamer of dust slithered across a reddish hillside. "The Scourge of God," Haroun said. "Let's get moving."

Ragnarson collected the boys, got the animals organized. Haroun filled the hole he had dug, wishing he could leave it poisoned.

As they set off, Bragi chirruped, "Let's see if we can't pull those old mountains in today."

Haroun scowled. The mercenary was moody, likely to become cheerful at the most unreasonable moments.

The mountains were as bad as the desert. There were no trails except those stamped out by game. One by one, they lost animals. Occasionally, because they were trying to keep the beasts with them, and because they were so exhausted, they made but four miles in a day. Lost, without roadmarks, scavenging to stay alive, their days piled into weeks.

"How much longer?" Bragi asked. It had been a month since Al Rhemish, three weeks since they had seen any sign of pursuit.

Haroun shook his head. "I don't know. Sorry. I just know Tamerice and Kavelin are on the other side." They seldom spoke now. There were moments when Haroun hated his companions. He was responsible for them. He could not give up while they persevered.

Exhaustion. Muscles knotting with cramps. Dysentery from strange water and bad food. Every step a major undertaking. Every mile an odyssey. Constant hunger. Countless bruises and abrasions from stumbling in his weakness. Time had no end and no beginning, no yesterday or tomorrow, just an eternal now in which one more step had to be taken. He was losing track of why he was doing this. The boys had forgotten long since. Their existence consisted of staying with him.

Bragi was taking it best. He had evaded the agony and ignominy of dysentery. He had grown up on the wild edge of the mountains of Trolledyngja. He had developed more stamina, if not more will. As Haroun weakened, leadership gradually shifted. The mercenary assumed ever more of the physical labor.

"Should have stopped to rest," Haroun muttered to himself. "Should have laid up somewhere to get our strength back." But Nassef was back there, coming on like a force of nature, as tortured as his quarry, yet implacable in his hunt. Wasn't he? Why did Nassef hate him so?

A horse whinnied. Bragi shouted. Haroun turned.

The animal had lost its footing. It kicked the oldest boy. Both plunged down a slope only slightly less steep than a cliff. The boy gave only one weak cry, hardly protesting this release from torment.

Haroun could find no grief in his heart. In fact, he suffered a disgusting flutter of satisfaction. One less load to carry.

Bragi said, "The animals will kill us all if we keep dragging them along. One way or another."

Haroun stared down the long slope. Should he see about the boy? What the hell was his name? He couldn't remember. He shrugged. "Leave them." He resumed walking.

Days dragged past. Nights piled upon each other. They pushed ever deeper into the Kapenrungs. Haroun did not know when they crossed the summit, for that land all looked identical. He no longer believed it ended. The maps lied. The mountains went on to the edge of the world.

One morning he wakened in misery and said, "I'm not moving today." His will had cracked.

Bragi raised an eyebrow, jerked a thumb in the direction of the desert.

"They've given up. They must have. They would have caught us by now." He looked around. Strange, strange country. Jebal al Alf Dhulquarneni were nothing like this. Those mountains were dry and almost lifeless, with rounded backs. These were far taller, all jagged, covered with trees bigger than anything he'd ever imagined. The air was chill. Snow, which he had seen only at the most distant remove before, lurked in every shadow. The air stank of conifer. It was alien territory. He was homesick.

Bragi, though, had taken on life. He seemed comfortable for the first time since Haroun had met him. "This something like the country you came from?"

"A little."

"You don't say much about your people. How come?"

"Not much to tell." Bragi scanned their surroundings intently. "If we're not going to travel we ought to get someplace where we can watch without getting caught on the trail."

"Scout around. I'll clean up."

"Right." The northerner was gone fifteen minutes. "Found it. Dead tree down up yonder. Ferns and moss behind it. We can lay in the shade and see anything coming." He pointed. "Go past those rocks, then climb up behind. Try not to leave tracks. I'll come last."

Haroun guided his charges up and settled down. Bragi joined them moments later, picking his resting place with care. "Wish I had a bow. Command the trail from here. Think they gave up, eh? Why, when they were willing to kill themselves in the desert?"

"Maybe they did."

"Think so?"

"No. Not Nassef. Good things don't happen to me.

21

And that would be the best...." Tears sprang into his eyes. He brushed them away. So his family were dead. So Megelin had died. He would not yield to grief. "Tell me about your people."

"I already did."

"Tell me."

Bragi saw his need. "My father ran a stead called Draukenbring. Our family and a few others used to get together to go raiding during the summers." Haroun got little sense from the youth's story, but his talking was enough. "... old king died my father and the Thane ended up on opposite sides ... Haaken found what he wanted when we joined the Guild."

"You didn't? You already had your own squad."

"No. I don't know what I want, but it isn't that. Maybe just to go home."

Again moisture collected in the corners of Haroun's eyes. He smote the ferns. He couldn't become homesick! It was too late for unproductive emotion. He turned the conversation to cities Bragi had visited. Megelin Radetic had come from Hellin Daimiel.

Shadows were growing in the canyon bottom when Ragnarson said, "Don't look like we're going to have visitors today. I'm going to set some snares. You can eat squirrel, can't you?"

Haroun managed a feeble smile. Bragi was baffled by the dietary laws. "Yes."

"Hallelujah. Why don't you find a place to camp?"

Unbent by the sarcasm, Haroun levered himself upright, leaned on the fallen tree. Amazing, the changes in life. A king, and he had to do for himself. He'd never had to when he was a Wahlig's fourth son.

"People up ahead," Ragnarson said. Haroun raised a questioning eyebrow. "Can't you smell the smoke?"

"No. But I believe you." Twice Bragi had taken detours around mountain hamlets, not trusting the natives.

Inimical or not, their presence was reassuring. Civilization could not be far.

"I'll go scout it out."

"All right." Close now. So close. But to what? Though they had pushed less hard since deciding the Scourge of God had given up, Haroun remained too weary, too depressed, to determine a future course.

Get away from Nassef. Get over the mountains. One down and the other almost accomplished. Vaguely, somewhere in the mists: hammer the Royalist ideal into a weapon that would destroy the Disciple and his bandit captains. But he knew no specifics, had no neat plan ready to unveil. He was tempted to follow Ragnarson when he rejoined his mercenary brethren.

Bragi certainly smelled the end of their flight. He kept talking about getting back to his unit, to his brother, or at least to Guild headquarters at High Crag, where they would know what had become of Hawkwind's companies.

Haroun wanted to be a king less than Bragi wanted to be a soldier. Become a mercenary? Really? It would be a life circumscribed by clearly stated rules. He would know where he stood. "Foolish," he whispered. Destiny had assigned him a role. He couldn't shed it simply because he didn't like it.

Ragnarson returned. "About twenty of your people up there. Almost as ragged as we are. Couldn't tell if they'd be friendly or not. You go take a look."

"Uhm." They should be friendly. El Murid's partisans had no cause to cross the mountains. He crept forward, eavesdropped.

They were Royalists. They had no better idea where they were than did he and Ragnarson. But they did know there were refugee camps somewhere nearby. A chain of camps had been financed by the Wahlig of el Aswad and his friends, at the suggestion of Megelin Radetic, back when it had become apparent that the Disciple was a serious threat.

Haroun stole back and told Bragi, "They're friends. We ought to join forces."

The northerner looked dubious.

"We wouldn't have to worry about natives anymore."

"Maybe. But after what I've been through I don't trust anybody."

"I'll talk to them."

"But . . ."

"I'm going."

"Hey," Haroun said. "There's one of my father's captains. Beloul! Hey! Over here!" He waved.

They had been in camp half an hour. The two boys had collapsed and been forgotten. Haroun had wandered dazedly, unable to believe he'd made it, looking for someone he knew. Ragnarson had tagged along, eyeing everyone warily.

The man called Beloul set his axe aside, stared. His face blossomed. "My Lord!"

Haroun flung himself at the man. "I thought everybody was dead."

"Almost. I'd feared for you as well. But I had faith in the teacher. And I was right. Here you are."

Haroun's face clouded. "Megelin didn't make it. He died of wounds. Here. You remember Bragi Ragnarson? One of Hawkwind's men? He saved my life at the salt lake, and during the siege of el Aswad? Well, he did it again at Al Rhemish. He got cut off from his outfit." Haroun could not shut up. "Bragi, this is Beloul. He was one of the garrison at Sebil el Selib when El Murid attacked it way back when."

"I remember seeing him around el Aswad."

"He was the only survivor. He joined my father and was one of his best captains."

Bragi asked, "How do I get to High Crag from here? Soon as I rest up a little. . . ." They were not listening.

"Everyone! Everyone!" Beloul shouted. "The King! Hail the King!"

"Oh, don't do that," Haroun pleaded. And, "We got lost in the mountains. I thought we'd never get through."

Beloul kept shouting. People gathered, but with little enthusiasm. Fear and despair stamped every weary face.

"Who else made it, Beloul?"

"Too early to tell. I haven't been here long myself. Where is the teacher?"

Haroun scowled. The man was not listening. "He didn't make it. They all died, except a couple kids. The Scourge of God himself was after us. Took us a month to shake him."

"Sorry to hear it. We could use the old man's counsel."

"I know. It's a weak trade, Megelin for a crown. He saved me for a kingship. So what am I king of? This isn't much. I'm the poorest monarch who ever lived."

"Not so. Tell him," Beloul appealed to the refugees.

Some nodded. Some shook their heads. Which depended on what each thought was expected.

"Your father's party established dozens of camps, Lord. You'll have a people and an army."

"An army? Aren't you tired of fighting, Beloul?"

"El Murid still lives." For Beloul that was answer enough. While El Murid lived Sebil el Selib and his family remained unavenged. He had been at war for twelve years. He would remain so as long as the Disciple survived. "I'll send word to the other camps. We'll see what we have before we start planning."

"Got messengers going west," Bragi said, "let me go along. All right?" No one answered. He spat irritably.

Haroun said, "Right now I'm content just to be here. I'm exhausted, Beloul. Put me to sleep somewhere."

He slept and loafed for three days. Then, so stiff he could barely walk, he left his hut and surveyed his new domain.

The camp surrounded a peak in the northern Kapenrungs. So many trees! He could not get used to the trees. When he stared through gaps created by axes, he saw an endless array of forest. It disturbed him as much as the desert disturbed Ragnarson.

He hadn't seen the mercenary for a while. What had become of him?

Beloul reported, "Forty-three people came in today, Lord. The mountains are crawling with refugees."

"Can we handle them?"

"The teacher's friend knew what he was doing. He put in the right tools and stores."

"Even so, we should move some out. This is a resting place, not the end of the journey." He glanced at the peak. Beloul was erecting blockhouses and a palisade. "Where's my friend?"

"He left with the westbound courier. Very determined lad. Wanted to get back to his own people."

For a moment Haroun felt vacant. The time of flight had created a bond. He would miss the big northerner. "I owe him my life three times, Beloul. And I'm powerless to do anything in return."

"I let him have a horse, Lord."

Haroun scowled. Not much of a reward. Then he indicated the fortifications. "Why all that?"

"We'll need bases when we start striking into Hammad al Nakir. Al Rhemish isn't that far."

"If you know the way through."

Beloul smiled. "True."

Haroun looked at the trees, at the river coursing along the foot of the mountain. It was hard to believe his homeland wasn't far away. "It's so peaceful here, Beloul."

"Only for a while, Lord."

"I know. The world will catch up."

Chapter Three: *THE FAT BOY*

Sweat rolled off the fat boy. He sat in the dust and mutely cursed the Master. This was the season for the north, not the boiling, rain-plagued delta of the Roë. Necremnos had been bad in springtime, Throyes worse a month ago. Argon, in summer, was Hell. The old man was crazy.

He opened one dark eye, cocked his brown, moon-shaped face, studied the Master.

Was there ever such a wreck? The shadow of the Foreign Quarter Gate helped, but even midnight could no longer conceal his age and debility, nor his weakening mind, nor his blindness.

The old man was napping.

The fat boy's hand darted to a tattered leather bag, whipped back clutching a rocklike bun.

The Master's cane cracked dust. "Little ingrate! Damned thief! Steal from an old man. . . ."

Yes, he was past it. Once getting food had been difficult. Just a year ago the problem had required total concentration.

The old man tried to rise. His legs betrayed him. He tumbled backward, cane flailing.

"I heard that! You snickered. You'll rue the day. . . ."

27

Passersby ignored them. And that was a dire portent.

Once the Master had drawn them against their wills. With his tricks and banter he had stripped the smartest of their money.

Sing-song, the old man called, "Brush aside a veil, see through the eyes of time, penetrate the mists, unlock the doors of fate. . . ." He attempted a sleight-of-hand involving a black cloth and crystal ball, bungled it.

The fat boy shook his head. The fool. He could not admit that he was past it.

The fat boy hated that old man. He had traveled with the itinerant charlatan all his life. Not once had the old man mouthed a kind word. Always he had strained his imagination to torment the child. He had never permitted the boy a name. Yet the fat boy had not run away. Till recently the very idea had been alien.

Sometimes, when he managed the price, the old man would surround prodigious quantities of wine. Then he would mumble of having been court jester to a powerful man. The fat boy, somehow, had been involved in their falling out. Now he paid the price, whether it had been his fault or not.

The old man had instilled a strong guilt in his companion.

He meant it to be his security in his declining years.

The fat boy, brown as the earthen street, sweated, swatted flies, and wrestled temptation. He knew he could survive on his own. He had the skills.

Sometimes, when the Master dozed, he performed himself. He was a superb ventriloquist. He spoke through the old man's props, usually the ape's skull or the stuffed owl. Occasionally he used the mangy, emaciated donkey that carried their gear. When feeling bold he would put words into the Master's mouth.

He had gotten caught once. The old man had beaten him half to death.

That old man wore a list of names, varying according

to whom he thought was chasing him. Feager and Sajac were his favorites. The boy was sure both were false.

He chased the secret of a true name doggedly. It might be a clue to his own identity.

Finding out whom he was, now, was the main reason he did nothing to improve his condition.

He was unrelated to Sajac, that he knew. The old man was tall, lean, and pale. He had faded grey eyes and blondish hair. He was a westerner.

Yet the boy's earliest memories were of the far east. Of Matayanga. Escalon. The fabled cities of Janin, Nemic, Shoustal-Watka, and Tatarian. They had even penetrated the wild Segasture Range, where the Theon Sing Monasteries, from their high crags, overlooked the shadowed reaches of the Dread Empire.

Even then he had wondered why he and Sajac were together, and what drove the man to keep moving and moving.

Sajac appeared to be sleeping again.

Hunger clawed at the boy's belly. He could not remember not being hungry.

His hands darted.

Nothing. The sack was empty.

The old man did not react. This time he *was* asleep.

Time to do something about their naked larder.

Coming by money honestly was hard enough in the best of times. . . .

He waddled along, looking incomparably clumsy and slow. And, though he was not fast, he was quick. Quick and subtle. And daring.

He took the guard captain's purse with a touch so deft that the man did not cry out till he had entered a sweltering tavern and asked for wine.

By then the fat boy was three blocks away, buying pastries.

His liability was that he was too memorable.

The guard captain, though, committed a tactical error.

He shouted his promises of punishment before having his criminal in hand.

The fat boy squealed and took off. He could be enslaved, if not maimed or beheaded.

He made his escape, and returned to Sajac before the old man wakened.

His heart pounded on long after he had regained his breath. This was his third close call this week. The odds were turning long. People would start watching for a fat brown boy with quick hands. It was time to move on.

But the old man would not. He meant to put down roots this time.

Something had to be done.

Sajac wakened suddenly. "What have you been up to now?" he snapped. "Stealing my food again?" He seized his cane, probed the bun sack. "Eh?"

It was full.

The fat boy smiled. He always bought the hard rolls because the old man had bad teeth.

"Thieving, I'll warrant!" Sajac staggered up. "I'll teach you, you little pimple...."

The fat boy hadn't the strength to run. He whimpered. The old man plied his cane.

Something had to be done.

Once his persecutor tired, the fat boy whined, "Master, was man to see you hour passing."

The time had come.

"What man? I didn't see anyone."

"Came while Master meditated. Was great man of city. Offered obols thirty for guaranteed divination of chicken entrail, to choose between suitors of daughter. One poor, one rich. Man prefers rich, girl loves poor. To keep secret from daughter, same said come by midnight. Self, told same Master was in possession of sovereign specific to overcome love, same being available for obols twenty extra."

"Liar!" But the cane fell without force. "Twenty and

thirty? At midnight?" That was a lot of wine, a lot of forgetfulness.

"Truth told, Master."

"Where?"

"On High Street. By Front Road, near Fadem. Will leave gate open."

"Fifty obols?" Sajac chuckled evilly. "Get me my potions. I'll mix him something fit to grow hair on a frog."

The fat boy, generally, could sleep under the worst conditions. But he could not doze while awaiting midnight.

The rains came, as always, an hour after nightfall. The old man huddled in his cloak, the fat boy in his rags. The time came to confess his lie or go on.

He went on.

He put the Master astride the mangy donkey, led the animal through silent streets, up hills and down, by back ways, making turns for confusion's sake. Neither robbers nor watchmen bothered them.

Their course took them past the seat of the Fadema's government, the Fadem. Still no one challenged them.

Finally they came to the place the fat boy had chosen.

Argon sits on a triangular island, connected to other delta islands by floating causeways. The apex of the triangle points upriver, and it is there that the girdling streams are narrowest. It is there that the ancient engineers built the walls their tallest, with their feet in the river itself.

A hundred feet below, and a quarter mile south, lay one of the pontoons. It linked Argon with suburbs on a neighboring island. Beyond, in the deeper darkness, lay fertile rice islands, the foundation of Argon's wealth.

The fat boy did not care. Economics meant nothing to him.

"Is necessary to walk from here," he said. "Great Lord say bring no beast to mess garden."

The old man grumbled, but let the boy help him down.

"Is this way." He took Sajac's arm.

"Damn you!" the old man snarled a minute later, rising from a rainwater pool nearly four inches deep. "That's twice." *Whack!* "You did it on purpose." *Whack!* "Next time go around."

"Am humblest apologizer, Master. Promise. Will be more careful." A grin tore at the corners of his mouth.

"Woe! Is pool across path again."

"Go around."

"Is impossible of accomplishment. Is flowerbeds on sides. Great Lord would be angered." He paused. "Ah. Is only four feet wide. Self, will jump across. Will catch Master when same jumps after." He positioned the old man carefully, grunted prodigiously.

He cast his voice to say, "Hai! Was easy, Master. But jump hard to make sure."

The old man cursed and thrashed the air with his cane.

"Come, Master. Please? Great Lord will be angry if augurs come late. Jump. Self will catch."

The fat boy's heart hammered. His blood pounded in his ears. Surely the old man would hear their infantry-tramp thundering. . . .

Sajac mouthed a final curse, crouched, hurled himself forward.

He did not begin screaming till he had fallen halfway to the river.

The tension broke. The fat boy flung his arms into the air and danced. . . .

"Here! What's going on up there?"

A police watchman was hurrying up the cline to the ramparts. The fat boy ran to the donkey. But the animal would not move.

He would have to brazen it out.

The watchman walked into a storm of tears. "Woe!" the fat boy cried. "Am foolishest of fools."

"What happened, son?"

The fat boy blubbered. He was very good at that. "Grandfather of self, only relative in whole world, just jumped from wall. Am idiot. Believed same only wanted to look on river by night for last time." He made a show of trying to control himself.

"Only relative left. Was wasting sickness. Much pain. No more money for opium. Self, am stupidest of stupids. Should have known. . . ."

"There, there, son. It'll be all right. Maybe it was for the best, eh? If the pain was that bad?"

That watchman had patrolled the same beat for years. He had seen all kinds go off the wall. Jilted lovers. Dishonored husbands. Guilty consciences. Just plain folks.

Most of them did it by daylight, wanting an audience for their final world-diddling gesture. But a man with cancer would not be mad at the whole world, just its gods. And those little perverts could see just fine at night. His suspicions were not aroused.

"Come on down to the barracks. We can put you up there tonight. Then we'll see what we can do for you in the morning."

The fat boy did not know when to quit. He protested, wailed, made a show of trying to throw himself after his departed relative.

The policeman, deciding he needed detention for his own safety, dragged him to the police barracks.

A less enthusiastic despair would have allowed the boy to have gone his own way. The lawman would not have demurred. His world was filled with parentless, street-running children.

The same watchman woke the boy from his first-ever sleep in a real bed. "Good morning, lad. Time to see the Captain."

The fat boy had a premonition. How many guard captains could there be? Not many. He could not risk meeting this one. "Self, am famished. Dying by starvation."

"I think we can arrange something." The policeman gave him an odd, calculating look.

The boy decided he had better show more grief. He turned it on, as if suddenly realizing that he had not just awakened from a bad dream.

The watchman seemed satisfied.

He gorged himself at the mess hall. And filled his pockets while no one was watching. Then, when he could stall no more, he followed the watchman to the Captain's quarters.

He got himself out a side door while the patrolman made his report. He had recognized the officer's voice. His premonition had been valid.

They almost caught him in the stables. The donkey did not want to leave such rich fodder. But the fat boy got her moving in time to evade the Captain's notice.

He decided to abandon Argon altogether. The Captain was bound to do his sums and order a general search. Sajac had taught him long ago that the best way to avoid police was to be out of town when they started looking.

Could he bluff his way past the causeway guards? They might not let a kid leave by himself.

He managed it. He was a crafty and confusing liar.

The child-fugitive from Argon joined the ranks of the visibly unemployed who nevertheless survived. He did so by employing the dubious skills he had learned from Sajac, and others of the old man's ilk whom they had encountered in their journeys.

For several years he wandered the route he had shared with Sajac, from Throyes to Necremnos, to Argon, and round again, with stops in most of the villages between. One summer he traveled to Matayanga and Escalon. Another, he journeyed down the western shore of the Sea of Kotsüm, beneath the brooding scarps of Jebal al Alf Dhulquarneni, but that route showed no promise. The people were too savage and excitable.

They used human skin, back in those dread mountains,

to make the parchment on which they scribbled their grimoires.

He picked up several more languages, none of which he learned well. He stayed nowhere long enough to become proficient. Or he simply did not care.

He developed evil habits. Money fled through his fingers like grains of sand. There were girls, and wine. . . .

But gambling was his downfall. He could not resist a game of chance. He left a series of bad debts. The list of places he had to avoid grew too long to remember.

And he persevered in his stealing, thereby committing the double sin, making enemies on both sides of the law.

It caught up with him in Necremnos.

Mornings and evenings he did the usual phony sorcerer spiel.

"Hai! Great Lady! Before eyes of woman renown for beauty and wisdom sits student of famed Grand Master Istwan of Matayanga, self, working way west at Master's command, to seek knowledge of great minds beyond Mountains of M'Hand. Am young, true, but trained in all manner of secrets beauteous. Am also Divinator Primus. Can show how to win love, or tell if man loves already. Have in hand certain rare and secret beauty potions hitherto concocted for wives of Monitor of Escalon only, ladies known across nethermost east for teenlike beauty unto fiftieth year."

The appeal went on and on, tailored to any woman who showed interest. He sold a lot of swamp water and odiferous juices and ichors.

Between his morning and evening shifts he prowled the marketplaces, picking pockets.

And by night he squandered his take.

Then a pickpocket victim recognized him while he was at his more innocent trade.

He tried bluffing it out, packing his gear and loading the donkey while he argued. But when a policeman showed signs of believing his accuser, he fled.

He was no more agile or fleet than he had been in

Argon. He relied on cunning. Cunning was his edge on the rest of the world.

Cunning betrayed him.

The place he chose to go to ground was an outpost of a gambler he had bilked the autumn before.

"Seize him!" was his first intimation of disaster.

A pair of hoodlums, one lank and scarred, the other fat and scarred, piled on.

Beyond their flailing limbs the youth spied a man who had promised him a slow flaying at their parting.

He panicked.

From his sleeve he slipped the knife he used to cut pursestrings.

And an instant later his lean attacker wore a second, scarlet-gushing mouth below one opened in a silent scream.

Blood drenched the fat boy. It was hot and salty. He lost his breakfast as he writhed to get away from the other man.

This was nothing like getting an old fool to jump off a wall.

The gambler stared with wide, angry eyes as the fat boy charged him.

The fat hoodlum tripped the boy. The gambler scuttled out the back door. The youth bounced up, discovered that his antagonist had produced a knife of his own.

A crowd had begun gathering. It was time for him to leave.

His opponent would not let him.

He wanted to delay the fat boy till his employer brought reinforcements.

The youth feigned a rush, whipped to one side. He darted out the back door while the fat man was off balance.

It became a hell night. He scrambled across rooftops and crawled through sewers. Half the city was after him. Watchmen were everywhere. Hoodlums turned out by the hundred, lured by a bounty the gambler posted.

It was time to seek greener pastures. But only one direction lay open now. The west to which he had so long claimed to be bound.

He had not yet learned his lessons. He fully intended to pursue his habitual lifestyle once he crossed the mountains.

Even there he would be pursued by a doom of his own devising.

From a safely distant hilltop he laughed at, and hurled mockeries at, Necremnos.

Grinning, he told himself, "Am fine mocker. Finest mocker. Greatest mocker. Is good idea. Henceforth, sir," and he pounded his chest with his fist, "I dub thee Mocker."

It was the nearest thing to a name he would ever have.

He travelled south by remote trails till he reached a staging town on the outskirts of Throyes, where he wrangled a waterboy's job with a caravan bound for Vorgreberg, in Kavelin, in the Lesser Kingdoms, west of the Mountains of M'Hand.

The caravan crossed vast, uninhabited plains, rounded the ruins of Gog-Ahlan, then climbed into mountains more tall and inhospitable than any Mocker had seen in the far east. The trail snaked through the narrow confines of the Savernake Gap, past its grim guardian fortress, Maisak, and descended to a town called Baxendala.

There, after a girl and some wine, Mocker fell to dicing with the locals.

He got caught cheating.

This time he was on the run in a land where he spoke not a word of the language.

In Vorgreberg he lasted long enough to pick up a smattering of several western tongues. He was a fast, if incomplete, study.

Chapter Four: *THE MOST HOLY MRAZKIM SHRINES*

Day after day El Murid sat at Meryem's bedside. Sometimes his daughter or Sidi would join him. They would share prayers. His captains sought him there when they needed instructions. It was there that his generals Karim and el-Kader came with the gift-news that they had won an astonishing victory over Royalist forces near the ruins of Ilkazar. That battle's outcome was more significant than his seizure of Al Rhemish. It broke the back of Royalist resistance. Hammad al Nakir was his.

It was at Meryem's side that, in time, an emaciated, dessicated Nassef finally appeared to report, "Yousif's brat eluded me. But Radetic paid the price."

El Murid merely nodded.

"How is she, Micah?"

"No change. Still unconscious. After all this time. The fates are cruel, Nassef. They give with one hand and take away with the other."

"That sounds like something I'd say. You're supposed to put it, 'The Lord giveth, and the Lord taketh away.'"

"Yes. I should, shouldn't I? Again the Evil One insinuates himself into my mind. He leaves no opportunity begging, does he?"

"That's the nature of the Beast."

"It's a hard path the Lord sets me, Nassef. I wish I understood where he's leading me. Meryem never hurt anybody. If she ever did, she paid for it a hundredfold just by being the Disciple's wife. Why should this happen now? With the victory at hand? With the naming of her daughter so near? When we could finally start living the semblance of a normal life?"

"She'll be avenged, Micah."

"Avenged? Who's left to avenge her on?"

"Yousif's son. Haroun. The pretender to the throne."

"He'll die anyway. The Harish have consecrated his name already."

"All right. Someone, then. Micah, we've got work to do. Disharhun starts tomorrow. You can't stay closed up. The faithful are gathering. We've promised them this festival for years. You have to put your personal agony aside."

El Murid sighed. "You're right, of course. I've been feeling sorry for myself. Just a little while longer. You. You look awful. Was it bad?"

"Words can't describe it. They did something sorcerous to us. I'm the only one who survived. And I can't remember what happened. I lost five days of my life out there. There was a tower. . . ." But he wasn't sure.

"The Lord saw you through. He understood my need."

"I have to rest, Micah. I don't have anything left. I won't be much help the next few days."

"Take as long as you need. Heal. I'll need you more than ever if I lose Meryem."

El Murid prayed again after Nassef departed. This time he asked only that his wife be allowed to witness the christening of her daughter.

That had meant so much to her.

It was the wildest, hugest, most joyous Disharhun in living memory. The faithful came from the nethermost marches of Hammad al Nakir to share the victorious

40

holiday with their Disciple. Some came from so far away that they did not arrive till Mashad, the last of the High Holy Days. But that was in time. That was the day when El Murid would accept his victory and proclaim the Kingdom of Peace. And they would have been present on the most important date in the history of the Faith.

The crowds were so huge that a special scaffold had to be erected as a speaking platform. Only a few specially invited guests were allowed into the Shrines themselves. Only the Disciple's oldest followers would witness the christening.

Shortly before noon El Murid strode from the Shrines and mounted the scaffolding. This would be his first annual Declaration to the Kingdom. The mob chanted, "El-Murid-El-Murid." They stamped their feet and clapped rhythmically. The Disciple held up his arms, begging for silence.

The blazing sun flamed off the amulet that had been given him by his angel. The crowd ohed and ahed.

The religion was changing beyond El Murid's vision. He saw himself as just a voice, a teacher chosen to point out a few truths. But in the minds and hearts of his followers he was more. In remote parts of the desert he was worshipped as the Lord in Flesh.

He was unaware of this revisionism.

His first Mashad speech said nothing new. He proclaimed the Kingdom of Peace, reiterated religious law, offered amnesty to former enemies, and ordered every able-bodied man of Hammad al Nakir to appear at the next spring hosting. The Lord willing, the infidel nations would then be chastised and the rights of the Empire restored.

Men who had visited Al Rhemish before, to celebrate other High Holy Days, marvelled at the dirth of foreign factors and ambassadors. The infidel were not recognizing El-Murid's claim to temporal power.

El Murid was weak when he left the scaffold. Pain

ripped at his arm and leg. He summoned his physician. Esmat gave him what he wanted. He no longer argued with his master.

One hundred men had been invited to the christening, along with their favorite wives. El Murid wanted it to be a precedent-setting ceremony. His daughter was to approach the Most Holy Altar attired in bridal white. She would both receive her name and wed herself to the Lord.

He meant it to be an inarguable declaration of his choice of successor.

"She's beautiful, isn't she?" Meryem said huskily as the girl approached the altar.

"Yes." His prayers had been answered. Meryem had come out of her coma. But her limbs were paralysed. Servants had had to clothe her and carry her here on a litter.

El Murid recalled how proud she had looked on her white camel. How bold, how beautiful, how defiant she had been that first venture into Al Rhemish! Everything went misty. He took Meryem's hand and held it tightly throughout the ceremony. The girl was nearly an adult. There was little parents could contribute. She could handle her own responses.

When the newly-appointed High Priest of the Shrine asked, "And by what name shall this child of God be called?" El Murid squeezed Meryem's hand more tightly. Only she knew the answer. This was the moment for which she had lived.

"Yasmid," Meryem replied. Her voice was strong. It rang like a carillon. El Murid felt a surge of hope. He saw another rise in Nassef. "Call her Yasmid, the Daughter of the Disciple."

She squeezed his hand in return. He felt the joy coursing through her.

Her recovery lasted only minutes more. She lapsed into coma before the ceremony's conclusion. She passed to Paradise before morning.

The end was so certain that Nassef ordered Al Rhemish dressed for mourning shortly after sundown.

El Murid had been so drained by constant concern that the event itself left him numb. He could shed no tears. The little energy he had he devoted to Yasmid, Sidi, and Nassef.

The ever-calm, self-possessed Nassef had gone to pieces. More than to El Murid himself, Meryem had been all he had had in the world.

"She is asleep in the arms of the Lord," satisfied no one.

Nassef's response was to plunge into his work with redoubled energy, as if to take his grief out on the world. Some nights he skipped sleep altogether.

Sidi simply withdrew. And Yasmid became more like her mother at the same age. She was brash, bold, and fond of embarrassing her father's associates. She had a low tolerance for pomposity, self-importance, and inflexible conservatism. And she could argue doctrine with a skill that beggared her father's.

For that reason alone the new priesthood gradually accepted the notion of her succession.

She spent a lot of time dogging her uncle as he poured over his maps and tactical studies. She knew more about his plans than did anyone else alive. A half-serious story went the rounds, to the effect that she would succeed her uncle too.

The wave of the idealist had crested, but had not begun to recede. People still worried honestly about goals and doctrinal purity. The inevitable, post-revolutionary wave of the bureaucrat had not begun to gather.

Yasmid would not be challenged till professional administrators supplanted professional revolutionaries.

Nassef dumped the pacification of Hammad al Nakir onto el-Kader. He made a crony named el Nadim his satrap on the east coast and Throyen marches. He and Karim focused their attentions west of the Sahel, on lands El Murid was determined to restore to Imperial dominion. They spent month after month in the careful reinterpretation and reiteration of plans Nassef had nurtured for years.

Occasionally accompanied by his son, El Murid sat in on some of their staff meetings. He had his mission and his children, and nothing more. The pain in his limbs was unrelenting. He could no longer pretend, even to himself, that he was not dependent upon Esmat's drugs.

Despite a close watch, he could not resolve his increasingly ambiguous feelings toward Nassef. His brother-in-law was a chimera. Perhaps even he did not know where he stood.

Nassef's headquarters became cluttered with artwork. Years earlier he had employed several skilled artists to travel the west. He had called in their work: detailed maps, drawings and specifications of fortifications, sketches of prominent westerners with outlines of their personal strengths and weaknesses. He adjusted his master plan as information came in.

"The base plan is this," he told El Murid. "An explosion out of the Sahel, apparently without direction. Then one strong force materializing and heading toward Hellin Daimiel. When they think we're committed, we wheel and overrun Simballawein to clear our rear against our push north."

"Ipopotam. . . ."

"Eager to please, my agents say. They'll stay neutral till it's too late. With Simballawein taken, we turn on Hellin Daimiel. But when they withdraw behind their walls we by-pass them again. We push to the Scarlotti. We seize the fords and ferries so help can't get across from the north. All this time raiders will be roaming the Lesser Kingdoms, keeping them too busy to threaten our flank. In fact, after I've got everybody's attention, el Nadim will cross Throyen territory and attack Kavelin through the Savernake Gap. If he breaks through we'll have the Lesser Kingdoms in a vice. They'll collapse. If everything goes right, we'll overrun every kingdom south of the Scarlotti before summer's end."

El Murid examined the maps. "That's a lot of territory, Nassef."

"I know. It's chancy. It depends on the speed of our horses and confusion of our enemies. We can't fight them on their terms. Wadi el Kuf proved that. We have to make them fight our way."

"You're the general, Nassef. You don't have to justify to me."

"As long as I'm winning."

El Murid frowned, unsure what he meant.

Later that day he called for Mowaffak Hali, a senior officer of the Invincibles, who had been conducting an investigation for him. "Well, Mowaffak? It's getting close to the hosting. Am I in the hands of bandits?"

Hali was a fanatic, but he tried to be honest. He did not create answers in hopes they were what his master wanted to hear.

"Nothing damning, Lord. They've given up plundering their own people. I suppose that's a good sign. In private, they're excited about plundering the infidel. I couldn't trace most of the specie that went west. Some apparently went to pay spies. Some apparently bought arms. Some remains in the banks at Hellin Daimiel. And a lot have disappeared. So what can I say?"

"What's your feeling, Mowaffak?"

"I'm baffled, Lord. I lean one way one day, the other the next. I try to leave my personal feelings out."

El Murid smiled. "I've reached this point a dozen times, Mowaffak. And every time I end up doing the same thing. I let it go because Nassef is so useful. I let it go, and hope he'll eventually reveal the real Nassef. I thought an independent viewer might see something I'd missed."

"We don't punish our hands when they fail us by dropping something. I don't like the Scourge of God. I don't trust him, either. Yet he has no equal. Karim is good. El-Kader is good. And yet they are but shadows of the master. I say the Lord wrought well when he brought you two together. Let him undertake to keep you together."

"And yet. . . ."

"The day he becomes a liability will be the last day of his life, Lord. A silver dagger will find him."

"That's a comfort, Mowaffak. I sometimes wonder if I deserve the affection of the Invincibles."

Mowaffak seemed startled. "My Lord, if you didn't you wouldn't have won our love."

"Thank you, Mowaffak. You reassure me, even if you can't ease my confusion."

Disharhun was coming again. Each day made him more nervous. The moment of no return was hurtling toward him like a falling star. It would be too late once the Children of Hammad al Nakir crossed the Sahel. The great war would continue till the Empire was restored or his people had been trampled into the dust.

Warriors were arriving when he asked Nassef, "Should we put it off a year? So we'd have more time to get ready?"

"No. Don't get the jitters. Time is our enemy. The west is weak and confused. Not sure we'll attack. But they're bumbling along, getting ready. In a year they'd know and be organized."

El Murid made his Mashad speech to the assembled host. He was awed by its vastness. Fifty thousand men faced him. They had gathered at *his* command. And as many more were moving toward the Sahel already.

Hardly a grown man would stay home this summer.

He exhorted them to carry the Word, then returned to the Shrines. He was prepared to remain near the Most Holy Altar, praying, till the trend of the campaign became clear.

The first reports seemed too good to be true. Yasmid told him it was going better than Nassef had hoped.

Then Mowaffak Hali came to him. "Lord, I need your advice."

"How so?"

"A man named Allaf Shaheed, a captain of the Invincibles, has made a dangerous mistake. The question is how we should react."

"Explain."

"A force of Invincibles encountered Guild General Hawkwind in the domains of Hellin Daimiel. Foolishly, they offered battle. Hawkwind shattered them."

"And that has what to do with this Shaheed?"

"He assumed command of the survivors. While fleeing he chanced on a Guild landhold. He slew everyone there."

"So?"

"We're not at war with the Guild proper, Lord. We're at war with people who employ Guildsmen. That's a critical distinction. They demand that it be observed."

"They demand? Of me, Mowaffak? The Lord makes demands of El Murid. Not men."

"Perhaps, Lord. But should we needlessly incur the hatred of ten thousand men as dedicated as our own Harish? Twice have they invoked what they call the Sanctions of Nonverid and gone to war as an order. Each time they eradicated their enemies root and branch. Were they to muster their full strength and march against Al Rhemish not even the Scourge of God could stop them."

"I think you exaggerate, Mowaffak. And I won't be dictated to by infidels."

"I merely suggest that we not add to our burdens, Lord. That we make a gesture to placate the old men of High Crag. The Guild scattered, taken piecemeal, is far less dangerous than the Guild faced as a body."

El Murid reflected. He saw the sense of Hali's argument. Wadi el Kuf had been impressive. But there was also the fact that petitioning the Guild at any level constituted an admission of weakness.

There was no weakness in the Lord.

"Relieve Shaheed. Return him to Al Rhemish. Otherwise, do nothing but instruct your captains not to let it happen again."

"As you command, Lord." Mowaffak Hali grew pale. He had survived Wadi el Kuf. He hoped never to witness such a slaughter again.

He debated with himself for a day before finding room in his conscience for disobedience.

He sent three messengers by three routes, each bearing letters begging understanding and offering restitution. But the Lord was not with him. Every envoy perished enroute.

Chapter Five: *WAR CLOUDS*

Bragi reached High Crag after a four month journey through refugee camps scattered across the Lesser Kingdoms. The castle was an ancient, draughty stone pile perched atop a windy, sea-battered headland jutting from the coast north of Dunno Scuttari. He looked up the long slope to the gates, recalling the misery he had endured during recruit training, and almost turned back. Only his concern for his brother drew him onward.

He explained his circumstances to the gatekeeper. The gatekeeper told him to report to the sergeant of the guard. The sergeant sent him to a lieutenant, who passed him on to a captain, who told him to spend the night in barracks because he could expect to tell his story a dozen more times before anyone decided what to do with him. He was listed missing in action, presumed killed. His death bonus had been paid to his brother. The bonus would have to be repaid.

"I don't care about all that," Bragi said. "I just want to get back to my brother and my company. Where are they?"

"Sanguinet's Company? Down near Hellin Daimiel. Simballawein is negotiating for reinforcements for the

Guild garrison there. There's talk that El Murid plans a holy war. Wants to resurrect the Empire."

"Why can't I just catch up?"

"As soon as you've gone the route here."

He remained stuck at High Crag for three months.

Haaken stared. "I don't believe it. Where the hell did you come from?" He was a burly youth even bigger than his foster brother. He approached Bragi warily, circled him. "It's you. It's really you. Damn it. Oh, damnit. After all the heartaches I went through."

Someone hollered back among the tents. "You lying son of a bitch!" A soldier charged onto the drill field. "I'll crap! It *is* him. What the hell are you doing here, Bragi?" He was a tall, lean, tan, ginger-haired youth named Reskird Kildragon, Haaken's friend and the only other Trolledyngjan in the company.

Haaken threw an arm around Bragi. "It's really you. I'll be damned. We were sure you were dead."

"Why the hell didn't you keep riding somewhere?" Kildragon demanded. "Haaken, how are we going to pay back that death bounty?"

Bragi laughed. "Hasn't changed a bit, has he?" he asked Haaken.

"Too damned stupid. Can't *beat* sense into him. Tell the guys, Reskird."

"Yeah." Kildragon winked at Ragnarson.

"So talk," Haaken said. "How did you get out of Al Rhemish? Where have you been? Maybe you *should* have gone somewhere else. We're probably headed down to Simballawein. The Disciple is up to something. We'll probably be in the thick of it. Well? Can't you say anything?"

Grinning, Bragi replied, "Maybe. If you'd shut up long enough. You realize you've said more in the last five minutes than you usually say in a year?"

The rest of Ragnarson's squadmates appeared, ambling out nonchalantly, as if only mildly curious. "Oh-oh," Haaken said. "Here comes Lieutenant Trubacik."

"Lieutenant?"

"Been lots of promotions. Sanguinet is a captain now."

Bragi sucked spittle between his teeth, nervous.

"You're late, Ragnarson," Trubacik snapped. "You were due on guard duty ten months ago." He chuckled at his own wit. "Captain wants to see you."

A messenger came in on a lathered horse. Sanguinet ordered the camp gates closed and the troops into company formation. "Gentlemen, it's begun," he announced. "We're headed for Simballawein. General Hawkwind will join us there."

Five hell-days on the road, marching forty or fifty miles each day. Then a messenger overtook them with word that a regiment of Invincibles had butted heads with Hawkwind and gotten the short end. Only a handful had escaped.

The walls of Simballawein hove into view. "It's as big as Itaskia," Ragnarson muttered to Haaken.

"Bigger, I think." Cheering crowds waited outside the gates. "Think we'd won the war already. Hell, a city ain't nothing but a box trap."

"Gloom, despair, and blessed misery," Kildragon chided. "Come in out of the fog and look around, Haaken. Take a gander at them girls. Check the look in their eyes. I mean, they're ready to attack." He waved at the nearest.

"Sanguinet's going to. . . ."

A girl rushed Reskird. She shoved flowers into his hands, fell into step beside him. She chattered. Kildragon chattered back. Lack of a common tongue didn't hamper communication.

Haaken's jaw dropped. He pasted on a sickly smile and started waving. "Hello, hello," he croaked.

"Smooth," Bragi observed. "You're a real sweet talker, little brother." He straightened his pack and tried to look appealing without showing off. They had given him his squad leader's post back, provisionally, because Haaken would not keep it in his stead. He was supposed to show a certain decorum.

He caught his captain watching him. Sanguinet wore an amused smirk. For reasons Ragnarson could not comprehend he had become a pet project of Sanguinet's soon after he had enlisted. That did not make life easier. Sanguinet rode him harder than he did anyone else.

They had stumbled into soldier's heaven. The drinking was free, the women were easy, the people were desperate to please, and the duty was light. For the first time Bragi found himself enjoying soldiering.

The idyll lasted two weeks.

The horizons were masked by smoke. Nassef's warriors were not charitable conquerers. Anything they could not drive off or carry away they burned or killed. The Scourge of God appeared to be developing a vicious image deliberately.

"Sure are a lot of them," Bragi observed.

"Too many," Haaken said.

The Scourge of God had been closing in for days. Only a few outlying strongholds remained unsubdued.

"Must be a hundred thousand of them," Reskird guessed.

He was not overestimating much. The excitement of war and easy plunder had penetrated Hammad al Nakir's nethermost reaches. Thousands who cared not a fig for El Murid's revelations had answered his call to arms.

They might doubt his religious pretensions and social tinkering, but they loved his message of Imperial redemption and dominance, of historical rectification. The west had brought Ilkazar low. Now the hammer was in the other hand.

Reskird was having trouble concealing his trepidation. "Tents like whitecaps on the sea," he murmured.

"Horses can't climb walls," Bragi reminded. And, "We'll make chopped meat out of them if they storm us."

Simballawein's defenders numbered twenty-five hundred Guildsmen and ten thousand experienced native troops. The Grand Council had armed a horde of city folk as well, but their value was doubtful. Even so, General Hawkwind believed he could ensure the city's safety.

"Something will go wrong," Haaken prophesied.

For once his pessimism proved well-founded.

Nassef had laid his groundwork early and well. His agents had performed perfectly. The attack began straight-forwardly, concentrating on the south walls, which were held by native troops and city militia. Hordes of desert warriors rushed in to perish beneath the ramparts. As Bragi had observed, it was not their kind of warfare. The few engines they had bothered to build were almost laughably crude and vulnerable.

But Nassef knew his troops. That was why he had begun sugaring the path long before the invasion began.

In Simballawein, as everywhere, there was a breed of man loyal only to gold, and a class interested only in the political main chance. Nassef's agents had structured a pro-El Murid government-in-waiting from the latter. The quislings had used desert gold to hire desperadoes willing to betray their city.

They attacked Simballawein's South Gate from within, while its defenders were preoccupied with the attack from without. They opened the gate.

Scimitars flashed. Horsemen howled through the gateway. Iron-shod hooves sent sparks flying from cobbled streets. Arrows streaked from saddle-bows.

Arrows and javelins answered from windows and rooftops, but the unskilled citizen-soldiers could not stem the flood. They received conflicting orders from conspirators who had infiltrated their organization. Hastily assembled companies raced off to peaceful sectors. Panic spread. And all the while horsemen charged through the lost gate and spread out as swiftly as oil on water.

The panic spread to the rest of the city.

Panic had become Nassef's favorite weapon during his eastern campaigns. He had exploited it in his seizure of Al Rhemish. Now he was intent on teaching the western kingdoms the terror of the horseman who moved like lightning, who appeared and vanished, and struck where least expected.

Simballawein was like a dinosaur. Its immense size kept it from dying immediately.

The youths on the north wall watched the fires bloody the underbellies of the clouds and listened to the moans of a city collapsing.

"I think it's getting closer," Reskird said.

They knew what was happening. This was Simballawein's last independent night. And they were scared.

"How come we're just sitting here?" one of the soldiers asked.

"I don't know," Bragi admitted. "The Captain will let us know what to do."

"So damned hot," Haaken muttered. The heat of the fires could be felt this far away.

"I don't want to second-guess Hawkwind. . . ."

"Then don't, Reskird," Haaken grumbled.

"I was just going to say. . . ."

"Ragnarson?" Lieutenant Trubacik carefully stepped over the legs of lounging soldiers. The ramparts were narrow.

"Here, sir."

"Report to the Captain."

"Yes sir."

Trubacik moved to the next squad. "Haven?"

Bragi went to Sanguinet's command post. "Gather round," the Captain said softly, when everyone had arrived. "And keep your voices down. All right. Here's the word. There's no hope of holding. The situation has deteriorated too much. The General has informed the Grand Council. Come midnight, we're pulling out."

Voices buzzed.

"Keep it down. Somebody out there might speak Itaskian. Gentlemen, I want you to speak to your men. The enemy main force has moved around to the south, but we're still going to have to fight. On the march. Discipline is going to make the difference. And we're going to have to give a little extra. We're green. There's going to be veterans in front of us and behind us, but we've still got to take care of our part of the line."

Bragi did not like it. Hawkwind thought he could fight his way through a larger, more mobile army?

"Maintaining discipline is a must. We're taking civilians with us. The Grand Councilors, their families, and the Tyrant. The Tyrant will bring his own escort, but don't count on them if it gets tight. We're in the narrow passage. We can't count on anybody but our brothers."

Ragnarson began to understand what it meant to be a Guildsman.

He also saw how Hawkwind could justify abandoning a commission. With Simballawein's rulers deserting their people, he would be following his commissioners.

"The march will be short. We'll hit a bay on the coast twelve miles north of here. A fleet is waiting to pick us up."

"Why not sail from here?" somebody asked.

"The waterfront is in enemy hands. That's all, men. There isn't much time. Explain to your people. Discipline and silence. Discipline and silence."

The group dispersed. Similar assemblies broke up elsewhere.

"It's crazy," Reskird protested. "They'll get us all killed."

"How much chance have we got here?" Bragi demanded. "Haaken, find me a dirty sock."

"What?"

"Get me a sock. I'm going to cram it in his mouth and

keep it there 'til we're aboard ship. I don't want him shooting his mouth off out there and getting us wiped out."

"Hey!" Reskird protested.

"That's the last noise I want to hear out of you tonight. Get your stuff. Here comes Trubacik."

"Ready, Ragnarson?"

"Ready, sir."

"Take them down to the street. The captain will form you up."

The wait in the dark street, behind the gate, seemed eternal. Even Sanguinet became impatient. Several Grand Councilors were late.

Native soldiers kept drifting in and joining the Tyrant's bodyguard. The Guildsmen became nervous. News of the proposed breakout was spreading. The enemy would hear before long.

Hawkwind reviewed his troops during the delay. He was a small, slim man in his fifties. He looked like a harmless shopkeeper, not the most devastating captain of the age. Till one looked him in the eye.

Bragi saw raw power in the man. Raw power and pure will. Only death Herself could best a man like General Sir Tury Hawkwind.

Hawkwind completed the review, then informed the Tyrant he would wait no longer. The gates opened. Ragnarson was surprised how quietly they moved.

A moment later he was double-timing into jeopardy. Enemy watchfires formed constellations on the hills and plains. He clutched his weapons and kit to keep them from clattering, and tried not to be afraid.

But he was scared. Badly scared. Again. After all he had survived, he felt his capacity for fear should have been blunted.

They started north on the road that had brought Sanguinet's Company south. They would leave it later and follow another to the coast.

First contact came quickly. Nassef's men were alert.

56

But they were not ready for a sally in force. The Guildsmen cut through easily.

Bragi suddenly understood why Hawkwind had chosen to flee at midnight. Darkness negated the enemy's speed and maneuverability. Only suicides galloped around when they couldn't see.

Nevertheless, Nassef's men kept getting in the way. And when they slowed the column, their brethren overtook it from behind.

The fighting seldom reached Bragi's company. He and Haaken occupied themselves carrying a Guildsman who had fallen and nearly been left behind. They did not talk much.

An hour fled. Miles passed. Another hour trudged into the warehouse of time. Hawkwind kept moving. The enemy could not place a preponderance of strength into his path.

Hours and miles. The sky began lightening.

"I hear the breakers," Haaken gasped. Their burden had become agonizingly heavy.

Bragi snorted. "Even if we were close, you couldn't hear the surf over the noise we're making."

But Haaken was right. They tramped through an olive grove and there lay the sea. A galaxy of lanterns sparkled on the water as ships signalled their whereabouts.

"The ships," Haaken muttered to himself. "I see the ships."

The run ended ten minutes later. The secundus and tercio started digging in. Longboats began carrying Councilors to the vessels.

It was a big fleet. Some of the ships had escaped Simballawein. Some, Hellin Daimiel had sent against this contingency. The Daimiellians wanted to salvage Guildsmen who might stiffen their own defenses.

El Murid's men attacked, but without verve or organization. These were not fanatics, they were plunderers. They saw no profit in trying to obliterate a beaten foe. The Guildsmen repulsed them easily.

Bragi's company was one of the last into the boats.

He was digging an arrowhead from Reskird's shoulder when Sanguinet said, "You boys might have the stuff after all."

Bragi was startled. He had not noticed the captain getting aboard.

"Sir?"

"I saw you pick up a man and carry him to the beach."

"He was one of ours."

"You'll make it, Ragnarson. So will your brother. The man was dead the last three miles."

"What? I never noticed."

"What's wrong with your sidekick there? He don't stay this quiet when he's asleep."

"I told him to shut up. He was getting on my nerves."

"Oh? Maybe he'll make a Guildsman too."

"Maybe. You can talk now, Reskird. You made your point."

But Kildragon refused. He was sulking.

The fleet made Hellin Daimiel three days later.

Nassef's horde had raced them northward. The roads out of the city had been cut. A noose was tightening fast. In a few days the sea would be the city's only means of communication.

Hellin Daimiel was not Simballawein. Nassef's confederates were caught and hung before they did any harm.

Bragi's company spent six weeks there, remaining till Hawkwind and the ruling council were sure the city was in no immediate danger.

"Company meeting," Lieutenant Trubacik told Ragnarson one morning. "The rumors were right. We're moving out."

Sanguinet was sour. "The Citadel is sending us to the Lesser Kingdoms. Nassef isn't interested in Hellin Daimiel right now. Meanwhile, Itaskia and the other northern states are raising an army. We're supposed to keep Nassef from clearing his eastern flank, to threaten him into staying south of the Scarlotti till the northern army arrives. It'll be tough, especially if the Kaveliners don't hold in the Savernake Gap.

"We're going to Altea. I guess it's mainly a moral gesture. One company can't do much. My opinion is that we'll be wasting ourselves. The Citadel should assemble the whole brotherhood and take the initiative. But High Crag didn't ask me what I thought.

"We'll board ships in the morning. They'll ferry us to Dunno Scuttari. We'll transfer to river boats there. We'll off-load somewhere in eastern Altea and play hit-and-run.

"Gentlemen, we're the best warriors in the world. But this time I think somebody is a little too sure of us. Break it to your men gently."

Sanguinet entertained only a few questions. He did not have any answers.

Reskird had ended his sulk in the taverns and whorehouses of the city. He was his old self. "You look like death on a stick," he told Bragi. "What's up?"

"They're shipping us to the Lesser Kingdoms."

"Huh?"

"Altea, specifically. On our own. You'd better hope that Sanguinet is as good a captain as he was a sergeant."

Haaken had no comment. He just shook his head gloomily.

Chapter Six: *THE WANDERER*

The fat youth's arms and legs pistoned wildly. He had done it again. The boys behind him had never heard of the concept mercy.

His donkey, for once, was cooperative. She trotted beside him, eyes rolling forlornly, as if to ask if he would ever learn his lesson. He was headed for an early bout with cut-throat-itis, an often fatal disease.

He was on a downhill slide, this Mocker. The town he was leaving was called Lieneke. It was hardly more than a village. A chance aggregation of bumpkins. And even they had caught on to his cheating.

A fragment of the message had begun to penetrate his brain. He was going to have to do things differently from now on. Assuming he got away this time.

The boys of Lieneke were a determined, persistent lot, but they did not have enough at stake. Fat and lazy though he was, Mocker had stamina. He kept windmilling till they gave up the chase.

He did not go on any farther than it took to get out of sight. Then he collapsed by the roadside and did not move for two days.

He did some hard thinking during that time, and

finally convinced himself that he did not have what it took to cheat his way through life.

But what else could he do? His only skills were those he had learned from Sajac and his ilk.

He ought to find a patron, he thought. Somebody stupid but buried in inherited wealth. He smiled wryly, then steeled himself for a serious effort to avoid games of chance and outright thefts.

His visible profession was socially acceptable. Sure, he obtained money under false pretenses, but his customers were fooling themselves. The popular attitude was a tolerant *caveat emptor*. People gullible enough to buy his crazy advice and noxious beauty aids deserved whatever they got.

He finally moved on when a combination of hunger and fear caught up with him. The passage of a party of knights caused the fear.

He had encountered a similar band near Vorgreberg several weeks earlier. The men-at-arms had beaten him simply because he was a foreigner. He had not accepted his beating graciously, and that had not helped. He was a wicked little fighter when cornered. He had hurt several of them badly. They might have killed him had a knight not interceded.

Kavelin was a state typical of the Lesser Kingdoms. Those minor principalities were a crazy hodge-podge where social chaos was the norm. They were lands of weak kings, strong barons, and byzantine politics. National boundaries seldom defined or confined loyalties, alliances, or conspiracies. Wars between nobles were everyday occurrences. Uncontrolled sub-infeudation had reached illogical extremes. The robber baron was an endemic social disease. The blank-shield highwayman-knight was a neighborhood character.

It was the sort of region for which a Mocker was made.

Western Kavelin was in confusion at the moment. The barons there were at one another's throats. Their little armies were plundering the innocent far more often than battling one another. A lot of loot was floating around.

Mocker decided that Damhorst, which appeared to be an islet of peace amidst all the excitement, was the perfect place to launch his abbreviated career.

Damhorst was a town of ten thousand, prosperous, quiet, and pleasant. The grim old castle perched on a crag above the town was intimidating enough to compel good behavior. Baron Breitbarth had a cruel reputation with wrongdoers.

Damhorst's prosperity was in part due to the fact that bands of soldiers from the fighting came there to dispose of their plunder, receiving ridiculously low prices.

A representative cross-section of Mocker's peers had located themselves around the town square. The fat youth moved in and fit in. Even his coloring and accent were unremarkable.

The fates immediately tried his resolve. His traditional pitch was not geared to milking soldiers looking for escape from yesterday and tomorrow. His forte was conning vain women. But the ladies he encountered there were mostly world-wise women of doubtful repute. They did not need his wares to help sell what his usual customers had trouble giving away.

But the fates occasionally relent. And sometimes they try to make amends for dealing out a lifetime of dirty tricks by yielding one golden opportunity.

It was a pleasant day. Mocker had to admit that Kavelin was pleasant most of the time. Politics were the true foul climate plaguing the little kingdom.

The leaves had begun to turn. He found them a great amazement. There were few trees in the lands from which he hailed. The swirls and bursts of color in Kavelin's forests made him wish he were a painter, so that he could capture their fleeting beauty for all time.

It was a warm and listless day. He sat on his mat, amidst his props, and regarded his world with no more than half an eye. Not even the fact that he hadn't a copper daunted him. He was at peace with, and one with, his universe. He was caught in one of those all too rare moments of perfectly harmonious rightness.

Then he saw her.

She was beautiful. Young and pretty and filled with sorrow. And lost. She meandered around the square dazedly, as if she had nowhere to go and had forgotten how to get there. She seemed frail and completely vulnerable.

Mocker felt the touch of a strange emotion. It might have been compassion. He could not have named it himself. The concept was alien.

Nevertheless, the emotion was there and he responded. When her random wandering brought her near he queried softly, "Lady?"

She glanced his way and saw a pair of hand puppets flanking a round brown face. The right hand puppet bowed graciously.

The other whistled.

The first barked, "Manners, Polo, you churl!" and zipped over to wallop the whistler. "Behave before lady of quality."

Mocker winked over his forearm. He wore a thin little smile.

She was younger than he had guessed at first. Not more than eighteen.

The first puppet bowed again and said, "Self, beg thousand pardons, noble lady. Peasant Polo was born in barn and raised by tomcat of more than usual lack of couth or morals." He took a few more whacks at the other puppet. "Barbarian."

When the first puppet returned to Mocker's right, Polo whistled again. The first moaned, "Hai! What can be done with savage like that? Want to slap manners into same?"

She smiled. "I think he's kind of cute."

Polo did a shy routine while the first puppet cried in

bewilderment, "Woe! Will never civilize same when beautiful lady rewards crudeness with heart-stopping smile."

"You're new here, aren't you?" The girl directed the question to Mocker.

"Came to town three days passing, lately from east, beyond Mountains of M'Hand."

"So far! I've never even been to Vorgreberg. I thought when I married Wulf.... But it's silly to worry about might-have-beens, isn't it?"

"Assuredly. Tomorrow too full of just-could-be to chase might-have-been lost in yesterday."

First Puppet hid behind his little arms. "You hear that, Polo? Big guy is spouting philosophical nonsense again."

"Will make first class fertilizer when spread on cabbage patch, Tubal," Polo replied. "We ignore him, eh? Hey, lady, you hear joke about priest and magic staff?"

Tubal sputtered. "Polo, peasant like you would disgust devil himself. Behave. Or I ask big guy to feed you to skull."

"Skull ain't biting," said a third voice as Mocker cast his into the prop's mouth. "On diet. Have to lose weight."

Mocker himself said, "Being mere street mummer, have no right to pry. But self sense great despair in lady and am saddened. Day is too fair for grief."

"Oh. My husband.... Sir Wulf Heerboth. He died last night. I didn't sleep at all."

Tubal and Polo exchanged glances. They turned to peer at Mocker. He shrugged. He was at a loss. "Is great pity one so fair should be widowed so young."

"We had such precious little time.... What am I saying? I'm almost glad. He was a beast. My father arranged the marriage. It was two years of torment, that's what it was. Now I'm free of that."

Mocker began to see the parameters. In part she was grieving because she was supposed to, in part feeling guilty for feeling released, and in part feeling insecure in the face of a future without a protector.

"Beautiful lady like you, knight's lady. . . . Noblemen will come swarming when mourning period elapses. Self, guarantee it. Certain as self is magus primus of Occlidian Circle. Be not afraid, lady. And be not ashamed for glad feelings for freedom from slavery to wicked husband. Never, never make self into what family and friends expect. Is road to misery absolute. Self, speak from certain knowledge."

"Oh-oh," said Polo. "Here we go. Tall tale time."

"That seems like awfully deep thinking for someone your age."

Mocker doubted that she was more than a year older than he, but he did not protest.

Tubal replied, "Big guy was born in hole in ground. Deep hole."

The girl smiled. "Well. . . ."

"Is deep subject, too. Of varying depth. In Shoustal-Wotka. . . ."

"What's your name, mummer?"

He could not generate one on the spur of the moment, so confessed, "Self, am ashamed. Don't know. Call self Mocker in own mind."

"What about your parents?"

"Never knew same."

"You were an orphan?"

He shrugged. He did not think so. He liked to believe that Sajac had carried him off out of spite for his parents, that even now they were looking for him. He might be a missing prince, or the lost son of a great mercantile house. "Maybeso."

"That's awful. Don't you have anybody?"

"Old man, once. Travelled with same for while. He died."

A tiny fraction of his mind kept telling him that he was getting himself into trouble. There were two kinds of people in his world: marks, and people he left alone because they could stir more trouble than he could handle. This woman fit neither category neatly. That made her doubly dangerous. He did not know which way to jump.

"That's sad," she said. "My father is still alive, and that's kind of sad too. I just know he's going to try to get his hands on everything Wulf left me."

Ping! went a little something in the back of Mocker's mind. "This father. . . . Same is superstitious? Self, being most skilled of tricksters. . . ."

"I couldn't do anything to my own father! Even if he did marry me off hoping Wulf would get himself killed. It wouldn't be right. . . ."

Tubal interrupted. "Was remark made, not too long passing, to effect don't allow friends and family to run life. Big guy was close to truth."

"You don't know my father."

"Truth told," Mocker replied. "And same does not know portly purveyor of punditries. So. Things equal to same thing are equal. Something like that. Hai! Lady. Self, being easily embarrassed, cannot forever call conversant 'beautiful lady.' Same must have name."

"Oh. Yes. Kirsten. Kirsten Heerboth."

"Kirsten. Has beautiful ring. Like carillon. Appropriate. Kirsten, we make deal, maybeso? For small emolument, self, being mighty engineer, will undertake to prevent predations of pestilential parent. Also rapacities of others of same ilk. Am easily satisfied, being wanderer mainly interested in visiting foreign lands, needing only bed and board. Would be willing to begin with latter."

"I don't know. . . . It doesn't seem. . . . Are you really hungry?"

"Hungry?" Polo said. "Big guy is putting eye on horse across square, same being prizest mount of Chief Justiciar of Damhorst."

"Well, come along then. I don't guess it'll hurt to give you dinner. But you'll have to promise me something."

Mocker sighed. "Same being?"

"Let Polo tell me about the priest and the magic staff."

"Disgusting!" Tubal growled as Mocker stuffed him into his travelling kit. "Absolutely shocking," the puppet muttered from inside.

Mocker grinned.

Kirsten maintained a small townhouse on the edge of Damhorst, in the shadow of Baron Breitbarth's grim old castle. An elderly maid-cook constituted her staff. Sir Wulf had been one of those highwayman-knights, and only marginally successful. He had left Kirsten the house, one gold trade noble, and a small leather bag of jewels she had found inside his shirt after he died in her arms. The gold would carry her a month or two, and the jewels several years more, but she was hardly fixed for life.

Mocker reiterated his remark to the effect that her beauty was her fortune.

The visit for a meal turned into a month-long stay. Daily, Mocker would spread his mat in the square—he insisted that he had his pride—and would pursue his routines. Sometimes he was successful. People enjoyed the entertainment portions of his spiel. More often than not, Kirsten would come and watch. He seemed to have an infinite store of blarney.

Evenings he amused her with tales from the east. She was particularly fond of Tubal and Polo, who were famous puppet-show characters east of the Mountains of M'Hand. The contest of city-slicker with simple farm boy seemed to have a universal appeal. The traditional plays were all adaptable to rural or urban audiences.

Time, proximity, and loneliness worked their devious magics. Mocker and Kirsten became more than accomplices, then more than friends.

Handling Kirsten's father took little imagination. Mocker used earnings from the square to pay a couple of thugs to escort the man out of town. He had no trouble understanding the message in his lumps and bruises. He kept travelling.

Kirsten never learned about that, of course. She remained amazed that the old man had paid but the one friendly visit.

Mocker began to feel vaguely lost. He had had plans. Nebulous things, to be sure, but they had been plans. They were going by the board because of a chance-met woman.

He had become involved with a human being on more than an adversary or use level. He did not know how to handle it. Nothing like it had ever happened before.

The deeper he got, the more uncomfortable he became.

He almost panicked the day Kirsten mentioned that she had been to see a priest, and that the priest wanted to see him too. He barely restrained himself from flight.

A few days afterward Kirsten swore, "Damn! Do you have any money on you? Mine's gone."

He lied, shaking his head. "Has been abominable week. Autumn rains. Getting too cold, too muddy."

"I guess it means selling the jewels. I talked to Tolvar last week. The goldsmith on the High Street. He said he'd make me a good price. Why don't you run them over and see what he'll offer?"

"Self? By night? In town thick with rogues and thieves?" His heart hammered. He could not picture himself lasting five minutes with a fortune like that on him.

His world-view crippled him. He saw in everyone the thief he was himself.

"You can handle yourself, darling. I've seen you. Besides, who would know that you're carrying them?"

"Everybodys. Self, being nervous, would worry too loud. . . ."

"Don't be silly." She shoved the leather bag into his pudgy hands. "Go on. Or we won't have anything to eat tomorrow."

He went. His intentions were honorable. Kirsten was his first love. Temptation did not bite him till he entered the High Street itself.

He froze.

He thought about everything jewels could buy. About Kirsten and an imminent visit to a priest. About opportunities in games of chance opened by unlimited betting funds. About that damned priest. . . .

He panicked. This time he did run.

He did not realize that he had left his donkey and props till he was over the border into the kingdom of Altea.

By then it was too late. He could not go back. He had damned himself with Kirsten forever.

It hurt. A lot. For weeks the pain kept him contained within himself, and out of trouble.

But the ache just would not go away. He began drinking to deaden it. And in Alperin, a small town in southern Altea, while drunk, he wandered into a dice game.

His luck was terrible. His mental state contributed nothing to intelligent betting. Before they let him go he was broke again, having retained just enough common sense to have earlier re-equipped himself with the tools of his dubious trade.

The exigencies of surviving an Altean winter banished Kirsten from his thoughts. He had no time for her. She fled him forever.

With her went his proud resolutions about gambling and thieving.

He ceased giving a damn about tomorrow. His future looked too bleak. He could no longer scrutinize it. And the less he cared, the bleaker it became.

He had fallen into a paradoxical trap. Though filled with a lust for life and learning, he was systematically eradicating tomorrows with wine and stupid crimes.

Tamerice lay south of Altea, a long snake of a kingdom squished between the Kapenrung Mountains and the Altean frontier. Mocker drifted into Tamerice with spring. His successes had been just frequent enough to keep body and soul together. His weight had declined. He had developed a shakiness which occasionally betrayed him when he tried one of his more complicated tricks.

He drew his best response when he stooped to entertaining. Tamericians enjoyed the Tubal and Polo plays. But a false pride or unconscious death wish drove him. He performed only when gnawing hunger compelled it.

He reached the town of Raemdouck the day after a carnival had arrived, and spread his mat beside the road the Raemdouckers followed to the field where the carnival had raised its tents. A pre-selected traffic helped him marginally.

His third morning there, before traffic picked up, he had a visitor. The man was tall, lean, and had tight, dark eyes in a hard face. Policeman? Bandit? Mocker wondered nervously.

The man sat down facing him, stared for more than a minute.

Mocker wriggled. A demon ground coarse salt into his nerve endings.

"I'm Damo Sparen," his visitor finally announced. His voice was as cold and hard as his appearance. "I own the carnival. I've been watching you."

Mocker shrugged. Was he supposed to beg forgiveness for bleeding off a miniscule portion of the man's revenues?

"You're interesting. One of the nastier cases of self-abuse I've seen. Talent bleeds out of you, and you waste it to the last ounce. Do you *want* to die young?"

Mocker gulped. "Maybeso. In thousand years, or two." He grinned weakly. He was scared. "What is going on here?"

"I wanted to tell you something. I'm no diviner, but this prediction doesn't require the skills of a necromancer. You will die. Soon. Unless you mend your ways."

Mocker's fear tightened its noose.

"You keep cutting purses, somebody's going to cut your throat. Before summer's done. You're too damned clumsy."

71

Mocker swallowed the lump in that throat. He was bewildered. The man sounded like an evangelist.

"My eastern friend, I'm going to give you a chance to see Old Man Winter again. I'm looking for someone with your talents and not much conscience. I could use you. If we could dry you out and knock a little sense in your head. You've got the skills, but they're in bad shape."

"Self, am unsure hearing is accurate. Explicate, please. Am being offered position?"

"Conditionally. I need a ventriloquist and magician. My performers usually get a share of the net. In your case that won't hold unless you shape up. I'll give you food, found, and lessons in whatever you don't already have. Hypnotism, for instance. Make it a trial period of three months. If you stop the drinking and stealing. . . . Don't try to bullshit me, my friend. I told you I've been watching you.

"Even without a share it's more than you've got now. Like I said, you won't last the summer this way."

Mocker hemmed and hawed. He could not believe the man was serious. Nevertheless, he decided to take a chance. He could be no worse off.

It was a fateful decision. Damo Sparen would quickly shape the raw Mocker clay into the man he would become.

Sparen was a westerner, and older, but was Mocker's spiritual brother. Their black, lazy souls had been struck on the same dies.

While supervising Mocker's higher education, Sparen became his first real friend.

"One thing you've got to learn," Sparen told him early on. "Discipline. Your troubles all stem from a lack of discipline."

Mocker sputtered.

"I mean self-discipline, not the poundings you got from Sajac. They're part of your problem, too. You don't know how to handle your freedom.

"My friend, you made it this far on sheer talent. But

72

you've got to learn some things that don't come instinctively. You've refused so far. So you've been hungry a lot.

"Sparen's First Law: Always make the mark think he's smarter than you are. Make him think it's him doing the con. Greed will carry it for you then.

"Second Law: Don't work a con where you're boosting. Or vice versa. I warned you before, don't steal around the carnival. Yesterday you cut a purse within a hundred feet of your puppet show. Don't let it happen again. I'm not patient. You could get my whole operation broken up.

"Third Law: Don't aggravate the underworld. You got to stay in good with those guys. They're organized. You leave a bad marker with Three Fingers in Hellin Daimiel and run off to Octylya, when you get there the Dragon's men will be waiting. With knives. They like to do each other little favors.

"Fourth Law: Think big. That crap of sitting in the street selling mud packs made with cat's piss ain't got no future. You'll be doing the same thing fifty years from now. Just like Sajac."

Mocker finally interjected, "Self, am able to do only what is known to self."

"Then suppose you stop scheming and stealing long enough to learn something? You're secure here. You don't have to take risks. Expand your talents instead. Look at me, Mocker. I started out where you are now. Today I've got a villa on the Auszura Littoral. A duke is my next door neighbor. I've got copra plantations in Simballawein. I've got mines in Anstokin."

"Hai! And still. . . ."

"And still I travel with the carnival? Of course. It's in my blood. It's in yours. We can't resist the challenge. Of what the carnival represents. One more sucker taken for everything but his greedy smile. But I don't do that kind of thing as Sparen. Sparen and his carnival are cover.

73

Sparen is an honest and respected businessman. People trust him enough to loan him money."

For once in his life Mocker listened.

"You had what you needed when you got a hold of those jewels. Working capital. More than I started with. How in heaven's name could you have wasted it that way?"

"Self, am mystified. Am bambazoolooed. Am utterly ignorant of course to pursue."

"That's good. That's a beautiful touch. The way you talk. Never change it. If they can't understand you, they can't ever be sure their losses weren't their own fault. At worst, you'll get a little more getaway time. And it'll help convince them they're smarter that you are."

"First Law."

"Exactly."

Mocker's secondary education proceeded apace. He began to learn the self-restraint that had been missing most of his life. Sparen gave a little heavy-handed encouragement, in the form of a gigantic thug named Gouch who was always there, sap in hand, when temptation stalked too close.

"I think we're getting somewhere, my friend," Sparen told him late that summer. And he meant the word friend. They had become as close as two men could. "I think you're ready to be a partner."

"Hai! Good. Self, have several ideas. . . ."

"This war thing has got me scared," Sparen told him, trampling his enthusiasm. "They're bully-ragging Throyes. If those crazies take over and come out of Hammad al Nakir, they'll crawl all over the Lesser Kingdoms. They'll ruin us. I've seen what a war can do to business. Luckily, this carnival business isn't the only one. There're a few better suited to wartime. It's time to start getting ready. Just in case." Sparen downed a long draft of wine. "You know, I never had a son. Not that I could acknowledge. I think I've kind of found one now."

Mocker's eyes narrowed. Was this just talk born of a mating 'twixt wine and melancholy?

"Well, that's neither here nor there. We've got to find you a trade name. Magellin the Magician strikes me. I used to have a partner who went by that. But I caught him shorting the accounts. Had to elevate his spirit to a higher plane and lower his flesh to the fishes. It was a sad occasion. I cried for an hour. I thought he was a good friend. Don't you do that to me, you hear?"

"Is farthest thing from mind, guaranteed. Have developed healthy respect for Gouch and own neck. Have learned to mend ways."

Which was not strictly true. He had learned a lot of wicked and wonderful things from Sparen and Gouch, but mending his ways was not one of them. He never could stifle his urge to cut a purse, or to squander his takings gambling.

What he did learn was how to manage theft with finesse, while Gouch was watching, so that he alone knew what was going on.

Chapter Seven: *THE EXILES*

The first assassins reached the mountain camp with the spring thaw. Six good men died stopping them. "Always in threes," Haroun gasped. He was pale and soaked with sweat. "Harish always come in threes. What moves men like that, Beloul? They knew they were going to die."

Beloul shrugged and shook his head. "They believe in their cause, Lord."

A second team materialized almost immediately, and a third followed close behind. Haroun imagined an endless line of smiling, vacant-eyed men coming to die for their prophet, each certain of immediate entry into paradise.

Distinguishing friend from foe was impossible in the ongoing refugee chaos.

"Beloul, I can't stay here," Haroun declared after the third attack left eight followers dead. "I'm a sitting target. They won't stop as long as they know where to find me."

"Let them come. I'll strip every newcomer and look for the Harish tattoo." The cultists wore a tattoo over the heart. It faded after death, purportedly when the soul ascended to paradise.

"They'll send men without it. I'm moving out. I'll drift from camp to camp. I have to show the flag anyway, don't I?" Winter boredom moved him as much as did the attacks. He was driven by a youthful eagerness to be moving, to be doing. He selected a half dozen companions and departed.

The camps heightened his appreciation of his mission. He was appalled.

The break with Hammad al Nakir meant a break with a fragile culture and briefly settled past. In some places the ancient desert ways, the nomadic, pre-Royal ways, were reemerging.

"What's wrong with plundering foreigners?" asked a captain in a camp run by an old functionary named Shadek el Senoussi.

"*We* are the foreigners here, you idiot!" Haroun glanced at el Senoussi. The man's face was a mask. "And these people are more understanding than I would be were our roles reversed. I'll tell you a thing, Shadek. If your men bother your neighbors again I'll swing the headsman's blade myself. Quesani law endures, even in exile. Its protection extends to everyone who welcomed us in our extremity."

"I hear, Lord." The old man wore a slight smile now. Haroun had a distinct feeling he approved.

"This is the end of it, then. If it chokes you, tough. Treat your neighbors as equals. We need their help."

Rebellion smouldered in el Senoussi's men. Haroun glared back. The old man needed replacing. He commanded too much personal loyalty.

Few of the camp leaders were enthusiastic about him. Some were spiritual brothers of El Murid's generals: born bandits smelling opportunity in chaos. Others simply did not like being commanded by an untried youth.

He drifted westward, accompanied only by his bodyguards. He met and assessed all his captains. Then he began to seek allies.

He discovered that a claimed kingship opened no doors.

"We'll see," he grumbled after yet another rejection. "They'll sing a different song when the Scourge of God begins hammering the Lesser Kingdoms."

"Let them burn," one guard suggested.

"Will he really come?" another asked.

"Someone will. My old teacher called it historical inertia. Nothing can stop it. Not even the deaths of Nassef and El Murid."

"Many men will die, then."

"Too many, and a lot of them ours. The Disciple doesn't know what he's doing."

He tried. He tried bravely and hard, and won no support anywhere. And he went on, his mission driving him mercilessly. His guards began to fear he was obsessed.

Finally, he admitted defeat. There would be no help while the Lesser Kingdoms were not directly threatened. He returned to the camps.

He was in el Senoussi's encampment when Harish assassins found him again. Three teams attacked together. They slew his bodyguards. They slew half a score of Shadek's men. They wounded Haroun twice before el Senoussi rescued him.

"Dismiss me, Lord!" the old man begged. "My failure cannot be excused."

"Stop that. It couldn't be helped. Ouch! Careful, man!" A horse trainer was dressing his wounds. "We have a savage, determined enemy, Shadek. This is going to keep on till we're killed or we destroy him."

"I should have seen through them, Lord."

"May be. May be. But how?" Haroun grew thoughtful. The attack had shaken el Senoussi, yet he seemed more upset because it had happened at his camp than because it had happened to his king.

El Senoussi, Haroun recalled, was an appointee of King Aboud's, a lifelong functionary. He'd spent decades shunning blame and appropriating credit. "Forget the Harish, Shadek. They're like the weather. We have

to live with them. Meantime, we have fires to put out."
The assassins had started several. Billowing smoke still
climbed the sky.

The log blockhouse that was the camp's bailey, and a
hutment against the palisade, stubbornly resisted the
firemen. The swiftness with which the flames had taken
hold bespoke careful preparation.

"Why did they go to the trouble?" Haroun wondered.
"They could have killed me if they hadn't wasted the
time."

"I don't know, Lord."

The answer came three hours later.

A sentinel called, "Invincibles!"

"Here?" Haroun demanded. "In Tamerice?" He peered
over the stockade.

Horsemen were coming out of a nearby wood. They
wore Invincible white.

"Must be a hundred of them, Lord," el Senoussi
estimated. "The fires must have been a signal."

"So it would seem." Haroun surveyed the encampment.
Women and children were moving provisions into the
charred blockhouse. They looked scared, but were not
panicking. El Senoussi had drilled them well.

"Lord, escape while you can. I only have eighty-three
men. Some of them are wounded."

"I'll stay. What good a King who always runs away?"

"He's alive when his moment comes."

"Let them come. I was trained in the Power." He
spoke from bravado and frustration. He wanted to hit
back.

El Senoussi backed away. "A sorcerer-king?"

Haroun saw the fear-reflections of the kings of Ilkazar
gleaming in the man's eyes.

"No. Hardly. But maybe I can blow a little smoke into
their eyes."

The Invincibles knew what they were doing. Their
intelligence was perfect. Their first attack penetrated

the stockade despite Haroun's shaghûnry and a ferocious defense.

"They're getting through where the hutment burned," Haroun shouted. He whirled. El Senoussi was barking orders. Warriors grabbed saddle bows and sped arrows into the throng in the gap, but the Invincibles entered the compound anyway.

"Go to the blockhouse, sire," el Senoussi urged. "You're just one more sword out here. You can bedevil them with your witchery from there."

Haroun allowed himself to be guided through the tumult. He saw the sense of Shadek's argument.

He *was* more effective from the blockhouse. He did little things and quickly betrayed individual enemies. The Invincibles gave up.

"That was close," Haroun told el Senoussi.

"It's not over. They're not going away. They're circling the camp."

Haroun looked over the palisade. "Some are circling. Some look like they're going for help."

"You'd better leave tonight, Lord."

It was the practical, logical, pragmatic course, but Haroun did not like it. "They'll be waiting for me to try. Or for somebody going after help."

"Naturally. But would they expect us to attack? They believe their own reputation. If we sallied without trying to get away. . . ."

"It might confuse them because it doesn't make much sense."

"It does if it gets you away, Lord."

"I don't understand you, Shadek."

"Don't try, Lord. Just go. And send help."

Haroun fled during el Senoussi's third sally. He went afoot, creeping like a thief, grinding his teeth because his wounds ached. He trudged doggedly through the night, ignoring his pain.

Dawn caught him fifteen miles northeast of the encampment. That put him just twenty from Tamerice's capital, Feagenbruch. The nearest refugee camp was more than forty miles away. He decided to try the capital.

It was risky. Tamerice's nobles might be so timorous they would ignore this compromise of the kingdom's sovereignty.

If they did react, though, they would make independent witnesses to an agression. Tamerice and its neighbors might assume a more bellicose stance toward El Murid.

That chance was worth the risk. El Senoussi's was only an interim encampment. Its loss would not constitute a significant defeat.

The Invincibles wanted to destroy him, not the camp, anyway. The big, important camps they would like to raid were all in the far north.

Haroun was known in Feagenbruch, and not well liked. He had aggravated the lords of that city with his importunities before.

He used his wounds, youth, and title to obtain entrée. He spoke well while explaining to the king's seneschal. He spoke even better once shown into the presence of the king himself.

"It's an outrage, Majesty," the seneschal opined. "We can't let such arrogance go unchallenged."

"Then gather what knights you can muster. Lead them yourself. Cousin," the king told Haroun, "accept my hospitality while this temerity is being rewarded."

"I thank you, Cousin," Haroun replied. He smiled softly. Indirectly, the man had recognized his claim to the Peacock Throne.

At week's end news came that the Invincibles had been defeated and harried back into the Kapenrung Mountains. El Senoussi's people had survived.

The shock waves of the incursion would, in time, course throughout the Lesser Kingdoms, stimulating the growth of animosity toward El Murid.

The Lesser Kingdoms were small and often impotent, but each was jealous of its independence and sovereignty.

Nationalism was stronger there than in the larger kingdoms.

Haroun met a man while he was waiting for the news.

It was an inconsequential thing then, but in time would shape the destinies of kingdoms.

Bored with Tamerice's squalid palace, which was a hovel compared even to Haroun's own boyhood home, he began sampling the excitements of the spring fair set up in the meadow north of town.

One afternoon he was watching the swordswallower when he sensed the approach of a wrongness. He could identify no positive threat. That puzzled him. Usually his intuition was more precise. He looked around.

He had come without guards. If ever there was a time for the Harish to strike, this was it. He damned himself for taking an unnecessary risk.

He reached with his shaghûn's senses.

That godawful palace. . . . Tamerice's rulers were a barbarous lot. Unlettered thick-wits disguising themselves in the trappings of noblemen. Feh! The only conversationalist there was a treasury clerk hired out of Hellin Daimiel. . . .

Only one individual stood out of the crowd of lean farmers and ginger-haired city folk. Short, fat, brown, apparently of Haroun's own age, he was an obvious alien. There was a hint of the desert about him, yet Haroun could not recall ever having seen a fat poor man there.

He let his senses dwell on the fat youth.

He *was* the source of the wrongness.

He's insane if he thinks he can get away with murder here, Haroun thought. He grabbed that notion, turned it over to look at its belly side.

The fat youth was no Harish crazy. Haroun sensed that quickly. He was up to something else.

Haroun's curiosity rose. He allowed himself to be stalked.

He had seen the fat man earlier. He was one of the

carnival performers. He did a good, if sometimes confusing, job of entertaining.

The fat youth was quick and deft. Haroun did not miss his purse for half a minute.

An instant's distraction was all it took, that one brief moment when the sword swallower breathed fire and Haroun was trying to puzzle out the mechanics of the trick.

He whirled when the realization hit him.

The fat youth was gone.

Bin Yousif smiled grimly. This thief was good, but he was a fool.

Haroun loosened his weapons and strolled toward the tent behind the booth where the fat youth had performed earlier.

Coins clinked inside the tent.

Haroun peeped through a tear. The youth was counting and grinning. His back was to the entrance.

Doubly a fool, Haroun thought. He entered the tent with the stealth of a ferret. He waited with his dagger bare.

The youth suddenly sensed his presence. He whirled, trying to rise.

Haroun's dagger pricked his throat. "Down!"

He plopped. Haroun thrust out a palm. His eyes were cold and hard and merciless. The fat youth's were frightened and calculating. "My money." Haroun's voice was soft and dangerous.

The thief started to say something, thought better of it. He handed Haroun his purse.

"The rest." He had seen the gold piece disappear. The youth was good, but he knew the tricks too. "Good. Now tell me why I shouldn't have you hung."

The youth began twitching.

So did Haroun's hand. His dagger pricked a dark throat again. "I was trained in the Power. You can't move fast enough to surprise me."

The youth stared at him.

"Do you know who I am?"

"No."

"Haroun bin Yousif."

The thief frowned, puzzled. Then, "Same being called King Without Throne?"

"Yes."

"So?"

"So you picked the wrong man, Lard Bottom. I could have you dangling from a royal gallows. But it's just occurred to me that that might be a waste. In my country we learn not to waste anything. I've just gotten the notion that you might be useful. If we could control your thievery."

"Same old song. Am foolishest of fools. Will never learn." The fat youth crossed his legs and folded his arms. "Self, am utterly indifferent to politics."

"The dagger rests in my hand, Tubby. That should make you a little concerned. Your choice is to work or hang. I'll pay you for the work if you do any good." He had been sculpting an odd-shaped little intrigue in the back of his mind for several months. This fat man with the unusual skills might be the character to execute it.

If he failed, so what? The world would be rid of a bandit.

Calculation flickered across the thief's face. He seemed to be thinking of agreeing for the moment so he could run later. Haroun smiled gently.

"Ten seconds. Then I'm leaving. With you, or to call the law."

"Woe!" the fat man cried. "Is infamous riddle of rock and hard place. Am bestruckt by horny dilemma. Am in narrow passage, between devil and deep. Am beset by quandary of epical dimension. Am driven to deepest depths of desperate, despairing desperation. . . ."

"Huh?" Haroun became confused by the verbal pyrotechnics. "Time's running out, Tubby."

"So much for tactic of bogglement and bewilderment. Only one course remaining: last refuge of mentally disadvantaged. Reason. Hai! Lord! Is impossible for self to leave carnival. Am partner in same. Junior partner, very, under closest scrutiny of baleful eye of paranoid senior partner, Damo Sparen, and incorruptible, house-size thug name of Gouch."

"Can't say I blame him. You travelling or hanging?"

"Hai! Lord! Have mercy. Am but humble fool. . . ."

"Pull that knife and you'll be a humble fool with a hole in his windpipe."

"Woe," the youth muttered. "Stars promised evil day. Should have paid attention." He got to his feet slowly. Haroun offered no help. "Will need several minutes to collect accoutrements."

"I'm not buying a baggage train."

"Self, am accustomed to company of certain tools. Am professional, not so? Carpenterses, same need hammers, saws. . . ."

"Hurry it up."

The fat man was gaining confidence. He saw that Haroun was reluctant to strike. "Show some manners, sand rat. Self, am in tight place, maybeso, but can yell and have whole carnival here in minute."

"Including your redoubtable senior partner? How excited would he be about your thieving?"

"Same taught self gentle art." He did not put enough conviction into it to daunt Haroun.

"No doubt. Is that why he watches you?"

The youth shrugged, started packing. "Has strange moments, Damo Sparen. Self, cannot understand same. Is like father sometimes, maybeso, and sometimes like jailor."

"All fathers are that way. What's your name? I can't call you Tubby forever."

"Is all same. Am Magellin the Magician here, sometimes."

Haroun started slightly. "I had a good friend named Megelin. They're too much alike. Try something else."

"Am known to self as Mocker. Same being from inconsequential incident long time passing, in nethermost east, before circumstance brought self on quest to west."

"Quest? And you ended up in a sideshow?"

Mocker chuckled weakly. "Self, must remember conversant is aspirant king. Must select words more precisionly, same being subject to interpretation by noble standard. Not knight's quest. Not holy quest. Simple search for place where enemy blades could not reach."

"Oh?" Haroun thumbed the edge of his knife. "Then you have a habit of making stupid mistakes."

Mocker caught the lilt of danger dancing along the edges of Haroun's words. "Not so! Have turned over new leaf. Have finally learned lesson. Present trap being otherwise impossible to escape, have seen light illuminating great truth heretofore eluding humble, foolish self. Truth is: is nothing free. When same seems in reach, then duck head. Fates are laying trap."

"I hope you learned. But you look too old to teach. How long does it take to stuff that junk in a bag?"

Mocker was stalling while trying to decide if he should yell for help. They both knew it. "Junk?" Mocker wailed. "Lord. . . ."

He looked at Haroun. The thin, leathery-skinned youth did not appear nervous. His self-confidence was too much for Mocker. He jerked his bag shut. "Is enough to get by. Sparen will care for rest. Now, must leave note for same, in explanation, or same will set hound Gouch on trail. Woe be unto man with Gouch for enemy."

"You read and write?"

Mocker held up fingers in a *little bit* sign. "Same skill being courtesy of cruel taskmaster, senior partner. Teaching, teaching. Always is teaching. Everythings."

"Do it quick. Make it good. And honest. You won't be back in a half hour to tear it up." Haroun could commiserate with the fat youth. How Radetic had driven him in his reading, writing, and language lessons!

Mocker was cunning enough not to assume that his captor was illiterate. He wrote a simple parting note saying that he would return in a few days. He had chanced on an opportunity to profit from the confusion along the border. He wrote in the language of Hellin Daimiel, which was the *lingua franca* of the Lesser Kingdoms, and Haroun's best foreign language.

"Is there anything else?" Haroun demanded.

"Donkey, that is oldest friend of self. Is in corral."

"You lead. I'll be a step behind you." He shook his head, muttering. "Might have known. Best friends with a jackass." He let Mocker leave before sheathing his dagger.

Two men were waiting outside. Mocker stood there with his mouth open, speechless. He seemed caught in the gap between relief and fear.

"What's this?" Haroun demanded.

Mocker found his tongue. "Sparen. Gouch."

Haroun had no trouble guessing which was which. Gouch would be the mountain of beef blocking their way past the performance booth. "Move this creature," he told the smaller man, who was seated on a crate.

"Where're you going, Mocker?" Sparen asked. He ignored Haroun. "Would you be taking anything with you?"

"Donkey. . . ."

Haroun pushed past the fat youth. "Move it," he told Gouch.

Gouch seemed to be deaf. Sparen said, "I wasn't talking to you, boy."

"I have spoken twice. I won't speak again."

Sparen's irritation showed. "You've got a mouth, boy. Gouch, shut him up."

Gouch moved quicker than a snake striking

Haroun moved faster. He cut the big man three times, not too badly.

Mocker tried to run. Haroun tripped him, wheeled on Sparen. "I'd guess Gouch is a valuable property. Move him or lose him."

"You have a point. Gouch, step back. I'll handle this myself."

Haroun took Mocker's elbow, started forward.

"I didn't say you could go, boy," Sparen said. "I just decided to kill you myself."

"Take care, Damo," Mocker said. "Is trained in Power."

"Isn't everybody in this business?"

"Is slight and arrogant, but is one known as King Without Throne."

Sparen spat to one side. "Right. And I'm the Lost Prince of Libiannin."

Haroun took advantage of the diversion of the exchange to palm a blow-tube. He raised his hand, coughed.

Sparen saw it coming, but too late. He made one violent thrust, then collapsed. An expression of incredulity contorted his features.

Gouch and Mocker crowded Sparen. "What did you do?" Gouch demanded. He shook Sparen. "Mr. Sparen, wake up." The giant seemed unaware of his own wounds. "Tell me what to do, Mr. Sparen. Should I break them?"

"Come on," Haroun snarled, grabbing Mocker's shoulder. "The big guy's got this figured as your fault." He was thinking he would have to get a lot of use out of this Mocker to repay himself for all this trouble.

A little later, Mocker remarked, "Sparen was friend of self. Not very trusting friend, but best friend even so."

Haroun heard the gentle threat. He saw the promise of murder in his companion's eyes. "I didn't kill him. The dart was coated with a nerve poison that causes temporary paralysis. It comes from the jungles south of Hammad al Nakir. He'll be all right in a couple of hours, except for a headache and a bad temper."

He hoped. The drug was fatal about a quarter of the time.

The more Haroun observed his companion, the more he became sure Mocker would make a dangerous enemy. The fat and incurable optimism hid a lean, conscienceless killer.

They were halfway to el Senoussi's encampment, several days later, when they encountered the refugees. These were not desert-born fugitives from the wrath of the Disciple. They were natives fleeing El Murid's minions.

The El Murid Wars had begun, and troops of desert riders were in Tamerice already.

They gave Haroun a hold on the fat man.

There was no point continuing southward. He turned back, heading for a camp in Altea. Invincible patrols forced them into hiding several times.

North of Feagenbruch they came across the burned wagons of the Sparen carnival. Sparen himself was among the dead, but Gouch had survived. They found him, wounded, lying beneath a mound of desert warriors.

Mocker studied Sparen for a long time. "Was paranoid fool, sometimes, maybeso, this man. But was friend. In some way, even, was like father. There is blood now, Haroun bin Yousif. Same must be cleansed in blood. Self, am now interested in politics." He moved to Gouch. "Gouch. You. Big fellow. Get up. Is work to do."

Incredibly, Gouch rose out of his pile of victims.

"They slew both my fathers," Haroun whispered.

It would be a long time before Mocker understood that remark.

He soothed Gouch's tears and wounds and fears and listened while the King Without A Throne explained the part he could play in bringing about the downfall of the Disciple.

Chapter Eight: *THE LONELY CITY*

Al Rhemish was a lonely city that first summer of the wars. All the Disciple's intimates had abandoned him for the excitement and loot of the west.

He often strolled the dusty streets with his children, having trouble accepting his fortune. He ached continuously in the vacuum left by Meryem's passing.

His loneliness grew as the victories mounted and the euphoria of the stay-at-homes transmogrified into a worshipful awe of the man who had dreamed the dream and made the turnaround possible.

"They're trying to make *me* their God," he told his children. "And I can't seem to stop them."

"They already call you The Lord in Flesh some places," Yasmid told him. She not only had the boldness her mother had shown when young; she also possessed that adult self-assurance El Murid had developed after his first encounter with his angel. She seemed an *old* child, an adult looking out of a half-grown body. Even he was disturbed by her excessively grownup perceptions.

Sidi, on the other hand, threatened to remain an infant forever.

"I issue edicts. They ignore them. And the men I set to police heresies become the worst offenders." He was thinking of Mowaffak Hali. Mowaffak was smitten by the man-worshipping disease.

"People want something they can touch, Father. Something they can see. That's human nature."

"What do you think, Sidi?" The Disciple took every opportunity to include his son in everything. One day Yasmid would have to depend on her brother the way he depended on Nassef.

"I don't know." Sidi was surly. He did not give a damn about the Lord's work. The Evil One was in him. He was the antithesis of his sister in everything. He afflicted his father with a desperate pain.

El Murid had trouble handling his feelings toward Sidi. The boy had done nothing blatant. Yet. But the Disciple smelled wickedness in him, the way a camel smelled water. Sidi would be trouble one day, if not for his father, then for Yasmid when she became Disciple.

El Murid felt trapped between jaws of faith and family. Rather than deal with it, he was letting everything slide during the boy's formative years.

He prayed a lot. Each night he begged the Lord to channel Sidi's wickedness in useful directions, as He had done with Nassef. And he begged foregiveness for the continuous quiet anger he bore because of Meryem's untimely passing.

Yasmid had taken Meryem's place, becoming confidant and crying shoulder.

El Murid was strong in his faith, but could never still the lonely, frightened boy within him. That boy had to have someone. . . .

"Papa, you should find another wife."

They were climbing the side of the bowl containing Al Rhemish. Twice weekly he made a hadj to the place where Meryem had fallen. The habit had become part of his legend.

"Your mother was my only love." He had faced this argument before, from Nassef and Mowaffak Hali.

"You don't have to love her like you did Mother. Everyone knows how you felt about her."

"You've been talking to Nassef."

"No. Does he think you should get married too?"

"Then Hali."

"No."

"Somebody. Honey, I know what you're going to say. I've heard it all before. I should wed a woman from the noble class in order to cement relations with the aristocracy. I have to gain their trust so our best people stop deserting to that child-king, Haroun."

"It's true. It would help."

"May be. But I don't compromise with the enemies of the Lord. I don't traffic with the damned, except to punish them for their wickedness."

"Papa, that'll cause trouble someday. You've got to give to get."

"It's caused trouble since the day I met your mother. And today I sit on the Peacock Throne, never having yielded. You sound like your uncle again. You're talking politics. And politics disgust me."

Yasmid was not repeating something she had heard, but she did not tell him so. He had grown argumentative lately. Prolonged disagreement sent him into furies. "Politics is how people work things out," she said.

"It's how they scheme and maneuver to take advantage of each other."

The Lord was the center and source of all power, and El Murid was his spokesman on earth. He saw no need for any politics but the monolith with himself at its apex, giving commands the Chosen should execute without question.

That vision was his alone. A vicious new politics entered the movement the moment it achieved its initial goal. His captains fought like starving dogs for those crumbs of power which dribbled through his fingers. They savaged one another for the spoils of the new order. Hardly a day passed when he did not have to rule on some dispute over responsibility or precedence.

"They're more interested in themselves than in the movement. Even the old faithful are falling into the trap." He paused to order his thinking. "Maybe we were too successful too suddenly. After twelve years, victory just jumped into our hands. Now things are so good they don't have to stand shoulder to shoulder against the world."

He dreaded the chance that the intrigues and machinations would become habitual. That had happened to the Royalists. During their final years they had done little but accuse one another and indulge their private vices.

He felt impotent. Evil seeds were sprouting, and he could do little to stunt their growth. All the preaching in eternity could not save the man who refused to be saved.

El Murid had grown. He had begun to see the weaknesses in his movement, the potential for evil flanking every inch of the path of righteousness. He had begun to realize that the fall for the true believer could be swift and hard and, worse, unrecognized until too late.

The knowledge did nothing to banish the depression initiated by loneliness.

When he could stand it no more he always called for Esmat.

They reached the site of Meryem's fall.

"Will they ever finish?" Sidi asked, indicating the monument El Murid had ordered raised. A quarter had been completed. Unused stone stood in piles now falling into disordered heaps.

"Even our stonemasons wanted to see the old Imperial provinces. Could I force them to stay when they wanted to carry the Truth to the infidel?"

"They didn't care about the truth, Papa. They just thought stealing from foreigners was easier than working."

El Murid nodded. The Host of Illumination was fat

with men whose skills could be better utilized at home. A black, rigid moment of fear enfolded him in cold tentacles. Hammad al Nakir boasted few skilled artisans. A military disaster could destroy the class and shove the nation a long step back toward barbarism. The centuries had not changed his people enough. They still preferred plundering to building.

He altered the course of the conversation. "What I need more than a respite from bickering is water. Millions of gallons of water."

"What?" Yasmid had been about to suggest that he have Nassef send captured artisans to replace native craftsmen gone to war.

"Water. That's the biggest thing we lost when the Empire fell. I don't know how. . . . Maybe only Varthlokkur himself could bring back the rains."

Sidi showed some interest, so he forged ahead. "The soil is fertile enough some places. But there isn't any water. And because of that there's so little vegetation that what rain does fall just runs away. . . . You see, in Imperial times they cut most of the wild trees for lumber and firewood. Then the barbarians came. Some places they plowed salt into the earth. Some places their cattle and sheep stripped the land. And then the wizard Varthlokkur stopped the rains. . . ."

Yasmid considered him with a half-amused smile. "What have you been doing, Papa? Going to school on the sly?"

"No, reading some studies done by the foreigner, Radetic. I discovered them after we took Al Rhemish. It's curious. Yousif shared a lot of my goals."

"Haven't you always said that the minions of the Evil One sometimes do the Lord's work unwittingly?"

"And it's true. But don't breathe a word of this. I'm going to adopt the foreigner's ideas. Once the Empire is resurrected and we have the people to do the work. Radetic believed the old lushness could be restored, though it would take three or four generations to get the life-river turned into the new channel. That made him despair. But I like it. I've got to give the Chosen distant goals. Otherwise the Kingdom of Peace will lapse into its old bickering ways."

"You never mentioned this before."

El Murid leaned against the memorial's base and gazed across the valley. He tried to imagine how it had looked in old times. There had been a shallow lake. The Most Holy Mrazkim Shrines had stood on a low, man-made island. The slopes surrounding the lake had boasted rich citrus groves.

Barbarian invaders had cut the trees for firewood.

"It used to be too far away to even dream. Now there's at least a chance. One of these days. . . . Well, it all depends on your uncle. If he wins the war. . . . Then we can start."

He looked at the barren valley. For an instant he saw the beauty that had been, and might again be.

"We could bring the water from the Kapenrung Mountains. There're still traces of the old canals. . . . But enough of that." He turned, knelt, prayed for Meryem's soul. Yasmid and his son joined him, Sidi reluctantly. When he rose, he said, "Let's go jump into the witch's cauldron and see what silliness they're up to today."

Yasmid wore an awed look as she followed her father. She had seen a whole new facet of a man. Her father had depths she had never suspected.

A morning of unpromising beginnings was becoming a cheerful day for the Disciple. He had revealed his most secret dream and no one had laughed. Even unimaginative Sidi had grasped the grandeur of the vision. Maybe, just maybe, he could get through the day without Esmat.

He discovered that Mowaffak Hali had rushed home from the war zone.

"I'm seeing you first because I know your business must be serious, Mowaffak. What is it?"

"Two things, Lord. The least important is that we've

lost track of the pretender, Haroun bin Yousif. He's gone underground since the attack in Tamerice. He's contacted only a few rebel leaders, and he no longer haunts the courts of the Lesser Kingdoms. Our agents can't find him."

"Time will deliver him to us. What else?"

"A grave development. I got this from my man in the Scourge of God's staff, who overheard one of your brother-in-law's spies reporting. The Itaskians and their allies have decided not to wait for us to come to them. They're sending an army south. They've chosen the Duke of Greyfells to command it. He's a cousin of the Itaskian king, and reportedly a good soldier."

"That's a pity, Mowaffak. I'd hoped we could finish in the south before we had to deal with Itaskia."

"It's the strongest of our foes, Lord. And the richest. And probably has the best leaders. And they'll have Iwa Skolovda, Dvar, and Prost Kamenets supporting them. The Scourge of God will face tough going north of the Scarlotti."

"Maybe. But I know Nassef. If I were a sinful man and laid wagers, I'd bet that he planned for this before he crossed the Sahel."

"I hope so, Lord. The sheer weight of our enemies intimidates me."

The remark echoed El Murid's fears. He wished he could share them with Hali, but dared not. His absolute assurance made the Invincibles what they were. Doubt would destroy them.

"Let's hope all our friends feel the pressure, Mowaffak. The movement is stumbling over its own success. Spread the news."

"As you command, Lord." Hali's tone betrayed doubts. "Can the Invincibles do something to stem this threat, Lord?"

"Study this Duke, Mowaffak. How competent is he? Would his army survive without him? Who would relace him? How competent is that man? You understand?"

"Completely, Lord. Politics being what they are, his replacement might be a bungler."

"Exactly. Oh. While you're here. I need your advice concerning el Nadim's eastern army."

"Lord?"

"He's gone over the Scourge of God's head. Appealed to me for permission to give up trying to force the Savernake Gap. Yet Nassef told me that maintaining the breakthrough threat is vital."

"What's el Nadim's problem?"

"He claims his enemies are decimating him with sorcery. That his Throyen levies are ready to revolt. They make up most of his army and think we're getting them killed just to be rid of them."

"That's not impossible, Lord. The Scourge of God is using native auxiliaries in the west. I've seen him allow them to take a merciless beating. But I agree when he says we need the eastern threat. It forces the enemy into a static strategy that leaves us the initiative. Once Kavelin and Altea fall, it won't matter. I can muster a few companies of Invincibles and send them east. They'd give el Nadim more backbone."

"And flexibility, I'd think. He hasn't been one of our more imaginative generals."

"Perhaps not. But he's reliable. He'll carry out his orders if they kill him. And he's our only sectarian leader who is a true believer. He came to it late, after he became one of Nassef's henchmen, and I think it's why he drew the remote assignment. The Scourge of God doesn't want him watching over his shoulder anymore."

"You're politicking, Mowaffak."

"Lord!" Hali grinned. "So I am, in my way. I guess it's part of being human."

"Probably. We don't always realize what we're doing. It's the blatant, premeditated backstabbing that aggravates me. Send those companies to el Nadim."

"As you command, Lord."

"Tell Yassir he can start sending in the whiners and complainers."

The following month was a good one. The occupied territories grew more pacified. The conquest of the Lesser Kingdoms proceeded inexorably, though Nassef had given Karim a minimum of warriors with whom to accomplish the task. The Scarlotti fords and ferries, as far east as Altea's western frontier, had been closed. Nassef crossed the river above Dunno Scuttari and completed that city's encirclement. He was achieving objectives ahead of schedule. Even el Nadim's troubles were no cause for despair. His success or failure remained peripheral to Nassef's strategy. Only his presence was essential.

Then El Murid received the letter from his brother-in-law.

"Yasmid. Sidi. Come hear what your uncle has to say." He scanned the letter twice more. "He wants us to come accept the surrender of Dunno Scuttari. He says it won't be long."

"Papa, let's go!" Yasmid enthused. "Please? Say we can! I want to see the west. And think what it would mean to the warriors to see you there with them."

He laughed. "It would be dangerous, Yasmid."

"We could pretend we were somebody else. Somebody who isn't important."

"Salt merchants," Sidi proposed.

"Salt merchants are important," El Murid protested, going along for the fun. His father had been a salt merchant.

"Sure, Papa. Salt merchants," Yasmid said. "You know all about that. We could make your bodyguards dress like merchants and ride camels."

"They'd still look like thugs."

"But. . . ."

"That's enough. Your uncle hasn't taken the city, and I don't think he can. He hasn't been any trouble for

Hellin Daimiel, and that should be an easier nut. We'll wait and see."

"Papa, he's just saving Hellin Daimiel for later."

"We'll wait and see. Remember, there's an Itaskian army to worry about now. We don't know what they'll do."

Yasmid smiled. She had the battle halfway won.

El Murid assumed a wry smile. He knew what she was thinking. He decided he was a weak-spined fool. He had so much trouble denying his children anything.

A grave Esmat approached him eleven days later.

"What is it, Esmat? You look grey."

The physician gulped. "Lord, the courier from Ipopotam hasn't arrived. He's four days overdue."

A chill climbed El Murid's spine. "How much of the pain-killer do we have?" He could not bring himself to call the opiate anything else.

"Perhaps enough for two months, Lord. It depends on the size and frequency of the dosages."

Which depends on how much pressure I have to endure, El Murid thought. "Then the failure of one courier doesn't much matter, does it? If you're afraid your stock will be depleted, send another man. Or double the next regular purchase."

"I intend doing both, Lord. If nothing else, that will answer the critical question."

"Question? What question?"

"Whether or not our enemies have discovered our need and begun intercepting our couriers."

This time the chill grated like the progress of a glacier. "Esmat. . . . Is that possible?"

"All things are possible, Lord. And this's a fear I've carried for several years. We've reached the point where the drug's withdrawal would leave the movement without a head for some time. It might take months to overcome the withdrawal pains."

"Is it bad, Esmat?" he asked softly.

"Extremely, Lord."

"Esmat, do whatever you have to. Secure the supply. This is a critical hour. I don't dare become ineffective. You should have mentioned our vulnerability before."

"Perhaps. I did not wish to offend. . . ."

"It's too late to take offense. The drug comes from a plant, does it not? A poppy? Can we grow our own?"

"I'm no horticulturist, Lord. And they have a monopoly. They guard seeds and fields. . . ."

"Can they guard themselves against the Host of Illumination?"

"Of course not. But we have treaties of friendship. Our word of honor would be destroyed. . . . We negotiated them specifically to insure our access to the drug. They might burn the fields if they thought that was why we were invading."

"Nassef negotiated those instruments before we went to war. Does that mean he knows?"

"Many people know, Lord. It's not something that can be kept secret long."

El Murid bowed his head, half in shame, half in fear. "Do what you can. And I'll do what I have to."

"As you command, Lord."

Chapter Nine: *THE ITASKIANS*

Haroun took his leave of Mocker and Gouch in northern Cardine, just east of that kingdom's frontier with the domains of Dunno Scuttari. "The patrols are thick," he warned. "Take care."

Mocker laughed. "Self, will be so circumspect that even eye of lofty eagle will not detect same. Am valiant fighter, true, able to best whole company in combat, but am uncertain of ability against whole army. Even with stalwart Gouch at back."

Bin Yousif had observed the fat man in action the day before, when they had stumbled into one of Nassef's patrols. Sparen had taught him superbly. Mocker's quickness, deftness, and endurance with a blade were preternatural. He was a swordsman born.

"Gouch, keep him out of trouble."

"I will, Mister. He'll be so good you won't even know him."

"Don't let him con you out of the cash." He had given the big man some expense money.

"Don't you worry, Mister. I know him. I watched him when he worked for Mister Sparen. We'll do this job, then come back for the next one."

There was a simple assurance about Gouch that Haroun

found both charming and disturbing. Megelin had taught him to see the world as a slippery serpent, changeable, colored in shades of untrustworthiness. Gouch's naive worldview was the antithesis of Radetic's.

"I think you will. Good luck." He turned his back on them and the donkey, strolled to his mount and companions.

"You think they'll do it?" Beloul asked.

Haroun glanced back. The two were waddling south already. The fat man walked that way because of his obesity, Gouch because of his still tender injuries.

"Who knows? If they don't, we're not out anything."

"So. Northward we ride," Beloul mused. "You're sure they'll be waiting across the river?"

He meant the Royalist army, which was supposed to have assembled in Vorhangs, the little kingdom across the Scarlotti. Haroun guessed between one and two thousand men would answer his call to arms.

He hoped, by employing them judiciously in support of the western armies, to make them a bargaining counter in his negotiations for aid in recovering the Peacock Throne.

"We'll find out, Beloul."

A few hours later, as they considered how to cross the Scarlotti, a messenger overtook them. "Lord," he gasped, "the Scourge of God has crossed the river."

"What?" Beloul demanded. "When? Where?"

"Just upriver of Dunno Scuttari. They started sending boats over four days ago. Took the Scuttarians by surprise. He has twenty thousand men on the north bank now."

"He's crazy," Beloul growled. "He's still vulnerable from the Lesser Kingdoms, and the Itaskians will be coming down behind him."

"No, he's not," Haroun countered. "Call El Murid crazy if you want, but not Nassef. He's got a reason if he sneezes."

"The risk is all on the north bank," el Senoussi

remarked. "Nobody on this side can challenge him. We'd better find out what he's up to."

"Yes." Haroun told the messenger, "Go back to your company. Tell your captain to find out what Nassef is doing. Tell him to send word to me at the camp in Kendel."

"Kendel?" el Senoussi asked. "We're going that far north?"

"I asked the Itaskian general to meet me. The Kendel camp isn't far out of his way. Somebody trade horses with this man. His won't survive the return trip."

"Thank you, Lord," the messenger said. "Will you take care of her? She's a good animal."

"Of course."

"Isn't that dangerous?" Beloul asked once the messenger departed. "How long before the Harish get wind of your whereabouts now?"

"You think they'd venture that far from home?"

"To the ends of the earth, Lord, if El Murid willed it."

"I guess they would. Guard my back well, then."

They crossed the Scarlotti during the night, the hard way. Still dripping, exhausted, they joined their warriors in the morning.

Haroun was not impressed by his army. It was a ragged mob compared to that his father had commanded. These men had just one outstanding quality: they were survivors.

"Can you do anything with them?" he asked Beloul.

"Of course. Most were soldiers at home. They're still soldiers. They just don't look pretty."

"They look like bandits."

Beloul shrugged. "I'll try to shape them up."

Haroun allowed a day of rest, then led his bedraggled host northward.

The warriors griped. Most had made long journeys south to the meeting place. The biggest refugee camps had attached themselves to the skirts of cities seemingly safe from the Scourge of God.

It took a week of hard riding to reach the Kendel encampment. Twice they were mistaken for Nassef's men and narrowly avoided fighting allies. Nassef had the peoples between the Scarlotti and Porthune spooked.

Haroun reached the camp only to discover that the Itaskian Duke had not responded to his request for a meeting. Yet the combined northern armies were amarch, moving south in small stages, and the main body was just forty miles from the encampment.

"He don't seem eager to make Nassef's acquaintance," Beloul observed. "Even the biggest, heaviest army can move faster than that."

"I smell the corruption of politics on this breeze, Beloul. It stinks like an old, old corpse."

"We'll have to make a showing for the men. It's a pity we came so far for nothing."

"We will. Tomorrow I'll go to him."

"Lord?"

"Let's inspect this camp, Beloul. People ought to know we care."

He had seen more than he wanted already. These people were living in the most primitive conditions imaginable. Their homes consisted of stick piles that did nothing but block the sun's rays.

"This will be a death camp come winter, Beloul. This isn't Hammad al Nakir. The winters get cold. These people will freeze. What happened to that Gamil Meguid who's supposed to be in charge?"

"He disappeared right after we got here."

"Oh?"

"Yes."

"Keep an eye on him."

"I mean to. Wait. I think that's him. With the foreigner."

Meguid was a small, fussy sort from western Hammad al Nakir. He and el Senoussi were old acquaintances. His hands fluttered when he talked, and his left cheek twitched constantly. He was overawed by his king's presence.

"My Lord King," he gurgled. "May I present Count Diekes Ronstadt. Our neighbor and benefactor. Count, His Most Serene Majesty. . . ."

"Enough, Meguid. Ronstadt? I've heard that name before."

The Count was a big man. He had muscles everywhere and an impressive mane of silver hair. Haroun had the feeling that his powerful dark eyes were probing the soft white underbelly of his soul. A quick, warm smile fluttered across the Count's pale lips. It was a smile that proclaimed its bearer an amused observer of the human condition.

"That could be, lad. We had a friend in common. Megelin Radetic."

"Of course! His roommate at the Rebsamen. . . . You're the one who was always getting him in trouble."

"In and out again. He was the most naive kid. . . . But brilliant. A genius. He could do anything. I wouldn't have survived without him. We exchanged the occasional letter. I was crushed when I heard what happened."

"The world is poorer for his absence. I'm impoverished. I would have made him my vizier. My marshal."

"A new departure, Megelin as warrior. But there wasn't anything he couldn't do when he put his mind to it. Come with me. Gamil wants to show off our new camp."

"Megelin managed both jobs for my father, in fact if not in name. What new camp?"

"Gamil supposed you'd be put off by this mess. He was scared you'd fire him. So he rushed over and asked me if we couldn't show you what all we've been doing."

"All right. Show me. He's right. This place appalls me."

"Follow me, then. We're building in the valley on the other side of that ridge. The water supply is better, the bottom ground more level, and there's good clay for building."

Haroun went along. Beloul, el Senoussi, and the others crowded around him, their hands near their weapons. "What is your part in this?" Haroun asked Ronstadt.

"This is my county. My fief. It's primitive and sparsely peopled. I'm combining a favor to an old friend with a favor to myself. Megelin wrote a few years back and suggested it. I liked the idea."

Count Ronstadt led them to a man-made clearing in the bottom of a wide, heavily forested valley, on the banks of a small, slow river. The clearing contained dozens of buildings in various stages of construction.

"Getting ready for winter is our main concern this year. Your people are living mostly by hunting. Next spring, though, they should be ready to try farming."

Haroun examined several of the incomplete houses. They were constructed of bricks of sun-baked clay. The refugees were making no use of the plentiful logs. Those they sawed into lengths and rolled into the river.

"I'm pleased, friend of my friend," Haroun said. "I see you have your own people helping. That's really too much."

"They're only teaching. They'll be back to their own work soon."

"How many people can you take here?" The refugees were unpopular everywhere, yet the migration from the desert had not peaked.

"How many here now, Gamil?" Ronstadt asked.

"Nearly five thousand, Count. But the official census lists about eight."

"My arms are open," Ronstadt told Haroun. "My fief is virgin. It could support thousands more. But the King is nervous. He ordered me to make a head count, then freeze it there. He doesn't want me getting too strong. We fudged a little. I want to tame this whole valley. I can't without Gamil's cheap labor."

"That's your deal with Meguid?"

"And a generous one by most standards. Since I'm not bellicose, the feudal burden is light."

"Ah. And their responsibilities to myself as their King?"

Ronstadt became less animated. "They no longer live in Hammad al Nakir. This is Kendel."

Haroun stifled a surge of anger.

Beloul took his elbow gently. "The logic is unassailable, Lord. We can't expect to get something for nothing. And this gentleman seems willing to give more for less."

"I'll let them help you where they can," Ronstadt said. "As long as it's not done at my expense."

Haroun remained angry. This being king without a throne was more frustrating than he had anticipated. Too much depended on the good will of people who owed him nothing.

He had to create a political currency before these westerners would take him seriously. He had to have something they wanted to exchange for what they could give.

His absolute imperative would have to be to retain the loyalties of the refugees. He could not permit them to become assimilated, nor to forget their grievances. They had to remain politically viable as contestants for power in Hammad al Nakir.

"Gamil says you want to meet the Duke of Greyfells," Ronstadt said. "Can I give you some advice?"

"What?"

"Don't waste your time."

"What?"

"He's not your man. He's a political animal, a political creation, a political opportunist. He got command only because the Itaskian Crown had to cut a deal with its opposition. You can't help him with his ambitions. He won't give you a place to squat."

"You know him?"

"He's a distant relative. By marriage. So is the man you *should* see. Everybody in the north is related to everybody else."

"Who should we see?" Beloul asked. "If the Duke is no good, who is?"

"Itaskia's Minister of War. He's the Duke's superior, and his enemy. And he has the ear of the Itaskian King. I'll give you a letter of introduction."

Next morning, while riding to meet Greyfells, Haroun asked, "What do you think of our benefactor?"

Beloul shrugged. "Time will tell."

"A not unenlightened man," el Senoussi opined. "Meguid thinks well of him. And trusts him."

The others agreed with Beloul.

"How Greyfells treats us will tell us a lot about him."

The Duke was easy to find. His army had not moved twenty miles in the past three days.

Ronstadt was right. Greyfells would have nothing to do with Haroun. Bin Yousif made it only as far as the entrance to the ducal pavillion, where he waited while an aide tried to get him in.

Radetic had taught him some Itaskian. Enough for him to follow the drift of the abuse Greyfells heaped on the aide for bothering him with the requests of "bandy-legged, camel-thieving rabble."

The aide returned red-faced and apologetic. Haroun said only, "Tell him that he'll regret his arrogance."

"Well?" Beloul asked when he rejoined his captains.

"The Count was right. He wouldn't talk to me."

"Then let's follow up on Ronstadt's suggestion. Itaskia isn't that far."

"I guess a few days more won't matter."

They crossed the Great Bridge three days later, guided by an impatient native sergeant.

"The glory that was," el Senoussi intoned. "Thus it was in Ilkazar in the Empire's prime."

Few of them had seen the like of the waterfront. The river traffic was incredible. Hellin Daimiel and Dunno Scuttari were becoming increasingly dependent on supplies brought in by ship. A river of wealth was flowing from the treasuries of the besieged cities to the coffers of Itaskian merchants.

The sergeant pushed and nagged and finally guided

them to a kremlin at city's center. He took them into a building and up several levels to an anteroom where a gimpy old man snatched Haroun's letter of introduction. He disappeared through a fancily carved doorway. He was not gone long. "His Lordship will see you now. You." He indicated Haroun. "The rest stay out here."

"That was fast," Haroun breathed. He started toward the doorway. His followers milled uncertainly, paths blocked by the old man.

A thin, short, middle-aged man came to greet Haroun. He offered his hand. "They told me you were young. I didn't expect you to be this young."

"Count Ronstadt in Kendel suggested I see you."

"And direct. I like that, though you young people overdo it. I presume my cousin disappointed you?"

"The Duke of Greyfells. He was unpleasant."

"He usually is. Somebody forgot to teach him his manners. I never cease being amazed that he's built such a strong following. I was more amazed when he outmaneuvered me on the command appointment."

"I hear he's a good soldier."

"When it serves his purpose. I imagine he'll try to use this as a stepping-stone to the throne. He makes no secret of his long-range goal."

Haroun shook his head slowly. "What's the attraction? It's nothing but headaches and heartaches for me."

The Minister shrugged. "Come. Sit down. I think we've got agreements to agree."

Haroun sat. He studied the Minister. And the thin man considered him from behind steepled fingers.

Haroun saw someone in complete control of his destiny, someone as sure of himself as was El Murid. A hard man. He'd make a bitter enemy.

The Minister saw a boy compelled to become a man. The strain of caring was making him old before his time. Creeping cynicism had begun tightening his brow. It had given his young mouth the lemon-biting look.

And he sensed a hardness, an implacability that approached fanaticism.

"What agreements?" Haroun asked.

"First, tell me what you think of El Murid's goals. His war goals. I don't give a damn about the religious issues."

"Restoration of the Empire? It's a fool's dream. This isn't the world of yesterday. There're real countries out here now. And, geopolitically, Hammad al Nakir isn't suited to the role of the great unifier." He recounted some of Megelin's thoughts on the subject, dwelling on his homeland's lack of a centralized administrative tradition and the absence of an educated class capable of administering. Ilkazar had had those, and the peoples the Empire had conquered had, for the most part, been little beyond the tribal stage.

"How old are you?"

"Nineteen."

"You had remarkable teachers, then. I know men with forty years experience in statecraft who couldn't put it that clearly. But you didn't tell me what I want to know. Do you subscribe to the imperial dream?"

"No. The Disciple and I come together only when he says we have to re-establish the dignity and security of the nation."

"Yes. You were well taught." The Minister smiled. "I suppose I can accept that. Let me confess to a small dream of my own. I want to make Itaskia the predominant state in the west. We're already the strongest, but conquest isn't my ideal. More an assumption of moral and mercantile dominion. Today's kingdoms are too diverse for unification."

They were speaking Daimiellian, Haroun's strongest foreign language. The Minister's confession made him determined to improve his Itaskian. "I believe the word you want is hegemony."

The Minister smiled again. "You may be right. Now, to the point. We can help each other."

"I know you can help me. That's why I'm here. But what can I do for you?"

"First, understand that I perceive El Murid as the principal threat to my dream. Yet he's also an asset. If he's defeated before he does much more damage, my hopes might come to life of their own accord. The destruction in the south, and the siege of Hellin Daimiel, have elevated Itaskia to a position of moral as well as military dominance. Economic domination is on its way. Cultural dominance shouldn't be far behind."

"I can help turn him back. But I need money, arms, and places for my people to live. Most especially, I need the arms."

"Even so. Listen. You have enemies who aren't mine. I have foes who aren't yours. And that's where we can help each other. Suppose we trade enemies? If you follow my meaning."

"I'm not sure I do."

"A man is more vulnerable to the dagger of an enemy he doesn't know, wouldn't you say?"

"I see. You want to trade murders."

"Crudely put, but yes. I'll give you arms and money if you'll make three commitments. The first is to go ahead and fight El Murid. The second is to abolish his imperialism if you win. And the third, bluntly, is to provide me with undercover knife work, or whatever, when I need to make a move from which I can dissociate myself."

A classic schemer, Haroun thought. What he wants is his own underground army. "Do you have designs on the Itaskian throne yourself?"

"Me? Good heavens, no! Why on earth would I? I'm safer and happier where I am, pulling the strings. I take it you have reservations."

"It sounds like a sweetheart deal. Too good to be true."

"Maybe from your viewpoint. But you don't know Itaskian politics. Or me. I'm not talking about cutting one throat tomorrow. I'm talking the long run. A lifetime of trade-offs. A perpetual alliance. Our problems aren't going to be resolved in a summer. Nor in ten summers, nor even by our achieving what we think we want. Do you see? Consider, too, the fact that I'm sticking my neck out here. I'm offering you a secret treaty. That could get me thrown out on my ear if certain parties got wind of it."

Haroun knew he might spend his life grasping for something beyond his reach. The old sorcerer in that ruined watchtower had shown him the possibilities.

He turned his inner ear to intuition and the Invisible Crown.

"I'll take the chance. You've got a bargain."

"Forever? It's said your father was a man of his word."

"Yes. And I'm my father's son."

The thin man rose, offered a hand. Haroun took it.

"This is all the contract we'll ever have," the Minister told him. "Nobody but you and me should know about it."

"And I'll never be able to invoke it for immunity, no doubt."

"Unfortunately. That's the nature of the game. But remember, you have me at the same disadvantage."

Haroun did not see it, but refrained from so saying. As the Minister had remarked, he did not know Itaskian politics. And he had searched the west and been offered no other deal at all. Beggars could not choose.

"What do you want right now?" he asked.

"Nothing. Just help stop El Murid. I have to survive that crisis first." The Minister turned, walked to a huge wall map of the west. He examined it briefly, one finger tracing a line from Itaskia toward Dunno Scuttari. "If you'll take some men to Hempstead Heath, about twelve miles south of the South Town Gate on the Octylyan Road, my people will meet you with a shipment of weapons. A gesture of good faith on my part. How does that sound?"

"Again, too good to be true. You don't know the disappointments we've suffered."

"But I do. Why do you think you got in so quickly? I've been studying this thing for eight months. These weapons. They're not the best. They're old, non-standard, captured arms. The kind we use for foreign aid and arming the militia. I can scatter them around without having to account for them."

"Anything is better than bare hands. Not so? I'll be there waiting."

But he was not. He had to deputize el Senoussi for the job.

The messenger had come from Dunno Scuttari. Haroun found Nassef's apparent plans less interesting than the messenger's serendipitous acquisition of facts about Duke Greyfells.

Patiently, probably for the dozenth time, the man told his story. "Lord, as I was passing the camp of the Itaskian host—which I dared because I wanted to see this army that everyone expects to be the salvation of the south—I saw riders come forth. I could not flee without being seen, so I concealed myself in the forest. They passed within ten yards of me, Lord. Their captain was the bandit Karim. He had with him several Itaskians of lofty station. They and Karim's men shared jests as old friends might."

"Karim? You're sure?"

"I have seen Karim several times, Lord. I've heard him speak. This was the same man. There's some treachery afoot."

"Then this Duke. . . . He wouldn't treat with the legitimate King of Hammad al Nakir. He wouldn't share his thinking with his allies. He practically whipped me from his camp. . . . No wonder. Karim was there at the time."

Beloul muttered, "A scorpion. Poisonous vermin. He makes common cause with bandits."

"Ah, Beloul. Think. The scorpion dies beneath the boot of the man who knows its ways. Perhaps fate has tossed us a meager gift. Shadek. Meet those men bringing us arms. Beloul. Collect our warriors. Let them know we're on the spoor of the villain Karim. Let them know that it's a hot trail. The rest of us will start after him now. If we catch him before he rejoins his army. . . ." He laughed evilly.

Beloul's grin was as wicked. He had a special hatred for Karim. Karim was one of the butchers of Sebil el Selib.

"As you command, Lord."

The Fates were toying with the young King. Karim led him a merry chase into the south. The old bandit was in enemy territory and knew it. He was wasting no time. Haroun did not overtake him till he was making the river crossing into northwestern Altea. Haroun could do nothing but curse and watch. Six hundred of Karim's warriors lined the south bank.

Haroun had to wait for Beloul before he could force the crossing, hurling all his strength against the handful Karim had left. By then he was a day behind, and Karim was aware of how narrowly he had escaped.

Chapter Ten: *ALTEAN VENTURES*

The arrows made *whisk*ing sounds when they streaked over the riverboat, and *thump*ed when they hit its side. The barrage was desultory. The range was extreme for the short desert bow.

"They're going to follow us to the end of the river," Haaken grumped.

Nassef had tightened his noose round Dunno Scuttari before their departure. They had sailed under fire, and the attack had continued every day since. No damage had been done, but constant pursuit was depressing. Sooner or later the Guildsmen would have to fight, if only to make their landing.

The riverboat was a small galley. Most of its regular crew had been left behind. Guildsmen had to take their turns at the oars. Neither the primus nor even the non-coms were exempt.

The labor left Kildragon surly. "If I'd wanted a career pulling an oar I would've gone home to Trolledyngja," he grumbled every time his turn came up.

"You'll get to put it down quick enough," Bragi promised. "Then you can entertain us with your philosophizing about the life of an infantryman. The Captain says we're in for some hard marching."

Haaken and Reskird muttered subversively.

"You had your fun. In Simballawein you chased skirts. In Hellin Daimiel you chased skirts. In Dunno Scuttari you didn't have to do anything but keep the girls happy. Now all of a sudden you start bitching because you have to earn your allowances."

"I think that corporal's belt has gone to his head," Reskird observed.

"I noticed," Haaken said.

"Come on. . . . Why don't you get your stuff ready? We're going ashore tonight."

They had been delayed five weeks in Dunno Scuttari, first for lack of transport, then to await the proper phase of the moon. The first few hours ashore would be critical. They would need all the light they could get.

Darkness, moonrise and the hour of peril came all too quickly.

"There it is," Bragi said, indicating the mouth of a tributary of the Scarlotti. "Fifteen minutes."

They landed at a village just above the sidestream, while El Murid's men were scurrying around in search of a ford. Captain Sanguinet hoped his company could vanish into the night before its pursuers got across.

The Altean villagers greeted them as enthusiastically as had the people of Simballawein.

"Keep your hands to yourself, Kildragon," Bragi growled as he formed his squad. "We don't have time for that."

Haaken chuckled softy. In Dunno Scuttari his brother had earned the reputation of being the squad's most devoted pursuer of "split-tail."

"Professional jealousy," Reskird remarked.

"Pot calling the kettle black, for sure," Haaken agreed.

"Come on, guys," Bragi said. "We're in a tight spot." He was edgy, and becoming more so. He had a bad feeling about this Altean campaign. He smelled disaster cooking. And Trolledyngjans were wont to put a lot of stock in omens and forebodings.

118

"Ready here?" Sanguinet asked.

"Ready, Captain," Bragi replied.

"What's all the hollering over there?" Reskird asked as soon as Sanguinet left. He craned his neck in an effort to see.

Bragi hoisted his pack. "They probably just figured out that we're not going to hang around and protect them." He needed no familiarity with the language to interpret the outrage being vented by the village elders. "Get your packs on."

They moved out to the curses of men and wails of women. Bragi ached inside because the little ones were crying.

They did not even know why.

Sanguinet set a hard pace, heading southeastward. He did not let up often, and then only for a few minutes at a time, to confer with the guides the Altean monarchy had sent to meet them. The march to the Bergwold, the forest they were to use as a base, was almost a hundred miles, and the Captain wanted to make it without a major interruption.

Dawn came and the company marched on. Villages, farms, manors, small castles, hove up ahead, slipped by, and drifted past like slow, lonely ships. The countryside showed no evidence of the passage of raiders, though the peasants vanished from the fields whenever the weary Guildsmen trudged into view.

Here and there, Sanguinet exchanged news with the masters of the various manors and castles. It was more neighborhood gossip than concrete fact. Karim had not yet turned his attention to Altea. The only real fighting had taken place down along the border with Tamerice. Crown Prince Raithel had beaten back three modest incursions.

Bragi wondered why everything was so quiet. He had expected almost continuous fighting. What Karim was doing to the Lesser Kingdoms had been a constant source of conversation during the trip upriver. Of the little states below the Scarlotti, only Altea, and Kavelin, which Altea geographically screened, remained unsubdued. Bragi had expected to be too late for the whirlwind's passage.

Something strange was going on and the entire Altean nation felt it. Nassef's protegé was not one to lightly abandon the unstoppable inertia his forces had gained.

Twenty-eight hours of grueling marching brought the company to the northern verges of the Bergwold, so-called because of its proximity to Colberg Castle, a ruined fortress which had played a critical role in Altea's early history. The Alteans considered it a national monument. The passing Guildsmen saw nothing but crumbling walls looking spectral in the moonlight.

None of them knew anything about the kingdom they were supposed to help preserve. Of all of them only Lieutenant Trubacik spoke the language.

Those facts had weighed on Bragi throughout the march. As Reskird had observed, his corporal's belt had gone to his head. He had begun to take leadership seriously.

And there was little to do but think while walking.

Even the Captain was exhausted. The company broke discipline that first night. Not one spadeful of earth got turned along the camp perimeter.

The lapse lasted only that night. Next day Sanguinet moved deeper into the wood and commenced work on a semi-permanent base camp. Scouts made contact with a band of desert Royalists using the Bergwold for the same purpose. Sanguinet concluded a loose alliance.

For weeks they did little but patrol the farmland surrounding the forest. The patrols were half-hearted. The desert horsemen covered more territory faster, and the local nobility went out of their way to keep Sanguinet posted.

Such was the Guild's reputation

"It feels good," Bragi confided to his brother. "One

lousy company and these people figure the kingdom is saved."

"What happens when we don't live up to expectation?" Haaken grumped. Then, "Maybe that's why we're here. Morale. Maybe High Crag knows what it's doing."

"Maybe." Bragi's tone carried the skepticism every line soldier feels for the intellectuals of his trade.

He and his men did a lot of fishing and poking around the Colberg. More interesting diversions were not available.

Word finally came that the enemy was moving. Prince Raithel had met them and been defeated. He was retreating northward and needed reinforcements.

"Here we go again," Haaken grumbled as he shouldered his pack. "Why don't we just wait till they come here?"

"The Master Strategist has spoken," said Reskird. "Bragi, get him an appointment with the Captain."

"I got a sock if you want it, Bragi."

Ragnarson ignored them. Haaken's and Reskird's bickering had become ritualized. There was no rancor in it. It had become a time-passing game.

They never saw Raithel's army. The company found its own enemies twelve miles south of the Colberg.

"Oh-oh," Reskird groaned in his soothsayer's voice. "Trouble."

Royalist outriders galloped past the column in a panic, coming from the crossroad the company had passed a half mile back.

"You the official doom-crier now?" Haaken demanded.

"Company conference!" Sanguinet shouted after stopping one of the horsemen. "Come on! Move it!"

The Captain put it bluntly. "We're in for it. There's a mob of El Murid's men coming down that side road back there. We can't outrun them. They've already spotted us." He flung a hand at a brushy sugarloaf hill a mile away. The road snaked around its western base. "We'll go up yon hill and dig in. If you're religious, pray your ass off. There's a thousand of the bastards." He exaggerated. There were five hundred of the enemy. But that was trouble enough.

Bragi's squad stood to their weapons while their back-ups dug in. "Some friends," Haaken grumbled, watching the last of the Royalists gallop away. "We might've had a chance with their help."

"We still stand a damned good chance," Bragi said. "We're Guildsmen, remember?"

Reskird glanced over his shoulder. "Look at that dirt fly."

The secundus and tercio flailed at the earth. "Nothing like an unfriendly sword to motivate a man," Bragi observed.

The enemy reached the foot of the hill and halted. His commanders conferred. They seemed reluctant to attack.

"Hey!" Bragi said. "Some of those guys are westerners. Haaken. Can you make out their colors? Aren't they the same as those guys we met in Itaskia wore? Right after we came out of the mountains?"

Haaken peered. "I think you're right. Greyfells. Maybe this is another gang of Royalists."

"How come ours ran off, then?"

Sanguinet came to stand beside Ragnarson. "Itaskians?"

"Yes sir. Those are Greyfells colors."

"Lieutenant Trubacik. Take a white flag down. Find out who they are."

The command argument below continued till Trubacik approached and said something.

It electrified his listeners.

A man with wild grey hair cut Trubacik down.

A deep-throated roar rose from the hillside.

"We did something wrong," Bragi said. "But what?"

"Don't worry about it now," Sanguinet told him. "Worry about staying alive. They've made up their minds. They're coming."

The wild-haired horseman whipped his followers into line for a charge.

"Behind the ditch," Sanguinet ordered. "Primus, stand to your spears and shields. Bowmen, make every arrow count while they're coming through the brush. Men, if we turn their first attack we'll have our bluff in."

The enemy commander sent most of his warriors, holding only about eighty in reserve. Their animals struggled with the brush and the steep slope. The better Guild bowmen began taking them at extreme range. At least fifty did not reach the ditch, which lay just above the worst part of the slope.

The first riders up tried to jump the ditch but their animals had been ridden hard before being compelled to scale the hillside. Only a handful made the leap successfully. The others found their hindquarters dropping into the trench. They floundered around, blocking the progress of those behind them. Guild spearmen filled the trench with dead and dying animals.

The slower attackers walked their mounts into the ditch and up its farther side—into the thrusting spears. More animals went down. Only a handful maintained the momentum to crash the Guild battle line.

Guild arrows kept pounding into those farther down the slope.

Horsemen began leaping from their saddles and throwing themselves at the shield wall.

That was what Sanguinet wanted.

Bragi dropped his bloody spear and started plying his sword. The enemy kept coming. His dead and wounded carpeted the slope and filled the ditch.

Ragnarson pushed an attacker away with his shield. Three more leapt to take the man's place. He took one, but their combined weight forced him back a step. Perforce, Haaken and Reskird adjusted their positions so they could keep their shields locked with his.

A few riders answered the Guild arrows with shafts of

their own. They did no damage because the secundus and tercio turtled with their shields.

Though the assault lasted only minutes, Bragi thought it an eternity before El Murid's warriors began to waver. At least a hundred of their number, and as many horses, had fallen.

The man with the wild hair rallied them. They began pressing again.

It was a slaughter without respite. Six, seven, eight of the desert horsemen went down for every Guildsman. But their captain kept driving them forward.

If that fool keeps on, he'll lose his whole command, Bragi thought. *Why's he so desperate to wipe us out?*

Then he heard Sanguinet shouting behind the line.

He dared not turn, but knew what had happened. The warriors who had not joined the initial assault had raced around the hill to attack from the rear. Sanguinet was trying to stop them.

The Captain succeeded, but only at the cost of taking his archers away from their bows.

The pressure on the main line redoubled. The shield wall began cracking. Desert warriors pushed into the gaps.

Bragi, Haaken, and Reskird soon found themselves isolated. They backed into a triangle and kept fighting as weary horses pushed past. "Andy! Raul!" Bragi shouted. "Push over here and link back up. Haaken, step backward when I say. Reskird, be ready to fit them in." He kept stabbing and cutting while he shouted.

The cohesiveness of the Guild line continued to dissolve.

A strange, fearless calm came over Ragnarson as death approached. His mind became detached from the body involved in the fighting. He saw what needed doing and tried to get it done.

He managed to reform his squad, having lost only two men.

His calm communicated itself to the others. Their panic declined. They settled down to the grim business of fighting the way they had been taught, maximizing their chances of surviving.

Bragi kept his men in a hard little square, moving when he could to incorporate other members of the company. He kept yelling, "Get their horses! We can murder them on the ground."

The man with the wild hair concurred. Too many of his men were being forced to their feet, where their sabers and small round shields were of little value against heavy infantry. He saw his battalion being destroyed by an inferior force. The gradual regathering of the Guild platoons promised to worsen the casualty ratio.

He was upslope of the Company now. He started gathering riders for another charge, one that would shatter the Guild formation more thoroughly and leave the individual infantrymen vulnerable to his horsemen.

Bragi took advantage of the lessening pressure to include more Guildsmen in his little phalanx and move them to a rock outcrop they could use as a core for their formation.

"Get the wounded back in the rocks," he ordered. "Haaken? See those guys over there? Take a couple men and see if you can help them get over here. You. With the bow. Cover them."

He stamped around the rock as if this were his company, gathering more men, recovering weapons and shields, and keeping one eye on the charge the horsemen were about to throw down the hill.

He gathered some forty able men, and a dozen wounded, before the charge. Despite constant harassment, the rest of the company had managed to coalesce into strong knots. Most had moved to the downhill side of the trench.

"Here they come," said Kildragon.

"All right. Reskird, take over on the left side. Haaken, you take care of the right. I'll stay here. You men, don't let them bluff you. They don't have the balls to ride through us into the rocks."

The charge did what the enemy commander wanted,

though again he paid a terrible price. It shattered every Guild grouping but Bragi's. The hillside swirled with furious individual combats.

The chances of the Company surviving did not look good.

The horsemen sheered round Bragi's group, trying to cut at its flanks. "Get their horses!" he kept shouting. "Somebody with a bow, get that sonofabitch with the grey hair." Nobody did so, so he snatched up a fallen bow and tried himself. He had no luck either.

But a minute later, when the man, cursing, rode closer while trying to force his riders to push straight in, Bragi got his horse by throwing a spear. The animal dropped to its haunches, dumping its rider over its rump.

"Haaken! Grab that bastard!"

Despite furiously raining blows and pounding hooves, Haaken snaked out, grabbed a handful of grey hair, and hurled himself back. He threw the groggy enemy captain at Bragi.

Ragnarson was not gentle with him either. He hoisted the captive overhead so his followers could see that he had been taken.

The Guildsmen cheered.

Bragi did not get the results he wanted. The enemy did not give up. But many of them did back off to talk it over, giving the Guildsmen a chance to reform.

Reskird said, "Those guys aren't going to turn tail just because you got their Number One."

"It was worth a shot. Maybe I shouldn't have. They might take time to think out how to get rid of us easier." Bragi glanced down at the grey-haired man. He had become docile. His lips moved, but no sound came forth. "Hey. He's praying."

"Wouldn't you? Hell, I'd be praying now if I knew a god I could trust."

"Thought you was high on the Grey Walker because he saved your ass when your ship got rammed."

"Yeah? Look what he got me into."

"Bragi," Haaken called. "Come here."

Ragnarson pushed to his brother's side. "What?"

"Out there. More of them." Haaken pointed with his chin.

The horsemen were barely discernable. They were not on the road, where dust would have given them away earlier.

There were two columns, splitting from one. They seemed intent on surrounding the hill.

"Damn! And we could've been out of this now if those chicken-shit Royalists had helped. They could've kept that bunch from getting behind us."

"Here they come again!" Kildragon yelled.

Bragi sighed and forced his weary muscles to lift sword and shield once more. This was it. The end. And he didn't even know what he was dying for, unless it were simply brotherhood and the honor of the Guild.

Well, Ragnar had always said you should make your death a moment to remember. And if you couldn't be remembered by your friends, you should leave your enemies with tales they could tell their grandchildren during the long, cold winter nights.

The charge came hard. It should have spelled the end of Sanguinet's Company. But it began weakening almost immediately. Even as he shouted about getting the horses, Bragi sensed the uncertainty of the foe. In minutes their attack became half-hearted. Soon afterward they began showing their backs.

"What the hell?" Bragi asked the air. "Haaken. They're running. Running like hell. What happened?"

Reskird suggested, "Those guys down there must be on our side."

At that most of the Guildsmen surrendered to exhaustion and collapsed on their shields. They did not wait for confirmation. But Bragi dragged himself to the top of the rock outcrop. "Hey, Reskird! For once in your miserable life you guessed right. Whoo-ee! Look at them bastards ride!"

The rumbling of hooves and wailing, hair-raising Royalist warcries swept around both sides of the hill.

"What god did you pick this time, Reskird?" Bragi demanded headily. "We owe him a whole flock of sheep. Wow! I don't think any of them will get away." He eased back down and stretched himself on his shield. "Ah. This sure is nice."

And Haaken, dropping beside him, gripping his upper arm, said, "We made it. I don't believe it. We made it." He was shaking so much he could do nothing but hang on.

"Just lay back and look at that sky," Bragi told him. "Look at those clouds. Aren't they the most beautiful things you ever saw?"

Haaken did as he was told. "Yeah. Yeah."

Bragi let everybody enjoy a few minutes of unexpected life. Then he forced himself to his feet and said, "All right, if you're not wounded, let's start picking up the pieces. We've got a lot of brothers hurt and scattered all over hell. Try to get everybody to gather around here. I'm going to find the Captain and see what he wants we should do. Haaken, pick a couple guys with strong stomachs and finish off their wounded."

He found his captain a few minutes later. He was still kneeling over Sanguinet's mutilated body when Reskird shouted, "Hey! Bragi! Come here!"

Ragnarson rose, looked, saw Reskird facing a group of Royalist horsemen. He gathered his sword and shield and trudged back. "Sanguinet is dead," he said in Trolledyngjan. "So are Tomas and Klaus. Who's going to take over?" He surveyed the horsemen. "Well I'll be damned!"

"That's one I paid you back, Bragi." Haroun grinned.

Reskird whispered, "Isn't that that Haroun guy from when we was commissioned at el Aswad?"

"Yeah," Bragi said. "We were handling them, Haroun."

"What are you doing here?"

"High Crag detached us to Altea. To give the locals a little backbone."

An older Royalist asked, "Your men did this?" He indicated the carnage.

"They wouldn't leave us alone," Bragi replied, making a sour joke of it. "We would've cleaned up on them good if your boys hadn't chickened out on us."

Haroun said, "Pardon me?"

Bragi explained that a group of Royalists had left the company to its fate. Haroun's face darkened.

"We met some of them. We thought they were messengers. I'll find their captain. I'll show him this. Then I'll hang him."

Haaken called, "You want I should croak the old guy too, Bragi?"

"No. Give him to these guys. They might get something out of him."

Haaken pulled their captive out of the rocks, where he had concealed himself.

"Wahla!" several horsemen cried.

"Karim!" Haroun shouted. "Ah!" He began laughing. His followers joined in, pummeling one another like joyous children.

"What is it?" Bragi asked.

"You've caught Karim. The great Karim, who is second to the Scourge of God himself. There will be rejoicing when the world hears of this. And many tears will be shed in the councils of the usurper. Oh, how the Scourge of God will rage! My friend, you have given us our first great victory. My spirit soars! I feel the tide turning! The Fates no longer vie against us. But what became of the northern traitors who rode with him?"

"I don't know. I wish I did. I'd like to get my hands on them. They caused this. This Karim didn't want to attack."

"You recognized them?"

"Yes. We thought they were your people at first. Then this Karim killed our Lieutenant."

"They wanted no witnesses to their treachery. They

129

were going to meet with Nassef. To betray the northern host. We've been chasing them more than a week."

"You caught Karim. Take him if you want. Will you excuse me? Many of my brothers are injured."

Haroun grinned at Karim. "Beloul. Do you have anything special in mind?"

"Lord, you know I do. All the torments of all the hundreds who died at Sebil el Selib."

Karim sprang at Haaken, seized his sword. He ran himself through before he could be stopped.

"A brave man for a former bandit," Haroun observed.

Because none of the surviving noncoms seemed inclined, Bragi began putting the company together again. One hundred twelve Guildsmen had survived. Fifty-three, miraculously, had come through unscathed.

"We'll shed tears for these for a long time," Bragi told Haaken. He and the young king stoods facing the long rank of graves the Royalists had helped dig. "There were some great men among them."

Haroun nodded. He knew what it meant to lose old comrades.

Chapter Eleven: *VICTORY GIFTS*

El Murid and his party departed the Sahel at Kasr Helal, travelling as salt merchants desperately seeking a supplier. The war threatened to destroy the trade. Salt prices were soaring as the flow into the desert dwindled.

It was at Kasr Helal that, unrecognized by the garrison commander, El Murid learned that, to obtain salt, traders had to deal with a Mustaph el-Kader, an uncle of Nassef's General el-Kader. The elder el-Kader was disposing of stockpiles from the captured Diamiellian works.

El Murid had heard of Mustaph el-Kader. He was infamous as a procurer and as a supplier of religiously proscribed wine. What was a man like that doing controlling the salt supply?

"Don't whine at me!" the garrison commander snapped when the Disciple protested.

"But. . . . To deal with whoremasters and thieves, at usurious prices. . . ."

"You want salt? Good. You buy from who we tell you to. If you don't like it, go home."

El Murid turned to Hali, who was supposed to be his master of accounts. "Mowaffak?"

Hali controlled himself. "We'll do what we have to,

131

and pass the costs along. But nobody's going to love us. I wonder, Captain, what the Disciple would think of your profiteering."

"What he don't know won't hurt him. But complain if you want. He'll tell you to go pound sand. It's his brother-in-law's game. He won't turn on his own kin, will he?"

That was not the desert way. Family was concrete while truth, justice and sometimes even God's law were subjective.

"Who knows the heart of the Disciple?" Hali asked. "Surely not a bandit disguised as an officer in the Host of Illumination."

"A True Believer, eh? Get out of here. You're wasting my time. You guys are a royal pain in the ass, you know that?"

When they had gotten beyond the captain's hearing, El Murid murmured, "Nassef is doing it again, Mowaffak. If it isn't one thing, it's something else. He's driving me to distraction."

"Something has to be done, Lord."

"Of course. How do these things happen? Why hasn't anyone complained?"

"Maybe they have and the complaint hasn't been passed on. Maybe they never had the chance. Our most reliable people follow the heaviest fighting. Nassef bears your writ of command over the Invincibles. He's been exercising it, possibly to keep them away from evidence of evils such as this."

"Mowaffak, hear me. I speak for the Lord. You will chose one hundred men of irreproachable repute. Men immune to blandishment and extortion. Reclaim their white robes and return them to their original professions. They are to travel throughout the Kingdom of Peace, including both Hammad al Nakir and all the new provinces, unmasking evils such as this. They aren't to distinguish between the grievances of the faithful and the infidel, nor those of the desert-born and foreigner, nor of the mighty and the weak. All men will be equal

132

before their judgment. I will arm them with letters giving them absolute authority in anything they care to judge, and will back them completely, even against my own family. Even if I disagree with their judgments. This exploitation must stop."

"And who will watch the watchers?" Hali murmured to himself.

"I will, Mowaffak. And I'll be the most terrible judge of all. And Mowaffak. Collect this barbarous captain when we leave. We'll chastise him, and release him to spread the news that El Murid walks among the Chosen, as one of them, hunting their oppressors."

"How much longer will you tolerate the Scourge of God, Lord?" Hali asked, returning to a subject dear to his heart.

"How long will the fighting last? The day we begin beating swords into plowshares, then I'll have no use for captains of war."

It was at Kasr Helal, too, that Esmat told him another Ipopotam courier had failed to return. That made three who had vanished; two regular couriers and the special messenger sent after the disappearance of the first.

"Your worst fears have been realized, Esmat. Three men lost strains a belief in chance. Select six warriors from my bodyguard. Send them. Then another to see what happens to them. Do it right away, and tell them to ride hard. How long can we last?"

"Perhaps forty days, Lord. If luck rides with us."

He wanted to admonish Esmat for the pagan remark, but could not invoke the Lord now. That would be to claim God's countenance of his secret shame.

From Kasr Helal El Murid travelled northwestward, toward Dunno Scuttari and Nassef's promised spectacle. He and his companions often paused to ogle what they thought were great wonders. El Murid lingered over structures bequeathed to the present by the engineers of the Empire. Then the flame of the Empire of tomorrow burned in his eyes, and Hali would remind him that they were travelling incognito. He had had few opportunities to preach since Disharhun. The words piled up within him.

Even the towns and little cities were splendid, despite Nassef's rapine. But never had he imagined such splendor as burst upon him when first he gazed upon Dunno Scuttari.

"Oh, Papa!" Yasmid cried. "It's magnificent! So big and. . . . and magnificent!"

"Your uncle tells me he's going to make it a gift to me. What would I do with a city? You think it's beautiful? I'll give it to you. Assuming Nassef can take it."

"He can, Papa. I know he can."

"What about me?" Sidi demanded surlily.

"There are other cities. Which one do you want? Hellin Daimiel?"

"I don't want another city. I want. . . ."

"Let him have this one, Papa. It's beautiful, but I'd rather have Hellin Daimiel. That's where everything interesting. . . ."

"He said *I* could have Hellin Daimiel, Yasmid."

"What you're going to get, Sidi, is a taste of the strap. Act your age. You're not four years old anymore."

"How come she always gets her own way? When do we get to see the ocean? I want to see the ocean."

El Murid's hand whipped out. "There are times, Sidi, when you disgust me," he said as the boy rubbed his cheek. El Murid glanced at Mowaffak Hali, who pretended an intense interest in the River Scarlotti. "There are times when I'm tempted to foster you with the poor tribesmen of the Sahel so you'll learn to appreciate what you have and stop whining about what you don't."

El Murid stopped. The boy was not listening.

"Mowaffak, have someone find the Scourge of God and tell him we're here."

Nassef himself came to greet them. He was an adolescent mass of uncontrolled emotion. He had happy smiles and ferocious hugs for everyone.

El Murid easily identified the indelible tracks loneliness had stamped into Nassef's face. He saw them in his own face whenever he glanced into a mirror.

"I'm glad you came," Nassef enthused. "So much work went into this. It would have been a sin if you'd have missed it."

El Murid noted how attentive Nassef was to Yasmid, with his little jokes, his teasing, his mock flirtation. He indulged in an old speculation. Did Nassef have designs on the girl? She was on the brink of marriageability. For Nassef to wed her would be a great coup for the ambitious Nassef who sometimes thrust his head out of the shadows surrounding the several Nassefs the Disciple knew.

There were those who would frown on a man marrying his niece, but it was not without precedent. Many of Ilkazar's emperors had married their own sisters.

A few months earlier Hali had brought El Murid a chart of succession found in the apartment of Megelin Radetic at el Aswad, the fortress the Wahlig of el Aswad had abandoned shortly before the assault on Al Rhemish. What El Murid had seen in that chart had startled him. And had revivified all the specters that had haunted him throughout his association with his brother-in-law.

If Radetic had guessed correctly, Nassef had powerful motives for pursuing Yasmid. Only Haroun bin Yousif stood between Nassef and the throne on that chart. A marriage could lead to Crown and Disciplate conjoined.

El Murid had visited his wife's father on the way west. The old man, who had disinherited his children in the beginning, had been on his deathbed. El Murid had introduced the old chieftain to his grandchildren. They had conquered him immediately. He had recanted. There had been tears of forgiveness and of reconciliation.

"Nassef."

"Lord?"

"I came by way of el Aquila."

A strained longing shone on Nassef's face.

135

"I saw him, yes. And these two stole his heart. He said they were just like you and Meryem at the same ages. He forgave us all. He wanted me to tell you that."

For an instant a tear glinted in Nassef's eye. "Then I can go home? I can see him again?"

"No. You know the Fates were never that kind. He was on his deathbed when we arrived. We stayed till the Dark Lady came for him. He had a gentle, peaceful death."

"And my mother?"

"She abides, but I don't think she'll survive him long."

"I'll visit her as soon as we go into winter quarters. What did he think about me?"

"Pray for him, Nassef. He never accepted the Faith. He died an unbeliever. But he was proud of his son and daughter. He talked incessantly of the things you've accomplished. He said he always knew you'd go far."

Nassef glowed through his sorrow.

Mowaffak Hali watched with the cold eyes of a raptor. For a man who abhors politics, his prophet thought, Mowaffak can play them craftily.

Nassef wasted little time getting on with the event that had drawn the Disciple to Dunno Scuttari. The next day he ferried the family across the river and guided them to a pavillion on a hilltop.

"You won't be able to see much, really," he said. "But what there is you can see best from here. In the morning."

"What is it, Nassef?" Yasmid demanded.

"A surprise, Little Dove. Get up early and you'll see."

"Come on, Nassef," she breathed. Already, unconsciously, she was adopting the little wiles a woman uses to bend a man to her will.

"No, I'm not telling. Not even you. You'll wait like everybody else." He gestured downriver, toward the eastern end of the fortress island. "They'll be the most surprised."

Yasmid's pleading and flirting went for naught. This, Nassef said without verbalizing, would be his greatest triumph. It was his game. It would be played his way, by his rules.

El Murid, uncharacteristically, had an image of an unconfident roué stalking a virgin who had spurned the advances of countless lovers with more to offer. A roué who did not disguise his intent to use her once and pass her on—yet one who had staked his fortunes and ego on the successful outcome of an otherwise inconsequential affair.

And so he gained yet another perspective on this stranger who was his oldest acquaintance. There seemed to be no end to the faces of Nassef.

That night El Murid stood outside his pavillion and marvelled at the magnitude of the Host of Illumination. Its campfires covered the countryside on both banks of the river. It seemed that whole shoals of stars had descended to the plains and hills. "So many...." he murmured. "All brought here by *my* dreams."

Nassef had told him that he had recruited almost twenty thousand westerners. The Word, or parts thereof, stirred sympathetic resonances in some western hearts. The New Empire was battling its way from the womb.

Yasmid began tormenting him before sunrise. "Papa. Come on. Come and see what Nassef did. You won't believe it when you see it."

It was hours before his usual rising time. He preferred to work late and sleep late. He fought her till it became obvious that her determination was the greater. Accepting defeat grouchily, he rose. He dressed and followed her to the pavillion's exit.

"All right, brat. Show me this miracle and get it over with. I need my sleep."

"Can't you see, Papa? It's right there. Look at the river, Papa."

He peered down at the Scarlotti.

The river was not there.

The once vast flood had dwindled to a few lakes connected by one murky stream a dozen yards wide. Great expanses of mud lay exposed to the breeze and the rising sun. The breezes shifted while he wrestled with his awe. A foul odor assailed his nostrils.

"How in the world . . . ?"

Nassef came striding toward the pavillion. Weariness seemed to drag him down, yet when he saw them watching, his step took on a boyish bounce. A broad grin captured his face. "What do you think?" he shouted.

The roué has broken his beloved maidenhead, El Murid thought. And now he comes to gloat, to adore himself publicly, to brag. . . .

He snorted softly. "What did you do?" he demanded. "How can you dry up a river overnight?"

"You can't. What you do is impress a couple hundred thousand people and make them dig a new riverbed. I started as soon as we got here. I got the idea from *The Wizards of Ilkazar.* Where the poet tells about Varthlokkur sending the earthquake to demolish the walls and a building collapses into the Aeos and dams it and floods part of the city. I thought, why didn't they dam it upriver? Then they could have gotten in through the water gate. Then I thought, why not reroute the river? It would just spill over a dam."

Nassef babbled on. This ingenious stroke clearly meant more to him than just adding the jewel of another city to his diadem of clever conquests. He had invested of his *self*, like a child undertaking a severely ambitious project in hopes of winning paternal approval.

El Murid remembered Nassef once mentioning his trouble communicating with other children. He realized that in his superbly competent campaigns, and especially in this conquest, his brother-in-law was trying to make a statement to the world.

What was it? A simple, "I exist! Notice me!" Or something more complex?

Something more complex, surely. Nothing about Nassef was simple.

"Some of my men are in the city already," Nassef told

him. "They went down in boats during the night and waited for the water level to fall below the bottom of the water gate grates. They've occupied the area inside. I had other men laying plank roads across the mud as the river fell. Those should be done by now. The Host should be entering the city. They should surrender before nightfall."

Nassef was overoptimistic. Led, cajoled, and bullied by stubborn Guildsmen, the defenders resisted for nine days, yielding their inner strongholds only when overwhelmed. By the fifth day Nassef was frantic. The stone and earth dam shunting the Scarlotti was weakening. And he had yet to capture one of the fortified causeways connecting the inner and outer islands with the riverbanks.

He drove his forced laborers to prodigies and kept the dam intact. On the seventh day the Invincibles captured a causeway.

That sealed the city's fate. Nassef had acquired indefinite access.

On the eighth day a messenger arrived from the Lesser Kingdoms.

Nassef had no color and was shaking when he approached El Murid afterward. "Micah. . . . My Lord Disciple. They've slain Karim. Bin Yousif's rabble and some Guildsmen. They got him in Altea. Karim. . . . He was like a father to me. I'd sent him on a critical secret mission. He was coming back. He may have been successful. If he was, he was bringing us the chance to finish the war before winter."

El Murid frowned as he listened. Nassef seemed lost in the chaos of his thoughts, some of which he was verbalizing. He had never seen his brother-in-law this devastated, this indecisive, this much at a loss for what to do. The possible death of Karim was not something he had calculated into his plans. His habit of anticipating contingencies had failed him. Fate had found his blind spot. He had not taken into account the mortality of himself and his intimates.

"Men die in wartime, Nassef. And they won't all be soldiers we don't know, mourned only in some remote mud hut. Meryem's passing should have taught you that."

"The lesson didn't sink in. One dirty trick. . . . That whole campaign is going to go to Hell now. Karim was the only one who understood what I wanted. The only one who knew the whole plan. I wonder if they got anything out of him? What kind of an arrangement did he make . . . ? I have to go out there. I'm the only one who can keep it moving. The only one who can get that whoreson bin Yousif. I'll leave el-Kader here. He knows this project. He can finish up."

Before El Murid commented or could ask questions his brother-in-law rushed away. An hour later Mowaffak reported that Nassef had ridden east with a large band of Invincibles.

El-Kader assumed Nassef's role smoothly. He forced Dunno Scuttari's surrender the following day.

Nassef's dam collapsed the day following that. The flood severely damaged the dike facings on the city's outer island. Natives muttered about omens.

We have had too much talk about Fate and omens lately, El Murid thought. And I am as guilty as the worst of them. It's time for a sermon of admonition. We're back-sliding.

He was preparing the speech when Esmat relayed the report from the observer they had sent to Ipopotam.

"The lot? All six killed?" El Murid demanded. "That's hard to believe, Esmat. They were the best."

"Nevertheless, Lord. Our man didn't see who or how, unfortunately. He simply found them dead on the road. The natives wouldn't tell him what had happened. He returned before he suffered the same fate."

"All right. It's too late to save the next regular courier. What's our supply look like? We should be in fair shape.

Things have been going well. I haven't called you much lately."

"True, Lord. I'd guess sixteen days. Longer if we ration."

"Oh. Not as good as I thought. Too tight, in fact." His nerves began to fray. "Find el-Kader."

The argument with el-Kader became bitter. Stunned by the Disciple's suggestion, the general said, "Just abandon the confrontation line, Lord? With an enemy army on its way? Why? What kind of sense is that?"

El Murid felt foolish as he replied, "The Lord wills it."

"What?" Sarcastically, el-Kader observed, "Then the Lord has become a ninny overnight. And I can't credit that. Lord, we have treaties with Ipopotam. How are we supposed to seduce our enemies if we can't keep faith with our friends?"

"It has to be done," El Murid insisted. But he could muster none of the fiery conviction that usually fueled his statements. El-Kader's resistance stiffened. It was plain that his prophet's demands had nothing to do with the Lord's will. "General, it's necessary that my domains encompass those of Ipopotam."

"Oh?" el-Kader mused. "*Your* domains?" Louder, "I think I understand, Lord. And I suggest you find a diplomatic solution. The Itaskians are moving. Their army is like none we've faced before. I'll need every man to fight them. The future of the Kingdom of Peace will be decided on the Scarlotti, not in Ipopotam."

"There isn't time. . . . Are you refusing me?"

"I'm sorry, Lord. I am. I must. My conscience won't let me favor one man's vice over the welfare of the Host of Illumination."

El Murid exploded. "How admirable you are, el-Kader. I'd applaud did I not know you a thief and profiteer. I take it that it's within the scope of your conscience to let your relatives plunder their countrymen?"

El-Kader's face became taut. But he ignored the remark. "Lord, if the Itaskians defeat us. . . ."

"I order you to move against Ipopotam!" He was becoming more frightened with every second of delay.

"And I refuse, Lord. With all due respect. However, if you get the Scourge of God to direct me otherwise...."

"There isn't time for that!" El Murid glared at the richly decorated walls of what, till a few days earlier, had been the private audience chamber of the King of Dunno Scuttari. He whirled and stalked to a tall, massive wooden door. He shoved, shouted, "Mowaffak!"

El-Kader stiffened. It was no secret that Hali was El Murid's liaison with the Harish cult.

Hali stepped inside. His eyes were cold. His face was dead.

"Will you reconsider, General?" El Murid demanded.

"I'll give you the western recruits and ten thousand of our own people. Nothing more. I won't go myself. I have to defend the Scarlotti line."

El Murid's jaw tightened. This el-Kader was stubborn. Not even fear of the Harish would compel him to abandon his duty. He would yield nothing more.

He was a valuable man. No need wasting him in anger. "Mowaffak, I appoint you commander of the army just created. We're going to occupy Ipopotam."

Hali's right eyebrow rose almost imperceptibly. "As you command, Lord. When shall we begin?" El Murid glanced away. El-Kader did not. Hali shrugged as if to say, "What can I do?"

"Immediately, Mowaffak. And I'll accompany you." A growing, unreasoning panic taunted him. He felt the walls of the universe closing in. "That's all. Both of you. Get out of here. Give the orders. There isn't much time."

Two days after the Disciple's departure southward, two bedraggled, confused Itaskian survivors of Karim's Altean debacle reached Dunno Scuttari. There consternation and confusion deepened when they could locate no one who knew anything about the negotiations which had brought them south. El-Kader had them thrown into a dungeon.

The general continued preparing for the advent of the northern army, unaware that its commander and his own were co-conspirators.

Sidi and Yasmid, left behind by their father, drove their Invincible babysitters to distraction with their bickering. They always squabbled when their father was absent.

Sidi was young, but perfectly aware that he was being deprived of his patrimony. He was possessed by a growing, diamond-hard hatred for his sister.

Chapter Twelve: *END OF A LEGEND*

The death of Karim did not halt the invasion of Altea. The Host of Illumination came on, but its advance became confused, frenetic, without direction. The war bands simply roamed, killed, raped, and destroyed. The warriors did not know what their goals were.

"I'm exhausted, Beloul," Haroun said. "There're just too many of them." He lay back on a grassy hillside, staring at a sky that promised rain. "This charging here to stop this band and there to. . . ."

Beloul settled to the grass beside him, sitting cross-legged. "It's grinding us all down, Lord." He plucked a stem of grass and rolled it between his fingers, squeezing out the juice. "We can't sustain it."

"We have to. If they break through here. . . . If they finish Altea and Kavelin, and manage their treachery with the Itaskian Duke. . . . What'll be left? It'll be over."

"I doubt it, Lord. The Guildsmen will continue. We'll fight. And the thieves will fall out soon enough. Can you imagine El Murid being satisfied with half the spoils? When he wants an empire spanning Ilkazar's historical boundaries?"

"Despair stalks me, Beloul. I don't think he can be stopped. He's done the impossible."

"No war is over till the last battle is fought, Lord."

"You begin to sound like Radetic."

Beloul shrugged. "With age comes wisdom, Lord. And Radetic was both old and wise. For a foreigner. Let us recount our victories instead of forecounting our defeats. Karim is gone. The Duke's treachery has been forestalled."

"Who's that there?"

"What?"

"Someone's coming."

"Looks like Shadek."

El Senoussi cantered up. "There's news from Dunno Scuttari, Lord."

"At last. You look grim, Shadek. Is it that bad?"

"It's worse, Lord. A man's face can't express it."

Haroun threw an *I told you* look at Beloul. "Well?"

"The Scourge of God has kept his promise. He took the city."

Haroun surged into a sitting position. "What? Don't joke, Shadek. That's impossible."

"Nevertheless, Lord."

"But how? Where did he get the sailors and boats? How did he scale the inner walls?"

"The Scourge of God sees things hidden from us ordinary mortals, Lord. He does the thing that would occur to no one else. He and the Disciple rode into the city, Lord."

"They surrendered without a fight? You can't make me believe that, Shadek."

"No. They fought. Valiantly. But the Scourge of God changed the course of the river and attacked them through the city's watergate. That huge bridge he was building from the north bank? That engineers said would never work? Just a diversion."

Softly, Haroun asked, "What do you say now, Beloul? You know how that's going to hit them north of the river? They'll give up without a fight. He can't be stopped anymore."

"The final battle isn't lost or won, Lord."

"Yes, yes, I know. Megelin junior. But it's only a matter of time. Shadek. . . . You have that grey look. I take it there's more."

"Indeed, Lord. There's more. The Scourge of God has decided to replace Karim with himself. He's probably here by now."

"I expected that. He takes defeat personally. What else?"

"El Murid has given his pet Invincible, Mowaffak Hali, his own army. And ordered him to occupy Ipopotam."

Haroun grinned. "Ha! So! You hear that, Beloul? The fat man and his friend did their job. He's desperate. This'll destroy the credibility of his diplomacy. Nobody will believe him anymore. If only the northern army would strike while he's gone and Nassef is out here. . . ."

"I doubt that would help much, Lord," el Senoussi opined. "El-Kader commands the Host. He's no moron. At worst he would persevere till the Scourge of God bailed him out."

Haroun frowned. "You insist on extinguishing every spark of hope, don't you Shadek?"

"I'm sorry, Lord. I but relate the truths I see."

"Yes. I know. So. The Scourge of God has come to our part of the board. How can we make his stay here miserable?"

Sadly, Haroun had to admit that there was little they could do. His army hadn't the strength or the staying power. The predations of the roving war parties were crushing the Altean will to resist. Crown Prince Raithel's army was the sole native force still solid and reliable. The Prince's men, too, were exhausted.

"What about those Guildsmen?" el Senoussi asked.

"Still licking their wounds in the Bergwold," Beloul replied. "I was up there the other day. That boy is trying to rebuild with Altean stragglers. He had a little over two hundred men. Maybe three."

"They won't be much help, then."

"Only as a rallying point. That battle on the hill didn't hurt their reputation."

Haroun observed, "We may all end up hiding in the Bergwold. Shadek, locate the Scourge of God. Keep an eye on him."

Nassef found Prince Raithel first, just fifteen miles west of the Colberg. He shattered the Altean army. The Prince barely escaped with his life. Two thirds of his soldiers did not.

Nassef then turned to Haroun. He started boxing the Royalists in.

Altea seemed to be taking its last pained gasps of freedom. Only the Bergwold and a handful of fortified towns remained unconquered.

The fat man wakened suddenly, every nerve shrieking that something was wrong. Frozen by fear, he moved nothing but his eyelids.

The campfire had burned low, but still cast a red glow. He probed the shadows. Nothing.

What was it?

There was a frightening stillness to the night. He turned till he could make out the huge, blanket-buried lump of Gouch.

There was a fly walking on the big man's naked eyeball. Its wings caught the glow of the coals, giving the eye an eerie look of motion.

Mocker hurled himself at the big man. "Gouch! You wake up." His hands closed on an arm grown cold. "Hai! Gouch! Come on. Self, am frightened by game."

He knew it was no game. The fly had betrayed the truth.

Gouch had taken terrible wounds in their last fight. They had slain six Invincibles! A half dozen of the most determined fighters in the world. It had been too big a task.

It was a miracle that the big man had lasted this long.

"Woe! Gouch! Please! Do not leave self alone."

They had become close. Mocker, though he had expected the worst, could not accept it.

"Am accursed," he muttered. "Am carrier of death, like bearer of plague. Should be expunged from face of earth."

For a time he just sat beside his friend, damning himself, mourning, and wondering what he would do now. Finally, he rose and began collecting rocks. The cairn he built was not much, but it showed that he cared. He would not have made the effort for anyone else.

He muttered as he worked. "Self, am in no wise able to continue task here. Enemy catching on. Same being intelligent, will send bigger party next time round. Same will be inhamperable. Must assay alternate course, designed to inconvenience religious dolts."

He fluttered round the camp till sunrise. Then he loaded his donkey and headed north, toward lands where he might more effectively prosecute his personal war. He narrowly avoided colliding with El Murid's southbound invasion force.

The Duke of Greyfells, who had moved south slowly while awaiting confirmation of his negotiations with Karim, finally learned of Karim's death. He was furious. Then he learned that Nassef had replaced his subordinate in the Lesser Kingdoms.

Altea was a remote theater. He would not be noticed there.

In disguise, guarded by his most intimate supporters, he rode south to renegotiate treacheries that had promised him the Itaskian Crown and partition of the west.

His second in command, a bitter enemy, allowed him a headstart, then rushed the northern army toward Dunno Scuttari.

It met el-Kader and the Host of Illumination on a plain near the town of Pircheaen, twenty-two miles north of the Scarlotti. The armies skirmished throughout a brisk autumn day. Neither commander was prepared to commit himself. The exchanges of the second day were more savage but no more conclusive. Both sides claimed victory.

El-Kader withdrew during the night. But the Itaskians did not follow up with an advance toward Dunno Scuttari. Instead, they turned east, hoping to force a crossing of the River Scarlotti somewhere away from the most heavily defended crossings.

El-Kader recrossed the river, then marched parallel to the Itaskians.

"We're in a bad spot," Beloul told his king. He held a crude map of the area west of the Bergwold. "He's hemmed us in. He has men here, here, here. . . ." One by one, he indicated the locations of eight war bands, each at least the equal of Haroun's own. The Royalists were surrounded on all but the Bergwold side.

"Can we break out?"

"Maybe. But it looks grim."

Haroun sighed, surveyed the countryside. There was not an enemy in sight, yet the cage door had been slammed shut. He glanced down at his hands. They were shaking. He was afraid his nerve was going. He desperately needed a rest. "Which group is he with?"

"Here. South of the Bergwold."

"All right. That's where we'll try to break out."

"Lord? Attack the Scourge of God himself?"

"Yes. We'll just have to fight the harder. And hope. Beloul?"

"Lord?"

"Tell the men our only hope is to slay the Scourge of God. That's going to be the whole point of the attack."

"As you command, Lord."

Sorrowfully, uncertainly, Haroun watched his little army prepare for what might be its last battle. Why did he bother? It seemed every peril he evaded led to a worse. "Let's go!" He swung into his saddle.

"We might do it!" he shrieked an hour later.

The surprised enemy force, backboned by a handful of Invincibles, could not get organized. Haroun flailed about himself, wailing Royalist warcries. His men, smelling success, were hurling themselves on their enemies with more passion than he had anticipated. Some were just yards from the Scourge of God.

Hatred seared the air as he and Nassef glared at one another. The hate drew them like powerful lodestones. But the meeting was not fated. The swirl of battle pushed them ever farther apart.

In time, Haroun moaned to Beloul, "They reacted too damned fast." The tide was turning. And a scout had brought word that another war band was approaching.

"Yet the Scourge of God remains in peril, Lord. Look. The Invincibles keep getting tangled up trying to protect him."

"Don't humor me, Beloul. I have eyes."

The fighting drifted toward the Colberg. All the valor and sacrifice of the Royalist champions was in vain. The Invincibles rallied their less enthusiastic companions and began closing a circle around them. When asked for suggestions, el Senoussi could contribute only, "Maybe we could make a stand in the ruins, Lord."

"Maybe. Where are the damned Guildsmen? Didn't you send a messenger?"

"Beloul did, Lord. I don't know where they are. Maybe they're getting even."

"Not that Ragnarson. . . . Look. There they are."

An infantry company came double-timing from beyond the Colberg.

"You're right, Lord. And just in time."

"They pay their debts."

Ragnarson opened an escapeway for the Royalists.

"Why didn't you keep after them?" bin Yousif demanded as Ragnarson shepherded him toward the Colberg. "We could have had the Scourge of God."

"Bitch and gripe. How the hell was I supposed to

know? Your message said stand by to bail you out if you got in over your head. I barely got here in time to do that. Haaken, get those Altean clowns into close order. Look, your kingship, I just saved your ass. Again. You want me to throw you back? Or to worry about keeping it saved? That isn't the only gang of those guys around. There's one only four miles north of here."

Beloul protested, "Lord, these masterless curs need a lesson in manners."

"Look behind us, Beloul."

He hated looking back himself. That part of his force which remained was no larger than the company led by the young Guildsman. Most of the rest had scattered. It would take days for the survivors to reform.

"Hey, Bragi," a Guildsman shouted. "We'd better get into the woods. They're ready to come after us."

Haroun glanced back. The second war band had arrived. "Your man is right. We'd better run."

They entered the tangle of the Bergwold in time. Nassef's riders showed no inclination to follow them. Ragnarson laughed. "They've tried before. We taught them a lesson. If they're going to come in, they have to get off horses. They don't like that. Move your men ahead. I'll screen you."

"Bragi. They're going to try it after all."

Haroun listened to the courses of men Nassef had ordered into the wood. "You're right. They don't like it."

"They're going to like it a lot less in a little while. Haaken. Reskird. We'll set the ambush at the deep ravine."

The fight was little more than a skirmish. Nassef's men quickly retreated to the forest's edge.

They came again the following morning, this time seriously. The Scourge of God had gathered all his men for the sweep.

"There's way too many of them," Regnarson told

Haroun. "They can cover the whole Bergwold. We can't play hide and seek."

Haroun nodded as he studied the Guildsman's Bergwold maps. "These are good." Megelin would have been pleased with their quality. "You read?" he asked.

"Only enough to follow those. It's part of the training, but the war broke before we got to reading and writing. Captain Sanguinet and Lieutenant Trubacik drew those. They taught all the noncoms how to read them."

"My friend, we've gotten ourselves into a classic situation here. Whatever we do is wrong. We can't run and we don't dare fight."

"Between a rock and a hard place, as we say at home."

"Nassef wants you as bad as he wants me. He was fond of Karim. What do you think we should do?"

Ragnarson shrugged. "You was trained to lead. Now would be a great time to start. I got this job because nobody else would take it. It's all I can do to figure out what to do with the volunteers we've been getting."

"Have you gotten many?"

"A lot. Your friend Nassef has been kicking ass all over the country. Most of them don't seem to know where else to go."

Dawn's light was seeping into the dank, misty forest when Regnarson's brother appeared. "They're coming, Bragi. Two lines deep. We won't have a chance if they make contact."

"Could we break through?" Haroun asked.

"That's what they want us to try, I think. Then the whole mob could close in."

"And if we run, they'll be waiting on the other side of the forest."

"That's how I'd set it up."

"Let's do it anyway. We'll locate them and I'll attack with my horsemen. You run for Alperin after they start chasing me. It's only twelve miles. Its walls are strong and it has its own garrison. I can circle around and catch up with you there."

"I don't like it," Ragnarson said. "What good will it do? We'll still be surrounded."

"But with a wall to protect us, and people to help."

"The Scourge of God hasn't been intimidated by walls yet." Nevertheless, Ragnarson acquiesced. He could muster no plan of his own. "All right," he grumbled. "I kind of stumbled into this, you know. I kind of hoped I could make some kind of showing before High Crag replaced Sanguinet. I thought this was my big chance."

Haroun smiled thinly. "Look what I'm going to lose. A whole kingdom. It's so huge. It stretches as far as I can throw a rock."

"Yeah. Haaken! Reskird! Let's move out."

Haroun came to respect the Guildsmen even more. The passage through the wood took a day and a night and most of another day. The warrior brothers seldom rested, and frequently spent their own strength to help the weaker of their allies. And many of them were burdened with wounded. He questioned Ragnarson about it, but the youth could not explain. That was the way his brotherhood did things.

Yet the Guildsmen were no less weary than the others, Haroun saw. They just seemed to have more will.

And these, he thought, are the Guild children. No wonder old generals like Hawkwind and Lauder, with their select followers, were so feared.

The sun was well to the west when they reached the nether verge of the Bergwold. Haroun considered the time of day. "We'd have a better chance of pulling it off after dark."

Ragnarson agreed. "We can use the rest. Send some of your people to scout it out. They're better at it than mine. Mine can't see anybody out there, and I think that's too good to be true."

"You're right. Beloul!" Haroun called. "I have a job for you." He explained what he wanted.

The sun had set before Beloul returned to say, "Lord, he's there. The Scourge of God himself, with the Invincibles. They're hiding in a ravine beside the road to Alperin. They don't know that we're here yet. And from what I could overhear, they're exhausted from their ride around the forest."

Haroun translated for Ragnarson. He added, "Let's give it another hour. Then I'll try to draw them off to the south."

"Make it two hours and you'll have the moon."

The time rushed away. The moon seemed to streak into the sky. Suddenly, Haroun was on his mount and Altean countryside was rushing beneath him. He was kicking his mare because she was reluctant to run in the weak light. To his left, one of his followers went down as his mount stumbled.

Nassef was not ready for him. Not for him to come smashing straight in behind a swarm of arrows. The Invincibles remained disorganized for the critical few minutes Haroun needed to lead his band past and take them flying into the night.

Then they came after him.

He could see little, looking back to the northwest, but he could hear the thundering hooves and the exultant warcries.

The Invincibles, like their Guild enemies, were tenacious. Haroun could not shake them. His success consisted of staying ahead. Gradually he swung round northward, circling back toward Alperin.

"Why are we doing this, Lord?" el Senoussi wanted to know. "Why aren't we escaping? Towns are traps."

Haroun did not answer for a while. He did not know how to put it into words. "There's a duty, Shadek. A responsibility. How can I explain? You imply an argument, and the sense of it is incontestable. Radetic would have commended you. Mine is purely emotional. Maybe it's the hand of fate that moves me. But I do have a feeling this Ragnarson might be critical to my future. To all our futures."

"You're the King, Lord."

Haroun laughed. It was a weak, drained gesture. "I love your enthusiasm, Shadek. You're like an oasis after six days of hard desert. You shelter me from the sandstorms of tomorrow."

El Senoussi chuckled. "Thank you, Lord."

Moments later, Beloul said, "Something's wrong, Lord. They're not pushing us as hard as they should be."

"I've noticed. We must be doing what they want."

"I told you, Lord," said el Senoussi.

Daylight arrived. And Haroun learned why the Invincibles had relaxed. He had come back to Alperin.

"Damn! He's outfoxed us again." There was fierce fighting at the town gate. "He let the Guildsmen get there so he could catch them with their gates open."

"Would that we had such a plotter in our ranks, Lord," said el Senoussi.

"Be patient, Shadek. He's teaching me."

"Indeed, Lord. What now?"

"What about our friends back there? In no hurry, eh? Unless we try to break away? Let's see if we can get up on yon hill and watch for a while. Our friends might get so interested they'll give us a chance to get away."

He spoke lightly, as if unconcerned, but he was sure this was the last day of his life.

The Invincibles allowed them the hilltop and did not offer battle immediately. The Scourge of God seemed content to delay his gratification while he dealt with the Guildsmen.

"That's the end of some brave boys," Beloul said gently.

Haroun glanced at the town gate. Fanatics in white were flooding through. "Yes. A pity."

"That Nassef is one crafty bastard," Haaken told Bragi as the Alteans defending the gate collapsed. They had made a valiant stand. Their task had been hopeless, but they had held long enough.

"He thought on his feet," Bragi replied. "He outguessed us. We've got to pay the price. Let's just hope this trick is something he's not expecting. Come on, Reskird!" he shouted. "Quit screwing around over there. They're coming." He could see most of the curved street running from the gate. Horsemen swept toward them like a sudden spring flood, forced on by those behind them.

Alperin was typical of towns that spent centuries constrained within walls. It had had to grow upward and together instead of spreading. Its streets were narrow and twisted. Its buildings stood three, four and sometimes five storeys high, often overhanging the cobbled streets.

It was a bad place for horsemen to engage bowmen who had taken to the rooftops.

Arrows swarmed down onto the Invincibles and their animals. The desert warriors tried fighting back with their saddle bows, but could find few targets. The Guildsmen exposed themselves only long enough to loose their shafts.

The Invincibles still entering the town kept forcing their fellows into the deadly streets.

"Keep it up! Keep it up!" Bragi screamed. He scuttled across a steep slate roof. "We're going to do it, Haaken! We're going to do it! They don't know what's happening."

He was right. The Invincibles, absolutely certain of victory and unable, because of the twisting streets, to see that the slaughter was not localized, kept driving into the killing rain.

"Haaken, I'm going to find that Altean captain. What was his name?"

"Karathel."

"Yeah. Maybe he can rally his men and grab the gates again. We can trap them in here and murder them all."

"Bragi."

"What?"

"Don't push your luck. Things can change. They still outnumber us a skillion to one. We should just worry about getting out alive. Just make them back off."

"Yeah. Okay." But Bragi was not listening. He was

too excited to accept the possibility of disaster. He had
thought on his feet too. He had turned Nassef's trap into
a counter-trap. He was flying high. "Be back in a few
minutes."

He scrambled from roof to roof, moving toward the
wall, parallel to the street. He paused occasionally to
loose an arrow. He had told his men to concentrate on
leaders. Confused followers could be dispatched later.

Nowhere did he see anything to warrant Haaken's
pessimism. The streets were filled with dead men. It
was a target shoot.

His trip proved needless. Karathel's thinking paral-
leled his own. His was counterattacking when Bragi
arrived. The Invincibles at the gate were hard pressed.

Then more Invincibles attacked from outside. They over-
ran the Alteans while Bragi watched, feeling completely
helpless.

"Damn!" he snarled. "Damn! Damn! Damn! We had it
in the palm of our hand."

Haaken's warning came back. Nassef had thousands
of men in Altea. If they kept converging nothing could
prevent their victory.

He could see Haroun's men on their hill, watching,
unable to help. He sighed. "Just not enough people."

Below, the new wave of Invincibles surged into the
deathtrap streets. It was time to rejoin Haaken. If this
was the end, they should go down together.

He found his path barred. Some not too bright Invincible had fired a building in hopes of driving the Guildsmen
off its roof. He had overlooked the fact that the fire
would be as hard on the men in the narrow street. Bragi
decided to descend and circle round the burning house.

He dropped into a tight alleyway lying behind a long
row of shops and houses. He had taken no more than a
dozen steps when horsemen overtook him

He whirled, let an arrow fly. A man groaned. He
loosed a second shaft into the flesh under a man's chin
as a horse reared over his head. He fumbled for a third

arrow, dropped it, clawed at his sword. The certainty of death nearly paralyzed him.

The third rider let out a strangled wail and fled, though he had been in perfect position to split Bragi's head with his saber.

Bragi stood there a moment, stunned. "What the hell?" He glanced at the men he had downed. The Invincible was still alive, groaning. The other was stone dead.

"What the hell?" Bragi said again. Then he shrugged. "Why look the old gift horse in the mouth?" He ran while the running was good.

"Something's happened," Haaken said when Bragi finally found him. "Look how they're howling and carrying on. And hardly fighting back."

Regnarson looked into the street. He loosed an arrow. "Looks like they've gone crazy. I don't get it. But keep hitting them."

"We won't be able to much longer. We're about out of arrows."

"Use them all. We'll worry about what to do next when we have to."

The arrow shortage never mattered. Within minutes those Invincibles who could were flying out the gate, where Haroun's men took advantage of their confusion and despair to hurt them further.

Haroun rode into the jubilant town an hour later. "Look at his face," Bragi whispered to Kildragon. "He's *glowing*. I never saw anybody look like that."

"I don't know how you did it, my friend," Haroun said softly, awed. "I don't even care. But today will live in memory ever green."

"What? Come on. We didn't. . . . We survived, that's all."

"No. You did more. Much more. Today El Murid lost his war. The Invincibles have been broken. Now it's only a matter of time till the Disciple has been destroyed."

"What the hell are you raving about? So we finally

won one. It didn't amount to that much. And the rest of them will be after us in a day or two."

Bin Yousif considered him momentarily. "You really don't know, do you? I forget, you don't speak my language well. Listen, my friend. Outside. That's a death song the Invincibles are singing. And inside, that's a victory song by my people. They're not singing for today, but for the war. You did two things. You destroyed the biggest band of Invincibles El Murid had left. And you slew the Scourge of God. You. Yourself."

"That man in the alley . . . ?" Bragi muttered to himself. "But. . . ." He sat down on a stone wall surrounding a fountain. "Really?"

"Really. And it'll change the whole shape of the war."

Chapter Thirteen: *THE ENTERTAINER*

The fat youth crouched in the scraggly brush and studied the enemy encampment. Fifty Invincibles guarding two children. What made them so important?

He had come close to stumbling into them. He had made cover just in time. His curiosity was aroused. Two children!

He had been headed north, skirting the edge of the Sahel, making for Altea, where he hoped to rejoin bin Yousif. But now the north had fled his mind. This might be a chance to strike a real blow on behalf of Sparen and Gouch.

He shook. "Fat one, O flabby friend, am in no wise able to brave fifty swords of enemies implacable as Lady Death Herself. Only fool would do same.

"Pusillanimous pretender," he answered himself. "Is potential opportunity of unparalleled magnitude. Must at least investigate. Establish identity of protected children. Same might be of tremendous value. Elimination of same might be mighty blow against fell empire of madman El Murid."

Mocker was easily frightened. Sajac had kept him afraid for years. But the constant pressure had schooled him to control his fear.

He was scared silly when he led his donkey into the encampment, pretending less familiarity with the desert tongue than he possessed.

"Go away, vagabond," a sentry told him.

Mocker just looked puzzled and, more brokenly than usual, claimed a right to use the spring. He offered to entertain the band in return for his supper.

He had learned some of the desert tongue during his half-forgotten trek down the coast of the Sea of Kotsüm, and had picked up more while traveling with Haroun. He understood most of what was being said around him.

Thus it was that, shortly after the Invincible commander let him lay out his bedroll, he learned who the children were.

Malicious glee almost overcame him.

They were the spawn of the Disciple himself! Ah, but weren't the Fates playing a curious game? The general at Dunno Scuttari, el-Kader, had ordered them moved to the safety of the Sahel. He was concerned about the approach of the northern army.

What sweet opportunity! The children of El Murid! He nearly forgot his fear.

His devilish mind began darting around like a whole swarm of gnats. How best to exploit this chance encounter?

First he would have to infatuate the children and attach himself to their party.

How? The Invincibles were keeping them carefully segregated.

He opened his packs as evening settled in. He joined some of the younger Invincibles at their campfire. Sealing his eyes, he commenced the dexterity drills he had so often cursed Sparen for forcing upon him. They amounted to little more than making a common object—a copper coin in this case—appear and disappear between his fingers.

"Sorcery!" someone muttered. Mocker heard the fear in the voice.

He opened his eyes, smiled gently. "Oh, no, my friend. No witchcraft. Is simplest trick of prestidigitation. See? Coin is on back of hand. Is finger game. Watch." He pulled a short stick from the fire and made it appear and disappear, slowly and clumsily enough for the warriors to get the drift. "You see?"

Stage magicians were not unknown in the desert, but they had shown no eagerness to perform since El Murid's ascension. The Disciple's followers were too sensitive about sorcery.

"Hey! I think I saw it," said a warrior. "Do it again, would you?" The man squatted in order to see better.

"Self, am humblest of entertainers," Mocker said. "Have been perilously buffeted by winds of war."

"Got you," the warrior said. "That's neat. Could you teach me how to do it? I've got a kid brother who would love something like that."

Mocker shrugged. "Self, can try. But take warning. Is more difficult of achieving than looks betray. Takes much practice. Self, am professional, yet must practice two hours daily."

"That's all right. Just the coin trick. Come on." The warrior, who was hardly older than Mocker, produced a coin of his own. Several others crowded around, equally interested.

Within twenty minutes that fat youth had three students and an audience of a dozen. The watchers taunted the trainees whenever their fingers betrayed them. Mocker provided a natter of invented self-history with his instructions. His biography was an epic of how the war, in the form of marauding Guildsmen, had robbed him of his position as jester to a minor Libianninese nobleman. The Guildsmen, he claimed, had erroneously concluded that the knight was collaborating with the Scourge of God. They had hung the man and burned his manor.

Mocker claimed that only a miraculous escape had saved him from the same fate.

"So uncivilized, this west! Understand that war is facet of mankind. Have studied with leading philosophers and know same. But barbarisms practised by combatants here. . . . Self, am soured on whole end of earth. Am determined to return to east of childhood, where sanity reigns supreme."

The Invincibles took no offense. He seemed to be condemning their enemies more than themselves.

Their captain heard most of the tale. Mocker kept a close, if surreptitious, eye on the man, but could not detect a reaction. His fireside companions seemed satisfied, but their opinions were not critical. The captain's was.

Then he noticed the face in the shadows. A girl's face. How long had she been watching? And listening?

"Enough of teaching now. Is boring for soldiers out in wilderness, maybeso? Self, will do show. Same being entertaining enough, audience might reward self with copper or two to sustain same during hardship of eastward journey, maybeso." He recovered the rest of his tools and props.

He relied heavily on the stage magic, but after a while broke it up with Tubal and Polo. His audience did not respond. The Children of Hammad al Nakir were not familiar with urban-rural conflicts, and were too conservative to appreciate the ribaldry.

"No fun at all, these people," Mocker muttered to himself. "No imagination. Men of friend Haroun howled at same stories."

Two faces now watched from the shadows. He returned to the stage magic, carefully playing to that select audience.

He studied the children as much as he dared, feeling for something that might reach them. He thought the girl was the one he would win. The boy seemed sour, surly and impossible to impress.

He thought wrong. The boy was the one who defied the captain's glare and came to the fireside. "Can you teach me those tricks?" he demanded.

Mocker scanned the faces of the Invincibles. He found no guideposts. He spread his hands, shrugged. "Maybeso. All things are possible with faith. Show self hands."

"What?"

"Hands. Self, must see hands to say if true skill can be developed."

Sidi offered his hands. Mocker took them, studied their backs, then their palms. "Training is possible," he announced. "Fingers are thin enough. But not very long. Will be problem. Will require much hard practice. Get coin. Will begin. . . ."

"Some other time," the captain said. "He needs his sleep now. We've spent too long on this as it is."

Mocker shrugged. "Am sorry, young sir."

Sidi glared at the captain. Suddenly, he whirled and stamped toward his sister. Mocker thought he heard a muttered, "I never get anything I want."

Mocker turned in with the warriors, but was a long time falling asleep. What had gone wrong? Was it too late to do something more? They would travel on in the morning, leaving him here to watch opportunity vanish into the badlands. . . . Did he dare try something tonight? No. That would be suicidal. That damned captain would cut him down before he got out of his bedroll.

The captain wakened him next morning. He had been lying there half awake, trying to ignore the racket made by the rising warriors. "Pack your things, Entertainer," he ordered. "You're coming with us."

"Eh? Hai! Not into desert. Am bound for. . . ."

The captain glared. "So you'll make a detour. The one you were were fishing for. That's what last night was all about, wasn't it? So drop the pretense. Pack your things. You've found your new sponsor."

Mocker stared at the ground. He fought fear. This man was dangerously perceptive.

165

The captain leaned closer. "The Lord Sidi and Lady Yasmid insist on having you. I won't defy them. But I'll be watching, fat man. One misstep and you're dead."

Mocker shook all over. He had had no illusions before, but with the captain having voiced his suspicion he became more terrified than ever. He rushed to his donkey.

He irritated the captain further when the party got under way. He was the only one walking. But Sidi took a proprietary interest in him, shielding him from the Invincible, acting like a child with a new pet.

Mocker faked smiles and mumbled to himself, "Am going to repay this patronization with compound interest, Lord."

The Sahel he liked even less than he did Sidi.

Between Hammad al Nakir proper and the domains of the coastal states lay a strip of land which made the interior desert attractive by comparison. A legacy of the Fall, a natural killing zone, it varied in depth from forty to one hundred miles. Virtually waterless and lifeless, it consisted almost entirely of sharp, low mountains and tortuous, rocky gorges. It was the cruelest of lands. The few people who survived there were among the poorest and most primitive alive. They hated outsiders.

And they were El Murid's, heart and soul. Most of the current crop of Invincibles sprang from the Sahel. The sons of the Sahel saw more promise in El Murid's dreams than did the Children of Hammad al Nakir proper.

Mocker walked that barren land and wept for himself. However was he going to win his way back through this maze of dead hills and unseen sentinels? The watchful Sahel tribesmen were everywhere. Lean, ragged savages, they scared hell out of him each time they visited their brethren of the bodyguard.

He tried to keep them out of mind. Sufficient unto the day the evil thereof.

After three thoughtful days he selected the girl as his primary target. El Murid's movement would miss her more than it would Sidi. The heart of the insane beast would not miss a beat if she were to take over when the Disciple's last day came.

The boy was a useless little snot. If he assumed the mantle his father's movement would rush headlong toward the graveyard of history.

The fat man had begun, occasionally, to think politically. Haroun bin Yousif had set his feet upon the path.

He wanted to cause his enemies all the pain he could. Removing their future prophetess seemed the surest way.

He could not get close to the girl. His usual winning techniques seemed wasted on her. Though she often watched his entertainments, and sometimes observed Sidi's private lessons, she never betrayed amusement or delight. The Invincible captain was more responsive.

She had to be an inhuman monster. A child with no child in her at all. That was spooky enough in a grownup. In a kid it was horribly unnatural.

He worked hard with Sidi. The boy had no talent and a lot of impatience. He had to praise him constantly to keep him interested. Sidi was the only channel to Yasmid.

"Self, have decided," he announced one morning, after the Invincibles had set up a semi-permanent camp just behind the Sahel. "Will show favorite pupil secret of mesmerism after all." He had decided to go ahead with his final, most desperate, most perilous line of attack.

He had been priming it from the beginning, of course, just in case, mentioning hypnotism, when playing coy. His excuse for dropping the subject was always the best: the Invincibles might accuse him of witchcraft. And there was the problem of finding a reliably close-mouthed subject on whom to practice.

Sidi had been voluntering his sister for almost as long as Mocker had been tempting him.

"Now?" Sidi demanded. He was excited. Mocker watched the green burn in his eyes. Damo Sparen certainly had been a student of the human race, the fat man reflected. He had been guiding the Disciple's son according to the Sparen precepts, letting the boy do all the work. He was ready. A lust for power over people boiled within him.

"Soon, Lord. If same can be managed unbeknownst to white-clad savages. Same being simple skill learnable by anyones, but subject to gross misinterpretation by superstitious, self must protect self. . . ."

"Tonight. Come to my tent tonight. My sister will be there. I promise."

Mocker nodded. He kept his mouth shut, let the boy have his head.

Sidi was the perfect mark, so avaricious and self-centered that he had no time for suspicions. Mocker was ashamed. This was like robbing a blind man.

But the stakes! Oh, the stakes!

He worried about the captain all day. That man was the essence of vigilance. He would have to be the first to die. . . .

He dared leave no one like the captain alive on his backtrail. The captain had that same abiding quality exemplified by Haroun's man Beloul. He would come till he had gotten his revenge.

Not all the Invincibles remained cold and aloof. Several of Mocker's pupils became quite friendly. He swapped jokes and quips with them, and regaled them with endlessly shifting, slippery lies about his misadventures in the east. They answered him with lies of their own.

Darkness finally fell. He let a few hours drag past. Finally, heart hammering, he crept to Sidi's tent. No one challenged him.

It was a night without a moon, but he knew the guard only pretended not to notice him. What if the man suffered a fit of conscience and reported this to his commander?

"Lord?" Mocker whispered, his nerves howling. "Is self. Can same enter?"

"Come on! It's about time. Where have you been?"

Mocker slipped into the tent. "Waiting for camp to fall asleep." He smiled. Yasmid was there.

She had brought one of her handmaidens. That was a complication he had not foreseen.

Could he hypnotize three at one time? He had never tried. And a life or death situation made it a hell of a time to start.

As if to soothe his nerves, he began tumbling a coin amongst his chubby fingers, making it appear and disappear. "All is ready?" he asked. "All are agreed? Lady? Self, will not undertake task if same offends. . . ."

"Get on with it." Yasmid smiled thinly. "Entertainer, I'm here because I'm interested. But we have to finish before the guards change watches."

"Is not so simple like skinning goat, Lady. Stage must be set."

"So set it."

There was no doubt who was in charge here. Not Sidi. Mocker smiled wanly. Had the girl been using her brother all along?

He assumed the lotus position. "If Lady will sit facing self? All right. Lord, will do same here?" He patted the carpeted earth with his left hand. Beckoning the handmaiden, "You, sit here, please." He patted with his right hand. "Lord Sidi, and you, Miss, you must watch self close. So what self does. Is impossible of explaining, but easy to show. Lady Yasmid, you concentrate on coin here. Put all else out of mind. Never let eyes wander from same. See same turn in candlelight? Bright, dark, bright, like day, like night. . . ." His voice became a low monotone. She strained to hear. He stared into her eyes, droning about the coin, and secretly prayed that the other two would be trapped by it as well.

"Now sleep comes. Blessed sleep. Respite from all trials of daytimes. Sleep." He went on far longer than Sparen had deemed necessary. He wanted to be sure. The stakes were high. "Eyelids feel like same are weighted with lead. Unable to open eyes." It began to get to him.

He finally dared glance at Sidi and the maid.

He had them!

His heart hammered. Oh, the wonder of it! He began talking rapidly, first to the maid, then to Sidi, sketching what he wanted remembered should they be interrupted from outside. Yasmid he told not to remember anything. Then, to her, "You will begin to see good side of portly friend of brother Sidi. Will want to ease lot of same. . . . Wait."

To himself, he muttered, "Is famous case of putting cart before horse. Self, am being too anxious. Must take time, do thing right. First must find true feelings and natural weak points hidden in female mind, same being foundation stones self must assemble into working structure." He began questioning Yasmid about her feelings. About everyone and everything.

"Very interesting," he murmured a half hour later, having discovered that while she worshipped her father and his notion of a Kingdom of Peace, she secretly loathed her father's war. It had claimed the life of her mother, and that she believed too great a price to pay for a dream.

Her father's warriors, especially Nassef, awed her, but she saw them as instruments of impatience. She was convinced that her father's ideals were invincible in themselves, that they could conquer the world by their own innate superiority. Were westerners not enlisting in the Host of Illumination? Had the Faith not caught on even in Throyes? El Murid needed but give them time.

But she was no pacifist. There was a savage, vengeful strain in her. She wanted the Royalists hunted and slain to the last of their number. They were unrepentant tools of the Evil One, and as such deserved only to be reunited with their dark master.

Mocker strove to reinforce her anti-war feelings. Then he resumed working on her attitudes toward himself.

He wanted her convinced that he was a good and

trustworthy friend, that she could confide in him when she dared go to no one else.

Someone stirred outside the tent. "Lord? It's almost time to change the guard."

"Just a minute," Mocker replied, managing a creditable Sidi-like whine. Working hastily, he again told the three what he wanted remembered. Then he wakened Yasmid and her handmaiden with simple fingersnaps.

"What's the matter with Sidi?" Yasmid demanded. The boy was snoring.

"Woe," Mocker said. "Fell asleep short time passing. Self, feared to shake awake lest same be considered crime. In homeland of self touching of royal personage is deemed capital offense. Being cautious by nature, thought leaving same sleep was prudenter course."

"We're not royalty, Entertainer. We've never claimed to be. We're just spokesmen for the Lord. The brat may wish he was a prince. . . . Nobody would pay attention if he complained."

Mocker watched her carefully. Her reserve seemed to have faded. Maybe he had succeeded. "Maybeso. Still, must ask Lady to do wakening honors. Self would feel more comfortable. Must depart, anyways. Is almost time for watch change. Captain would be irate did same catch nocturnal visitant to beautiful lady in his charge."

He caught her blush as he turned to leave. It climbed her cheeks till it peeped over her veil. He grinned at the darkness as he left the tent.

He had not lost his touch.

In two days he had Yasmid chattering like an old friend. She followed him around the camp, her devotion testing the captain's indulgence. Mocker heard her whole life's tale, and much about her fears and dreams.

As Yasmid drew closer, Sidi withdrew. The boy was selfish and jealous and did not hide it. Mocker was afraid he would back-stab him for turning to his sister.

Yasmid came to him the third morning, her face ashen, her mind numb.

"What is problem, Lady?" he asked softly. "Evil tidings? Self, saw messenger arrive hour passing. Am sorry, if so."

"The Scourge of God is dead."

"Eh? Same being famed Nassef, high general to Lady's father?"

"Yes. My uncle Nassef. The man I planned to marry."

"Is sad. Very sad. Self, will do whatever to ease pain of same."

"Thank you. You're a kind man, Entertainer." She seemed compelled to rehearse the details. "It happened at some little town in Altea. The same Guildsmen who killed Karim did it. Only three hundred of them, they say. They slew my uncle and more than a thousand Invincibles, and nobody knows how many regular warriors. The Invincibles haven't been so humiliated since Wadi el Kuf. How can that be, Entertainer?"

He took her pale, cool little hands in his. "Self, am no military genius, admitted. But know strange things happen when men fight. Sometimes. . . ."

She was not listening. She had turned her attention inward. Some of the turmoil there found its way to her lips.

"This is a merciless war, fat man. It claimed my mother last year. It nearly claimed my father at Wadi el Kuf. Now it's taken my uncle. What next? Who? Me? My father again? Sidi? There's got to be a way to stop it. Think for me. Please?"

"Might note, just for purpose of establishing philosophical point, that war is having same effect on many thousands other families. Including family of enemy, Haroun."

"I don't care about. . . ."

"Self, am but humblest wandering mummer, Lady. Simple entertainer. Yet can say this with certitude. Whole war really rests in hands of two men, one being father of yourself, who started same, and archenemy Haroun bin Yousif, who will not let same end." He glanced around to see if anyone were in hearing. In a softer voice, he added, "Make peace between same and peace for rest of world would follow surely as dawn follows night."

She scowled. Then confusion took over. "That's impossible. There's too much blood between them now."

"Not so. Admitted, am not familiar of bin Yousif. But saw same few months passing, at castle of former master of self, where same was seeking aid. Same did not know self was overhearing. Was lamenting war to captain name of Bellous. . . ."

"Beloul?"

"Hai! Just so. Beloul. Old grey-haired guy with nasty temper. Was lamenting to same inability of self to make peace without loss of face to self or El Murid. In meantimes, best young men of desert were dying at hands of one another, and soon none would be left."

"I've heard my father say that. And weep about it. How much more mighty we would be if the Royalists became one with the Kingdom of Peace."

Mocker glanced round again. They were still alone. He whispered, "Sajac the Wise."

Yasmid's eyes went glassy. The fat youth smiled. "Sparen, you were hard master. Am finally appreciating beneficence of same. Lady Yasmid. Hear me. Is good chance of stopping war by meeting with Haroun. Sometime soon, in hour or two, summon self and present idea that self should escort Lady to see same, same probably being in Altea. Sneaky-like, by night, so guards committed to father and war don't prevent." He added a few refining touches, then said, "Will go to sleep now, Lady. Will waken when self asks what is wrong, remembering nothing but agony of uncle's death."

He waited twenty seconds, then plunged forward dramatically. "Lady! Speak! What is wrong?"

Yasmid opened tear-filled eyes. "What?"

"Mercy!" Mocker swore. "Self was frightened. . . . Seemed Lady was fainting."

173

"Me?" she asked. Confusedly, "Nassef. . . . I was thinking about my uncle."

"Is greatest of great shames of great war. Man was genius absolute. Passing of same will be drastic blow to Disciple, maybeso." He settled back onto his boulder seat feeling smug.

Then he noticed the captain eyeing him from the horse picket. The man's expression was inscrutable, but it sent cold-clawed monsters lumbering along his spine. The way the Invincible's eyes drilled into him!

"Is great tragedy Lady has suffered. Self, would suggest time alone, in tent, to deal with grief privately." He moved on to watch several Invincibles practice their swordsmanship. He studied them as if he were unaccustomed to the flash and clash of steel.

The Invincibles practiced daily, both mounted and dismounted, singly and in formation. They were a determined bunch. And Mocker always watched them.

Damo Sparen had been a hard teacher. His lessons had survived his passing well. Among them had been, know your enemy's strengths and weaknesses beforehand.

Mocker knew every man in the encampment now—except that damned captain. He knew he could best any of them except, possibly, the captain. And he had no intention of meeting the man. The captain he intended to share Gouch's fate. Death in the night.

Yasmid summoned him that afternoon. He went reluctantly, no longer certain he wanted to harvest what he had sown.

"Entertainer, are you my friend?" she asked.

"Assuredly, Lady." He tried to appear baffled. Pleasure kept trying to fight its way through. He had not been sure this would work.

"I have a boon to beg, then. A huge one."

"Anything, Lady. Self, exist to serve."

"We were speaking of prospects for peace. You mentioned bin Yousif. . . . I've had a wild idea. A really insane, improbable idea that just might end this hideous war. But I need your help."

"Aid of self? In ending war? Am entertainer and would-be student philosophic, Lady, not diplomat. Am in no wise able. . . ."

"I just want you to ride with me. To be my protector."

"Protector, Lady? When fifty of bravest men of desert . . . ."

"Those brave men are my father's creatures. They'd never permit what I have in mind."

"Same being?"

"Slipping away from here tonight. Riding hard, northward, through the desert and the Kapenrungs, into Altea, to find the King Without A Throne and make peace."

It was exactly what he wanted to hear. It was hard to pretend shock when he was so elated. "Lady!"

"I know it's crazy. That's why I think it might work. You said yourself that Haroun wants peace as much as I do."

"Truth told. But. . . ."

"Enough. I know the risks, but I'm going to try it. The only question is, will you go with me? Will you help me? Or must I try it alone?"

"Alone, Lady? In this mad world? Would be remiss to permit same, same being suicidal. Am frightened. Am terrified, must admit. Am natural-born coward. But will accompany. For sake of Lady, not of peace." He thought that was a nice touch.

"Then come to my tent after the first watch change. I'll know the guard. He'll do whatever I tell him as long as he doesn't know what's going on. You may have to hit him. Be gentle. He's a good man."

"Self? Attack Invincible? Woe! Lady, am anything but fighter."

"I know. I didn't say you had to fight him. Knock him in the back of the head when he isn't looking."

It was not as simple, of course, as either of them hoped.

Mocker's first move, before approaching Yasmid's tent, was to make an exit without challenge possible. He began with the captain because he wanted no cool head available when it came time to organize a pursuit.

That part was almost too easy. It was anticlimatic. Like plucking a ripe plum. The man was hard asleep. He died without a sound or struggle.

There were six men on perimeter guard duty. Mocker eliminated them next, in the silent way Sparen had taught him. He approached each as a friend, told them he could not sleep, then took them suddenly. That bloody treachery done, he turned to the guards at Sidi's and Yasmid's tents. Finally, he selected two horses from the now restless picket line, readied them, threw what provisions he could behind their saddles, and went to collect his prize.

In his nervousness his donkey and props slipped his mind.

His nerves kept humming like the taut catgut of a carnival fiddle. Every step took time. Each passing minute increased the risk of discovery.

He was almost too scared to think. He proceeded by rote, persevering in an oft-rehearsed scenario.

He scratched on Yasmid's tent. "Lady?"

A head popped out. He squeaked in surprise. "Ready?" she asked.

He nodded. "Have horses set to go. Come. Quietly."

"You're shaking."

"Am terrified, must confess. Come. Before alarm goes up."

"Where's the guard?"

"Bashed same over noggin and dragged behind Sidi's tent. Come. Hurry." He could not give her time to think, to ask questions.

Yasmid came forth. Mocker gawked. She had donned male clothing. She made a passable boy.

A moan came from behind her brother's tent. And a demon with a savage hand seized Mocker's vitals. One of his victims had survived! "Hurry, Lady!" He dragged her toward the horses.

"Captain!" Sidi shrieked, his whining voice tormenting the night. "Captain!"

A sleepy Invincible materialized in Mocker's path. The fat man struck him down, seized his sword, and plunged on. He did not loosen his grip on the girl.

"Why did you do that" Yasmid gasped.

Mocker flung her toward the horses. "Get on!" he snarled. "Talk later." He whirled, crossed blades with the nearest of three pursuers. He dropped the man, and the next, in the wink of an eye. The third backed off, astounded. Mocker scrambled onto a horse. Howling like a damned soul, he tried to scatter the rest. The animals did not go far. They were well trained. He screamed and kicked his mount into motion as a wave of Invincibles appeared. He swatted Yasmid's animal as he passed.

For a long time Yasmid was too busy hanging on and keeping up to ask questions. But she did not forget them. When the pursuit faded and the chance arose, she demanded, "Why did you do that? You weren't supposed to hurt anybody."

He glanced back, expecting the momentary materialization of a horde of vengeful Invincibles. "Self, wonder if bodyguards would play by same rule? Lady, am ashamed. Am coward, admitted. Panicked. Howsomever, retrospectively, must admit same was necessitated. Would not have made escape otherwise. Not so? And Invincibles would have cut self down like cur dog. Not so?"

Yasmid argued, but only half-heartedly. She had to admit that he would have been maltreated had they been caught.

The journey became an epic. The supplies he had secured did not last. Yasmid had brought money, but buying by the wayside was dangerous. It left trailmarkers. He drove himself and the girl hard. Death was close behind. The Invincibles would neither forgive nor give up.

Weary days came and went. Desert gave way to mountains. The mountains rose, then descended to the farmlands of Tamerice. Exhausted, Yasmid traveled in silence, devoting all her energy to keeping up. Though in friendlier lands, Mocker kept the pace hard, keeping her tired. She was having second thoughts. He did not want her finding the strength and will to slip away.

He stole native garb and made her wear it, that they might become less remarkable. He dressed her as a girl again, hoping fear of being taken for a local maiden would make her avoid her countrymen. Their taste for rape was legend.

He happened to glance back while scaling the first tall ridgeline inside Altea. A heavy dust cloud rose to the south. The riders creating it were too far back to be discerned, but he had no doubt whom they were.

He began asking the locals if they knew where bin Yousif was hiding. Most of them refused to talk. He almost panicked.

He had to find Haroun fast. His narrow lead would fade if he spent much time searching.

A garrulous peasant finally told him that bin Yousif was in the Bergwold, trying to rebuild the Royalist force Nassef had scattered before his death.

Neither in Tamerice nor Altea did they encounter an enemy patrol. He could not understand that. Someone should have been there to keep the defeated in line. He had expected to be ducking and dodging all the way.

He added that puzzle to his other worries.

"Almost there, Lady," he announced one morning, pointing. "See hill with ruin on top of same? Is famed Colberg, ancient castle of Altea. Forest called Bergwold lies beside."

"I don't know if I'm glad or not, Entertainer. But one thing is sure. I'm going to be happy to get off this nag."

"Assuredly. Self, am not rider. Am shank's mare man,

accustomed to walking. Am going to spend next two weeks lying on ample pillow of stomach." He glanced back. "Hai!"

A low white wave was rolling across the flat green countryside. Their pursuers were just a half mile behind.

He swatted Yasmid's mount with the flat of his saber, whipped his own, and began the race.

The Invincibles, on fresher animals, closed fast, but the fat man managed to reach the wood several hundred yards ahead. He flung himself off his horse, dragged Yasmid from hers, grabbed her hand and dragged her into the dense underbrush.

Chapter Fourteen: *SUMMER'S END*

Mowaffak Hali overcame the army of Ipopotam quite cleverly. He seized the poppy fields before they could be destroyed. But now bands of partisans roamed the countryside.

"They're a stiff-necked people, Lord," he admitted. "They won't accept amnesty."

"I don't want excuses, Mowaffak. I want them brought to heel."

"They're using the tactics we did before coming to power, Lord."

"Not exactly. There's a difference, Mowaffak. Aboud's people didn't know who their friends were. We do. Till they stop resisting slay every man you encounter. Burn their villages. Destroy their fields. Drive them into the forests. Pull down their heathen temples. Eradicate their devil-worshipping priests. And feed and treat kindly those who yield their arms."

"They're not wild dogs, Lord."

"I'm getting old, Mowaffak. There isn't an ounce of mercy in me anymore."

"I have news from the north, Lord. The northern host moved against us there."

A chill crawled over El Murid. His expression betrayed him.

"The news isn't bad, Lord. El-Kader turned them. And the Scourge of God has destroyed the Altean army. It's only a matter of time till he occupies Kavelin and links up with el Nadim."

"El-Kader succeeded without Nassef? This year's campaign is a success?"

"So it would seem. The Scourge of God is preoccupied with bin Yousif and the Guildsmen who slew Karim. He means to have his revenge. And yours, Lord."

El Murid became pensive. Mowaffak was politicking again. "I have my grievances with bin Yousif. But he's only a minor nuisance. Nassef is letting himself be distracted by a side issue. His warriors are needed against the army of the north. This is no time to indulge personal desire."

"My thought exactly, Lord."

Hali's expression betrayed him. Ipoptam was the grossest of side issues, of indulgences. Pacification was tying up thousands of warriors needed elsewhere.

"Go away, Mowaffak. Flog these people. Bring them to heel."

"As you command, Lord."

El Murid glared at Hali's retreating back. Once again Mowaffak had left him to wrestle with his conscience.

Mowaffak was right. But he dared not enter the moral and spiritual lists, to do battle with his addiction, while this war demanded his attention. The war between the soul and the flesh, when it came, would consume him. It would be total and without quarter.

Cued by his thinking, his old wounds began aching.

The Disciple's retinue were worried. Their master seemed to have lost his spirit, his zest, his drive. All too often he retreated into his own inner realms rather than face the crises staring at the Kingdom. Some, like Hali, begged Esmat for help.

What could he do? the physician asked. He simply did

not have the personal or moral courage to shed his procurer's role.

And because of that weakness, even Esmat himself held Esmat in contempt.

Altaf el-Kader was not known as an emotional man. His acquaintances knew him as one who let himself be rattled by nothing.

Nevertheless, he blew up when the crows of disaster fluttered in from Altea. Even his boldest subordinates could not approach him. But when the storm blew away, el-Kader was more cool than ever. He had, in a way, been reborn.

He spoke to the assembled captains of the Host of Illumination. "Gentlemen, you've heard the news. The Scourge of God has been sent to his reward by the same Guild scoundrels who robbed us of Karim's songs. The death of this one man, whom we revered and respected. . . ."

An angry mutter began among his listeners.

"Be quiet!" he snapped. "I won't fall into that trap, too. We have people in Altea. Let them deal with the matter. What you and I must do is prove that the Host isn't the Scourge of God. We have to show that we can win without him. Quickly and impressively, for both our friends and enemies. Our foes were wavering. The Disciple's messages have won us converts by the thousand. We can't let the one take heart and the other grow fearful."

He paused to let his words take root. Then, "Prepare to march. We'll make our demonstration by destroying the northern army."

The wings of fear descended, brushing the necks of men who had known no trepidation when Nassef had been in command. El-Kader bore it. He knew the biggest proving would have to be of himself to his captains.

"You have heard me," he said. "Go. Prepare. I'll tell you more as it becomes necessary."

He was adopting Nassef's approach, revealing his thinking to no one. That seemed to reassure them. They were accustomed to operating in the dark.

He had chosen his mission. He attacked it with a flare and determination never before shown. But never before had the final responsibility rested on Altaf el-Kader. Now he had to answer to no one but himself—so he demanded more of el-Kader than ever Nassef had.

Despite his statement concerning Altea, he marched eastward. The immediate assumption was that he meant to punish Nassef's slayers. That had been the style of the Scourge of God, to say one thing and do the opposite. He let his entourage believe that he had had a change of heart. What his followers believed would also be believed by his enemies.

He gathered to the Host all the garrisons along the way, including the men holding the river crossings.

The northern army immediately leapt the river behind him. Its crossing required several days.

El-Kader heard and smiled.

He had planned each move carefully during his day of isolation. He needed only a minimum of luck. . . .

He got more. The Fates, having served the enemy long enough, re-enlisted with the Host of Illumination. The Duke of Greyfalls, having learned of Nassef's demise, had abandoned his hunt for the Scourge of God. He rejoined his command during its crossing. The resulting uncertainty at the highest echelon permitted el-Kader to shake the northern scouts.

He immediately turned westward. In hard marches he passed below the northerners and swung back toward the river. He was lying in wait when Greyfalls started to march toward Dunno Scuttari.

El-Kader hit him in a land of low hills, attacking from the flanks. He gave his foe no time to organize. The might of the northern knights proved useless. The deadly Itaskian bowmen became scattered before they could bring the punishing power of their weapons to bear.

Only the stubborn formations of pikemen from Iwa Skolovda and Dvar withstood the fury of the first charge. They remained brief-lived islands of stability in a maelstrom of death.

The knights of the north, as was the noble wont in defeat, abandoned their footbound followers to el-Kader's untender mercy and flew for the river crossings. But their enemy had anticipated them. His riders were there before them. Not a quarter reached the northern shore.

The men they abandoned fared better.

The infantry fought on, having no choice. Broken into even small units, hunted mercilessly, the soldiers became scattered over a half dozen Lesser Kingdoms. Their losses, too, were brutal. Only one in three witnessed the coming of winter.

El-Kader called off the hunt ten days later. He wanted to go into winter quarters and to allow some warriors to return to their families.

Then came the news of Yasmid's disappearance.

Hali had debated with himself all morning. How could he tell his prophet? He sometimes let the reports slide, to save El Murid distress, but this time he had no choice. The news was too important. He finally requested an audience.

"Lord." He bowed.

The Disciple knew Mowaffak's bad news now. "What is it?" he snapped.

"An ill wind from the north, Lord."

"I saw that the second you came in. Why don't you just say it?"

"As you command, Lord. There're grim tidings for the Kingdom of Peace, Lord. The worst."

"Out with it, man. Don't play games with me."

Hali, devoted as he was, reached his limit. "Very well, Lord. Two items. The Scourge of God has been slain. And your daughter had been kidnapped."

El Murid did not respond immediately. Nor did he

move. His flesh became so pale that for a moment Hali feared he had suffered a stroke. But finally, in a soft, gentle voice, the Disciple said, "I know I've been short-tempered lately, Mowaffak. Sometimes I haven't been fair. But that's no cause to jest so cruelly."

"I wish I were joking, Lord. My pain would be less terrible. But the joke has been played by the Evil One."

"It's true, then?"

"Every word, Lord. And it hurts like my death wound to tell it."

"Nassef. Slain. It doesn't seem possible. And Yasmid carried off. How can that be? It would take an army to reach her, wouldn't it?"

"Guildsmen in the first instance, Lord. The same who slew Karim. They sent more than a thousand Invincibles with him. This has been a hard summer for our brotherhood. There aren't many of us left."

"And Yasmid?"

"The facts aren't clear. A rider brought the news. He was too near death to tell us much. He had ridden too hard with wounds too grave. El-Kader moved your children into Hammad al Nakir lest his confrontation with the north went wrong. Invincibles guarded them. How they failed I don't know. Someone got to your daughter. My brethren who survived the attack are in pursuit."

"That's not very clear, Mowaffak."

"I know, Lord. Yet it's the sum of my knowledge to the moment.

"Are these heathens pacified?"

Hali smiled thinly. "The survivors are behaving themselves, Lord."

"Then I'll get out of your hair. I'm returning north. I leave you and Ipopotam to one another. Decide how many men you need here. Keep as few as you can. El-Kader will need all the help he can get. Mowaffak?"

"Lord?"

"Leave me now. I need to be alone."

"As you command, Lord."

Hali paused at the door, considering the man he loved more than life itself. El Murid sat hunched as if in extreme pain, staring into the gentle glow of the amulet of his wrist. There were tears in his eyes, but his expression remained unreadable. Mowaffak guessed that he was wondering if the game were worth the candle.

He shook his head sadly. His prophet had sacrificed almost everything for the movement. What was left to give? Just himself and that brat, Sidi, who ought to be put out of his misery anyway.

Hali's heart hardened. Heads were going to roll over the Lady Yasmid's disappearance. There was no excuse for so grotesque a lapse of trust.

He ran into Esmat a moment later. "Good morning, Doctor. Give me a boon, will you? Tend our Lord. He's had a terrible shock."

Esmat watched the Invincible depart. He was astonished. Hali never had a kind word. . . . Something was bad wrong. He rushed to the Disciple's side.

El Murid departed Ipopotam two days later. He rode northward as hard as his old injuries would permit.

Rumor said the Altean Guildsmen carried Nassef's head on a pike, as a battle standard. Elsewhere the Guild seemed to have disappeared, but that band in the outbacks kept reminding everyone that their brotherhood was fighting its own private war.

What a cruel end for Nassef. . . . Would his niece join him in the arms of the Dark Lady? Had she done so already?

He would unleash the whole might of Hammad al Nakir if she were still alive.

But the power of the desert might have no meaning now. Its controlling genius was gone. Who could replace the Scourge of God?

El Murid snorted, deriding himself. At least he would not have to worry about treachery, betrayal or faithlessness anymore. He had no more need to worry about what he would do *with* Nassef, only what he would do without him.

Who would win the impossible victories? Who would give him the Al Rhemishs and Dunno Scuttaris of tomorrow? Who would recover the provinces north of the Scarlotti?

"Lord!" one of his lieutenants shouted. "A rider from the north! My God, Lord, el-Kader's done it! He's destroyed the northern army!"

"Is it true?" El Murid demanded.

"Absolutely, Lord! The message bore the seal of el-Kader himself."

"Find bin Gamel. Tell him to halt the army. We give praise to the Lord of Hosts, from whom all victories flow."

He was astounded. El-Kader? Victorious? The man was but the shadow of Nassef, a crony, a profiteer interested only in making his relatives rich off the chaos of war. The man had no imagination. . . . But he had won that battle at the ruins of Ilkazar. . . . Amazing.

Cold autumn winds were blowing when El Murid joined el-Kader. Those who worried about such things predicted an early, bitter winter. The weather had changed rapidly, as if to declare that first savage summer of war over at last.

El-Kader's encampment was nearly naked of warriors. "Where are all our soldiers?" the Disciple demanded. "Was your victory that expensive?"

"Lord? Oh, no. Some are hunting for your daughter. The others went home to their families. The hunters haven't found much, but we're sure she's still alive."

"How so?"

"There's been no news otherwise. And she would be of no value to bin Yousif dead, would she? Our dearest hope is that he'll keep her alive so he can use her against us. If he does, we'll get her back."

"*He* has her?"

"We think so, Lord. We traced the route of her

bodyguard, who were pursuing her, into Altea, where they were slaughtered by those Guildsmen he's tied in with."

"Guildsmen? Again? The ones who slew Karim and the Scourge of God?"

"The same, Lord. They're getting to be a damned nusiance."

"I want them a dead nuisance, General. I don't want to hear about them again until you can tell me they're all dead."

"Their chances of survival are poor, Lord. Thousands are looking for them."

"Looking? You don't know where they are?"

"No, Lord. They've vanished. They were operating out of a forest in Altea, but when we went after them there they were gone. So was bin Yousif, who is working with them. They fled about the time your daughter should have reached them."

"You will locate them."

"Of course, Lord."

One of el-Kader's orderlies approached, whispered to his commander. "You're sure?" the general asked.

"Absolutely, sir."

"Interesting." He turned to El Murid. "There's a delegation from the north asking permission to cross the Scarlotti. They want to open peace negotiations."

"Peace negotiations? What have they got to negotiate? They're beaten."

"Perhaps, Lord. But it won't cost to listen."

The thing made more sense when the delegates arrived. El Murid immediately caught the stench of back-stabbing politics.

Virtually all the northern states were represented. Only Trolledyngja, the Sharan tribes, and Freyland's kingdom, none of whom had been involved in the fighting, had failed to send someone. And the delegates fell into two obvious parties.

The conciliators represented the small states between

the Scarlotti and Porthune rivers, kingdoms which had had a foretaste of Illumination. The belligerents represented Itaskia and her northern allies.

El Murid greeted the ambassadors with benevolent smiles, and western style handshakes for the conciliators. The Duke of Greyfells seemed puzzled because he drew no special reaction.

El Murid had none of his own people introduced. It was a message to the northerners. He alone spoke for the Kingdom of Peace.

He spoke with el-Kader afterward. "General, is there anything we especially want from those people? Something we can't just take?"

"Not really, Lord. We can keep them divided. Oh. They could give us a little help with a few political problems."

"For instance?"

"The Guild. They could apply pressure to get the Lady Yasmid returned if she's in Guild hands. And you might mention your displeasure about the presence of refugee camps in their domains. While those exist, beyond our reach, they'll remain seedbeds of trouble."

"I see. Wouldn't that give them the impression we don't think we'll be able to break them up ourselves?"

"We will. In time. But what we should be doing here is lulling them. Letting them think they're buying peace. If we make the camps an issue we might get our enemies to pull their teeth for us. You might also insist that they hand over bin Yousif if they get the chance. No harm in getting the Lord's enemies to do the Lord's work, is there?"

"None whatsoever." El Murid rewarded el-Kader with one of his rare smiles. "All right. Let's play their game. And beat them at it."

Next morning El Murid hosted the ambassadors at a lavish breakfast. He had had his people prepare the finest meal possible. Every ingredient came from the recovered provinces. And on the practice fields overlooked by the breakfasters, el-Kader's officers ostentatiously drilled converts from the west.

The Disciple took his meal on a makeshift throne overlooking the assembly. During its course he summoned emissaries individually, and asked each: "Why did you come here?" and "What do you want?" Interpreters translated. Scribes recorded the responses as fast as they could scribble.

Most of the ambassadors admitted that they had come because their lieges had ordered them. In a dozen ways they claimed a desire to end the bloodshed.

"Peace? That has the simplest of solutions. Accept the Truth," the Disciple told each. Then he smiled and offered each emissary a prepared treaty. He had had every learned man in the Host up all night writing. "That, sir," he would say, "is take it or leave it. I am the Hand of the Lord on Earth. I won't dicker like a tradesman. Give me your answer at breakfast tomorrow."

A few, from remote kingdoms, tried to argue. Invincibles intimidated them into silence. Most just returned to their places, surveyed the terms offered, and sometimes seemed surprised.

El Murid was playing a game and enjoying himself immensely. Power could be so diverting. . . . He frowned, and silently admonished himself. This was no fit behavior for the Hand of the Lord.

In most cases his terms appeared liberal, but he could afford to give away things that he could not possess and to make promises he had no intention of keeping. The Law did not extend its protection to the Unbeliever. The only clause of real weight, with him, was that which permitted missionaries to carry the Truth into the unoccupied territories.

"Did you watch?" he asked el-Kader afterward, almost laughing. "Some of them were ready to kiss my hand."

"Yes, Lord. And they'd bite it if you glanced away. Lord, there was one who approached me privately. He wants to speak with you in his own behalf. I think we might profit."

"Which one?"

"Greyfells. The Itaskian."

"Why?"

"Politics. He claims to have made an arrangement with Karim, at Nassef's request. He says that's why Karim was killed. He could be telling the truth. What we know of Greyfells' movements, and of bin Yousif's and Karim's, would appear to support him."

"Let me see him, then. This might be interesting."

He wished that he had not left Mowaffak in Ipopotam. He could use a trustworthy, discreet sounding board just now.

So. Here was the spoor of another of Nassef's schemes. Greyfells' very involvement suggested its nature. No wonder Nassef had been eager to reach Altea after Karim's death. There had been covering up to do. And bin Yousif, blocking his claim on the Peacock Throne, had been there. . . .

"Nassef, Nassef," he murmured, "you're dead and you're still doing it to me."

Why had el-Kader brought this up? Wasn't he one of Nassef's cronies? Surely he had been tempted to assume the plot for his own.

Greyfells was a spare, hard man with shifty eyes and prematurely grey hair. There was an air of the fox about him. He seemed to be sneaking all the time. "My Lord Disciple," he said, bowing obsequiously.

El Murid told his interpreter, "Tell him to get to the point. I won't play word games. I'll throw him out if he tries that."

Greyfells listened with exaggerated innocence. He minced to the doorway when the interpreter finished, peeped out. "I have to be careful. I have enemies."

"Why shouldn't I let them have you?" El Murid demanded.

Greyfells told him the story that el-Kader had passed

along earlier, in more detail. He confessed his determination to usurp the Itaskian crown and carve his own empire.

El Murid was disgusted. If ever mortal woman had borne a child to the Evil One, this man's mother had. "This is all news to me, Duke. Like yourself, my brother-in-law had his own ambitions."

The Duke went pale.

El Murid grinned. Crafty Nassef! He had not been frank with Greyfells.

"I command the allied army, Lord. I decide when and where it fights." Greyfells spoke quickly and nervously, trying to salvage something.

"Then you made a poor decision not long ago." El Murid was on the verge of laughter now.

"That choice wasn't mine. But the political climate compelled me to live with it."

"You no longer have much of an army."

"It can be replaced. A dozen such could be raised. The plans are in the works." A little bluster restored his confidence. "We Itaskians don't make the same mistake twice."

"Perhaps not." El Murid moved the hand that had concealed his amulet. The living stone burned brightly. Its fire reflected off the Duke's eyes. "But others remain to be made. I see no profit in your proposal. If I detect an advantage later, I'll contact you."

"Your profit is the men you won't lose." Greyfells was plainly irked. "You'll have peace while you digest your conquests. Time to clean up loose ends like Altea, Kavelin and Hellin Daimiel. And you'd have no more worries about those Royalists who've flown into my territories."

The man appalled El Murid. *His* territories! "Produce bin Yousif. Hand him over to me, alive, and I'll give you anything you ask," El Murid lied. He felt no guilt over deceiving a tool of the Great Deceiver. "Deliver me the one thing I most want and I'll talk. Till then you're wasting your time."

Greyfells stared at him, and at the famous amulet. He saw he would never win his point by persuasion. He bowed. "Then I'd better return to my quarters before I'm missed. Good evening."

El Murid allowed a minute to pass. "El-Kader. What do you think?"

The general stepped from behind a concealing tapestry. "He seemed pretty explicit, Lord."

"Will he be of any value?"

"I doubt it. He'd betray us in an instant."

"Have your spies keep an eye on him, but ignore him otherwise. For now."

"As you command, Lord."

During the ensuing week, El Murid concluded treaties which guaranteed peace with all his enemies but Itaskia, Iwa Skolovda, Dvar and Prost Kamanets. Every treaty contained a provision stating that neither signatory would allow passage to the enemies of the other. The northerners would find it difficult to get at him without attacking former allies.

He was sure that that provision, and the one guaranteeing freedom of movement to his missionaries, would be violated often enough to provide his *casus belli* when he resumed his offensive.

He had no desire for an enduring peace outside the Kingdom's domain. He was negotiating merely to lull tomorrow's conquests.

He did not delude himself. The other signatories just wanted to buy time to strengthen their defenses.

The real puzzle was the whole-hearted bellicosity of the Itaskians. Why were they so war-hungry when there was no immediate threat to their territories or people? How were they profiting?

Thus ended the bloody summer known historically as the First El Murid War. Suddenly, the restoration of the Empire looked plausible.

The Disciple returned to Hammad al Nakir, first to Al Rhemish, then to Sebil el Selib, where he shared his griefs with his memories of yesterday. He received weekly updates from el-Kader, who was designing the next offensive according to what he could reconstruct of Nassef's plans.

The general's missives never brought the news El Murid wanted. Never a word about Yasmid.

Even his spies among the Royalists could discover nothing beyond the fact that the girl had, indeed, appeared at the Guild camp in the Bergwold in Altea.

At first the Disciple coped by spending endless hours in prayer. Later, after endowing Esmat with powers rivalling those once given Nassef, he sequestered himself in Al Rhemish's Most Holy Mrazkim Shrines and set about defeating his addiction.

Chapter Fifteen: *CAPTIVES*

Four Guildsmen dragged the captives to an outpost. They were none too gentle. The fat man kicked up a fuss, so they bound him, gagged him, and headbashed him several times even though he had been fleeing the Invincibles.

The female remained haughtily silent no matter what language was directed her way.

Kildragon took charge of them, but paid them little heed. He had Invincibles to dispose of. When he finished he detailed two men to escort them to the main encampment. He had listened to the fat man's story, but did not care to sort it out himself.

The fat man started the trip draped across the back of a donkey. His clothing and skin took a beating from the underbrush. He cursed continuously, in a dozen languages.

"Oh, shut up!" Yasmid finally snapped. "You got us into this. Take it like a man."

"Is impossible of doing same thrown across back of animal like sack of corn. Is ignominious fate for. . . ."

"Why don't you knock him in the head again?" Yasmid asked the Guildsmen, using the tongue of Hellin Daimiel.

"She can talk," one muttered in Itaskian.

"I've got a better idea," the other told Yasmid, replying in the language she had chosen. "We'll make him walk. Fat as he is, he'll run out of wind fast."

"You'd be surprised, soldier."

"Better put a choker on him, Karl," the other Guildsman suggested. "So he don't do a fast fade into the woods."

Thus it was that Mocker entered the camp of his ally led like a hound on a leash. The ignomity of it! His captive entered walking tall and proud and free, imperious as a queen, while he entered like a slave.

The Guildsmen took them inside a log stockade and across a compound to where Guildsmen and Royalists were involved in a complicated game of chance.

"Captain, Sergeant Kildragon sent some prisoners."

A big, shaggy youth looked them over. One of the older Royalists said something, then rushed toward one of the shabby barracks. The shaggy youth shrugged. "Hang on to them, Uthe. Beloul wants Haroun to look at them." He returned to his game.

Yasmid flinched, turned pale. She spoke no Itaskian, but had recognized the names. Beloul! The most dangerous of the Royalists. The one most driven by hatred and vengeance. The last vestige of her hope died. Fear replaced it. There would be no peace. Beloul! How could she have been such a fool?

A youth rushed across the compound, dark robes flying. Yasmid remembered his face. That night on the hill overlooking Al Rhemish. . . . He had aged, matured, hardened. . . .

"Why didn't you cut him loose, Beloul?" Haroun demanded. He applied a knife to the fiber binding the fat man's wrists. Shifting to Itaskian, he told Ragnarson, "The man is an agent of mine. I sent him to the far south. Was there a big man with him?"

"Just the split-tail, sir," one of the escorts replied. "We didn't know who he was. He didn't explain. Not so's anybody could understand, anyway."

"All right. All right. Get that gag off of him."

Mocker could hardly stand. He gripped the expanse of his belly, teetered, and dry-throatedly moaned, "Woe! That self should come to this after fighting way across thousand miles, hazarding life and limb at every step, constantly beset by hordes of desert madmen. . . ."

"You did a good job in Ipopotam," Haroun told him. He used the desert tongue because Mocker had. "Ended up pulling a whole army away from the main action. More than I dreamed. What happened to your man-mountain friend?"

"Do not mention same again. Same met one Invincible too many. Lies buried far from home, not even knowing why. Poor, stupid Gouch. Was good friend. Sparen will rest easy, knowing same has avenged self."

"I'm sorry. He was likeable—in his primitive way."

Yasmid exploded. "Entertainer! You know this. . . . This. . . . You're working for him?"

Mocker grinned. "Truth told, Lady. Self, am tricksey rogue, more than with fingers. Sometimes do pretty good with girls, too, maybeso."

"What's she talking about?" Haroun asked.

Mocker bowed, still grinning. "Hail, mighty king. Self, am pleased to present same to genuine princess, same being firstborn daughter of archfoe El Murid, Yasmid, captivated by self, at great peril, and brought forth from very heart of Desert of Death. As small token of appreciation, self would suggestion mighty king bestow upon same huge cash reward. Line up gold pieces, one for every wound, one for every insult suffered. . . ."

Haroun's eyes grew larger and larger. He really looked at Yasmid for the first time. "It's you. You've grown."

Their eyes locked for a long moment, as they had on that faraway night at Al Rhemish.

Yasmid launched a magnificent, almost artful tantrum. Her shrieks emptied the barracks. In moments she stood at the heart of a circle of two hundred men.

Haroun turned to Ragnarson. "The fat man has brought

us the Disciple's daughter. I don't know how. . . . Can
you believe it? It's incredible."

Bragi did not share his awe. But he saw the possibilities. "The Fates have taken a dislike to the man. He was
riding high a month ago. Now he's lost most of his
family."

Yasmid kept it up. Her anger gave way to hysteria. A
sea of evil gloating faces surrounded her. The legions of
the Evil One had fallen upon her. What would Haroun
do? Throw her to his men?

"Whew!" said Ragnarson. "She does go on, doesn't
she?"

"Is in mortal terror," Mocker opined.

"Shut up, girl!" Ragnarson thundered.

She did not. Of course. He had spoken in Itaskian. She
would not have had he used a tongue she did comprehend.

The Guildsman was not in the most tolerant of moods.
He had been losing badly in the game he had been
playing. But it was not anger alone that impelled him to
do what he did. Her hysteria had to be cracked.

He grabbed Yasmid, dragged her down, rolled her
across his lap, hiked her skirts, and began whacking her
bare bottom with his hand. She squirmed and squealed
for a moment, then refused to respond.

Ragnarson would never comprehend the indignity he
had done her, nor those she had suffered already. In his
culture women did not wear veils and girls usually got
excited when a guy bared their bottoms.

The fat man had forced her into native dress, and had
burned her veils. She had travelled in shame for days.
Now another barbarian had exposed her womanhood to
the whole camp. His followers laughed and jeered and
made crude observations about the hand-shaped birth-
mark on her behind.

Tears rolled from her eyes, but she refused to pleasure
them by begging or crying out.

Haroun was of the desert. He became livid. He slapped

Ragnarson's hand aside, yanked the girl to her feet, shoved her behind him. He poised on the balls of his feet, ready for anything. Yasmid crouched behind him, shaking, overcome by shame.

The laughter died. Guild eyes hardened. Ragnarson rose slowly, fists doubling.

"Hai!" Mocker cried. He whirled between the men, his robe flying. As he spun, he yelled, "Self, am wondering when celebration begins. Have made hero of self. Should receive great jubilee in honor, singing, drinking, unfortunately no wenching, but good time for all." He tried to turn a cartwheel, crashed to the dusty earth.

His antics broke the tension.

"Maybe he's right," Ragnarson said, after puzzling out the fat man's fractured Daimiellian.

"Beloul," Haroun said, "take the Lady Yasmid to my quarters."

Beloul's eyebrows rose. But he said only, "As you command, Lord."

Shifting languages, Haroun told Ragnarson, "You should be more careful of the sensibilities of other peoples. You subjected her to unforgivable humiliation. I'll probably have to guard against her taking her own life."

"What?" Bragi asked incredulously.

"That's ridiculous," his brother said.

"Perhaps. To you. You are the children of another land. You do things differently there. My people sometimes find your ways ridiculous."

"You mean she's the real thing?" Bragi asked. "She's not just some tramp your friend picked up on the road?"

"It's her."

"Then we've got some thinking to do. She's trouble."

"Such as?"

"You figure we've had El Murid's men in our hair before? You ain't seen nothing. If we keep her alive—and what good is she dead?—people are going to come looking for her. All of them with hook noses and wearing white. And your friend left a trail good enough for one mob to follow. There'll be more. Which means we've got to disappear. Fast."

"You're probably right. Let me think about it." Haroun strode after Beloul. He met his captain outside his hut. "How is she?"

"Mortified, Lord."

"Uhm. Beloul, find some cloth. Anything, so long as it's something she can use to make a veil and decent clothing."

"Lord?"

"You heard me." Haroun stepped into the shack that served him as home and headquarters.

Yasmid had seated herself on the dirt floor. Her head was down. She was crying silently, her whole body shaking. She did not look up.

"I apologize for my friends. They hail from faraway lands. They have different customs. They weren't trying to humiliate you."

Yasmid did not respond.

"I've told Beloul to find something you can make decent clothing from."

She did not look up, but in a small voice asked, "What are you going to do with me?"

"I? Nothing. Except keep you out of sight. So your father will worry."

"Aren't you going to kill me? Throw me to your men, or those barbarians, then cut my throat?"

"Why would I do that?"

"I'm your enemy. My uncle and my father killed your whole family."

"Your uncle was my enemy. Your father is my enemy. But you're not. I don't make war on women. You didn't. . . ."

"You killed my mother."

Haroun shrugged. "There was a battle on. I wasn't keeping track."

Yasmid pulled her knees up under her chin, hugged them in her arms. "He tricked me, didn't he?"

"Who?"

"The fat man." She knew, of course, but wanted to be told again. That would, somehow, make her feel less like an accomplice in the deceit. "He got me to come. . . . I thought I could make peace between you and my father."

"That would be difficult. Yes. He tricked you. That's his profession. And he's better than I suspected." Haroun sat on the earth facing her, wondering what made her seem unique.

It was nothing physical. She was an average looking girl, not at all striking. An active, outdoor life had weathered her more than the men of Hammad al Nakir liked. And she was much too assertive.

Yasmid stared into infinity. After a time, she murmured, "It's an interesting dilemma."

"What's that?"

"Whether I should slay myself and thus free the movement of concern and uncertainty, or preserve myself against its need."

The nature of his culture denied Haroun much knowledge of women. He knew them only through tradition and hand-me-down gossip from equally ignorant companions. The last thing he expected of a female was an ability to reason, to sacrifice, to be concerned about tomorrow. He remained silent, awed.

"I guess I should wait for a sign. Suicide is extreme. And if I'm alive there's always a chance of escape or rescue."

"As my fat friend might say, all things are possible." But some are unlikely, he thought. "Ask Beloul for whatever you need for sewing." He left the hut looking for Ragnarson.

"No, no, no," Bragi was telling an Altean who had just sped an arrow into a butt. "You're not remembering what I said about your elbow."

"I hit it, didn't I? Sir."

"Yeah. That time. But you're more likely to hit it every time. . . ."

"Excuse me," Haroun interrupted. "It's occurred to me that our best course might be to move into the Kapenrungs."

"What?"

"We should move to the mountains. They're more suited to the kind of war we'll have to fight now. More room to move around and stay ahead of the hunters. And close enough to Hammad al Nakir to give us the option of striking south. It's only a few days ride from the mountains to Al Rhemish."

"We were assigned to Altea."

"Specifically? Without any flexibility for the commander on the scene?"

"I don't know. They just said we were going to Altea. Maybe they told Sanguinet more. But he's not here to let me know."

"Sent you here and forgot you. Haven't you noticed? They haven't been in any hurry to replace your captain. They haven't even sent any orders. You're on your own."

"How do you figure to get from here to there without getting wiped out? They've got men everywhere."

"Consider our prisoner. They'll know who has her, and where we were last. Anyway, moving was your idea."

"Yeah."

Ragnarson did not debate long. He knew there would be no more miracles like Alperin. The first bands left that evening.

Haroun talked him into sending their men in parties of four, by as many routes as possible, travelling at night, so they would attract minimal attention. Haroun assigned one of his people to each group of Guildsmen, to guide them to Beloul's old refugee camp. Bragi sent his brother with the first night's travellers, and Kildragon with the second's. Bin Yousif, Mocker, and Yasmid vanished sometime during that night. Haroun left no word of his intentions or destination.

Ragnarson left the Bergwold on the last night, riding

with Beloul and two young Royalists. None of the three spoke a dialect he understood, and Beloul had wanted to be the last of his.

He looked back once. The Bergwold leaned toward him like a dark tidal wave frozen in mid rush. He felt a twinge of regret. The forest had become home.

There had been few moments of happiness since fleeing Draukenbring. But he and Haaken were still together, and healthy, and he had never asked the gods for more than that.

Beloul was a crafty traveller. He led them across the nights and miles without once bringing them face to face with another human being. He seemed to sense the approach of other travellers. Always, they were under cover when another night rider passed. Most of those were people of their own persuasion.

It was a skill his own men should learn. How could El Murid find them if even their friends never saw them moving?

These desert men were naturally cunning. Sneakery and deceit were their patrimony.

He wished he could communicate with Beloul better. The captain was one cunning old man.

Bragi had been trying to learn the desert tongue for ages. He had not made much headway. Its rules were different from any he knew, and there were countless dialects.

Thus it was that, when Beloul broke his own rule and stopped a dispatch rider, Ragnarson was bewildered by his companions' behavior. They went into a frenzy of angry excitement. It took half an hour for them to make him understand. El-Kader had destroyed the northern army.

That explained Beloul's sudden haste. This end of the world would fill with warriors hunting the daughter of their prophet. It was time to find a hole and pull it in after. He was glad Haroun had talked him into fleeing the Bergwold.

Four days later he threw his arms around Haaken and said, "Damn, it's good to see you. Good to see anybody who doesn't talk like a coop full of hens clucking."

"You hear? About the battle?"

"Yeah. But you have to fill me in. I missed most of the details."

"El Senoussi and I have been plotting. We figure we ought to recruit survivors. So we can build our own army."

"Tell me in the morning. Right now all I want to do is sleep. Face down. How do you figure to get guys to join when we can't pay? When we can't even guarantee them anything to eat?"

Haaken had no answer for that one.

Eventually, Ragnarson and Beloul did send their boldest followers, in ones and twos, to recruit not only survivors of the battle but anyone who wanted to enlist in the hidden army. That army grew as autumn progressed into winter. The recruits learned Guild ways on the march, while dodging and ambushing el-Kader's hunters.

Those hunters never realized whom they were skirmishing. The search for Yasmid was centered farther north, closer to the Bergwold.

They were turning Altea over.

Mocker turned up after a month, but Haroun remained invisible even to his best friends. He was gone so long that Beloul began worrying about having to find a new king.

It was then that Beloul realized that El Murid's offspring were now closest to the throne, through their mother.

Grinning evilly, he prepared special message packets meant to fall into enemy hands. They contained faked plans for an effort to alleviate Sidi's burden of life lest he be put forward as a Pretender by his father.

Beloul's purpose was to inform Sidi of his standing. The Disciple's son was but a boy, yet from what the fat man said he had qualities that would set sparks flying if he saw a chance for power.

The winter was a cold one and hard on the war-torn lands where marauding troops from both sides stripped the peasantry of its food stores. Anger stalked the snowy land like some hungry, legendary monster.

Everywhere, high and low, men schemed against the coming of spring, when they might seize their own particular breed of fortune and bend it to their will.

Chapter Sixteen: *THE MIDDLE WARS*

Assigning blame is not the task of the historian. Neither should he deny guilt where it exists. In later days even the chauvinist historian would admit that the north, personified by Duke Greyfells, provoked the second El Murid War.

Itaskian apologists pointed at the Guild and Haroun bin Yousif's Royalists and argued that the first summer of fighting did not possess a separate identity because those belligerents never made peace. But the Guild and Royalists were fighting different wars. Theirs merely shared some of the same battlefields as that of the allies. The Kingdom of Peace had established treaties with those enemies who could accept an accommodation short of annihilation. Even Itaskia's highest leadership, despite verbal belligerence, had accepted El Murid's redrawing of the western map. Once winter settled in, the first El Murid War was over.

The real question was when and why the next would begin.

Only the Disciple himself knew his intentions for his second summer of conquest. His warriors came from their homes and tribes, more numerous than ever. Remote, maundering, El Murid blessed them on Mashad, and sent them to join el-Kader in his watch on the Scarlotti. There they were joined by thousands of converts and adventurers from the recovered provinces.

El-Kader waited, daily expecting an attack order from Al Rhemish. The instruction did not come. El Murid had lost interest in the reconquest. His dream of greening the desert and his effort to conquer his addiction had become obsessions.

Among the faithful it was whispered that the Evil One himself had come to Al Rhemish and the Lord in Flesh was wrestling him within the confines of the Most Holy Mrazkim Shrines.

El-Kader distributed the Host along the Scarlotti in accordance with an order of battle mentioned by the Scourge of God months before his death. El-Kader's posture remained strictly defensive.

He sat. He waited.

Lord Greyfells and Itaskia's allies bullied several small states whose lords had concluded treaties with the Disciple. They abbrogated treaties at will, at swordpoint crossing kingdoms which had agreed not to permit passage of belligerents. They promoted palace revolutions and imprisoned uncooperative nobles. Greyfells' arrogant treatment alienated the masters of the smaller states.

Emissaries came to el-Kader begging him to withhold his wrath. Some volunteered intelligence in hopes of staying the fury of the Host. A few even petitioned its intercession, begging protection from the arrogance and rapacity of the Duke.

Greyfells did little to conceal his desire to carve out an empire of his own.

El-Kader bided his time, awaiting the will of the Disciple, allowing Greyfells to make himself ever more obnoxious.

His petitions to Al Rhemish went unanswered. El Murid could not stop wrestling the Evil One long enough to concern himself with his opponent's manifestations on the frontier.

El-Kader finally took the initiative. He summoned his captains. He presented them with the order of battle and told them that unless they heard otherwise they were to cross the Scarlotti in fifteen days. They were to speak of the plan to no one till the last minute. Certain kingdoms were to be treated as allies, not foemen.

He waited. He even went so far as to pray for word from Al Rhemish.

Responsibility had changed Altaf el-Kader. His office left him too busy with command to waste time profiteering.

The day came and still there was no command from Al Rhemish. He prayed once more that El Murid would forgive him for taking this on himself. Then he left his tent and crossed the river.

The Host of Illumination rolled north like a great tsunami, unexpected, unstoppable, everywhere swamping its foes. Greyfells, caught unprepared, found his rebuilt army adrift in enemy waters. War bands swarmed around it, nibbling at its extremities. He spent all his energies keeping it intact and avoiding battle with the Host. He showed his positive qualities in retreat.

Suffering inconsequential losses, el-Kader seized all the territories south of the River Porthune. Though the Scourge of God had expected that to take a season, el-Kader finished by Midsummer's Day.

In the absence of contrary instructions, smelling the blood of reeling foes, el-Kader breached that line while momentum and morale remained his allies. Some of his war bands ranged as far as the Silverbind, well within the Itaskian domain. A large force camped within sight of the city walls, and departed only when the whole garrison came out to fight. Panic swept the north. The grand alliance was within a whisper of collapse.

From the south frontier of Ipopotam to the Porthune, the west had been returned to the Empire. Only two small enclaves of resistance remained. Hawkwind's stubborn Guildsmen still directed the defense of Hellin

Daimiel. El-Kader ignored the city. It could do nothing to discomfit the Host.

Of High Crag he was not so tolerant. The home and heart of the Guild had to be destroyed. The warrior brotherhood backboned the resistance in the reoccupied provinces.

Ere ever he crossed the Scarlotti, el-Kader summoned Mowaffak Hali from Ipopotam and handed the Invincible the chore of reducing High Crag. Hali accepted the task with reservations. He doubted that it could be accomplished.

Mowaffak Hali was a thorough, methodical leader. He did not hurl the remnants of the Invincibles against High Crag's ancient walls. He gathered information and men of talent, and such additional warriors as he could obtain, for a slow, systematic reduction of the fortress. He built great engines. He employed miners. He did whatever needed doing to neutralize his opponents' advantages.

He might have succeeded had events elsewhere not compelled him to abandon the siege.

Far to the north, el-Kader had the misfortune to, at last, catch the elusive Greyfells.

The nearest town, Liston, gave the battle its name. The engagement was unusual. El-Kader amassed heavy cavalry for the first time in the Host's history. And Greyfells abjured the traditional western use of knights. Once el-Kader closed his trap and battle became unavoidable, the Duke ordered his horsemen to fight afoot.

Greyfells made his stand on the face and top of a rocky hill flanked by woods, with his pikemen and knights massed before his archers. The bowmen of Itaskia were renown, and in this engagement justified their fame. While the pikemen, supported by disgruntled noblemen, valiantly absorbed charge after charge, the archers darkened the sky with arrows.

Had el-Kader not grown over-optimistic, had he not been overconfident, had he listened to his advisers and waited a few days till the whole of the Host had gathered, he would have obliterated the northern might. Liston would have been the battle memoralized as ending the resistance to El Murid's Second Empire.

But he did not wait, and he did not try getting behind his enemies. And still he came within a gnat's eyebrow of success. In the end, he simply ran out of ready bow-fodder before his foes collapsed completely.

Greyfells had the advantage of him in that his troops believed that they had nowhere to run. They believed they had to win or perish. And win they did—in the sense that they compelled el-Kader to withdraw.

The importance of Liston could be weighed only in its effects on the hearts and minds of men. The number of dead on the field was of no consequence. That Greyfells could do nothing but lick his wounds afterward meant little. That el-Kader had not committed his whole strength was overlooked everywhere.

The Host of Illumination had been turned.

Western armies *could* withstand its onslaught. El Murid *could* be stopped.

The effect was magical. Enemies sprang from the earth. Some of el-Kader's allies changed sides again. Resistance stiffened everywhere.

El-Kader coped first by withdrawing across the Porthune, then by summoning every man he could from the south. The siege of High Crag, a project he cherished, he ordered abandoned. He drew strength away from Hellin Daimiel and the captains pursuing the growing guerrilla forces in the southern Lesser Kingdoms.

The summer campaign was in danger of collapse. He had to scatter his strength, flinging lesser armies here and there to stamp out sudden brushfires of resistance. He could not seize the breathing time to rejuvenate the Host and lead it in a grand, finishing surge northward, though he knew the Itaskians could no longer stop such a thrust.

Bin Yousif's Royalists were no help. They had adopted

the tactics developed by the Scourge of God in the days when the Kingdom of Peace had been but a dream. There were thousands of Royalists now. They and their Guild allies were keeping the provinces in turmoil. Their raids were becoming ever more widespread, like the growth of a cancer.

There was a bright side to the summer. El Nadim and the armies of the east, receiving no instructions from Al Rhemish either, abandoned their futile siege of the Savernake Gap and turned their attention to the Empire's old provinces behind the Mountains of M'Hand. El Nadim integrated Throyes into the New Empire. He forced pledges of fealty from old eastern tributaries as remote as Argon and Necremnos. His legates collected caravans of tribute and battalions of mercenaries. His missionaries carried the Truth to the masses, and were well received.

El Nadim's successes amazed the Faithful. He was the least regarded of the generals Nassef had created. Now, suddenly, with only a few thousand men actually of Hammad al Nakir, with almost no fighting, he had recovered territories more vast than the whole west.

Some whispered that el Nadim had been successful because he was a true believer, because he followed El Murid's teachings in handling his foes. There were those who said that el-Kader's troubles were the Lord's punishment for associating with profiteers.

El-Kader ignored the whispers. El Nadim's successes pleased him. The tribute of the east could be used in the west. Two summers of fighting had left a lot of desolation.

He, too, was applying El Murid's precepts—to the extent that they won favor amongst the populations of the recovered provinces.

He drove his warriors and allies hard, extinguishing any resistance he could identify. He recovered several bridgeheads across the Porthune, but the enemy regained a couple below the river. Both sides retained isolated pockets within the other's territory. Their smaller allies remained evanescent in their loyalties, shifting allegiances with each breath of fortune.

Winter, the season of peace, set in. It became the season of negotiation, the time of secret treaties and not so secret betrayals. Always there was an agent of the Itaskian Duke around, ever with an offer of double-edged treason.

And still el-Kader had received no orders from Al Rhemish.

None that he considered genuine, anyway. None signed in the Disciple's own hand.

Order did come. From someone. He ignored them. They were not from his prophet.

Nassef's death had been the signal for the formation of new cabals, for the beginning of the institutionalization of the movement. The greatest, the most praised and heroic of the revolutionaries was gone. The sedentary administrators-potential perceived a vacuum and were trying to fill it.

It was a foreshadowing of the social inevitability of all revolutions, though Altaf el-Kader could not understand.

He saw a gang of stay-at-homes isolating the Disciple and presuming to speak in his name, perverting his pure vision.

He knew a cure.

He had a few words with Mowaffak Hali, a man he did not like but who possessed the specific for this disease. Hali agreed. Something had to be done.

Hali bore el-Kader no love either, but in this they had to be allies. He gathered a few tattooed white robes and rode for the capital.

He was shocked by what he found. The Disciple was a ghost of a man, drained, without spirit. His struggle with the evil within him was consuming him.

Mowaffak spent one afternoon with the master he loved, then went into the desert and wept. Then he instructed the Harish and returned to the west. He redoubled his prayers on behalf of the man who had been, in hopes he would be again.

The third summer of fighting began like the second, with el-Kader trying to avoid his old mistakes. He began by making big gains, but bogged down just thirty miles from the Silverbind and Itaskia the City. For four grim months he maneuvered, met the enemy, maneuvered, and skirmished in an area of barely a hundred square miles. Greyfells had spent the winter preparing, screening the approaches to Itaskia and the Great Bridge with countless obstacles and redoubts. El-Kader could not break through.

It was some of the bitterest, most sustained, deadly and unimaginative fighting ever. The Duke pursued no higher purpose than stalling el-Kader. Defeating him would have obliterated any chance of profiting from the threat to Itaskia.

El-Kader strove to bleed the north till it could no longer withstand him.

Both generals spent lives profligately, though the Duke was the worst. A worried king resided less than a dozen leagues away, and willingly raised fresh levies.

El-Kader's failing was an inability to adjust to the changed nature of his army. He was a desert captain, born to the warfare of the wastelands. But the Host was no longer a horde of nomadic horsemen, riding like the wind, striking where it would, then melting away. That element remained, but in this third summer more than half the troops were westerners whose lack of mobility el-Kader abhorred and whose tactics he could not entirely encompass.

He considered throwing the known quantity of his countrymen like chaff into the wind, to let the breezes carry them where they would, behind Greyfells and along the banks of the Silverbind. But he did not. He did not trust his allies, and the defeat at Liston still haunted him.

So he endured four months of attrition, and, if gravemarkers were the totalizers of success, he was winning. But the Great Bridge seemed to arch into a bottomless pool of replacement battalions.

It was a pity that he had lost touch with Nassef's spy networks. The news of political conditions north of the Silverbind would have heartened him. Itaskia's peasantry were on the verge of revolt. The nobility were demanding Greyfells' recall. Bankers were threatening to call in their loans to the Crown. Merchants were howling about the interruption of overland trade. City dwellers were angry about rising food costs caused by exports to Hellin Daimiel and reduced production due to conscription of peasants into the replacement levies. Fathers and mothers were bitter about the losses of their sons.

Itaskia was as taut as a bowstring stretched till it was about to snap. El-Kader needed to give just the right nudge.

His choice of campaign style was an error. By letting the Duke set the standard of battle he had permitted himself to be diverted from his strength to a form of warfare he did not understand.

Then, as autumn approached, he made every soldier's most dreaded mistake.

He stepped into the shadow of the outstretched left hand of Fate.

He was doing what needed doing, directing an attack against a stubborn earth and log redoubt, when a random arrow struck his mount in the eye. The animal threw him, trampled him, and dragged him. Altaf el-Kader was a stubbon man. He held on for four days before finally yielding to the Dark Lady's charms.

His passing broke the will of an already dispirited army. Bits and pieces broke away. The most fanatic Faithful were dismayed.

The wrath of the Lord was upon them, and their hearts were filled with despair.

The Host was an eager, conquering horde no more. It had become a huge mob of war-weary men.

Mowaffak Hali assumed command, after riding all the way from Al Rhemish. He bore the mandate of the Disciple himself. But he arrived only after a chaotic, month-long interregnum.

He found the Host in disarray, dissolving, retreating, its captains squabbling amongst themselves instead of fighting the enemy.

He summoned a council. A Harish kill-dagger thrust into a balk of oak formed an intimidating centerpiece for the meeting. Hali spoke. He brooked no questions.

He told them he would be a hard taskmaster. He told them they were going to turn the campaign around. He told them he would have no patience with defeatism or failure. He told them that the Lord was with them even in their hour of despair, for he had descended upon the Most Holy Mrazkim Shrines and the Disciple and had renewed his pledge to the Faithful. He told them to keep their mouths shut, to listen, and to do what they were told when they were told. He caressed the kill-dagger with each of his directives, and each time that silver blade glowed a gentle blue.

He got his message across.

Methodically, Hali studied the situation and took hold of its problems. Systematically, he carved off chunks of northern strength and obliterated them. He was not a man of inspiration like Altaf el-Kader. He was no genius like Nassef el Habib. He was, simply, a determined workman. He knew his tools. He knew their limits and his own. He strained both. Animated by his will, the Host stopped, ceased falling apart and brought the enemy to a halt on the Porthune.

Winter came once more.

El Murid attained his victory over the demon within him. It was a long, grueling battle. Esmat served as his eyes and ears in the world. The physician screened his master from anything even mildly disturbing.

Even after El Murid recovered, Esmat confined outside news to the huge irrigation project El Murid had ordered begun before going into seclusion.

The drive had gone out of the Hand of the Lord on Earth. He knew the physician was intriguing, but did not protest. He *wanted* to escape his role as Disciple, and Esmat had deprived him of his chemical escape. . . .

He told himself he could quash Esmat's ambitions whenever he wanted.

He knew the movement would suffer during his absence. The Al Rhemish factions would play at a hundred intrigues, trying to push into the power vacuum, perhaps even attempting to suborn the generals in the field. . . .

He could not bring himself to care. With Yasmid gone, and no news of her fate. . . . He did not have much to live for anymore.

One man kept the Faith. One man kept the schemes and intrigues from becoming a gangrenous wound in the movement's corpus. One man battled and controlled the forces of devolution. Mowaffak Hali, Master of Assassins.

Hali did not like Esmat, but he did trust the physician. More than he should have. When Esmat said the Disciple was still fighting his addiction, Hali took his word. He would preserve the movement while it awaited the return of its prophet.

He did much of his waiting in Al Rhemish, in a big white tent from which grim-faced, fiery-eyed men ventured with silver daggers next to their hearts. The daggers had a habit of finding the hearts of the more dangerous conspirators.

Even the least of men shrank from the Invincible when they encountered him in the street. Esmat was terrified of him.

El Murid spent all his time sequestered in a vast suite hidden deep in the Shrines. He had had Esmat assemble a dozen tables in what once had been the priest' dining hall. He had shoved them together and covered them with maps and crude models reflecting northern Hammad al Nakir. Upon that vast board he planned his dream reconstruction.

He could wander round for hours, making marks, shuffling models, building his vision of the desert's tomorrow. Citrus groves. Lakes. Renewed forests. All to be created with the water that western prisoners were canaling down from the Kapenrung snows.

It was the day that el-Kader fell. His amulet began vibrating. It became hot. He cried out in surprise and pain. The jewel's glow intensified. Then it flashed so brightly that for a time he was blind.

A voice thundered through the Shrines: "Micah al Rhami, son of Sidi, that was named El Murid by mine angel, where art thou?"

The Disciple collapsed, burying his face in his arms. For a moment he could do nothing but shake in fear. Then, "Here, O Lord of Hosts." His voice was a tiny mouse squeak.

"Why hast thou forsaken me, Chosen of the Lord? Why hast thou abandoned me in the forenoon of mine triumph? Why dost thou lie in indolence, surrounding thyself with the wealth of nations?"

The fear ground him down. He grovelled and whimpered like a puppy at the feet of a cruel master. The voice boomed on, chastising him for his sloth, self-pity, and self-indulgence. He could not force a word of rebuttal past the whiteness of his lips.

"Rise up, Micah al Rhami. Rise up and become El Murid once more. Shed thy robe of ungodliness and minister to the Chosen once more. The Kingdom of Peace doth lie in great peril. Thy servant el-Kader hath been slain."

Five minutes passed before El Murid dared peep out of the shelter of his arms.

The light was gone. The voice had departed. His amulet had returned to normal. His wrist was an angry red. It ached.

He rose, looked around. He was badly shaken. The first time he called out his voice cracked. It was the mouse voice again.

Then the mouse roared. "Esmat!"

A terrified Esmat appeared instantly. His furtive gaze darted from shadow to shadow.

"Esmat, tell me the situation in the provinces."

"Lord. . . ."

"Did you see a light, Esmat? Did you hear a voice?"

"I heard a thundering, Lord. I saw lightning."

"You heard the voice of the Lord of Thunders telling me I was failing Him. You heard Him setting my feet on the Path once more. Tell me what I need to know, Esmat."

The physician started talking.

"Thank you," El Murid said when he finished. "It's worse than I thought. No wonder the Lord is vexed. Where is Mowaffak Hali these days?"

"He's in the city at the moment, Lord."

"Bring him. I need him to take command of the Host."

Esmat was puzzled, but asked no questions. He went for Hali, and as he walked told his friends what had happened in the Shrines. Few were pleased.

The news of el-Kader's passing reached Al Rhemish eleven days after Hali's departure. The Disciple's foreknowledge further dismayed those who had been profiting from his seclusion.

Three weeks later El Murid changed his mind. "Esmat, find me a messenger. I want to move el Nadim west. He's finished in the east, and I need Hali here."

"As you command, Lord." Esmat left looking pale. It looked like the profitable days were done.

El Murid did not rush Hali's recall. The threat of the man's return was enough to purge Al Rhemish of parasites. Nor did he hasten el Nadim's transfer. El Nadim and his strength would not be needed till spring.

The Disciple was, simply, proclaiming his return. He wanted the world to know that he was in command again, that he was El Murid once more, that the hiatus of will had ended.

The word spread across the Second Empire like ripples across a pond. An upswing of morale accompanied it. Countless believers reaffirmed their faith.

The era of stagnation ended. The movement took on new life. The gloom of the future vanished like a fog burned off by a hot, young sun.

Nevertheless, the Disciple could not expunge the gloom of the past from his own heart. His losses were a soul-burden he could not shed.

Chapter Seventeen: *THE GUERRILLAS*

Between them, Ragnarson and bin Yousif recruited seven thousand men in three years. The enemy no longer came to the Kapenrungs hunting them. They were all hardened veterans with nothing to lose.

Haroun directed field operations throughout the Lesser Kingdoms, through a score of sub-commanders. Many were men he had never met, men who had allied themselves with him because of his guerrilla successes.

He had learned the lessons of Nassef's campaign in Hammad al Nakir. Now, in the Lesser Kingdoms, the nights were his. He had begun to believe that he was at least the ghost of a king.

He selected the targets and chose the men who would attack them. He ran the spies and assassins who were making the enemy miserable. When a big operation came up he took the field himself.

His partner, Ragnarson, trained recruits.

Ragnarson was not happy. He had seen no real action in two years. The world had forgotten that he and his Guildsmen existed. He worked his tail off to make stubborn fighters of the hungry, ragged, dispirited leavings of lost battles, then Haroun sent them off to skulk in the woods like bandits.

"I just don't feel useful anymore," he complained. "My men don't feel useful. None of use have wielded a sharpened sword in so long that we've forgotten how."

"Uhm," his brother grunted. "Nor sheathed a sword of flesh in its proper place." Women were scarcer than gold in the mountains. The occasional wild hill woman stopped by and made sure gold and silver did not accumulate.

"We're not ready for heads-up fighting," Haroun insisted, as he had been doing since they had come to the mountains. "You keep looking at it like we should fight in one big mass. We may someday. If the war goes on long enough. But not yet, damnit! It'd be our last battle if we did."

"This hiding in the bushes and stabbing guys in the back is getting to me, especially since I don't get to do even that. It's not getting us anywhere. Ten years from now we're still going to be hiding in the same bushes."

"It worked for Nassef and it'll work for us. You just have to be patient."

"Bragi was born impatient," Haaken said. "Mother told me he was a month premature."

"I can see that. Well, I've been thinking about the problem. You may see action sooner than you want, my friend."

Ragnarson perked up. "How so?" His brother and Kildragon looked interested too. Beloul and el Senoussi continued to look bored.

"I got us together because I've had some news from Al Rhemish. Seems El Murid had a visit from his angel."

Ragnarson shuddered. He became uneasy whenever facing the notion that there might be something to El Murid's religious claptrap. "How does that do us any good?"

"It doesn't. My spy says that Disciple came out of seclusion spitting fire. He's ready to go again. He's going to recall Hali and replace him with el Nadim—and the eastern army."

"Sounds grim."

"Worse than grim. It'll mean the whole war. Some of us like to think the tide's turned. But we're deluding ourselves. My friend the Itaskian Minister is scared silly. Greyfells hasn't broken the Host. He's just squandered lives and wealth. Itaskia's allies are muttering about a separate peace. Any big setback will knock everything apart. And Itaskia can't go it alone."

Ragnarson frowned and shook his head. "We supposedly had them when we finished Nassef and Karim. It was a sure thing after el-Kader fell." He looked at Haroun sourly. "Now we have friends Mowaffak Hali and el Nadim and. . . ."

"I'll eliminate them."

"Exactly what I thought you'd say. And then what?"

"What do you mean?"

"I mean that this's one of those dragons that grows heads as fast as you chop them off. You're going to tell me that we'll have them by the shorthairs if we get rid of Hali and el Nadim. And I'm telling you that's a load of horse manure. There'll be another one step in just like el-Kader and Hali and el Nadim."

"You overestimate them. They weren't that good. They were lucky, and their opponents were that bad."

"And Nassef picked them all. Except Hali. Who are you kidding, Haroun? You know your own people and you know the west. The Host has always been outclassed in weapons and training, and a lot of times outnumbered. They've had more than luck going for them. The only guy who can handle them is Hawkwind, and nobody'll give him enough men to do any good."

Haroun shrugged. "Maybe you're right. Still. . . . Here's why I want to talk to you. I'm leaving you in charge here. I'm sending Mocker after el Nadim. Shadek, Beloul, and I are going to be away on personal business."

"Eh?"

"Beloul and Shadek have been nurturing a scheme. I can't tell you more right now. Except not to believe everything you hear the next couple of months."

"What am I supposed to do here? Sit and twiddle my thumbs all winter?"

"My spy system needs running. The raids have to be directed. Somebody has to take charge. Don't worry about it. I have faith in you. You'll manage."

Haroun looked around to make sure no one was eavesdropping. "Just ignore any strange stories you hear about me, Beloul and Shadek."

The would-be king drifted away in his mind to happier times to come. He had to sometimes. He had to remind himself that these grim todays would be worth the pain and deprivation. He had found little happiness in this struggle.

He vanished one winter night, taking with him Beloul, el Senoussi and a dozen of his toughest supporters. He left behind less than a ghost of an idea of his plans.

That was his way. Like his onetime archfoe Nassef, he could not share his thoughts. Ragnarson said he would have fought his war alone had it been possible.

Mocker departed later that same week, leading a mangy-looking donkey loaded with ridiculous impedimenta. For six months, through the length and breadth of the Lesser Kingdoms, Haroun's men had been risking their lives to accumulate that collection of junk.

"That's one guy I'm not sorry to see go," Kildragon observed. "I'd have killed him myself if it wasn't for Haroun protecting him. He can't do anything without cheating or stealing."

"He has his uses." Ragnarson rather liked the fat man, who could be entertaining. A man just had to have sense enough not to trust him.

"What're we going to do?" Kildragon asked. "I mean, we've got the whole thing to ourselves. We can try it our way now."

"Sit tight. Wait."

"You mean keep doing it his way?"

"For now. Because he's right. We'll just get ourselves killed doing it any other way."

"Well damn! Are we Guildsmen or are we bandits?"

"A little of both. I don't recall any Guild rule that says we have to do things thus and so, Reskird. Remember your first mission?"

"Stay alive. All right."

For two months Ragnarson let Haroun's organization, of which his Guild-oriented infantry made up a lesser part, roll along on its own impetus. Various warbands made desultory raids on remote outposts and terrorized natives who favored El Murid. Taking Haroun at his word, Bragi tried to ignore rumors that bin Yousif and Beloul had been slain.

The stories were dreadful. Some said el Senoussi had turned on his king, that he had made a deal with El Murid's son, Sidi.

"It's getting hard to keep those guys interested," Kildragon said of the Royalists. "They're ready to fall apart. You think el Senoussi really was playing a double game?"

"Nothing political surprises me anymore. But I never figured Shadek for smarts enough to work something that complicated."

"How do we make the troops believe?"

"We don't try. El Murid and Sidi have spies too. We want them to believe they're dead."

Haaken ducked into his brother's headquarters. "Hali's on the move, Bragi. Messenger says he got wind of the rumors about Haroun and decided to head home early. He figures it's some kind of trick."

"Damn! But he is the Disciple's moral and political enforcer, isn't he? Got anything more? Like what route he's taking?"

"No. You're not thinking of trying to stop him?"

"Damned right I am. It's just what we need. Get our old bones loosened up."

"But. . . ."

"This is what we've been waiting for. Don't you see? It's a chance to do something."

"If you're going to do anything you'd better move fast. This messenger only had a couple of days head start. Hali doesn't piddle around when he decides to go somewhere."

"Get the maps. Let's find the fastest roads to Hammad al Nakir. Reskird, go tell our people to get ready. Rations for two weeks, but otherwise we're travelling light."

Haaken spread the maps. Bragi considered them. "I only see three roads that look worth worrying about. We can get to these two ahead of him, but it'll be a footrace."

"Send Haroun's boys to that farthest one. They're used to long, hard rides."

"They might refuse."

"Take a chance. You're supposed to be in charge."

"Who should lead them? Who do you trust?"

"I'd say Metillah Amin."

"All right. Tell him to move out today. We'll start tomorrow."

"It's going to snow tonight."

"Can't help that. I'm going to have Reskird take care of this eastern road. You and me will take the middle one."

"That's a lot of walking. Let me have the east road."

"Nope." Bragi grinned.

All day, along the way, the locals came out to watch. The Guildsmen bowed their heads and slogged on. None of the watchers spoke. Very few smiled. The occasional snowball flew from a youthful hand.

"Haaken, Reskird, we'd better be nice to these folks."

"Aren't exactly friendly, are they?" Kildragon asked. "Guess you could say they're not on our side."

"Guess you could say."

A light snow began falling as they parted with Kildragon and his three hundred men. By noon next day Bragi and his three hundred were fighting a blizzard.

"Just like home," Haaken growled.

"It's a part of home I don't miss," Bragi replied. "I've never seen it this heavy in these parts."

"Nobody else has either. So naturally we've got to be out in the middle of it. We're crazy. You know that?"

"We should be there pretty soon."

"And then what? Sit and freeze our butts off till we find out that this Hali had an attack of smarts and holed up by a fire somewhere?"

"Nice to see you in a good mood, Haaken."

"Good mood?"

"I can always tell. You talk more. And it's all bitchcraft."

They would have missed their road had it not been for the town and a soldier who knew it. "That's Arno yonder, Captain," he said. "Right where we want to be."

"Here's where we make ourselves unpopular," Bragi said. And they did, by forcing the townspeople to quarter them while they waited. Nearly a thousand people lived in Arno, and none of them welcomed the Guildsmen. It was not a good feeling.

Bragi paid what he could, and made his men meet Guild behavior standards. It did little good.

Four days passed. The townspeople grew increasingly resentful. Like common folk everywhere, they just wanted to be left alone.

"Riders coming," a chilled and winded scout reported the fifth afternoon. "Four or five hundred. Look like Invincibles."

Haaken glared at his brother.

"Another fine mess I've gotten us into, eh?" Bragi asked. "Pass the word. And tell the civilians to get into their cellars."

Arno had no walls. What a place to die, Bragi thought

as he hurried toward the church. Its belfry commanded a good view of the countryside.

The afternoon sun blazed off fields of snow. He squinted. The Invincibles were hard to see. They blended with the background. They were walking, leading their animals.

He spied one man clad all in black. Curious. Black was not popular with El Murid's followers.

"How am I going to work this?" he wondered aloud. "They're not going to let us pull another Alperin."

A horseman forged ahead. Bragi galloped downstairs. "Haaken! They're sending a guy to scout. Have a couple men make like townspeople. Tell him everything's wonderful."

Haaken waved acknowledgement from the loft of the town inn. A few minutes later two men stepped into the road.

By then Ragnarson was back in the belfry and wondering if he should avoid a fight. He had a hollow sensation. Something was wrong. This one did not feel like a winner.

The north wind picked up. He shivered. This winter was getting bad. People in these parts did not know how to handle the cold and deep snow. Most of his men did not.

He could not picture them surviving a long retreat. Not harried by an enemy and burdened by wounded. "But Hali won't be used to it either," he reminded himself. "It'll be harder on his men."

The fighting would be savage. Refuge from the weather would be the prize. The loser would be out in the cold literally.

He watched as several Invincibles gathered around the returned scout. The man in black joined them, gesturing emphatically.

The meeting broke up. Invincibles readied weapons and spread out for an advance upon the town.

"So much for that idea," Bragi growled. He plunged

back downstairs. "They're coming in ready, Haaken," he shouted. He glanced up and down the road, at windows where his men waited with ready bows. "Damned weather. Maybe he'd have gone around."

Back up the tower he went, puffing and snorting. "This has got to stop," he gasped.

The Invincibles reached the first houses. They were careful. Each carried a bow or crossbow. "Maybe I should get out after dark," Bragi muttered.

It began. And it looked bad from the beginning. The Invincibles were cautious, determined and as systematic as their commander. They cleared the buildings one by one.

Hali did not try to obliterate anyone, just to get hold of warm quarters. He did not surround the town. His men did not prevent Bragi's from fleeing a building they could not hold.

A third of Arno belonged to Hali when Haaken clumped into the belfry. "Looks like we lose this one."

"Don't it?"

"We've got a problem."

"Besides looking at a cold night, what?"

"They're using sorcery."

"I haven't seen any.... They wouldn't. They're El Murid's men."

"Yeah? Go remind them. The one in black turns up anywhere we're doing okay."

"Hmm. Well. Get the wounded ready. We'll get out after dark."

Haaken thudded back downstairs. Bragi looked into the road. Several Invincibles were in easy range. He let fly. His arrows stalled their advance.

The man in black appeared. Bragi sped a shaft that missed.

The man turned slowly. His gaze climbed the church tower. His left hand rose, one finger pointing. A bluish nimbus surrounded him.

A monster voice bellowed in the belfry. Flat on the floor, Bragi clapped his hands to his ears. It did no good.

The sound went away.

A quarter inch layer of blue haze masked everything in line of sight of the man in black. Sorcery! Bragi thought, *Haaken, I'm convinced!*

The haze faded. He examined the wood underneath. It had turned an odd grey color. It flaked when he touched it.

He examined his bow. It looked sound. He peeped outside. The wizard faced the inn, his arm extended again.

"You sonofabitch, you asked for it."

His bow creaked at its moment of greatest tension. His arrow did not fly true. It smashed through the man's elbow.

"Well, damn my eyes! I never seen such whining and carrying on."

Several Invincibles hustled the wizard into a captured house. His departure did not alter the outcome. The explusion of Guildsmen continued.

Bragi nearly waited too long. He had to fight his way out of the church. Haaken's only comment was, "We've got to quit fooling around here, Bragi. We're going to have too many people hurt to get them all back to camp."

"Scavenge all the warm clothes and blankets you can. And tools so we can build shelters. Find some harness animals and carts. . . . "

"I took care of it already."

"You're not supposed to plunder. . . ."

Haaken shrugged. "I'll worry about it when they court-martial me. What's the difference? These people will hate us no matter what. Which you already thought about or you wouldn't have told me to clean them out."

"I got that wizard."

"Shaghûn."

"What?"

"Shaghûn. That's what they call a soldier-wizard."

"Like Haroun is supposed to be? What's he doing here? With Hali, of all people?"

Haaken shrugged.

"He's going to be damned mad. Who's in good shape? We've got to let Reskird and Amin know what's going on."

"I sent Chotty and Uthe Haas right after Hali showed."

"You're getting too damned efficient."

A soldier approached them. "Captain, they're moving into this block."

Ragnarson withdrew as the sun set. The Guildsmen marched dispiritedly, sullenly, weakly. The cold was gnawing their wills. Bragi had to remind them that they *were* Guildsmen.

Several of the wounded died during the night. The company paused to bury them next morning. A messenger from Metillah Amin overtook them while they were chopping graves in the icy earth.

Amin had heard the Hali was on the middle road. The messenger bore a belated warning and the news that Amin was on his way to help.

"We're back in business," Bragi announced. "Haaken, take some men to those woods over there and start building shelters."

"You're not serious." Haaken wore a look of disbelief. "You are serious."

"Damned right I am. And get some fires going first thing."

Haaken grumbled away with the men. Their disenchantment was unanimous. For a moment Bragi feared he faced a mutiny.

Guild discipline held. He concluded his conversation with the messenger.

He joined his men at their hastily built fires. They huddled near the flames, taking turns rushing into the cold to assemble shelters of boughs and packed snow.

When he felt half toasted on each side he rose and trudged toward Arno, to see for himself what Hali was doing.

Twice he had to hide from Invincible patrols. They were not strong and not enthusiastic about their job. They were not ranging far from town.

Hali was doing nothing but keeping warm. He seemed content to wait till the cold spell passed. Neither his men nor his animals were fit to face prolonged exposure.

Bragi crawled into a haystack to sleep that night. When he finally returned to camp he found Amin and his men crowding the fires and looking forlorn. He decided to give them a day of rest.

The temperature did not drop that night, and it rose next day. It kept rising and the snow began a fast melt. The ground was soggy during the march on Arno.

"Looks like the cold is over," Bragi observed.

"Yeah," Haaken replied. "Our buddy, Hali, will be getting ready to move."

Hali was getting ready, but not to move. He had his shaghûn, and the shaghûn could see beyond the range of mortal eyes. The Invincibles were cooking up a little surprise.

Bragi walked into it. The fighting became savage. Amin's men were in a bloody mood. Hali's people, backboned by the shaghûn, stomped the eagerness out of them. Come nightfall, with only a few houses retaken, Ragnarson sent a whole train of casualties back to his camp in the woods.

"This is stupid, Bragi," Haaken declared. "It's like the time Father got into it with Oleg Sorenson."

"What?" Amin asked.

"My father and another man got into a fight one time," Bragi explained. "They were both too proud to give up and neither one was strong enough to drop the other. So they beat each other half to death. They couldn't get out of bed for a week. And nothing had changed when they did. They went right at it again."

234

"That shaghûn has to go," Amin said. "They'll eat us alive if he doesn't. We can eat them if he does. It's that simple."

"So go do something about him."

Amin smiled. "You mock me. All right. Loan me three of your best bowmen."

Bragi peered at the man. "Do it, Haaken."

"You sure?"

"He is. Give him his shot."

"Whatever you say." Haaken went looking for men.

"Still testing?" Amin asked.

"Always. You know it."

Amin was one of those curiosities which turn up in every war, the soldier of schizophrenic loyalties and ideals. He was twenty-seven years old. He had been fighting for ten years. For the first seven he had served El Murid. He had been one of the Scourge of God's Commanders of a Thousand.

He had become disenchanted with his fellow officers during the invasion of the west. They were making a mockery of the Disciple's law, and he saw little evidence that El Murid himself cared. When Nassef perished and el-Kader assumed command, Amin expected wholesale looting in the recovered provinces. He deserted.

Time had proven him wrong, but by then it was too late for Metillah Amin. He went to the mountains and swore allegiance to the King Without A Throne. His name was entered on the Harish lists.

Metillah Amin was an unfortunate man, and the more so because he knew no life but that of the warrior. In the tale of the El Murid Wars he was to have little significance save that he symbolized all the thousands of young men who found the conflict a slayer, not a mother, of dreams.

Bragi and his brother watched Amin's team vanish into the darkness. "That's a man looking for death," Haaken observed.

"It's his only way out," Bragi replied. "But he's got

that fighter's determination, too. He can't just let it happen. He's got to earn it. Keep an eye on him. We'll hit them with everything if he gets lucky."

Haaken returned an hour later. He hunkered down and held his hands out to the fireplace. Bragi heard a rising clamor. "Well?"

"He earned it. But he got the job done. The shanghûn is gone."

"Dead?"

"As a wedge. For whatever good it'll do."

It did little immediate good. Hali's men were stubborn and desperate.

Uthe Haas, Haaken's messenger to Kildragon, returned next morning. He reported that Reskird was on his way.

"Ha!" said Bragi. "We've got them now." He sent another messenger to tell Kildragon to dig in across the road near the encampment in the woods. Then he gradually surrounded Arno, sneaking his strength to the north clumsily enough to be sure he would be detected. When he launched his "surprise" attack next morning Hali broke out to the south, driving down the road toward Hammad al Nakir and imagined safety.

The weather remained warm. The snow was almost gone. The earth was mush. The race was a slow one. Ragnarson and his infantrymen shambled along, pausing each few paces to knock the mud off their legs. Each time a man lifted a foot there was a *schluck*! as the mud surrendered its grip.

The Royalists and their foes exchanged the occasional arrow, but there was little fighting. From above, the road would have looked like a disorganized ant trail. The columns became ever more extended.

Bragi discovered some stony ground to his right. He guided his men into it and began gaining on Hali. Then his path suddenly dipped to a narrow, icy creek. By the time he crossed, Hali was in a brisk fight with Reskird and the Royalists. His men charged through the mud and closed the circle around the enemy.

Here Hali's men were at a disadvantage against Guild bows. The encounter was bloody and did not last long. Only a few dozen Invincibles escaped.

Ragnarson prowled the field with the Royalists, trying to find Hali's body. Night fell without his being able to determine if the game had been worth the candle. Investigations next morning proved nothing either.

"Ah, damn, Haaken. All this for nothing."

"Maybe. And maybe he died in the town."

Bragi would know nothing for sure for months. By then he would be back in the Kapenrungs, engrossed in another matter and indifferent to Hali's fate.

237

Chapter Eighteen: *THE ASSASSINS*

Haroun knelt beside the brook, drinking from cupped hands. He shivered in the chill mountain breeze. Beloul said, "Lord, I'm not comfortable with this."

"It is risky," Haroun admitted. "Beloul?"

"Lord?"

"Guard my back well."

"You think Shadek would . . . ?"

"I don't know."

"But. . . ."

"In politics you never know. He kept me informed all the way, but I'm still not sure. The question is, did he do the same with Sidi?"

Beloul smiled thinly. "Shadek is my friend, Lord. But even I couldn't say. Who knows a man's secret ambition?"

"Exactly. And in this case that's what's going to count. He's set it up so he can jump any way he wants. Just the way I would have done. I admire him for that. I didn't think he had the imagination."

Beloul smiled again.

"Now I'm wondering if I'll ever trust him, assuming he does jump my way."

"We shouldn't waste time worrying, Lord. Just be

alert. We'll all know when his moment of no return comes."

"Maybe. Do you think he'd be fool enough to trust Sidi's gratitude?"

"He would arrange some sort of self-protection, Lord."

"Uhm. I thought so."

Next day, even deeper into the mountains, Haroun told his companions, "I have to leave for a few days. Make camp here. Wait for me." His tone brooked no questions. Aside, to Beloul, he said, "Take care, my friend. Most of these men were chosen by Shadek."

"I know, Lord. I know."

The snows in the Kapenrungs were deep. Haroun found the going heavy. Most of it was uphill, which did not help.

He located the cabin more by the smell of smoke than by memory or sight. It was as white as the rest of the landscape and virtually invisible. A dog howled, protesting his presence. He approached cautiously.

It had been months since he had come here. Anything might have happened. He reached with his shaghûn-trained senses, feeling for a wrongness. There could be no better place for the Harish to lie in wait.

The door creaked inward. He stared at the rectangle of shadow, probing for a trap.

"Come in, damnit! You're letting all the warm air out." The unveiled face of an old, old woman drifted across the doorway. He pushed inside, slammed the door. One hand rested on his sword hilt.

Nothing. No danger.

He stamped the snow off his feet. A thin layer of white remained. It faded in the heat.

After the bitter cold the cabin was overpoweringly warm. He shed clothing fast, feeling slightly faint.

"How is she?" he asked.

"Well enough, considering she's trapped here a hundred miles from the Lord alone knows where." There was no deference in the woman's harsh old voice. "She's sleeping now."

Haroun glared at her.

She was his uncle Fuad's first wife's mother, the nearest living relative he could claim. She looked like a pessimistic artist's conception of Death. Wrinkled, bony, toothless, all clad in black. And mean as a snake. She resembled the harridans guarding the gates of Bragi's version of Hell, he reflected. He laughed softly. "You're a sweetheart, Fatim."

A ghost of a smile crossed her colorless lips. "You're here now, make yourself useful. Throw some wood on the fire. I'll have to cook extra tonight."

"That any way to talk to your king?"

"King? Of what?" She snorted derisively.

A voice squeaked in the loft.

"Nobody. Just your uncle, Haroun," the old woman replied.

A thin, dark, strange face peered down from the gloom. The firelight made it appear diabolic. "Hello, Seif," Haroun said. Seif was the son of Fatim's brother's son, and all she had left of her blood. He helped around the cabin.

A slow smile fought the half-dead muscles of Seif's face. In a moment he began working his way down the ladder. Haroun did not help. Seif insisted on doing for himself.

Reaching the floor, Seif turned, started toward Haroun. He dragged one leg. He held one clawed hand across his chest. It shuddered with effort. His head lolled to one side. A tail of spittle fell from the corner of his mouth.

Haroun concealed his aversion and threw his arms around the youth. "How have you been, Seif?"

"Well?" the old woman snarled. "Are you going to see her or not? Your timing is good, anyway."

Haroun released Seif. "I suppose I should. That's why I came."

"And about time, I'd say. What kind of man are you? It's been almost a year."

"I have my problems. Where is she? Hiding?"

"Asleep, I told you. Go see her, you fool."

The youth said something. Haroun could not make it out.

"And you keep your mouth shut, Seif. Let him find out for himself. It's his fault."

"Find out what?"

"She's not going to come to you. So go."

Haroun bowed to her superior wisdom and pushed through the hangings that divided the cabin.

She was lying on her back in the crude bed he and Seif had worked so hard to build. She was sleeping, smiling, her left arm flung above her head. She looked sweet and vulnerable. A month-old child lay cradled in the crook of her right arm, head near her breast. She seemed content.

"Well, I'll be damned," he whispered. He knelt and stared at the infant's face. "I'll be damned. Girl or boy, Fatim?"

"A son, Lord. An heir. She named him Megelin Micah."

"How beautiful. How thoughtful. How absolutely perfect." He reached out, touched the girl's cheek. "Darling?"

Her eyes opened. She smiled.

They were on the downside now, getting near the desert. There was just the occasional patch of snow, in the shadows of the trees. "Lord?" Beloul queried softly.

"Yes?"

"What's happened?"

"What? I don't follow you."

"You've changed. Somehow, while you were away, you became a different man. More whole, I think you'd say. Perhaps matured."

"I see."

Beloul awaited something more. Haroun said nothing, so he asked, "Might I know?"

"No. I'm sorry, old friend. Maybe somday."

"As you will, Lord."

He *had* changed, Haroun reflected. The birth of a son gave the world a different look. It made a man a bit more inclined toward caution. For three days he had been considering cancelling the expedition.

"Lord," el Senoussi called from up the column, "We're here."

Haroun scanned the mountainsides and canyon. He saw nothing unusual. "Now's the time, Beloul. He's got to jump one way or the other. Be ready."

Beloul pointed. "Down there, Lord. Smoke."

"I see it."

Shadek led the way down the steep trail. Haroun eyed his back, trying to postulate his thoughts from his posture.

No matter his intent, Shadek knew the significance of the moment. It would be too late to change his mind once he brought his king and Beloul into Sidi's camp as simple bladesmen.

Unless he were making a delivery.

Haroun grew more tense. That possibility had not occurred to him earlier.

El Senoussi's hand snapped up, signalling a halt. Haroun dropped his fingers to his sword. Shadek made his way up the file. "Lord, this is going to be tricky. I don't know what they plan. It could be a trap."

"It could be. Take a couple men down and find out. I'll wait here."

"As you command, Lord." El Senoussi picked two men and departed. They disappeared among the trees whence the smoke rose.

Haroun and Beloul waited with their swords lying across their laps. The rest of the men dismounted.

El Senoussi returned two hours later. He came all the way up instead of signalling from below. Beloul whispered, "I'm inclined to think he's sticking, Lord."

"We'll see."

El Senoussi arrived. "It looks like they'll play it straight, Lord. There's only ten of them, and Sidi himself."

"Let's go, then. Make sure he dies first if they try anything."

"That goes without saying, Lord. Listen up, men! We're going down. And I'll cut the heart out of the man who forgets and gives our Lord away. This is just a warrior named Abu bin Kahed." He stared down the trail again.

They clattered into Sidi's camp, suspiciously eyeing Sidi's men, who watched them suspiciously. This would be an uneasy alliance, Haroun reflected.

El Murid's son awaited them, his face a stony mask. He made no move to greet them. The war truly claimed the young, Haroun reflected. The boy had the look of a cruel, miserly old man.

They set out for Al Rhemish next morning, riding fast. El Murid had ended his seclusion. He was watching everyone. The night-stalking Harish were busier than ever before. Sidi did not want to be away long enough to invite unwelcome questions.

The parties travelled without mixing. There was little intercourse between them, and less trust.

Haroun and Beloul performed the chores of ordinary warriors. They did their turns cooking, currying animals, standing sentry duty. Sidi's people paid them no heed. Shadek's men showed them no special respect. He had selected smart, vigilant, veteran guerrillas.

It was noon of a warm winter's day when Haroun once again saw the Holy City, the city of his dreams, the city of the kings of Hammad al Nikir. He had to struggle to keep his feelings hidden.

The great bowl had changed. There was a broad, shallow lake where once pilgrims had camped during Disharhun. The Shrines and city now stood on an island reached by a rickety wooden causeway. The old ruins had been cleared. New structures had been raised. More were under construction, including giants that looked worthy of the capital of a new Empire. The stone piers of a permanent bridge were in place beside the wooden causeway.

The inner slopes of the bowl were covered with green grass. Camels and goats, horses and cattle grazed them. At the points of the compass four small sections had been enclosed with fences built from the rubble of the leveled ruins. Each enclosure contained arrow-straight rows of seedling trees. The all-important moisture descended the slopes from a ringing irrigation canal. Haroun could only guess whence the water had come.

He exchanged glances with Beloul.

"It's changed remarkably," Shadek told Sidi.

"The old fool's hobby," the boy said. "Greening the desert. A damned waste of money and manpower."

"It would seem a worthy goal, Lord."

Sidi gave Shadek a cruel look. "Perhaps. But it would consume the labor and wealth of a dozen generations, General."

Haroun knew the numbers. Megelin had shared them with him back when, while preparing suggestions for his father.

He sensed that Sidi was parroting something he had been told. There was a strong flavor of rote recital in his phrasing.

What fell puppet-masters were filling him with contempt for his father's dreams? And with insidious schemes for murder?

No doubt Sidi believed he was his own creature, was making his own decisions and pursuing his own ambitions. The poor naive child.

Sidi was a dead puppet and did not know it. How long would he last once his manipulators eliminated El Murid? Till the first time his will crossed theirs.

While he wallowed in the privileges of power, they would sink their claws into its instruments. If Sidi asserted himself he would find himself standing alone.

Would the Invincibles support the slayer of their prophet? A parricide? Never.

There was no one on whom Haroun would rather see the jaws of fate close. Sidi impressed him that negatively.

He looked down as they crossed the rickety bridge. The water made a nice moat. There were fish in it. Big ones. It was a shame El Murid could not have remained a loyal subject.

They wound through Al Rhemish past sites hard to recognize but difficult to forget. There. . . . That was where he had unhorsed the Disciple when he was six. His uncle Fuad had died yonder. And his father and brother Ali and King Aboud had made their stand against this wall. . . .

"Lord!" Beloul cautioned softly. "Take care. Your memories are showing."

Haroun stifled the emotion, became as much a gawker as his companions.

He did not like all he saw. There were too many white robes. Getting out would be difficult.

Sidi led them to a stable belonging to one of his backers. He told el Senoussi to sit tight till he was needed, and to keep his men off the streets.

They moved into the loft over the stable. "Not exactly where you'd look for a nest of assassins, is it?" Haroun murmured.

El Senoussi held a finger to his lips. "The walls have ears in this town. There were too many intrigues during the Disciple's seclusion."

"When do we act?" Beloul asked.

Shadek shrugged. "He needs time to arrange it. He'll want it to happen when he has an ironclad alibi. And he'll probably try to arrange it so something happens to us, whatever the outcome. We'd make dangerous witnesses. It might take him a month."

"One thing, Shadek," Haroun said. "Be obsequious. Fawn on him. Be the desert's number one lickspittle if you have to. But make believe he's taken us in, that he needn't fear us."

"That is my plan, Lord." El Senoussi looked like an artist watching a very personal piece of work, wrought with loving care, being reshaped by another artist. "I'm going to make him so sure of me that when the day comes he'll come tell me himself. We'll slay the pup then leap at the throat of the sire. I trust that meets with your approval, Lord?"

"Pardon me, Shadek. I worry. About everything. What about escape? That bridge will be trouble if they're chasing us."

"That was an unforeseen complication, Lord."

Haroun gave him a name and address and had him bring the man to the loft.

Nine weeks ground away. Haroun and Beloul spent every minute of every one inside that stable. "I'm going out of my mind," Haroun moaned. "The Disciple is going to die of old age before we move."

Beloul started to say something. A stir below interrupted. Shadek growled something. Men scrambled into hiding. "Sidi's coming," Beloul whispered.

"Another false alarm," Haroun predicted. "Just checking up on us."

The boy visited once a week, growing bolder each time. Only two bodyguards accompanied him now. Shadek met him on the ground level.

Men watched from every shadow. Sidi and el Senoussi spoke in low tones, Shadek apparently growing excited, Sidi baffled.

Thus it had gone every time, with Shadek throwing his arms around as he spoke.

In the middle of a sentence he grunted and began to dig at his ear with the nail of his little finger. Then he dropped like a stone.

Arrows flew. Sidi and his bodyguards flung about in a grim, drunken *danse macabre* under the impact of the shafts. Shadek snaked away. His men leapt from the shadows, made sure of their victims.

"Quick, quiet and easy," Haroun told Beloul. "We couldn't ask for anything more." He scrambled down and joined el Senoussi, who was slapping off dirt and straw.

"Shove them under that pile of hay," Shadek ordered. "You, you, get the horses saddled." He turned to Haroun. "Lord, we're expected at the Shrines in an hour."

"Who are we supposed to be?"

"A delegation of salt merchants presenting a petition for redress. The Disciple has a soft spot for the trade. We're supposed to raise hell about the officers managing the Daimiellian salt works. Sidi said it was a pet peeve."

"Good enough. Anything to get past the Invincibles." Haroun thumbed his dagger.

They all made sure their hidden blades were accessible. Their more obvious weapons they would surrender before being permitted to approach the Disciple.

"Let me do the talking," Shadek said. "I know a little about the salt trade. I'll scratch my ear again."

Every man appeared pale and nervous. The one Shadek assigned to manage the horses was visibly relieved.

Haroun surveyed the others. They looked too hardened to be simple caravaneers. Nobody would believe their story.

Throats tightened and stomachs churned as they passed through the series of guardians shielding the Disciple. Haroun was baffled. The white robes seemed unsuspicious. Hidden weapons got by them, apparently because they surrendered blades almost as well concealed and, perhaps, because no one had ever dared stalk the Disciple in the sanctity of the Shrine.

Haroun hoped his own bodyguards never became as complacent. The Harish had struck too close too often already.

He hung back a little when they entered El Murid's throne room, keeping his head down. Beloul lagged with him. The others masked them with their bodies. El Murid knew Haroun and might recognize Beloul.

Haroun could not avoid a hungry glance at the Peacock Throne. *That* was his self-proclaimed destiny. . . .

It was called the Peacock Throne because its tall back resembled the fan of a peacock displayed. The twelve-foot plumes had been fashioned of planks of rare woods. Over the centuries they had been set with gold, silver, gems, ivory, jet, pearls, turquoise and semiprecious stones in contrived, garish patterns. Dynasties of Ilkazar's Emperors and generations of Quesani kings had contributed to the gaudy mosaic. The Throne was the heart and symbol of power in Hammad al Nakir, as it had been for the Empire before.

And now this usurper, this jackal without a drop of royal blood, defiled the seat of kings. Haroun stifled his anger.

Another rose to replace it. This beast had slain his family. This monster had destroyed everything worthy and dear and had unleashed the hounds that dogged him even now.

He counted bodyguards cautiously.

Shadek halted a dozen paces from the Peacock Throne. After the courtly courtesies, he advanced a few steps. He began talking in a low, persuasive voice. El Murid leaned forward to listen. He nodded occasionally.

What was Shadek waiting for? Let's do it! Haroun screamed inside.

Shadek's hands flew as if in emphatic support of his argument, as they had with Sidi. Haroun tried to relax, to still his fears. He dared not let tension betray him.

A door burst inward. A man in tatters staggered through. A pair of ranking Invincibles supported him. Rag-man croaked, "No, Lord! Beware!"

Not a soul moved for a bewildered moment. Then El Murid yelped, "Mowaffak! What are you doing here? What's happened to you?"

"Assassins, Lord," Hali croaked, extending a shaky arm to point. "They're assassins."

Haroun dove for his dagger.

"Hali!" Beloul squealed. And charged.

Men flew this way and that. El Senoussi rushed the Disciple, got sidetracked. Haroun flung himself after Shadek, only to have his path blocked by Invincibles. The white robes had been taken off guard. They began going down. Soon they were outnumbered.

Haroun dispatched the man blocking his path. He skipped the body and started toward his old enemy. He met El Murid's gaze. There was no fear there.

"You're a bold one," the Disciple said. "I never expected you here."

Haroun smiled. It was a thin, cruel, wicked little smile. "It saddens me that you'll never see me on the Peacock Throne, usurper. Unless you manage from the Other Side."

"Your father and uncle were wont to speak in that vein. Who is watching whom from where?"

Haroun sprang.

El Murid raised his left hand. The glow of his amulet shown into Haroun's eyes. He spoke one word.

Thunder rolled. A brilliant flash filled the room. The Shrines quivered on their foundations.

Haroun's knees gave way. A darkness stole his vision. He tried to shout but his mouth was numb.

El Murid did not laugh, and that infuriated Haroun. The Disciple was the villain of the piece. Villains were supposed to crow in triumph when they won.

Hands seized his arms, lifted him. A remote voice said, "Get him out of here." Haroun tried to help. His feet would not untangle. His supporters slung him around helter-skelter as they fled along a stormy shore. Every breaker smashed in with a metallic roar and muted shouting. Twice they dumped him while they hurled back the waves.

His vision began to clear. His legs worked a little. His mind regained its ability to grasp sequential events.

Shadek's men were fighting their way out. They were good, hard men but they had failed in their mission. They were leaving no one behind to be captured and tortured into betraying those who did escape. They might have to slay a few of their own to manage but that had been understood beforehand.

The city seemed unnaturally calm after the chaos of the Shrines. "Let's don't anybody get in a hurry," el Senoussi cautioned as he helped Beloul hoist Haroun aboard a horse. "We don't want to attract attention."

Beloul laughed. "Somebody's bound to figure there's something wrong." He indicated a pair of Invincibles howling at the entrance to the Shrines.

Haroun tried to tell Shadek to get a move on. His tongue was not yet fit for duty.

Shadek led them toward the bridge spanning El Murid's lake, saying, "They didn't have any horses around. It'll take them a while to get the word out. We'll be long gone before they do."

He was wrong.

There was a new order in the Kingdom of Peace. Secretly, El Murid had withdrawn his ban on the practice of the dark arts. A few former shaghûns had rallied to his standard. Most were in the capital city with the Invincibles. They were not the shaghûns of old but they had their uses.

Like getting swift orders to the bridge defenders.

The assassins reached the city's edge and found the causeway held by two score alert and angry white robes. "So we turn back to Bassam's," Haroun told el Senoussi.

Excitement was afoot in the city now. Those first wild rumors which come before slower-footed truth leapt from house to house like flames through a dry, brushy canyon. People moved with more speed and less purpose, certain something was wrong but unsure what it was. The Invincibles were more in evidence, though not yet asking questions. "Shadek, we'd better ditch the animals. We're too memorable this way."

"Aye, Lord." El Senoussi returned to the stable. What better place to abandon horses?

Now to move to the place his agent Bassam had prepared. . . . The wounded were a problem. They would be more memorable than any number of horses.

The pragmatic course was obvious. Dispatch the badly injured. Hide them with Sidi and his bodyguards.

There were only two men to consider, men whose lives Haroun did not want to squander. Too many had been wasted in this cruel war. "Shadek, we just became lepers. We'll bind ourselves in rags and go by twos and threes. People will be too busy getting out of our way to look us over."

"Excellent idea, Lord."

Haroun walked with a man named Hassan who had taken a saber's bite in his thigh. "Unclean!" he moaned. "Lepers!" In a softer voice, he told his companion, "I'm starting to enjoy this."

The nervous mobs scattered ahead of them, reformed behind. People cursed them. Some muttered that the Disciple had extended his protection too far, that lepers should not be allowed to befoul the City of God. One overly bold child chucked a clod. Haroun shook a gnarly stick and howled incoherently. The child scampered away. Haroun laughed. "This is fun."

"Have you ever known a leper, Lord?"

"No. Why?"

"It's no fun for them. They rot. They stink. Their flesh falls away. They don't feel anything. If they're not careful they can injure themselves fatally. That happened to my sister."

"Oh. I'm sorry, Hassan." What else could he say?

Bassam, a long-time Royalist agent, had prepared them a place in the cellar beneath his house. Something of an innovation for a poor shopkeeper, he had begun digging it the day of their arrival. He had made no effort to conceal the work, going so far as to brag that it would be the finest cellar in the city.

He had lined its walls with sun-baked brick, then had erected a cross wall that concealed a narrow portion.

The surviving assassins moved in. Haroun's agent started bricking up the hole through which they had entered. "I stocked food and water for a month, Lord. Nothing tasty, but it'll keep you. I expect the stench will bother you most. People would wonder if I dumped too many chamberpots. Your fresh air will come through that wooden grate. You can see the street through it. Try not to get caught peeking."

Bassam left one loose block that could be removed for communication purposes. He did not take it out again for four days. "They've searched the house," he announced. "They're searching them all. El Murid has decreed that no one will enter or leave Al Rhemish till you're caught. Mowaffak Hali died yesterday, but you can't claim him. It was gangrene. He was attacked by Guildsmen coming home. The same band that accounted for Karim and the Scourge of God a few years ago."

"That damned Bragi," Haroun muttered. "Who told him he could leave camp?"

"Begging your pardon, Lord," Beloul said. "Did you think you could tell Guildsmen what to do? Consider their viewpoint."

"I can see it, Beloul. I don't have to like it."

"There's more, Lord," Bassam said. "El Murid rescinded the ban against shaghûnry. He admitted he's been trying to recruit them since his God visited the Shrines. The first division of el Nadim's army passed Al Rhemish today. He sent all he had with it. Lucky for us."

"Send down some wine," el Senoussi muttered. "We'll celebrate Hali's passing and mourn everything else."

"Wine is proscribed," Bassam retorted. "I follow the Disciple's law to the letter."

"No sense of humor, eh?"

Bassam ignored Shadek. "You may be here a while, Lord. He's damned angry. The Invincibles prowl day and night. You can't travel a hundred feet without being questioned."

Bassam paid his second visit three days later. The Invincibles had discovered Sidi's body. "He's more excited than ever, Lord. Crazy with grief and rage. Someone whispered in the right ears. News of the boy's plot reached him the same afternoon they found the corpses. He's tearing the city apart looking for the conspirators. They've caught a bunch trying to get out. The Invincibles are making them sing. The Disciple thinks they're hiding you."

"I wish him luck. I hope he hangs them all." Haroun laughed wickedly.

"I won't be down for a while, unless there's crucial news. I have to mind the shop every second. Half of our good citizens have turned thief."

Nine days passed. The cellar began to wear. Nerves frayed. Tempers flared. It promised to get worse. Haroun collected the weapons and piled them in a corner. He and Beloul took turns guarding them.

Bassam came in the middle of the night. "It's gotten no safer, Lord. If anything, it's worse. They're calling it the Reign of Terror. The Invincibles have become a pack of mad dogs. Their killings make less sense every day. I don't know how long it'll last. People are getting hungry. There'll be riots. And my own days may be numbered. If they take one of my men and he talks. . . ."

"Then we'd better get out now."

"You wouldn't have a prayer. They'd cut you down before you got out of sight of the shop. It's worth a man's life to walk the streets in broad daylight, Lord. Sit tight and hope it runs its course. Or that the riots start before they get on to us. They might even get sick of it themselves."

"And if they do take you?"

"I'll hold out as long as I can."

"And we'll be buried down here without knowing anything is wrong," el Senoussi growled. "Like sleepy birds caught in their nests."

"We'll fix that. Right now." In less than an hour Bassam rigged a bell that would ring at a tug on any of several cords concealed around the shop. Its installation required making a small hole through his expensive new wooden floor. He bemoaned the vandalism the whole time he was drilling.

"I won't ring unless I'm sure I'm caught," he said. "Can't guarantee I'll be able to then. I'll only do it if it won't give you away. If I do ring, you're on your own. I don't know how long I can hold out. I've never faced any real test of courage."

"Of course you have, Bassam. No coward would have hidden himself in the Disciple's shadow all this time."

"One last thing, Lord. El Nadim is camped outside town. His is the last division of the eastern army. It'll be a tough spring for the Disciple's enemies out west."

"That's the way it looks."

"That's a good man," Shadek said a moment after Bassam departed. "And a scared one. He's sure he won't last much longer."

"He's the best," Haroun agreed. "Beloul? You think our fat friend failed?"

"It does look like his luck ran out."

That cellar became worse than any prison. A prisoner had no hope, no essential belief in his existence as a free man, no knowledge that he could break out at will. The days were interminable. The nights were longer. The stench was as bad as promised. Haroun began worrying about disease. He made everybody take turns exercising.

Bassam seemed to have forgotten they existed.

Twice they heard the mutter of searchers beyond the false foundation wall. They held their breaths and weapons and waited for the worst.

The bell tinkled gently eight days after its installation.

Its voice was so soft Haroun was not immediately sure it was not just his nerves.

"They've taken him!" Shadek snarled. "Damn!"

"How long will he last?" Beloul asked.

"I don't know," Haroun replied. "He was right, in a way. Good intentions don't count for much if there's a hot iron gnawing on you. Hoist me up to the grate."

He peered into the dusty street. He watched the white robes take Bassam away. They had bound him so he could not fight and force them to kill him.

"They did get him. Damn! Brave in the shop and brave in the Shrines, when they're breaking your fingers and toes, are two different things."

"We'd better move out."

"Not before dark. We wouldn't have a prayer before then. Get with the exercises. We'll need to be loose."

"At least let's get out where we can give them a fight if they come back," Shadek suggested.

"All right. Knock the wall apart. Carefully! Keep the noise down. We'll put it back together. Make them break it down to find out if we're gone or not."

The foul tempers and abysmal morale evaporated, to be replaced by anxiety.

They spent a tense afternoon waiting for Invincibles to appear. None came. Beloul and Shadek took turns studying the movements of the patrols in the streets. Haroun and the others continued their exercises.

There was no moon that evening. The winter moon would not rise till early morning.

They moved out right after sentry change. Shadek and Beloul said the watch officers would not check back for at least an hour. They had determined that there were both posted sentries and walking patrols. The latter were the greater danger. They roamed at random, in twos and threes.

Shadek said, "Let's hope they've gotten a little lax. They've had their own way for a long time. They can't keep on edge forever, can they? When every civilian practically kisses their toes?"

"Uhm," Haroun grunted. "Beloul, go get your man."

Beloul would slay the nearest fixed guard and don his robe. Haroun would steal up on the next and do the same. The two were the party's masters of the deadly sneak.

Together they would approach additional guards acting as a random patrol. They would clear the way and provide disguises for their henchmen.

Had there been an early moon they could not have done it. The sentries were posted within sight of one another.

Beloul was as slow, patient and deadly as a serpent. He performed his task to perfection. Haroun had more trouble but managed without alerting the enemy.

Fourteen Invincibles perished. The band reached the new circumferential street El Murid was paving around his island. A garden strip twenty to fifty feet wide would lie between it and the water's edge. No alarm had risen.

They were discussing how best to get the non-swimmers across. A pair of Invincibles materialized. "What's up?" one asked.

Haroun started a casual reply. One of Shadek's men panicked, threw a swordstroke that missed.

The group exploded.

Too late. One of the white robes got his whistle to his lips before he went down.

"Into the water," Haroun snarled. "Help each other the best you can." Softly, to Beloul, "I knew it was going too well. Damn! I thought we might have time to steal horses."

The water was cold. Haroun cursed as he towed one of the non-swimmers across those places where the man could not touch bottom.

He forgot the chill once he heard the clamor of pursuit, once the torches began appearing on the island shore.

Chapter Nineteen: *THE SORCERER*

The miles grew longer every day. The hills grew steeper. Mocker worried about getting through Kavelin without being remembered, but Fate overlooked him.

The weather caused him misery enough.

He was in no real hurry. He spent the worst days holed up at wayside inns. Haroun had given him money, but where he could he paid his way by entertaining. He wanted to get his touch back. It had been years since he had played to strangers.

Not once did he allow himself to be drawn into a game of chance.

Three years in the witches' cauldron of war had matured him more than had three with the dubious Damo Sparen.

Slow as he traveled, winter was slower. He climbed into Kavelin's eastern mountains and the Savernake Gap during the worst time of year. At the last town, Baxendala, they warned him not to go on. They told him the pass would be snowed in, and the gods themselves only knew what awaited him beyond the King's last outpost, the fortress Maisak.

But Mocker recalled Baxendala, and was afraid Baxendala might remember him.

When he reached Maisak he was cursing himself for not staying. Winter in the Gap made winter in the Kapenrungs seem mild.

The Maisak garrison would not let him inside. El Nadim had assailed them with a hundred wiles. They were not willing to take a chance on so much as one little fat man.

He hunched his shoulders and trudged eastward, his donkey following faithfully.

Winter was not so harsh east of the mountains. He left the snow behind before he reached the ruins of Gog-Ahlan.

The nearby traders' town had become a ghost village haunted by a few optimistic souls trying to hold on till war's end. The fat man got good and drunk and warm there.

El Nadim, the townspeople assured him, had established his headquarters in Throyes. "Curious," Mocker mused, tramping down the road leading to that city. "Time and greed make friends of old enemies."

El Murid's faith had swept Throyes like the plague. The resulting changed political climate baffled the fat man. He did not understand religion at all. For him gods were, at best, excuses for failure.

He found Throyes in a state of high excitement, eager, already spending the riches el Nadim's troops would bring home. He was amazed. This was the Host of Illumination, in its halcyon days, all over again.

And he was supposed to stop it? Alone?

It looked like trying to stop an earthquake with his bare hands.

Nevertheless, he went to work.

He had been to Throyes before. Memories of him might not have faded. He changed careers, becoming, instead of a con artist, thief and street mummer, a faith healer.

The eastern part of El Murid's empire was more tolerant than the rest. El Nadim had made no effort to exterminate its wizards and occultists. In fact, he maintained a personal astrological adviser.

The fat man's little devil eyes glowed when he heard that. A chink! An avenue of approach. If he could eliminate that astrologer and appear at the right moment. . . .

He was out of practice. And the eastern astrology differed from the western.

He located an old woman willing to tutor him in exchange for his faith-healing tricks.

Getting the patter down and becoming deft took three weeks. He was beginning to fear he would not get near el Nadim in time. Elements of the eastern army were drifting west already, into Hammad al Nakir.

There remained the problem of approach. No street corner stargazer was going to get past el Nadim's guards.

Eliminating the general's starry-eyed adviser beforehand was out. He was a mystery man. Nobody knew who he was or what he looked like. His very existence was little more than a rumor. Some people thought he was an invention of el Nadim's enemies, meant to discredit him with El Murid.

Whatever, getting close quickly had become the priority.

The parting was almost painful, but Mocker finally turned loose of some of Haroun's money. A tailor outfitted him in superb imitation of a sorcerer's apprentice. Another gentleman, of less savory profession, forged him letters of introduction, in Necremnen, over the dread signature Aristithorn.

Aristithorn was a Necremnen wizard. His reputation was not a pleasant one. El Nadim would have to become very suspicious before bothering him with authentication requests.

Everything was ready. His excuses for vacillating had been exhausted. He had to move or confess himself a coward. He had to march up to the sentries outside el Nadim's headquarters and start lying, or to forget Damo, Gouch, and his promises to Haroun.

He did not tuck his tail and steal away. He marched.

His costume made an impressive rotundity of him.

Walking tall and arrogant, he seemed to rise above taller men. Curious eyes followed him, wondering, *Who is that important young man?*

He hoped.

He presented himself and his letters. He told the sentries, "Self, am called Nebud, apprentice primus to Lord Aristithorn, Mage of Prime Circle, Prince of Darkling Line, Lord of Foul Hills and Master of Nine Diabolisms. Am sent to Lord el Nadim by same, to assist in great work."

He spoke with all the hauteur he could muster, fearing the soldiers would laugh. Even his toes were shaking.

They did not laugh. Aristithorn was no joke. But neither did they seem impressed. Their senior disappeared briefly. He returned with an officer who asked a lot of questions. Mocker responded with odds and ends from his carefully rehearsed store of answers. The officer passed him on to a superior, who also asked questions.

And so on, and so on, till the fat man forgot his fear in his preoccupation with keeping his lies straight.

He thought himself free of preconceptions about el Nadim, but was not prepared for the creature who received him. The man was almost a dwarf. He was not old, but so hunched away from the world that oldness seemed to envelope him. He shook almost constantly. He looked no one in the eye. He stammered when he spoke.

This was a mighty general? This was the genius who had conquered the east? This little guy was scared of his own shadow.

This little guy had a mind. The Scourge of God had had faith in that. And from beyond timidity a man's brain had brought forth the miracle, uniting the middle east virtually without bloodshed.

El Nadim had to be taken seriously, no matter his appearance. He had done what he had done.

"I understand you were sent by the infamous Necremnen, Aristithorn."

262

Not sure if he were being interrogated, Mocker did not speak.

"I received no prior warning of your arrival. I did not request your presence. The wizard isn't one of my allies. So why are you here?" El Nadim seemed almost apologetic.

"Self, have asked self same question since moment Lord Aristithorn informed self that self would be coming to Throyes. Wizard is master of closed mouth. But was very explicit in orders. Aid el Nadim in all ways possible, as if same were true master of self, for period of one year, then return to Necremnos. Opinion of self: Master is well-known for interest in international affairs. Also for despite of problems born of needless conflict. Is aficionado of Old Empire. Would suspect lord will ask self questions to decide if El Murid and movement of same are worthy heirs to mantle of Ilkazar."

"I see. Some of my brethren in the Faith would consider that an insult to our Lord. A Necremnen wizard judging his fitness to found the New Empire. Moreover, the Disciple has banned all traffic with their ilk."

"Self, would think that time has come for same to recognize reality. Will need help of thaumaturgic nature, absolute, to achieve temporal goals. Is fact. Western kings and captains have been petitioning western wizards for years. Now same are beginning to see El Murid as genuine threat, same being inflexible in hatred for Wise. Same have voted to ally with enemies of Disciple come summer should Host of Illumination manage big success early."

El Nadim smiled a secretive smile, then frowned, looking over Mocker's shoulder. He seemed both amused and slightly puzzled. And Mocker was slightly amazed when the man said, "We've heard something of the sort ourselves. Frankly, I'm worried. But the Disciple isn't. Yet your sources among the Wise would be better than ours."

Mocker gulped. Had he made up a truth out of whole cloth?

"But what could you do for me?" el Nadim asked. "That my captains and astrological adviser cannot?"

"Am only apprentice, admitted. Still, am skilled in numerous minor wizardries and expert at various divinations. Could assist adviser."

El Nadim's eyes narrowed.

"Liar!" someone squealed behind Mocker.

He began turning. Too late. The blow smashed his rising hand back against the side of his skull. Head spinning, he dropped to his knees, then pitched forward at el Nadim's feet.

He could not see. He could not move. He could scarcely hear. He could not curse the malicious fate that had brought him to this improbable pass.

"That's enough, Feager!" el Nadim shouted. "Explain yourself."

"He's a fraud," said Mocker's one-time companion Sajac, the general's half-blind astrologer. "A complete fraud."

This can't be happening, Mocker thought. The old man could not have survived that fall. Yet he had. So why hadn't time finished him by now?

Mocker should have understood necessity. He was its child himself. Crawling from the Roë, battered and no longer able to compel someone to care for him, Sajac had had to adjust to survive. The need had had a remarkably rejuvenating and regenerating effect.

"Explain," el Nadim insisted.

Mocker could neither move nor speak, but his debility and pain did not prevent him from being amused. Sajac would not expose him. By doing so he would betray himself.

"Uh. . . ." Sajac said. "He was my assistant once. He tried to murder me."

Mocker was coming back. He croaked, "Is partial truth,

264

Lord. Was travelling companion of same long ago. More like slave, in truth."

His remark initiated a battle of wits and half-truths. Student and teacher ingeniously skirted betraying themselves. And Mocker gradually got the better of it.

He knew El Murid's law. It shielded children well. He kept describing the maltreatment he had suffered at Sajac's hands. The old man could but answer his charges with lies. El Nadim sensed them.

"Enough!" the general snapped, for the first time sounding like a commander. "You each hold some of the right. And neither of you is telling the whole truth. Feager, I won't anger Aristithorn needlessly."

Mocker sighed, smiling. He had won a round. "Self, am grateful for confidence, Lord. Shall endeavor to requite same with quality of service."

El Nadim summoned a lackey. The man led Mocker to the finest room he had ever seen. Sequestered there, he went around and around and around in his mind, trying to figure out how Sajac could have survived. And how he could finish what he had started without getting himself shoved six feet under.

He would have to stay a quick step ahead of the old man.

He ought to say the hell with it. He had done his share in Ipopotam and with Yasmid. Yasmid. What the devil had become of the girl? Haroun had made her disappear. . . . He imagined human bones scattered among the trees somewhere in the high Kapenrungs.

He received a summons from el Nadim next morning. "I want a divination," the general told him.

Mocker was puzzled. "Divination, Lord? What sort? Self, am poorly skilled as necromancer, entrail-reader, suchlike. Am best with stars, tarot, ching sticks."

"Feager gave me a reading earlier. Concerning my enterprise in the west. I want a second opinion. Even a third and fourth if you're willing to pursue more than one method."

"Will need to spend much time obtaining particulars to properly consult stars," Mocker said. "Preferring not to take word of colleague for same. Understand? So, for moment, we try cards, maybeso, same being quickest and easiest under circumstances."

He drew the book of plaques from within his robes, offered them to el Nadim. "Touch, Lord. Take. Mix up good, thinking questions while doing same."

El Nadim glanced at the expressionless guards spaced around the chamber walls. The Hand of the Law should not be seen flouting it.

The guards stared into nothing, as they always did.

El Nadim took the deck. He touched. He mixed. He returned the cards. Mocker hunkered down and began laying them out at the general's feet.

He had five cards down. His heart hammered. The sixth was a long time coming.

It was another bad one. He glanced up. Did he dare start over?

Subsequent cards made a worse picture still.

He could not lie outright. El Nadim might know something about reading the tarot.

"Bad, eh?"

"Not good, Lord. Great perils lie ahead. Self, would guess same not to be insuperable, but very unpredictable. Would like to do astrologic chart now, stars being more exact."

"That bad? All right. Ask your questions."

El Nadim's stars were no better than his cards. Mocker was sure Sajac had derived similarly bleak forecasts; el Nadim had sensed it and had hoped that an alternate divination would prove more hopeful.

"Nevertheless," el Nadim mused after the fat man had reported his findings. "Nevertheless, we're going. Tomorrow. El Murid himself has commanded it."

He seemed so sad and resigned that Mocker momentarily regretted having to make his prophecies become fact.

266

There were always good men among the enemy, and el Nadim was one of the best among today's foe. He was a genuinely warm, caring and just man. It was his humanity, not his battlefield genius, that had melded the middle east into a semblence of the Old Empire. He truly believed, in his gentle way, in El Murid's Law—and he possessed the will and might to enforce it.

The disease of nationalism had not yet infected the east. El Nadim's vision of Empire met needs there that had died long since in the fractious west.

Mocker could see that. Perhaps el Nadim saw it. But Al Rhemish did not. El Murid expected his general to plunge into an alien civilization, comprised of scores of divers cultures and kingdoms, and repeat a success he had wrought in an area where only three significant cultures existed.

"Foredoomed," Mocker muttered as he dogged el Nadim through Throycs' western gate. El Nadim would find suasion and right dealing of little value beyond the Kapenrungs. The lords of the west spoke and understood only one language, shared only one reality, one right, and the sword was its symbol.

Each day the fat man grew more nervous. Sajac lurked like death in the shadows, a constant reminder that the past has a way of coming back. To the west there were Invincibles who might remember him, who had less to lose than did the old man.

Sajac made his move after a lulling week.

Mocker guided his mount off the trail, swung down, hiked his robe, and squatted. And it was while he was in that inelegant pose that the Dark Lady reached out and tried to tap his shoulder.

A foot crunched gravel. A shadow moved swiftly, like nothing of the desert.

The fat man moved faster, diving, rolling and springing to his feet with blade in hand.

The assassin, a young Throyen soldier, gaped. No human being ought to move that fast, let alone a fat man.

Mocker moved in. His blade danced in the sunshine, flinging sprays of reflected light. Steel sang its song meeting steel. Then the soldier was staring forlornly at an empty hand.

"Self, am perplexed," Mocker said, forcing the man to sit on a rock. "Am beset by epical quandry. By all rights, should slay attacker as example to vituperative old man who sent same. Not so? Terrify greedy instantly? But am afflicted by disease called mercy. Will even withhold curse of revenge. . . ." A wicked smile danced across his round face. "No! Will not withhold same."

He began to whoop and holler and dance, though his sword's point remained unerringly centered on the soldier's Adams apple. He howled out a few spirited, obscene tavern songs in guttural, fractured Altean while gesturing as if summoning up the Lords of Darkness.

"There. Should do job. Have set curse of leprosy, my friend, same being very specific."

The soldier flushed. He could imagine no worse fate.

"Very specific," Mocker reiterated. "Same becomes incumbent only when recipient tells lie." He laughed. "Understand? One lie and curse begins to take effect. Within a few hours skin yellows. Within few days flesh starts to fall away. Smell grows like stench of old corpse. Listen! Should lord general summon erstwhile assassin as witness, report whole truth of situation, exact. Otherwise. . . ."

The fat man whirled, sheathed his blade, caught his mount, finished his wayside business, then returned to his place in the column. He kept bursting into giggles. That fool soldier had fallen for it.

The fat man muttered and cursed as the column approached Al Rhemish. His companions fussed and bothered. They were eager to visit the Holy City and Shrines. Mocker sweated constantly. This was the critical period. It was here that he was most likely to encounter a familiar face. It was here that Sidi now resided. It was here that Sajac would find his best opportunities.

El Nadim's army assembled on the lip of the bowl, looking down on Al Rhemish.

"Where are the divisions I sent ahead?" el Nadim asked no one in particular. They were nowhere to be seen. They were supposed to have awaited him here.

A lone Invincible came galloping across the bridge and upslope. "You're not to enter Al Rhemish," he shouted. "Our Lord bid me tell you to go on westward."

"But. . . ."

"That is the command of the Disciple." The messenger seemed uncomfortable. He was relaying orders he did not himself approve.

"We've come a long way. We want to pay homage at the Shrines."

"Perhaps when you're returning."

"What's going on? What's happened?" el Nadim demanded. "Something has, hasn't it?"

The messenger inclined his head slightly, but said only, "The Disciple has barred outsiders from the city." He indicated the bowl's south rim. "Even the pilgrims, who are old folks, women, and children."

"Even his generals? Will he see me?"

"No. I'm to offer his apologies and tell you that you'll understand in time. He said to remain steadfast in the Faith. He said his prayers will go with you." The messenger then wheeled and descended into the valley.

El Nadim waited a long time before saying, "We'll camp here tonight. He may change his mind."

There was no change of heart. Al Rhemish ignored the army's existence.

Mocker signed after the column began wending through the desert once more. He was safe. He could concentrate on Sajac.

The crazy old man was careful. He had received a convincing lesson in Argon.

Mocker found scorpions in his boots. He found a poisonous snake in his bedroll. A flung stone narrowly missed his mount while he was negotiating a particu-

larly nasty piece of mountainside trail. He found doc-
tored water in his canteen, and feared his food would be
poisoned if he stopped eating from the soldiers' common mess.

Sajac had his bullies. They made sure Mocker got
nowhere near him.

The problem became a challenge. Poison would have
suited Mocker's sense of propriety perfectly. An agent
that would cause heart failure. . . .

Heart failure. Sajac was old. His heart might be weak.
Scare him to death? Using sympathetic voodoo magic
like he and Gouch had seen in Ipopotam?

Notions and schemes fluttered through his head like
drunken butterflies. He was supposed to be a sorcerer,
wasn't he? Why didn't he get with the hoodoo and the
mojo and make the old bastard think he was on his way
out? Sajac could never be sure he *wasn't* Aristithorn's
apprentice.

In minutes Mocker was telling a soldier, "Self, am
tired of constant sniping." Sajac's attempts had become
common knowledge. "Look!" He held up a hideous, ven-
omous little lizard that looked more like an example of
primitive beaded artwork than it did an animal. "Found
same snoozing in donkey pack. Patience is at end. Am
casting curse taught by master Aristithorn. Will gnaw
heart of squamous old buzzard. Is slow curse. Sometimes takes months to kill victim. Beauty is in torture of
waiting. Will end come immediately? Tomorrow? Will
hurry to settle affairs maybe hasten same? Hee-hee. Was
exceedingly difficult of learning said curse, but am glad
today. Is even more beautiful because same curse can be
hastened any time with proper cabalistic processes.
Friend, self is not cruel. Do not like harming even monsters like bilious little villain of lizard. But, and am
ashamed to admit same, am going to enjoy watching
agonized waiting of nasty old back-stabber."

He careened around the force making similar declama-
tions. He let his imagination run with the nastiness of

the curse, till he was sure Sajac would hear of it from a dozen sources and be scared out of his pantaloons.

Still. . . . The news might have no impact. The old man was as cynical a non-believer as he.

Once his excitement waned he became certain that he had chosen the silliest possible means of striking back.

Yet Sajac began watching his every move, squinting his myopic little eyes. Mocker grinned a lot, wondered aloud when the end would come, organized a betting pool that would pay the man guessing the correct moment, and occasionally pretended to be aggravated enough to consider hurrying matters. Sajac began to cringe, to become defensive and irritable. His forecasts for el Nadim degenerated.

"See?" Mocker crowed all over camp. "Curse is devouring wicked old man."

El Nadim became critical of Sajac's work. He had Mocker second-guess every reading. Which only made the old man more nervous.

There were no more attempts on Mocker's life. Sajac shifted to attempts at negotiation and bribery. The fat man dismissed these with derisive laughter.

Sajac lost his eyesight suddenly, completely. Mocker moved closer, began tormenting him verbally. The old man's protectors faded away, sensing the shift of power.

The Kapenrungs were in sight. When el Nadim summoned him, Mocker fought down his evil glee and began marshaling the courage needed to lead the general astray. Blind, Sajac could no longer dispute his readings.

The general did not want a divination. He said, "I want you to stop persecuting the old man. He's tormented enough, don't you think? El Murid teaches us not to answer cruelty with cruelty, nor to prey upon the old simply because they're weak. You may have been justified in what you did in Argon. You saw yourself trapped. But that excuse no longer obtains."

Mocker sputtered in protest.

"Go. And cease tormenting that pathetic old man."

271

Mocker went. And, in spite of his hatred, he thought about what el Nadim had said. He took a look at himself. And he was not pleased.

He saw a cruel thing no better than the Sajac he had known back when, feeding its insecure ego on its ability to injure someone weaker.

The fat man was not given to extended introspection. He did not examine himself for long. He simply decided to pretend that Sajac had perished in his leap from Argon's wall.

He caught a taste of the cool breeze off the mountains, grinned, went off to badger one of el Nadim's captains.

When next he presented himself for a reading, he went armed with a crude map. "Lord," he said, "have been on job, guaranteed. Have come up with plan for circumventing dread forecasts of past. Relies on very positive attributes of Hammad al Nakir, for outflanking Fates. Can move too fast for same to keep track. Before same catch on, voila! Here is new general in back pastures of enemies." He waved his map wildly. "Hai! New Empire is victorious! Tiresome war is finished. Self, being genius to suggest plan, receive great reward, am finally able to leave employ of penurious wizard and go into business for self."

"Let's see the map. And let's hear your suggestion. Not about it."

Mocker surrendered the map. "See how Kapenrungs cut across to west, forming barrier? Suppose way could be found through same? Exiting in Tamerice, crossing Altea, Host could be over Scarlotti and far north before enemy spies realize same is coming. Same spies will be far to west watching traditional routes from Sahel. Not so? So. . . ."

"There are no passes through the Kapenrungs. And I don't have the whole army here even if there were." El Nadim's force, a quarter of his army, numbered twenty thousand.

"Latter is immaterial," Mocker said. "Spies can dog

forerunner forces, thinking same are whole army, thinking new general is there. As to pass, self did not come unprepared to reveal same." He sketched a jagged line with a pudgy finger. "So." The route was identical to that he and Yasmid had followed earlier. And it passed within fifteen miles of Haroun's present main camp.

"Last night, while army slept, notion came upon self. Ran round it like silly dog on leash, getting tangled and snarled. Then decided to take first-hand look. Hai! Leaving body was difficult of accomplishment. So much body to leave. But managed same, and flew to inspect mountains, discovering route just outlined. Will be difficult of crossing, assuredly, but not impossible of achievement."

He had concluded that he'd never manage to eliminate el Nadim himself. Not with any hope of getting out alive. So he had decided to lead the man into a position where Haroun could do his own killing. The presence of the army would be noted quickly if it entered the mountains.

"I like the basic notion. As to its practicality. . . . Let me think it over."

Did the general know these were Haroun's mountains? Mocker hoped not. But el Nadim never said anything about bin Yousif. It was almost as if he were pretending Haroun did not exist.

And what of these wild rumors they had been hearing, about Haroun and Beloul being dead, having been betrayed by Shadek el Senoussi? If they were true he might be guiding el Nadim to a toothless tiger, truly giving him the surprise maneuver he was promising.

"Must waste no time, Lord. Point of entry to mountains is near."

"I can read a map. Go away and let me think."

Next day the van turned northward. And Mocker found himself riding point, charged with showing the way and using his alleged thaumaturgic powers to anticipate danger.

Days crawled by. The mountains rose ever higher. The

air grew colder as the wintery north wind leaked between the peaks. They began to encounter snow. The fat man's nerves grew ever more frazzled.

They were out there watching. He could feel the touch of their eyes. He had seen signs no one else had recognized.

What would he do when the hammer fell? One side or the other, or both, would label him traitor.

Even he was surprised when the boulders began thundering down the canyon walls.

Men shouted. Horses reared and bolted. Boulders started knocking people around. Arrows zipped out of the sky. Mocker flung himself off his mount and scurried to the shelter of an overhang. He crouched there momentarily, getting the lay of his surroundings. Then he started creeping up the canyon. He wanted to disappear before anyone noticed.

He glanced back after he had crawled three hundred yards.

The canyon floor was a mess, and the mess was getting worse. Yet el Nadim's soldiers were counterattacking. They were headed upslope, darting from the protection of one tree to the next. El Nadim himself had arrived and, oblivious to stones and arrows, was whipping them on.

He spied Mocker among the rocks ahead. He intuited what had happened.

His arm snapped up. A finger pointed. His mouth worked. A dozen soldiers started toward the fat man.

The fat man hiked the skirts of his robe and ran.

Chapter Twenty: *END OF A LEGEND*

"Suppose they get past Reskird?" Haaken asked.

"Suppose. Suppose. All the time with the supposes," Ragnarson growled. "If they do, then we've wasted our time."

He was shaky and irritable. He had looked el Nadim over and now doubted his trap would work.

Kildragon, commanding a force of Royalists, was to attack el Nadim's van in a narrow place ten miles to the north. He was to use boulders and arrows till el Nadim decided he could not break through. When the general turned back he was to find escape to Hammad al Nakir cut off here. Ragnarson had assembled six thousand men, rushed them through the mountains, and gotten them into hiding barely in time to let el Nadim pass. Now he was digging in.

"Let's check the works," he said. He could not stand still. He was too worried about Kildragon.

"They should've reached Reskird yesterday," Haaken said, following his brother. "We should've heard something by now."

"I know." Ragnarson slouched, stared into a narrow trench.

At that point the canyon was two hundred yards wide

and had a relatively level floor. Its walls were sheer, towering bluffs of granite. There was a small, cold stream and dense stands of pine. Ragnarson's line lay across a meadow before one such stand.

He had assembled his infantry there and backed them with a few hundred Royalist horsemen. The remaining Royalists were either with Kildragon or hidden in a side canyon slightly to the north.

"The golden bridge," Haaken muttered. "Not to mention that we're outnumbered."

"I know." Ragnarson went on worrying. The golden bridge was a Hawkwind concept. It meant always showing the enemy an apparent route of flight. Men who saw no escape from a poor battle situation fought more stubbornly.

Ragnarson's dispositions left el Nadim with no easy avenue of flight. And the general had the numbers.

"Here comes Reskird's messenger."

The courier reported that Kildragon was holding. But, he announced, el Nadim had smelled the trap. A quarter of his force was headed south to make sure of his line of withdrawal.

"Maybe that's a break," Bragi mused. "If we can finish part of them before the main mob shows. . . ."

"We'll just tip our hand," Haaken replied.

"No. Send somebody over to tell those Royalists to stay out of sight unless this first bunch starts to whip us."

Haaken's courier vanished into the side canyon just in time. El Nadim's horsemen appeared only minutes later.

Bragi's men scurried around, getting to their places. El Nadim's men halted. They sent skirmishers forward. Nothing happened after the probe had been repulsed.

"Sent for instructions," Ragnarson guessed. "Should we stir them up?"

"Let's don't ask for trouble," Haaken replied. "They look too professional."

The easterners pitched camp in the Imperial fashion,

surrounding themselves with a trench and palisade. They were equally professional in mounting their morning attack.

The westerners repelled them easily. The easterners retired to their encampment and stayed put till the balance of el Nadim's force joined them.

"Guess they found out what they wanted to know," Bragi said when it became clear that no new attack would develop.

The damned easterners bounced from rock to rock like knobbly old mountain goats. The rate they were gaining, Mocker thought, he might as well sit down, save his breath and be fresh when they arrived.

He scooted between two jagged hunks of granite and headed for the nearest tangle of brush. He would ambush them. He squirmed in with the grace of a panicky bear cub.... And found himself face to face with a Royalist warrior.

The man knocked his sword away. Glee animated his leathery face. "You!" He grabbed Mocker's clothing and yanked him forward onto his belly. He jumped astride. The fat man protested, but without much volume.

"You cheated me one time too many, tubbo."

El Nadim's harriers charged into view. Not seeing their quarry, they paused to talk.

A blade caressed Mocker's throat. "One peep, fat boy, and it's all over."

Mocker lay very still. The soldiers began probing hiding places.

An arrow streaked off the mountainside. Then another and another. The soldiers fled whence they had come.

"Bring them out of there," someone ordered. He had an abominable accent.

Mocker felt his captor tense, torn between obedience and a lust to use his knife. His life hung in the balance. The balance needed tilting. "Hai!" he moaned. "Self, thought same was goner. Thought knives of pestilent

277

foemen would drink blood sure. Months of labor to bring same into trap wasted in blood. Would have been sad end for one of great heroes of war against madman of desert."

The someone who had spoken waded into the brush. Mocker's setting hen rose from his plump nest. A boot pushed against the fat man's side, rolled him over. He stared up into the unfriendly face of Reskird Kildragon.

"Hai! Arrived in nick, old friend. Not so happy about self anymore, men of el Nadim. For some strange reason have decided former master magician betrayed same into trap." He forced a laugh.

"I'm no friend of yours, fat man. Get up."

Mocker rose. Kildragon bent and recovered his sword. Mocker reached for it. The Trolledyngjan refused to yield it. "Sorry. Thank your heaven that I'm going to go against my better judgment and let you live. Come on. Before your playmates come back with help."

"Is wise decision," Mocker averred. "Self being intimate friend of Royalist chieftain Haroun. Like so." He held up a pair of chubby fingers pressed tightly together. "Same would be displeased to learn that old friend and chiefest agent met misfortune at hand of professed ally."

"I wouldn't lean on his protection too much, was I you," Kildragon told him, urging him up the mountainside with an ungentle shove. "The last word we had was that he's dead. That's been months, and nobody has said different since."

The fat man shivered despite the warmth generated by his exertion. He was going to have to get himself onto his best behavior. A lot of these people would be hunting excuses to pound him.

It just was not fair. Everywhere he went somebody was out to get him. The whole damned universe had it in for him.

Kildragon herded him up and across the mountainside and before long he was half-convinced the man was trying to work him to death. "Sit down," the Guildsman told him suddenly, planting him on a boulder. "And stay put."

He stayed put, more or less, for the next four days.

That mountainside provided a fair view of the canyon floor. He watched el Nadim make repeated, valiant, futile efforts to break through. The general finally reached the not unreasonable conclusion that doing so would not profit him anyway. It was well known that there were no decent passes through the Kapenrungs. Why believe one assertion of a man proven faithless in other ways?

Mocker tried to determine the fate of Sajac by examining the dead after el Nadim departed. He found no sign of the old man. Prisoners could not tell him anything. His Royalist companions would not deign to answer his questions.

He needed to know. Despite el Nadim's admonitions, blind or not, he did not want that nasty creature skulking around his backtrail.

"Woe!" he muttered after el Nadim cleared out. "Back along same old route. Is becoming boring routine, back and forth through mountains. Self, am more profound, being of broader adventurousness, wishing to see new lands. Same motivation brought self to west in first place."

He had lost his audience before he began. What was the point of a declamation when nobody was going to listen?

Kildragon's force followed el Nadim's rearguard without any great enthusiasm or alacrity. Four days of heavy fighting seemed an adequate contribution to the cause.

Four of them rode stumbling horses. Haroun and Beloul walked. They took turns falling and helping one another up.

They were the survivors, and not a one was not wounded and perilously exhausted. The Invincibles had hunted hard and well, and hunted still, but they had shaken the white robes for a while. The Invincibles needed a day or two to work themselves up for a charge into the enemy mountains.

"I heard a trumpet," el Senoussi muttered from his animal's back. "A long way off."

"The bugle of the angels, maybe," Beloul replied. "We're halfway between back there and nowhere. They never even heard of bugles out here."

El Senoussi was right. An hour later everyone could hear the occasional braying of trumpets and what sounded like a distant crash of battle. Sound carried well through the cold, still canyons.

"It's a big one," Haroun guessed. "Up here? How can that be?"

"Been seeing a lot of horse droppings since we got into this canyon," Beloul said. "Too many for our side."

The others had noticed too. No one had wanted to be first to mention bad sign.

"We're getting close," el Senoussi observed a little later. "Someone ought to go take a look before we walk into it."

"He's right. Beloul, take Hassan's horse."

Beloul groaned but did as he was told. He returned soon. "The Guildsmen and our warriors have part of el Nadim's army trapped," he reported. "It looks nasty."

"Who's winning?"

"I didn't ask."

Haroun groaned as he climbed to his feet. He ached everywhere. "What I need is a week to do nothing but sleep, but I guess I'd better show my face. Heaven knows what they've been thinking since we disappeared."

His companions sighed and slowly clambered into their saddles.

It took but a moment to discern what Ragnarson had done. He had drawn a kill line across the easterners' path and was trying to wipe them out.

"It didn't work like I figured," Ragnarson admitted once nightfall provided a moment to visit.

"How so?" Haroun's followers were ecstatic about his return. He was using the meeting as an excuse to escape their attentions.

"That charge from the rear. I don't know if it was ill-conceived or just came too soon. It looked like it was going to work, then el Nadim made a comeback. He's got your men trapped in that side canyon now. And there isn't a damned thing I can do."

Haroun replied, "They can abandon their animals and climb out. If they don't, they're so stupid they deserve whatever happens. I'll go over myself come morning."

"Don't know if we can hold *here.*"

"Think positive. You've gained us another victory. Maybe our most important since Alperin. El Nadim himself is trapped here. Imagine the impact. He's El Murid's last great general. The hero of the east. The end of the legacy of the Scourge of God. Mowaffak Hali, too, is a tale that's reached its end. He made it to Al Rhemish, then the gangrene took him. The Disciple was furious."

Ragnarson grinned. "We wondered what happened to the sonofabitch. We ragged his gang pretty good, but couldn't find him afterwards. So tell us about your pilgrimage to the Holy City. I take it your scheme didn't work."

"We came this close." Haroun held up a thumb and forefinger spaced an inch. "Then the Disciple used his amulet. Damned near wiped us out." He told the story to a quiet, sometimes incredulous audience.

"Get some sleep," Ragnarson advised when he finished. "I'll get you up if we have to run for it."

"Thoughtful of you."

Haroun and his travelling companions slept through most of the next day's fighting.

The Royalists fought like a new army. Their King had returned. Fate was on their side.

El Nadim's men fought well. It did them no good. They could not break out. Ragnarson began talking about asking el Nadim to surrender.

A refreshed Haroun disabused him of that daydream. "Some of his least enthusiastic soldiers might sneak over and give up. Don't look for him to. He's a true believer. He'll fight till we kill him. Or till he wins."

"I don't know if we can whip them," Bragi said. "We might end up getting hurt worse than they do if we try."

Haroun shrugged. "You're the one put his back to the desert."

El Nadim mounted his most ferocious attack yet. The Guild lines bowed and buckled and would have broken but for a timely rear attack by Kildragon.

Spent, the easterners withdrew into their encampment. Not a man was seen for days. "Looks like we play see who gets hungry first," Ragnarson said. "I damned sure ain't going after them. My momma's stupid babies all died young."

A Throyen officer came out under a white flag five days later. He asked for bin Yousif.

"News gets around, doesn't it?" Haaken muttered.

"Seems to," Bragi replied. He and his brother watched over bin Yousif's shoulder.

"We're ready to talk terms," the Throyen told Haroun.

"Why? You came out here looking for a fight. You get one and right away you want to call it off."

"There's no point fighting when there's nothing to gain. Were we to win, you'd just fade into the mountains. Were you to win, you'd have spent most of your men. It would be best for everyone if we disengaged."

Haroun translated for Bragi, who could not follow the Throyen dialect. Ragnarson said, "This guy is dangerous. He's got an off-center way of looking at things. Keep him talking."

Haroun asked questions. He translated the answers. "He's pretty much said it, Bragi. We quit fighting and go our separate ways."

"Where's the profit? He must have a good reason for this. Like maybe el Nadim is dead or hurt. Push him."

"Don't be too eager. They've still got the numbers." Nevertheless, Haroun pressed.

The Throyen responded, "I'll come see how you feel in a week."

Haroun translated. "I pushed too hard. I think they'd give up their weapons if we let them go."

"What's to keep them from hiking around the Kapenrungs and joining up with the rest of their mob?"

"What's to keep you from wiping them out once they give up their weapons?"

"We're Guildsmen. We don't operate that way."

"Maybe they have a sense of honor too. Look, all they're going to do is sit and wait us out. Right?"

"Looks like. And yes, we'd be better employed somewhere else."

"Ask for their parole. Weapons and parole. That's good enough for me." Haroun planned an active summer campaign. Having seen the chaos in Al Rhemish, he believed the tide of war had turned. He wanted to get into the thick and make so much noise his claims would catch the ears of all his allies.

"All right," Bragi said.

Haroun resumed dickering with the easterner.

El Nadim's force filed out of the trap next morning, leaving their arms in their encampment. Ragnarson and bin Yousif watched closely, ready for any treachery.

Ragnarson was depressed. "Another inconclusive contest, my friend. When are we going to make some real progress?"

Haroun insisted, "We've set another stone in El Murid's cairn. Be patient. This summer, or next summer at the latest, his house of sticks will fall. There's nothing to hold it together." He was bubbling. Could the Second Empire long endure now that its last hero had fallen?

Ragnarson believed it could. "It's not as easy as you pretend, Haroun. I keep telling you, it's not just a few men. But my big problem is I don't like what trying to stop them has done to us."

"Done to us? It hasn't done anything."

"If you believe that, you're blinder than I thought."

"What?"

"I don't know you well enough to tell about you. You're a closed person, and you've lived this all your life. But I can see what it's done to my brother. Haaken is a good mirror that shows me what it's done to me. I'm twenty, and I'm an old man. Anymore, my only concern is the next battle, and I don't much care about that. I'm just staying alive. There's more to this world. I can remember a time when I was supposed to get married next summer. I can't remember the girl's face, though. I've forgotten the dreams that went with her. I live from day to day. I can't see the end. I can't see it getting any better. You know, I really don't give a damn who sits on the Peacock Throne, or which god gets declared head honcho deity."

Haroun considered Ragnarson thoughtfully. He was afraid Bragi might be right. Megelin would have agreed. His father would not have. It was to their often antagonistic memories and shades that he answered.

They'd certainly lost their illusions, he thought. And maybe more, that they hadn't known they had. Bragi was right about one thing. They were just surviving, trying to get through a winnowing of survivors.

What Bragi didn't see was that it couldn't end till El Murid was overthrown. That beast would never stop fighting. He would do anything to make his mission bear fruit. Anything.

Ragnarson marched toward Hellin Daimiel. The lands through which he passed were preoccupied with spring planting. War was a terror of long ago or far away. There was little evidence of El Murid's occupation.

Each town had its missionary, and each county its imam, trying to convert the unbeliever. They had had their share of luck. Bragi saw scores of new places of worship built in the desert style.

284

The occupation had had its greatest impact on civil administration. The Disciple's followers had started from scratch in the desert and had brought new concepts with them, bypassing traditional forms. Though the feudal structures persisted, the old nobility was in decline.

Ragnarson found scant welcome along the way. The Disciple's propaganda effort had been successful. People were content with El Murid's Kingdom of Peace, or at least indifferent to it.

Ragnarson was near the bounds of the former domains of Hellin Daimiel when the rider he had sent ahead returned. The man had gotten through. Sir Tury Hawkwind agreed with Haroun's strategy.

Haroun and his Royalists were somewhere to the south, moving faster. They would deliver the first blow against Hellin Daimiel's besiegers. Curving in from the north, Ragnarson would deliver the follow-up. While the besiegers reeled, Hawkwind would sally with the city garrison.

El Murid's force at Hellin Daimiel was not big, nor was it comprised of the desert's best. Native auxiliaries, old men, warriors injured elsewhere. . . . Its value was psychological. Haroun figured its defeat would have repercussions far beyond the numbers involved.

Ragnarson encountered fugitive desert warriors while still a day away from the city. Haroun's punch had been sufficient. He and Hawkwind had broken the siege.

"I'll be damned!" Ragnarson swore. "We run our butts off and we're still too damned late. What the hell kind of justice is that?"

Haaken peered at him. He wore what looked like a sneer. "Be grateful for a little good luck, nitwit."

"That any way to talk to your captain, boy?"

Haaken grinned. "Captain for how much longer? We get to the city, you're going to come down a peg or nine. We'll be back with the real Guild. And real Guild officers. No more of this Colonel Ragnarson stuff."

Ragnarson stopped walking. His troops trudged past.

He had not thought of that. He was not sure he could handle falling back to corporal. He had been on the loose too long, running things his own way. He watched his men march by. They were not real Guildsmen, despite the standard heading the column. Not one in fifty had ever seen High Crag. Only sixty-seven of his original company survived. They were the officers and sergeants, the skeleton but not the flesh of his little army.

"You planning to make a career of blocking the road?" Haaken asked.

"It just hit me how much has happened since we left High Crag."

"A ton," Haaken agreed. Something struck him. "We haven't been given our allowances for three years. Man, can we ever have a time."

"If they pay us." Suddenly, Bragi's world was all gloom.

He did not find himself deprived of his makeshift army. When he reached Hellin Daimiel, Hawkwind and bin Yousif were already headed south, intent on liberating Libiannin, Simballawein and Ipopotam. "Guess they're trying to draw strength away from the fighting in the north," he hazarded.

Haaken did not care about the big picture. His attention was taken with the city.

The siege had been long and bitter. Some all-powerful monster of a god had uprooted all the happy, orderly, well-fed citizens of yore and had replaced them with a horde of lean, hard-eyed beggars. The rich merchants, the proud scholars, the bankers and artisans of olden Hellin Daimiel had come into a ghastly promised land. It flowed not with milk and honey but with poverty, malnutrition, and despair.

"What happened?" Ragnarson inquired of a girl not yet too frightened to talk to strangers. He had to explain several times to make her understand that he wanted to know why the city was in desperate shape when the

Itaskian naval and mercantile fleets had been supporting the city all along.

"Our money ran out," the girl explained. "They wanted
our museum treasures too. They forgot whom we are,"
she declared haughtily. The Diamiellians long had arro-
gated to themselves the roles of conservators and moder-
ators of western art and culture. "So they send just
enough to keep us barely alive."

"Thank you. I taste politics, Haaken."

"Uhm?"

"The Itaskians have destroyed Hellin Daimiel more
surely than the Host could have by sacking it. Wearing a
mask of charity. That's bloody cruel and cunning."

"What do you mean?"

"Remember Haroun telling about that Itaskian War
Minister? He got what he wanted. He's let the siege ruin
Hellin Daimiel. And all the time he was probably reminding their ambassadors of the great things Itaskia
was doing for them. Maybe that's why Greyfells piddled
around."

"Politicians," Haaken said. He expressed an extreme
disgust with that word.

"Exactly." Bragi was just as indignant. "Let's see if
we can't find someplace to get crazy. I've got three years
in the woods to get out of my system."

The vacation lasted only two days. One of Ragnarson's
men brought the bad news. "El Murid has left the desert,
Colonel. They don't know where he's headed. The
Daimiellians are in an uproar. They figure he'll come
straight here."

"Damn! Well, let's see if we can't give him a warm
welcome."

Chapter Twenty-One: *HIGHWATER*

Hard-eyed, El Murid glared at the pylons bearing the names of those who had died for the Faith. There were too many. Far too many. The obelisks formed a stone forest atop the south lip of the bowl containing Al Rhemish. The presence of his family stelae only worsened his mood.

It had taken a great act of will to lay Sidi beside his mother. He had been tempted to throw his traitorous get to the jackals.

"Esmat."

"Lord?" The physician was not pleased that his master had resumed his pilgrimages to his family's graves.

"The Lord charged me with bringing the Truth to the nations. I've been delegating that task. That is why so many have died. The Lord is reminding me of my vocation."

"I don't follow you, Lord."

"I began alone, Esmat. I was a child dying in the wastes when I was called. I brought the Truth out of the badlands. Hearts opened to it. I used them. I wasted them. I'm alone again. Alone and lost in the Great Erg of the soul. If I remain here again this summer, the entire Host of Illumination will be taken from me. More and bolder bands of assassins will remind me that the time alloted for my work is both borrowed and limited. This summer, Esmat, the Disciple becomes a warrior for the Lord, riding with the Host."

"Lord, you swore never to go to war again."

"Not so, Esmat. I vowed not to determine strategy for the Host. I swore I would leave the management of war to my generals. Assemble us an escort when we go back down."

"As you command, Lord."

"If the Lord calls me before thee, Esmat, lay me down beside Meryem. And if ever Yasmid should be found, let her lie at my other hand."

"So it shall be, Lord. Was there ever any doubt?"

"Thank you, Esmat. Come. Let us gird ourselves, for we face the hour of our trial."

"And the Lord our God, Who is the Lord of Hosts, shall trample thine enemies, O Chosen, and they shall drink the sour wine of their unbelief, and they shall be vanquished."

"Esmat! You amaze me. I thought you indifferent to the Teachings. I didn't know you could see beyond your own small ambitions."

The physician shook. How subtle the Disciple was, chiding him in this gentle way! His transgressions were known! They had been forgiven, but not forgotten. "I'm not well enough known, Lord, and by myself least of all. I'm so foolish I try to be something I'm not."

"That's the curse of humanity, Esmat. The wise man leashes it before it leads him into the shadow where pretensions are of no avail."

"I am a child in the light of thy wisdom, Lord."

El Murid gave him a hard look. Was that quote a gentle mockery?

His venture west did not begin immediately. News of el Nadim's demise delayed it. "The Lord has written the final paragraph of his message, Esmat," he said. "I stand alone on the battlefield, naked to the Evil One. I must wrestle his minions now, as I wrestled the Dark One himself in the Shrines."

"Hardly alone, Lord. The Host of Illumination is more vast than ever before."

"Who will wield it, Esmat?"

"Convene a council of leading men, Lord. Let them name candidates."

"Yes. Good. Gather the right people, Esmat."

He selected Syed Abd-er-Rahman, the man least popular with functionaries who obviously wanted a general they could manipulate. El Murid could not recall ever having met the man or even having heard of him. But he was popular with the military.

He started west two days after he granted the appointment.

The news of his coming swept ahead like a scorching wind. It blew his enemies into shadowed corners. It brought his friends forth. Crowds cheered his passing. In town after town he slowed his progress so he could touch the reaching hands of the Faithful, and bless them and their offspring, and sanctify their new places of worship.

"We'll ignore it," he decided when Esmat brought news of the collapse of the siege of Hellin Daimiel. "Let bin Yousif run himself ragged trying to distract me. His conquests mean nothing. He'll win no new followers. We'll eradicate his bandits after we've dealt with the Evil One's northern minions."

Syed Abd-er-Rahman was energetic. He wasted no time putting his own strategy into effect. He kept el Nadim's eastern army separate from the western, ordering it to advance up the coastline from Dunno Scuttari. The other army he sent directly toward Itaskia, after assembling it in the Lesser Kingdoms. He scattered a dozen smaller divisions between the armies, their mission to drift north unnoted. He fought his first battle before El Murid joined him.

Like so many before, it was inconclusive. Greyfells

stalled the western Host without shattering it. The Duke had not yet abandoned hope of a successful treachery.

Abd-er-Rahman had predicated his strategy on the Duke's political tunnel vision.

Hardly had Greyfells blunted the interior thrust than he had to rush west to forestall the coastal. In his absence Rahman rallied the western Host for another thrust.

El Murid joined him at that time.

He attended all the conferences. He listened to all the discussions and studied all the maps. He kept his opinions to himself. Wadi el Kuf still haunted him.

News came that Libiannin had fallen to Hawkwind and bin Yousif. The fighting had been bitter. El Murid shrugged the loss off. "They suffered heavy casualties. Let them spend their strength. If we send more men they'll just flee into the mountains. Let's worry about finishing Itaskia."

Greyfells halted the army on the coast. He had to extend himself to do so. The eastern troops were outnumbered but not war-weary. Their officers were eager to win themselves names.

Abd-er-Rahman started north again.

Greyfells finally recognized the trap. The two armies were going to slap him back and forth like a shuttlecock while Rahman's smaller divisions slipped past and created havoc behind him. If he withdrew and took up a defensive position along the approaches to Itaskia, one or the other army would bypass and cross the Silverbind. If the city itself were threatened he would lose his command and all hope of profiting from it.

He was in a corner, on thin ice, already. He no longer dared visit the city. The mob jeered and threw brickbats. The news from the south, about guerrillas and Guildsmen liberating coastal cities, worsened his position. People wanted to know why bin Yousif and Hawkwind could capture great cities while he could do nothing. Itaskia's allies were near the limit of their patience.

He had to win a big one.

Esmat stole glances hither and thither as he approached his master. There were no witnesses he could detect. "Lord," he whispered, "There's an enemy delegation to see you."

El Murid was startled. "Me?"

"Yes, Lord. The ones who contacted you several years ago."

"That Duke?"

"His people."

"Show them in." This might lead somewhere. If Itaskia's stubbornness could be neutralized. . . . Endless warfare did no one any good. His dream of greening the desert would never bear fruit if all the empire's energies had to be devoted to reducing intransigent enemies.

The Greyfells proposal remained unchanged. El Murid did not. His readmittance of the shaghûn to the army was but one sign.

"What I'll do," he told the emissaries, "is nominate the Duke viceroy over all the northern territories. Not just Itaskia, but Dvar, Iwa Skolovda, Prost Kamenets and Shara. He'll have plenipotentiary powers within the scope of the Empire and Faith. In return he must acknowledge the Empire's suzerainty, allow free movement of missionaries and produce a modest annual subscription for the restoration of the great works of Ilkazar. In time of war or unrest he'll have to produce levies for the defense of the Imperium."

The emissaries looked dubious, though El Murid was practically offering Greyfells an empire within his Empire. They said they would relay the proposal.

The Duke found it better than he had hoped. He was composing his acceptance when events intervened.

Abd-er-Rahman overtook the Itaskians at the Five Circles.

The Five Circles were the remains of a vast prehistoric monument. They formed a cross in the center of a grassy

plain astride the main road from Itaskia to the Lesser
Kingdoms. The plain was surrounded by hardwood
forests. The natives avoided the megaliths. The Power
was strong there. Witch covens gathered among them
for their bizarre midnight rituals.

Neither Greyfells nor El Murid could halt events once
the armies sighted one another. Abd-er-Rahman was
anxious to bring the battered Itaskians to battle. He
knew one sharp defeat would strip them of their allies.
He accepted the plain as a site of battle, though the
circles would serve the enemy as strongholds if their
formations broke.

He hit fast and hard, sending the whirlwind of his
light cavalry first, following with his heavy horse. The
northern knights scattered. Rahman's horsemen ploughed
into the Itaskian infantry. But for the circles, they would
have been slaughtered.

The fighting continued till dusk. The Itaskians could
not escape. Rahman's men could not overrun the outer
circles. Wherever they threatened to do so, troops from
the larger central circle sallied in support of their
comrades.

El Murid abandoned all thought of negotiation. At the
evening council he announced, "Tomorrow we eschew
the mundane. Tomorrow I call down the might of the
Lord of Hosts and seal the northern doom."

A hundred eyes stared curiously.

El Murid stared back. These men were warriors before they were disciples. Their faith was incidental to
their profession. The spirit of the Lord no longer impelled them.

He would refresh their ardor.

"Tomorrow I shall challenge the heathen. I shall show
them the wrath of the Lord. I shall smite them with the
fire of retribution and leave them weeping for their dark
master's protection. I shall set them running like whipped
dogs. Shaghûns, attend me."

There were but a handful of the witch-brethren with

Abd-er-Rahman's force. They were so few and their wizardry so pitiful, Rahman seldom bothered using them. El Murid spent an hour closeted with them.

Morning came. The Host arrayed itself. The Disciple strode forth clad in purest white. Two Invincibles accompanied him, bearing the standards of the Lord and of the Second Empire. The black-clad shaghûns followed. El Murid halted on a mound a long bowshot from the southernmost circle. The shaghûns formed a shallow crescent cupping him and his standard-bearers.

Enemy faces lined the top of the tumbled rock barrier. The Itaskians had felled the megaliths during the night. The Disciple felt the full weight of their nervousness and fear.

He dropped to one knee, bowed his head, offered up a prayer. Then he rose, surveyed his enemies, flung arms and face toward the sky.

"Hear me, O Lord of Hosts! Thy servant beseechest thee: Empty the cup of thine wrath upon these who cast dung upon thy Truth. Lend thy servant thine immeasurable power that he might requite them for their iniquity. Hear me, O Lord of Hosts!"

Few of his enemies understood who he was or comprehended what he screamed. But they did not need that knowledge to realize that a mighty doom was upon them.

El Murid's amulet blazed, cloaking him in blinding light. Cries of despair rose within the circle. Panic-driven arrows darted toward the man of fire. The Disciple's shaghûns turned the shafts.

El Murid flung his hands downward. Thunder groaned across the sky. The earth trembled. Stones cracked, broke, tumbled, crumbled, flew into the air and plunged down again. Lightning stalked the plain. Men shrieked.

El Murid lifted his arms and flung them down again. Again the sky spoke and hurled down its spears. Again mighty rocks cracked, broke, flew about, collapsed into mounds of gravel. The surviving Itaskians shrieked and wailed and looked for places to run.

El Murid signalled Abd-er-Rahman.

A light horse regiment swept forward. It scoured that circle clean. The men cowering in the other circles were too stunned to support their fellows.

El Murid and his escort stalked to a hummock facing the westernmost circle.

Arrows darkened the sky before the Disciple commenced his prayer. The shaghûns were hard-pressed to turn them. One did crease a standard-bearer as El Murid flung his fiery hands at the world's blue ceiling.

The Host scoured that circle. And the eastern one too. And cheered their Lord almost continuously. At long last this stubborn foe was to be put away.

Some of the men in the northern circle tried to flee. Rahman flung his cavalry after them. They died before they reached the woods, before comrades who could do nothing to save them.

The plain stunk of fear. The Host was showing no mercy at all, even refusing to take knights and lords for ransom.

The Host grew quiet. The Disciple had turned his eye to the central circle, where half the northern army awaited its doom. He took his station atop rubble left from the scouring of the southern circle. The Host crowded up behind him, eager for blood and plunder.

The Duke and his captains were waiting. As the arrows began to fly and the light to surround the Disciple, a dozen bold knights charged.

Rahman sent men to meet them. But not in time. El Murid's shaghûns were compelled to shift their attention to stopping them. The last fell twenty feet from El Murid.

The arrows fell like heavy winter snow while the witchmen were distracted.

The standards went down. Two shaghûns fell. The

arrow-storm thickened. The remaining shaghûns could not turn it all.

El Murid's blazing power did not shield him.

His concentration was such that the first shaft bothered him less than a bee's sting. He brought the lightning down. Inside the circle a hundred men died.

A second arrow passed through the Disciple's upraised right hand. Again he brought the fire down. Boulders hurtled about. Men and animals screamed. Rahman's riders moved up close enough to use their short saddle bows.

The third arrow buried itself in El Murid's left breast. Though it missed heart and lung, its momentum spun him around and flung him to the earth just as the lightning came down again and shattered the last of the megaliths protecting Greyfells' army.

Abd-er-Rahman attacked immediately, hoping to finish the enemy before his own men realized what had happened to their prophet. The Host swarmed into the central circle.

Esmat reached his master before the glory of the amulet faded. He shielded his eyes with his hands. "Lord?"

El Murid groaned. He should have been dead. The terrible vitality that had seen him through the desert in his youth and through the hellish aftermath of the defeat of Wadi el Kuf remained with him. Perhaps his amulet assisted. Esmat grabbed the fallen standards. He snarled at the shaghûns, "Help me make a stretcher." The witch-men stared dumbly. "Strip one of the bodies, you nitwits!" He glared toward the central circle.

The melee was wild and bloody. The warriors of the Host continued pouring in. Some quick-witted foeman was howling, "The Disciple is slain!"

Too many warriors saw Esmat and the shaghûns flee with the stretcher. They believed the cries.

Shouting, the physician tried to assemble El Murid's bodyguard. A handful of Invincibles remembered their honor.

Fickle, insane panic filled the Host as it teetered on the brink of final victory. Victory slipped away.

Esmat concealed himself and his master in a woodcutter's cottage ten miles south of the Five Circles. A dozen Invincibles accompanied him. Most remained in the woods watching for enemy patrols. Two he retained for their muscles.

Out in the dusk the Host was in dismayed flight, small bands of warriors flying hither and yon to escape the Itaskians, who were so bewildered by their good fortune they were doing nothing to follow up.

"Hold him!" Esmat snapped. "Forget who he is. We're trying to save a man, not a myth." The white robes remained unconvinced. Esmat argued, "If we don't save him, who will speak for the Lord?"

The Invincibles leaned into it. Esmat began with the simplest arrowhead.

El Murid groaned and screamed.

A sentry burst in. "Can't you keep him quiet?"

Esmat sighed. "The will of the Lord be done." He took drugs from his kit. He had wanted to avoid them. The Disciple had had so much difficulty whipping his addiction.

El Murid bled a lot, but remained too stubborn to die. Esmat removed four steel barbs.

"How soon will we be able to move?" the leader of the bodyguard asked.

"Not soon. He's hard to kill but slow to mend. We might have to stay here for weeks."

The white robe grimaced. "The will of God be done," he whispered.

They stayed put a month. Twice the Invincibles exterminated small Itaskian patrols. They endured. The Disciple banished his despair with repeated pretenses of agony. Esmat gave him drugs out of fear of the Invincibles. His master became an addict once more.

The Host had collapsed. The survivors had fled so

swiftly their enemies hadn't been able to overtake them. Abd-er-Rahman had been unable to rally them. But the collapse affected only the one force.

Where there were commanders of will and energy the Faithful hung together. Two of the small divisions penetrated the domains of Prost Kamenets. Another crossed the Silverbind and brought fire and sword to the unguarded Itaskian midlands. The army on the coast, after one savage encounter with the remnants of Greyfells' force, stunned the Itaskians by driving north and occupying their great harbor city of Portsmouth, where they settled in for a siege. Other divisions lurked near Greyfells, harassing his foragers.

A stalemate, of sorts, had been achieved.

Greyfells could not move south while strong formations threatened his homeland. The Faithful hadn't the will to resume the offensive.

In the south, Haroun and Hawkwind continued to whoop from town to castle, cutting a broad swath, rooting out supporters of the Disciple. They captured Simballawein and roared on into Ipopotam.

The military governor of the occupied provinces let them spend their vigor and spirit. Once they were far away, he collected scattered formations and reoccupied Libiannin, putting all unbelievers to the sword.

An overconfident Haroun badgered Hawkwind into racing north to recapture the city.

The trap snapped shut in a narrow valley a day's march from Libiannin. Hawkwind and bin Yousif left eight thousand dead upon the field. They had had only twelve thousand men going in. The survivors managed to get inside the unguarded walls of Libiannin. They were not welcomed as liberators. The enemies leagued them up.

"News of a great victory, Lord," Esmat said, having heard of southern events in the village he had just visited.

They were moving south in small stages. "The Royalist and Guild forces were all but destroyed in a battle near Libiannin. The survivors are trapped in the city."

The Disciple was alert and lucid. He saw the ramifications. And yet he could not rejoice.

He had done the Lord's work and the Lord's will and the Lord had betrayed him. The Lord had allowed him to be struck down an instant before the moment of victory. He had endured every possible humiliation, had suffered every possible loss for the Faith. . . . He had left the corpse of his belief sprawled between the bodies of his standard-bearers.

"Where are we now, Esmat?"

"In Vorhangs, Lord. Just a few days from Dunno Scuttari. We can convalesce there."

"Send a message to the garrison commander. Tell him I'm alive. Tell him to send couriers to all our captains apprizing them of that fact. Tell him I want a general armistice declared. Tell him to announce my offer to hold a general peace conference in Dunno Scuttari next month."

"Lord? Peace? What about the new Empire?"

"We'll settle for what we get out of the negotiations."

"We have enemies who won't make peace, Lord."

"The Guild? Bin Yousif's bandits? You said they're all but destroyed. We will invite High Crag, by all means. They must be war-weary enough to give up the sanctions they declared when the Invincibles massacred those old men. But there will be no peace with Royalists. Ever. Not while bin Yousif and I both live.

"Esmat, that battle is all I have left. They've killed everything else. My wife. My babies. Nassef. Even my faith in God and my Calling."

Esmat responded with quotations from his Teachings.

"I was naive then, Esmat. Sometimes hate is all a man has." And maybe it was that way for everyone he had labelled a minion of the Evil One. The drunk, the gambler, the whoremaster maybe each gravitated to his

300

niche not because of a devotion to evil—but because of some need only an odious life could fulfill. Maybe some men needed a diet rich in self-loathing.

His entrance into Dunno Scuttari made a grand excuse for a holiday. The Faithful turned out in their thousands to weep and cheer as if he had brought them a triumph for the Chosen. There was a threat of carnival in the river-tainted air. The happy-storm was not long delayed. The costumes and masks came out. The bulls were run in the streets. Believer consorted with infidel and shared tears of happiness.

El Murid blessed the revelers from a high balcony. He wore a thin smile.

Esmat wondered aloud at their joy.

"They rejoice not for me but for themselves, Esmat."

"Lord?"

"They rejoice not for any accomplishment, nor for my return. They rejoice because by surviving I've put the mask back over the secret face of tomorrow. I've relieved them of uncertainty."

"Then they'll be disappointed when they find out how much you'll yield to make peace."

The Disciple had decided to defy his God. His mission, he told himself, was to establish the Kingdom of Peace. He had been unable to do that sending men to war. . . .

"What of the painkiller?" he asked as an aside. "Is there a supply?"

"You once called me a confounded squirrel, Lord. We held Ipopotam for years. I acquired enough to last several lifetimes."

El Murid nodded absently. So long as there was enough to divert him from thoughts of his true motive for defying the Lord: pure childish spite for the arrows of betrayal that had fallen upon him at the Five Circles.

He returned to Esmat's earlier question. "They don't care which mask the unknowable wears. They just want it to wear one."

Allied emissaries began arriving two weeks later. "They

seem serious this time," the Disciple observed. "Especially Greyfells'."

"Perhaps they sense your own determination, Lord," Esmat replied.

"I doubt it." Already they were hard at their backstabbing and undercutting. Yet he was impressed. He would be dealing with men honestly able to make commitments and undertake obligations, all in an air of great publicity. Even the Guild had entered its delegation, captained by the formidable General Lauder. The Itaskians had sent their redoubtable War Minister as well as the slippery Greyfells. Something solid would come out of the sessions.

Within the formal process there was little dissent or maneuver. No one held a position of strength. After a week, El Murid told Esmat, "We're going to get there. We can wrap it in a month. We'll be in Al Rhemish before your old cohorts can put back everything they stole when they heard I was dead." He chuckled.

He had become an easier El Murid, taking a juvenile pleasure in disconcerting everyone with his frankness and new cynicism. People recalled that he was a salt merchant's son and muttered that blood would tell.

"Not long at all, Esmat. The only real thieves are the Itaskians, and they defeat themselves by working at cross-purposes. We'll come out better than I anticipated."

He had concluded a covert, long-term understanding with Duke Greyfells almost immediately. In private, the Duke showed a pragmatic honesty El Murid appreciated.

"And what of the Second Empire, Lord? Do we abandon the dream?"

"Not to worry, Esmat. Not to worry. We but buy a breathing space in which the dream may build new strength. The Faithful carried the Word to the shores of the Silverbind. They have sown the thunder. Those fields will yield up a rich bounty when next the Chosen come harvesting."

Esmat stared at his master and thought, Yes, but. . . .

302

Who would provide the magnetism and drive? Who would deliver the spark of divine insanity that made masses of men rush to their deaths for something they could not comprehend?

Not you, Lord, Esmat thought. Not you. You can't even sell yourself anymore.

He looked at his master and felt a great sorrow, felt as though something precious had been taken away while he was distracted. He did not know what it was. He did not understand the feeling. He thought himself a practical man.

Chapter Twenty-Two: *LAST BATTLE*

Haroun and Beloul stared down at their enemies. The encircling camp grew larger every day.

"This could get damned nasty, Lord," Beloul observed.

"You'd make a great prophet, Beloul." Haroun glanced along Libiannin's crumbling wall. Heavy engines would have no trouble breaching it.

The enemy really needn't waste time on engines. A concerted rush would carry the wall. He and Hawkwind hadn't the men to defend it, and the natives refused to help.

"What's happening, Beloul? Why haven't they attacked? Why hasn't the Itaskian fleet shown? They must know what's going on. They'd want to take us out, wouldn't they?"

He had had no contact with the world for weeks. The last he had heard, El Murid was reported slain in a huge battle with the Itaskians. His hopes had soared like exultant eagles. He had sent out messenger after messenger, till it seemed an endless parade of fishing smacks were leaving harbor, never to be seen again.

"We're marooned, Lord," Beloul said. "The world is getting on with business and has forgotten us. Maybe on purpose."

"But with the Disciple dead. . . ."

"Lord, nobody but us Royalists gives a damn if you ever sit the Peacock Throne. The Itaskians? They're glad to have us howling around down here keeping the Disciple's men busy. But are they going to spend lives for us? It wouldn't profit them."

Haroun grinned weakly. "Have mercy, O Slayer of Illusions."

"Here comes Shadek. He looks like a man about to slay a few dreams."

El Senoussi's face did have a grim cast. Haroun trembled. He smelled bad news.

"A boat came in, Lord," Shadek puffed.

"Well?"

"It brought a Guildsman, not one of our men. He's with Hawkwind now. He had a funny expression when he looked at me. Kind of a sad, aching look. Made me think of a headsman about to swing his sword on his brother."

Haroun's back suddenly felt cold. "What do you think, Beloul?"

"I think we better take care to watch our backs, Lord. I think we're going to find out why our messengers never came back."

"I was afraid you'd say that. I wish I'd pursued my shaghûn studies to the point where I could perform a divination. . . . Would they really turn on us?"

"Their interests aren't ours, Lord."

"I was afraid you'd say that, too."

Haaken and Reskird looked like men standing at the graveside of a friend suddenly struck down. Ragnarson was so angry he could not speak.

Orders had come. After all these years.

Bragi compelled himself to calm down. "How many people know about this?"

"Just us. And the courier." Kildragon indicated the man who had brought the message from General Lauder.

"Reskird, take that sonofabitch somewhere and keep him busy. Haaken, hustle down to the barracks and sort out everybody who was in our company when we left High Crag. Get them out of the way, then tell the others we've got a full kit formation in two hours. Ready to march."

Haaken eyed him suspiciously. "What are you up to?"

"Let's just say a permanent commission as captain isn't a big enough payoff for selling out a friend. Do what I told you."

"Bragi, you can't. . . ."

"Like hell I can't. I resigned from the Guild five minutes before that guy got here. You and Reskird both heard me."

"Bragi. . . ."

"I don't want to hear about it. You gather up your Guildsmen and hike them up to High Crag. Us non-Guildsmen are going to take a hike of our own."

"I just wanted to say I'm going with you."

Bragi studied him a moment. "Not this time, Haaken. You belong in the Guild. I don't. I've been thinking about this a long time. I don't fit. Not in what it would be in peacetime. I want to do too much that the Guild wouldn't allow. Like lay hands on lots of money. You can't be rich and be a Guildsman. You've got to give it all to the brotherhood. You, you don't need the things I do. You belong. So you just stay. In a couple years you'll have your own company. Someday. . . ."

Ragnarson's voice grew weaker as he spoke. Haaken was looking hurt. Bad hurt. He was trying to hold back tears.

They were brothers. Never had they been separated long. He was telling Haaken it was time they went their own ways. Haaken was hearing that he was not needed anymore, that he was not wanted, that he had been outgrown.

Bragi felt the pain too.

"I have to do this, Haaken. It's going to ruin me with

the Guild, but I have to. I don't want to drag you down too. I'll be back after it's over."

"Stop. No more explaining. We're grown men. You do what you have to do. Just go. . . . Get away. . . ."

Bragi peered at his brother intently. He had injured Haaken's pride. The man behind that taciturn exterior never forgot that he was adopted, never let himself think he was as good as other men. The little rejections became big in his mind. . . . Best to just end it now, before they said something that would cause real pain. "Gather your men, Haaken. You have your orders." Bragi walked away. There were tears in his eyes too.

He managed to round up enough mounts for his men, more by theft than legitimate means. He hustled his baffled troops out of town before news of the treacherous peace could reach their ears.

His outriders captured an enemy courier almost immediately. "Read this," he ordered his interpreter, handing him a captured dispatch.

"Let's see. All the usual greetings and salutations. To the Captain of the Host at Libiannin. . . . It's from El Murid himself. Here's the gist. The Disciple is heading south to participate in the final solution to the Royalist problem. His own words. That's it. He probably sent several couriers, just in case."

"Uhm? He would be ahead of his messenger, would he? Boys, we're going to double-hustle now. Let's see if we can't have a little surprise waiting for the sonofabitch."

Haroun placed a gentle, restraining hand on Shadek's elbow. El Senoussi was ready to launch a one-man crusade against Hawkwind's Guildsmen. "It wouldn't do any good, Shadek. They have their orders, like them or not."

The Guildsmen were trooping aboard ships that had come to take them out of the city. An embarrassed and displeased Sir Tury had posted guards to make sure no

Royalists joined the evacuation. The guards would not look their former comrades in the eye.

"So it goes, Shadek," Beloul observed. "The waters of politics run deep and dark. Occasionally there has to be a sacrificial lamb."

"Now's a damned poor time for you to go philosophical on us, Beloul," el Senoussi snapped. "Stop jacking your jaw and start finding a way out of this."

"I wonder what El Murid gave up to get us?" Haroun mused.

"I'm sure he gave the Guild and Itaskians their money's worth, Lord."

"I didn't think he cared anymore. He's ignored us lately."

"Maybe getting three-quarters killed gave him a more intimate perspective," Beloul suggested.

"Don't be facetious."

Hawkwind had stretched the letter of his orders and filled them in on current events. His news hadn't been good for the Royalist cause.

Haroun glanced across the far curve of the harbor. A pair of heavily fortified hills stood there. They were connected with the city by a long wall guarding a strip of coast only fifty yards wide. Many smaller ships were beached there. Quietly, Haroun's men were seizing those in hopes some Royalists could follow the Guildsmen to sea.

"How many can we get out?" Shadek asked.

"Maybe a thousand," Beloul replied. "If the Guildsmen's brave rescuers don't stand off the roads and keep us bottled."

Haroun glared at the troopships. "Think the treachery runs that deep?"

Beloul shrugged. "Time will tell, Lord."

One by one, the transports stood out to sea. Haroun, Beloul and el Senoussi watched in silence. Shortly after the last warped away from the quay a runner arrived.

He gasped, "Lord, there're warships ready to come into the channel."

"Uh-huh," Shadek said, congratulating himself.

Haroun felt the color leave his face. "What flag?"

"Scuttarian, Lord."

"And Dunno Scuttari is in the Disciple's bag. Beloul, forget your little navy. Looks like our only choice is to take as many with us as we can. Shadek, round the men up and send them to the wall. It won't be long."

"Maybe we can negotiate something," Beloul suggested.

"Would you bargain with them if the roles were reversed?"

Beloul laughed sourly. "I see what you mean, Lord."

Push as he might, Ragnarson could not match El Murid's pace. The Disciple reached Libiannin fifteen hours ahead but too late in the day to launch the attack he had come to enjoy.

Ragnarson's outriders captured a courier who apprised them of the true state of affairs.

"We keep going tonight," Bragi announced. "Maybe we can get there in time to do some good. I'm going to ride ahead."

He gathered a small band and surged ahead outdistancing his main force. He scouted Libiannin's environs, found what he wanted and rejoined his command as the sky began to lighten.

The hill he had selected overlooked the enemy main camp. Its base was just a mile from Libiannin's wall. The remains of an Imperial fortification crowned it. A small party of desert scouts occupied the ruins.

Ragnarson sent his sneakiest people forward. His main force reached the peak of the hill fifteen minutes later. The enemy there were all dead. "Perfect." He assembled his captains. "What I want is. . . ."

El Murid and his people had their attention fixed on Libiannin. Ragnarson's men dug in for an hour before they were noticed. By then the Host had arrayed itself for the assault on the city.

Bragi went downhill, well below his foremost trench. He stood with hands on hips and said, "You folks go right ahead. Don't mind us." No one could hear, of course, but that was unnecessary. His stance conveyed his message. "But be careful about turning your backs on me."

He walked back uphill, listened to his men cuss and grumble as they deepened their trenches. They were not pleased by what they saw below. They were badly outnumbered.

One of Ragnarson's officers who was in the know asked, "What kind of standard should we show? We need something new if we just represent ourselves."

Despite his weariness and concern, Ragnarson was in a good mood. "Should be something unique, right? Something that will puzzle hell out of them. Tell you what. See if you can't find some red cloth. And some black. We'll make a flag like my father's sail. It'll drive them goofy."

Several officers got into the act, creating bizarre standards of their own.

The Host vacillated, racked by indecision. Bragi raised his standard, a black wolf's head on red. Baffled, the Disciple sent a deputation to investigate.

Bragi laughed at their questions while carefully concealing his true strength. He said, "The way I see it, you men have three choices. Attack Libiannin and have us jump on your backs. Attack us and have Haroun do the same. Or you can get smart and go the hell home."

One envoy glanced at the banner and for at least the fifth time asked, "Who are you?"

"I should let you find out the hard way." He could no longer resist a brag. "Ragnarson. Bragi Ragnarson. The Ragnarson that got rid of the Scourge of God, Mowaffak Hali and el-Nadim. Not to mention Karim. There's one name left on my list. Tell your nitwit boss I'll scratch his off too if he doesn't get out of here."

"That Guildsman from Altea? The Guild has made peace. You're out of line. This is between our Lord and bin Yousif."

"And me, Wormface. And me. I'm no Guildsman now."

One of Ragnarson's officers whispered, "Don't push them, sir. They may go."

"I'll carry this news to my Lord," an Invincible said. "It will help him reach his decision." He spun and raced down the hill.

"I don't like the way he said that," someone muttered.

"I think I goofed," Bragi admitted. "My name is right up by Haroun's on the Disciple's list. Stand to arms. Double-check the arrows."

"Can you tell what's happening, Lord?" Shadek asked. "My eyes aren't what they were."

"Mine aren't that good. Looks like somebody's dug in on that hill out there."

"Must be on our side," Beloul guessed. "Else they'd be all over us by now."

"But who? We have no friends anymore."

They waited and watched. The Host waited and baked in the increasingly uncomfortable sun.

"Couldn't you reach out with your shaghûn sensing, Lord?" Shadek asked.

"I don't know. I haven't used it for so long.... I'll give it a go."

Beloul and Shadek shooed the nearer warriors. Haroun seated himself, bent forward, sealed his eyes against the sun. He murmured poorly remembered exercises taught him long ago. A fleeting memory of el Aswad fluttered across his mind. Had that been him? That innocent child? It seemed like another boy in another century, roaming those desert hills with Megelin Radetic, spending those miserable hours with the lore-masters from the shadowed valleys of Jebal al Alf Dhulquarneni.

Slowly, slowly, the chant took shape. He took hold and repeated it till his mind had shed all distractions, then he reached out, reached out. . . .

A sound like a mouse's squeak crossed his motionless lips.

"All right." He lifted a hand. El Senoussi helped him rise. "I'll be damned," he muttered. "I'll be damned."

"Not a doubt of it, Lord," Beloul chided. "But did you learn anything?"

"I did indeed, Beloul. I did indeed. That's our fool friend Ragnarson out there. He's come to save us from the fury of the madman of the wastes."

Shadek and Beloul looked at him oddly. Beloul said, "Ragnarson? But he's Guild."

"You think we should tell him to go away?"

"Not just yet, Lord. Him decorating that hill improves the view marvellously."

And Shadek, "It gives a man a good feeling here inside, knowing there are people who will stick."

"Don't forget it if we get out alive, Shadek. We'll owe him bigger than ever. Let us, too, be men who can be counted upon by our friends."

"Not only our friends but our enemies, Lord."

"The Disciple must be in a dither," Beloul observed. "Like a starving dog stationed between two hunks of meat. Which should he jump first?"

"Except these two hunks will bite his behind if he turns his back."

"Take not too much heart, Lord," Shadek cautioned. "Ragnarson would have far fewer men than the Disciple. And El Murid has his amulet."

The Host went into motion. It split like some weird organism giving birth to another of its kind. Half came toward the city. The remainder faced about and advanced on Ragnarson's hill.

"And there's the answer," Beloul quipped. "The dog turns into two dogs."

"Tell the men they have to hang on till our allies finish their share of the Host," Haroun said.

"Let me be the first to congratulate you on your new-found optimism, Lord," Shadek said.

"No need to be sarcastic, Shadek."

"There's good and good, Lord, and some things could be better than they are. I'll speak to the men."

Haroun nodded. He returned to his semi-trance, supposing that, in this extremity, his small talent as a sorcerer would be more valuable than his talent as a swordsman. He tried to lay a slight, small cloud upon the minds of the men about to attack Libiannin.

At least six thousand horsemen swarmed up Ragnarson's hill. "Oh, damn!" he swore. "I didn't count on them splitting." He shouted and waved, letting his people know they could loose their shafts at will. Clouds of arrows arced toward the riders.

Few of these horsemen had faced the arrowstorms so often seen in the north. They received a rude shock.

Every man of Ragnarson's carried a bow. The pikemen and swordsmen of his front ranks loosed several shafts apiece before hefting their weapons and bracing to receive the charge. The regular archers never slackened fire. These infantrymen had borne the charge of el Nadim's cavalry and had survived. They had confidence in themselves and their officers. They faced the human tidal wave without losing their courage.

The Host left thousands dead on that hillside and countless more heaped before the trenches. The pikemen fended them off while the archers plinked. Yet the impetus of the attack was so massive, Ragnarson's front began to sag. It seemed the surviving horsemen might yet carry the day.

He committed his small reserve, ran back and forth behind the line cursing his bowmen for not shattering the attack.

For half an hour it hung in the balance. Then, here,

there, a few of the enemy began to slip away. The larger mass, almost entirely unhorsed after Ragnarson had ordered his bowmen to redirect their fire against the animals, began to give ground. Ragnarson ordered his wings forward to give the impression he meant to encircle.

Panic hit the enemy. They blew away like smoke on the wind.

"That was close," Bragi muttered. His men were exhausted but he had no mercy. "Sort out the wounded and get them up to the ruins," he ordered. "Archers, get down the hill and recover arrows. Move it! Come on, move it! Officers, I want to form for the advance. We've got to challenge them before they get their balance."

He had drums pound out the message of his coming. He had his men beat their shields with their swords. He hoped nerves in the Host would be so frayed his enemies would scatter.

El Murid had other ideas. He detached men from the assault on Libiannin and sent them to reorganize the survivors of the first wave for a second attack.

Ragnarson did to that second wave what he had done to the first, more thoroughly. The horsemen were less enthusiastic about facing the arrowstorm. They took longer reaching his pikemen and as a consequence suffered more from the blizzard of shafts. The enemy coming up afoot never closed with Ragnarson's line.

More drums. More shield banging. And again El Murid did not bluff. He pulled all his men away from the city.

This time he spearheaded the attack himself, pounding the hill with bolts of lightning called from the cloudless sky.

Ragnarson was proud of his soldiers. They did not let the sorcery panic them. They took cover and tried to hold their ground. When compelled to fall back they did so with discipline, fading toward the ruin.

They wrought incredible carnage while their arrows lasted. But this time the supply ran dry.

Bragi heard a distant whinny and sudden pounding of hooves. The Disciple's men had captured his mounts. "Looks like I miscalculated this time, don't it?" he told one of his officers.

"You're damned calm about it, Colonel."

Surprised, he realized he was calm. Even with the lightning stalking about. "Get back into the ruins. They'll have to come after us on foot. They're no good on the ground."

He ran hither and thither, establishing his companies amidst the tumbled stone. The majority of the foe were hanging back letting their prophet hammer the hill. El Murid was not much of a sharpshooter. Satisfied with his new dispositions, Bragi climbed to the ruin's highest point and stared toward the city. "All right, Haroun. This is your big chance."

Haroun surveyed his men. Their mounts pranced as if eager to be off to the fray. The warriors wore grins. They could not believe their good fortune. An absolute certainty of destruction had turned into a chance for escape.

"How soon, Lord?" Shadek asked.

Haroun peered at the hill. Ragnarson was in bad trouble. "A few minutes yet. Let a few hundred more dismount." He considered the street below. Beloul had finished passing along the line, vigorously pointing out that there was to be no run for freedom while El Murid's back was turned. They were to jump the Disciple from behind.

The more Beloul talked the fewer were the grins.

"Now, Shadek. Take the left wing. Beloul will 'go to the right."

"I'm thinking we ought to head east, then north, as hard as we can ride."

"What about our friends?"

El Senoussi shrugged.

"Who was it said something about people sticking? Sometimes I wonder how much I dare lean on you myself, Shadek."

"Lord!"

"The left wing, Shadek. Go after them as hard as you can, as long as you can. Let's not let El Murid duck the Dark Lady again."

"Suppose he won't let *you* duck?"

"Shadek."

"As you command, Lord."

Haroun led them out, spread them out and trotted them toward Ragnarson's hill. His coming was not wholly unanticipated. Many of the Disciple's horsemen came to meet him.

The lines crashed. Horses reared and screamed. Men shouted war- and death-cries. Lances cracked, swords clanged, shields whumped to the impact of savage blows. Dust rose till it choked the combatants, coating their colorful clothing a uniform ochre. And the Disciple's horsemen gave way.

Haroun howled and wailed, urging his men to finish it for once and all. His blood was up. He never thought to appeal to his people with arguments more convincing than love for their King. What matter to him that one man's death would mean they could return to loved ones unseen for years? *He* had no loved ones waiting in Hammad al Nakir. What matter that the passing of El Murid would permit their escape from sad roles as unwanted strangers in lands with grotesque customs? *He* was a stranger everywhere.

For Haroun—and Beloul—home was the hunt for the hated foe. Family were the men who shared the stalk.

A hand of fear passed over the battlefield. Its shadow fell heaviest upon the Chosen.

Haroun crowed and whipped his men forward.

The enemy broke and flew away like autumn leaves scattering in a sudden cold wind.

Beloul and Shadek drove their wings forward. Haroun,

wounded, kept pointing with his blade and cursing his men because they would not hurry.

Spears of lightning fell upon the battleground, failing to discriminate among targets. Horsemen pelted away from every point of impact.

Haroun tried to locate the Disciple. He descried a large band of Invincibles, but could not determine if El Murid were amongst them. He tried to force his way closer.

More and more of the Disciple's horsemen fled. Some flew eastward, toward Hammad al Nakir. Some galloped across the narrow plain and got inside Libiannin's undefended wall.

The fighting rolled this way and that, up and down Ragnarson's hill. All order vanished. Immense confusion set in. The dust made it difficult to distinguish friend from foe. Neither side could guess who might be winning. But the longer it went on, the more the once stout members of the Host chose the better part of valor.

Late in the afternoon the big band of Invincibles lost their nerve. They scattered. The morale of the Host collapsed. It dissolved in minutes.

"Enough," Haroun told Beloul, who wanted to give chase. "We got out alive. That's enough." He dismounted with exaggerated care. His legs quaked with weariness and reaction. He lowered himself to the earth and began cataloging his injuries.

Twenty minutes later Ragnarson limped down the hill. He was covered with gore. Some was his own. He rolled a corpse aside, seated himself on the trampled earth, loosed a weary sigh. "I'm going to be too stiff to move for a week. If they come back. . . ."

"They won't," Haroun promised. "They're going home. They've had enough. This was the last battle." Despair shadowed the corners of his soul. "The last battle. And the desert is still theirs." The groans and cries of wounded men nearly drowned his soft, sad voice. "I should have seen it before."

"What?"

"It will take more than killing El Murid to recover Hammad al Nakir."

He stared down the hill. The fallen lay in mounds and windrows, as though a big, wild tornado had slapped down in the midst of a parade. People from Libiannin were hurrying toward the field to join the looting. "Beloul, run those people off. You needn't be polite about it." A handful of Royalists, apparently with energy to spare, were working the dead already.

Haroun turned to Ragnarson. "My friend. . . . My friend. What are you doing here? Sir Tury had more room to refuse than you did."

Ragnarson wrapped his arms around his knees, rested his right cheek atop them. "What orders? This is *my* army." He tried to smile. It was too much work. "I'm my own man now."

The setting sun painted the seaward sky a fitting shade of blood. A cool breeze came off the water. Bold gulls drifted inland, curiosities aroused by the gathering ravens.

"They wouldn't be too harsh with you," Haroun guessed. "You won. Winners are easily forgiven."

"I don't want to go back. I wasn't born to be a soldier. Not the Guild type, anyway."

"What, then, my friend?"

"I don't know. Not right now. There'll be something. What about you?"

Haroun glanced at Shadek, at Beloul returning across the field of death. "There's an usurper on the Peacock Throne." A vast weariness entered his voice. He was tired unto death, and still the ghosts whispered in his ears. His father, Yousif, to his right, his uncle, Fuad, to his left. Contested by Megelin Radetic. "Still an usurper."

"There's one in my homeland too. The way I figure it, time and his own stupidity will take care of him."

"I'm not made for waiting."

Ragnarson shrugged. "It's your life. What ever happened to the fat guy? He was weird, but I liked him."

"Mocker? I thought he was with you."

"I haven't seen him since we split up. I figured he went with you."

"Curious."

"Maybe he headed east. He talked about it enough."

"He talked about everything. Probably somebody finally stuck a knife in him."

Ragnarson shrugged again.

Below, the groans and cries continued. More of their men were finding the ambition to search the dead.

Chapter Twenty-Three: *GOING HOME*

El Murid flung both hands skyward, beseeching another bolt from the firmament. He was half-mad with
frustration. The bandit Royalists were not overawed by
his power.

The blow felt like a hammer stroke against his ribs.
He felt bone crack. A whine ripped through his lips. The
earth hurtled up. He tried to reach, to soften his fall.
One arm would not respond. He hit the ground hard.
His bodyguards wailed in dismay.

As consciousness faded he heard hooves racing away.
He cracked one eyelid and watched his Invincibles flee.

The darkness came.

And the darkness went away.

A foot pushed against his ribs, rolled him over. A
scream boiled in his throat. He swallowed it, did not
breathe while the warrior went through his clothing.
The man cursed him. He carried no wealth upon his
person.

The warrior's eyes brightened when he discovered the
amulet. He removed it quickly and furtively, instantly
concealing it within his clothing.

The jewel had ebbed low. The looter never noted its
weak gleam.

El Murid confined his curses to his heart. The choice was the amulet or life. That was no choice.

A second warrior called, "You find anything?"

"Two lousy pieces of silver and a handful of copper. These guys are poorer than we are. This one's got decent boots, though. Look like they might fit."

The Disciple ground his teeth while the man yanked his boots from his feet.

The second warrior joined the first. "I found one of those silver kill-daggers. That ought to be worth something."

"Yeah? Let me see."

"Like hell."

"All right. All right. Hey, this one has a pretty fine sword here."

"Better than that knicked up hunk of Itaskian tin you're carrying."

El Murid wanted to laugh. The weapon had been given him in Dunno Scuttari only days ago. He'd never had it out of its scabbard. There was something ironic in that.

Even more ironic, he concluded after the warriors moved on, was the fact that his enemies were making no effort to learn if he were among the fallen. He did not understand their political apathy. They had him at their mercy.

How ironic it would be, too, if he were slain simply because he were found alive, with his killer never realizing the importance of the deathblow he dealt.

Darkness took the field into its arms. For a time, the more ambitious Royalists plundered by torchlight but eventually even the greediest opted for sleep.

The battlefield grew still and silent. El Murid waited. The pain kept him awake. When he was certain he would not give himself away, he began dragging himself from the field.

He had gone no more than a dozen yards when he

came upon his physician. "Oh, Esmat. What have you done? I thought you were one of the immortals and here you've abandoned me. My old friend. My last friend. Lying here for the ravens. It's cruel. All I can do is raise a stele for you."

Someone or something stirred a short way down the slope. El Murid froze. He did not move for a long time.

Somehow, the plunderers had overlooked Esmat's bag. He took it with him when he resumed dragging himself from the field. When he felt safer he crawled to a tree and used it to pull himself to his feet. He began stumbling eastward by the light of a crescent moon, his feet bleeding. Twice he paused to draw strength from the medicines in Esmat's bag.

Near dawn he encountered a riderless horse. He caught and calmed the beast and dragged himself into the saddle. He walked his new mount eastward.

Two weeks of agony brought him to the Sahel, where he fell into the arms of devoted followers. They nursed him and eventually carried him back to Al Rhemish where he secluded himself in the Most Holy Mrazkim Shrines.

His high ambitions had died their final death.

The Royalist warrior who plundered the Disciple's amulet sold it to a goldsmith in Libiannin after the Chosen there withdrew. The goldsmith in turn sold it to a woman of quality returning south to reclaim family estates near Simballawein. She had had the amulet for two months when it came to sudden life, cursing in a foreign tongue. Terrified, certain the thing was some dread sorcerer's toy that had been fobbed off on her by a dishonest artisan, she had her servants hurl it into a deep well. The well she ordered filled with earth and planted over.

So El Murid's amulet vanished from the earth, to the

bafflement of historians, the Faithful and, most of all, of him who had presented it to the Disciple.

The magic had gone out of El Murid's Movement. Literally.

Chapter Twenty—Four: *REVELATION*

The fat man was never more circumspect. He traversed an inhospitable land infested by piratical deserters from both the Itaskian army and Host of Illumination. These renegades preyed on everyone. The locals therefore greeted any stranger with violence, fearing he might be scouting for one of the bands.

Disorder held sway from the Scarlotti north to the Silverbind. He had survived that chaos. He had evaded misfortune week after week, making his way toward Portsmouth where the remnants of el Nadim's army yet awaited the Disciple's command.

"Self, am cast-iron fool," he berated himself at one juncture, forty miles from his destination. "Should be bound for easternmost east. Should be headed for lands where good sense is rule rather than exception, where man of skill and genius would have half chance to prosper."

His talents were wasted on this mad country. Its people were too damned suspicious and too impoverished. The to and fro of armies had destroyed tens of thousands of farms. Plunderers had carried off any wealth that had existed there. The natives had to scratch and fight to survive.

He was losing weight. Hunger was a monster trying to gnaw its way out of his guts. And he had no props with which to ply his trade even had he been able to gather the marks. He had had no time, and no money, to assemble a new inventory.

He never stopped asking himself what he was doing in this mad country, and still he went on. He had to get close to the eastern army. He had to *know*. He could not go on wondering if Sajac were out there somewhere, stumbling along on his backtrail, closing in for the kill.

That need to know had become an obsession. It drove him more mercilessly than any slavemaster's whip.

For the first time in his life he fell into the habit of introspection, trying to discover *why* this was so important to him. He encountered the shadowed reaches of his soul and recoiled. He dared not believe that such darknesses existed within him. He found his love-hatred for the old man the most repulsive monster hidden there. He wanted to be possessed of no feelings for Sajac at all. He wanted to be able to exterminate the old man like the louse he was—if he still existed.

He did not want to care about anybody but Mocker.

Yet he did care, not only about Sajac but about the friends he had made during his wartime adventures. He had grown fond of Haroun and Bragi, both of whom had treated him well and who had been understanding about his constant making an ass of himself.

Often, late in the night, he would waken and find himself afraid. It was not a mortal fear, a fear of this enemy land, nor was it a dread of specific enemies. It was a fear of having no more cause and no more friends and being totally alone.

He did not like that fear. It did not fit his image of himself as a man at war with the universe, beating it again and again by acuteness of wit. He did not want to be dependent on anyone, especially not emotionally.

He began to hear news of the eastern army as he neared Portsmouth. That last remnant of El Murid's might was preparing for a homeward march. An Itaskian force was camped outside the city ready to assume control when the easterners departed.

News was always a few days old. He lengthened his stride. He did not want to arrive only to discover that his quarry had departed by another route.

His always inimical fate must have dozed off. He ran head on into one of his rare strokes of fortune. He reached the city the morning the easterners departed. He ensconced himself on a rooftop for four long hours, reviewing the Host.

Nowhere did he see a blind old man.

The thing that drove him was not satisfied. It wanted the where, the why, and the how of the old man's separation from the Host. Cursing himself for a fool, he stalked the easterners down their road toward home.

On three different occasions he isolated a soldier and put him to the question. Two had not known Sajac. The third remembered the astrologer but had no idea what had become of him.

Mocker squealed in exasperation. He cursed the gods, one and all, with a fine impartiality. They were toying with him. They were playing a cruel game. He demanded that they cease their torment, and that they let him *know.*

He became so frustrated that, in one of the Lesser Kingdoms, after failing in a fourth attempt to isolate a soldier, he went to a priest for advice.

The priest was no help. Mocker refused to reveal enough of the story for the man to hazard offering advice. He simply told the fat man, "Nothing is certain in this life, my son. We live with mystery. We share a world shrouded in uncertainty. For those without faith, life becomes an interminable journey fraught with the perils of being unsure. Come. Let us pray together. Put your trust in the Lord."

Salvation was not what Mocker had in mind. He

stamped out of the rectory snarling about not getting caught in the world's oldest scam, about the effrontery of a priest who tried to con a master con artist.

He trailed the eastern army all the way to the Sahel.

He stood on a low swale staring at the barren hills, recalling what it had been like passing through them, going into the desert with Yasmid and the Invincibles. He could not penetrate those badlands without attracting the attention of the savage Sahel tribesmen.

"Woe!" he cried, after debating with himself for half a day. "Self, am accursed. Am doomed to remain wanderer in fear, ever watching backtrail lest doom steal upon self unnoticed." He again cursed all the gods and devils he knew, then turned westward, shambling shoulders slumped. Bragi and Haroun would be somewhere along the coast, he supposed.

Two days later he entered a village unscathed by war. The dogs did not growl and attack. They just barked out his arrival. The villagers did not rush out with hammers and knives and threaten to make pet food of him if he did not make himself scarce.

The townspeople were adherents of El Murid's Faith. He arrived during an hour of worship, while the muzzain was singing a prayer from the steeple of a church that once served another god. When prayers were over the villagers received Mocker with charity, offering him food and drink and asking only that he repay their kindness with a few hours of labor.

Work? Mocker? That was as implausible as asking the sun to stand still. Yet work he did, and marvelled at himself as he helped clean a stable. He tried entertaining with a few tricks but was admonished because they smacked of sorcery. The townsfolk were conservatives who hadn't warmed to the Disciple's shift in attitude toward the dark arts. In any case, the old man who lived in the temple had shown them all those tricks already.

Mocker's eyes grew huge. Old man? Tricks? Temple?

But. . . . Could it be . . . ? No. Impossible. Not a chance. Things did not happen that way. The gods did not torment you mercilessly, dangling your heart's desire just out of reach only to throw it into the dust at your feet, contemptuously, when you abandoned all hope. Did they?

He was so nervous and eager that he went to the extreme of taking a bath before attending the next service. He had learned that the old man in question was blind and on his last legs. The temple had taken him in out of charity. He had helped the priest where he could, which was very little, and in return received a place to lay his head, two meals a day and someone to bury him when he died.

A strong emotion hit Mocker when he heard this. He could not identify it immediately. Then he realized he was sad for this unknown old man, crippled and dying alone and unloved, nurtured only by the charity of strangers.

That feeling grew stronger as the hour of worship approached. It baffled him when he tried to probe it in an attempt to unearth its genesis and meaning. He became confused and, in an odd way, frightened. And he wondered constantly if this really could be Sajac.

He joined the worshippers as they drifted toward the temple. Several remarked on how clean and shiny he looked. He grinned idiotically and responded to a few feeble jests.

The nearer he approached the temple the more difficult it became to keep going. More and more of the villagers passed him. In the end, he stood a pace outside the temple door, alone, motionless, wondering what he would see when he stepped through. A feeble Sajac helping the priest? Or some complete stranger?

Three times he tried to take that last step. Three times something held him back. Then he turned and walked away.

In the final summation, he did not need to know. He

could walk away and let the pathetic creature in the temple be whomever he wanted.

The need had left him. Empathy had banished hatred. He resumed his westward journey.

Chapter Twenty-Five: *FINALE, WITH KING*

"There's an Itaskian wants to see you, Lord," Shadek announced from the entrance to Haroun's tent.

"Itaskian?" Haroun exchanged glances with Ragnarson. "What's he want?"

"An audience, Lord. He didn't say why."

"Who is he?"

Shadek shrugged. "A gentleman of quality. An older man."

"Uh-huh. Bring him here, then." Haroun's voice betrayed a great weariness.

"Now what?" Ragnarson wondered aloud.

"Who knows."

Their encampment was a hundred miles northeast of Libiannin. It lay a far ride from anywhere for anyone. The nearest known Itaskians were at Dunno Scuttari, not yet having returned north after their negotiations with the Disciple. The reports suggested that, despite the terms of the peace, they were trying to shake the hold the Faithful had on the kingdoms south of the Scarlotti.

Haroun was drifting toward the Kapenrungs, having nowhere to go but the old camps. Ragnarson had joined

him because he, too, had nowhere to go. He had dis-
banded his little army. His men had been anxious to
return home, to resume interrupted lives. Fewer than
twenty-five had remained with him. None knew what
they would do with their tomorrows.

Shadek returned. "The Itaskian, Lord." He held the
flap for a thin old man.

Haroun rose, face reddening. "My Lord Minister," he
growled, restraining himself with difficulty. "I am. . . .
shall we say I'm boggled by your audacity. Or stupidity.
Only a bold rogue or an idiot would come here after
what you did to us." Shifting to his own tongue, he
identified the man for Ragnarson.

"I?" the Minister asked. "Bold? Hardly. I'm in the
grip of an immense trepidation. My advisers are astonished that we lived long enough to reach you. They
don't believe you're sophisticated enough to distinguish
between this Itaskian and that."

"Why make distinctions?" Ragnarson growled. "One
father of lies is like another. The gods have blessed you,
Haroun. They've given you a peace offering. I know the
perfect way to dispose of this worm."

Haroun eyed the Minister. "I'm open to suggestions."

"In Trolledyngja we carry traitors from town to town
in a cart, hanging them gently. Just enough to make
them dance a little. When the traitor reaches Tonderhofn,
we draw and quarter him and send the quarters out to
the four winds as a warning."

"An interesting custom. I'd be tempted had I villages
through which to parade and a capital to call my own.
Had a snippet of treachery not arisen, I'd have the villages and capital. But nobody to slay. It's a problem. I
fear we'll have to settle for something less flashy."

The Minister refused to be intimidated. His stance
and gaze were those of a brave man who had under-
taken a hazardous mission willingly.

"I'm not pleased with you," Haroun told him. "But
you helped once. I'll let you say your piece."

"These are the facts, then. Whether you believe them or not. During the negotiations in Dunno Scuttari my cousin managed a secret understanding with El Murid. His agents then isolated my party for several days. During that time the articles of peace were implemented. The Guild came to shameful terms in return for a guarantee of their properties and livings south of the Scarlotti. My cousin then issued the orders that resulted in you becoming entrapped in Libiannin. I confess shame, sir, but I deny responsibility."

Haroun glared. The man did not respond.

Ragnarson said, "It *is* your fault. It's been clear since the wars started that Greyfells was dealing with El Murid. You didn't stop him."

"Who is this?" the Minister asked.

"My partner," Haroun replied. "Bragi Ragnarson. I want you to answer him."

"Ragnarson? Good. I've wanted to meet him. I'll answer him thus: He doesn't know Itaskian politics. It's impossible to control Greyfells without civil war."

Ragnarson snorted. "A dollop of poison."

"We'll let the question slide," Haroun said. "Get to the point. You want something."

"To reaffirm our private treaty."

"What treaty?"

"The one we made four years ago. I don't want it to fade away because the fighting has ended."

"Your war has ended. Not mine. Go on."

"El Murid is still El Murid. He hasn't given up. He's just backed off for a breather. He controls most everything south of the Scarlotti and has planted his ideals in fertile soil north of the river. If he tries again he may conquer us."

"So?"

"You said your war hasn't ended. I'm offering continued support. A strong Royalist movement will hamper El Murid. It might nibble away at his bastions outside the Sahel. And I still have those hidden ally needs I spoke about before. My cousin will change his strategy now. The occasional knife in the dark would be an invaluable tool."

"And, I guess, this aid wouldn't be sufficient to put me on the Peacock Throne. It'd be just enough to keep me going, to keep me a useful tool."

"We're getting bitter and cynical, aren't we?"

"You don't deny it."

"I have an operation in mind. It could net you the wealth to make you a power with which to be reckoned."

"Talk. I haven't yet decided to cut your throat."

"This is down the road a way, of course. Because the war has tied up the fleet, pirates have established themselves in the Red Isles. Their leader is a renegade wizard. We need somebody to go in and kill him. If that someone were nimble enough, he could escape with the pirate treasure before the fleet arrived to mop up."

Haroun glanced at Bragi. Ragnarson shrugged.

"You'd let this treasure get away?"

"It belonged to Hellin Daimiel."

"I see. Shadek, take the gentleman somewhere and make him comfortable."

El Senoussi took the Itaskian away.

"The man is cunning," Ragnarson observed.

"Oh?"

"He shined a pot of gold in your eyes and you forgot about Libiannin."

"Think he was telling the truth?"

"Anything is possible. Even that."

"You've got connections in Hellin Daimiel. Find out if they lost any treasure ships."

"Now?"

"You had something else to do?"

"I guess not." Creaking, Bragi rose. "Watch out for him, Haroun."

"I'm done with him. He won't see me again. I'm leaving too. Beloul! Sentry, find Beloul."

"Where you heading?"

"Nowhere important. Personal business. Take care."
Beloul pushed into the tent.

"I'm going away for a while, Beloul. You and Shadek
take over. Move back to the camps. Do whatever seems
appropriate. Try not to attract too much attention. The
next few years will be hard. It'll be a struggle to keep
the movement from falling apart."

"Where will you be, Lord?"

"Out of touch, Beloul. Use your own judgment."

"How long, Lord?"

"I don't know. It all depends."

"I see." Beloul's tone made it clear he did nothing of
the sort.

"Have a horse readied. And send someone to help
with my things."

Haroun climbed the mountain gingerly, feeling both
anticipation and guilty reluctance. He made a poor father and husband.

The old woman and her nephew were out gathering
firewood. They fled to the cabin when they spied him.
He made his approach openly and slowly, not wanting
to be taken for one of the Harish. He reached the cabin.
Its door stood open, presenting a dark and uncertain
rectangle.

"Yasmid?" he called. "Are you here?"

Minutes later he was seated with his woman beside
him and his son in his lap. He was free for a few hours,
days, or weeks. For the moment he was a husband, not a
king without a throne.

He would be happy here in his sanctuary. For a while.
Till his thoughts turned to the outer world once more.
He would try to stay, to be a simple husband, but the
Peacock Throne never ceased its night-whispered calling.
One day he would sally forth to battle again.

They knew, did Yasmid and little Megelin, but they
pretended his stay would last. They always pretended.

They always would, and would live each minute as if it might be their last.

"He's a sturdy little rascal, isn't he?" Haroun asked. Little Megelin gripped his forefingers and stared up with wise infant's eyes. A smile teased the child's soft, moist little lips.

Haroun wept. For all the children, he wept.

RETURNING CREATION

JANET MORRIS